THE
GOOD
LUCK
GIRLS

Charlotte
Nicole Davis

HOT
KEY
BOOKS

First published in Great Britain in 2019 by
HOT KEY BOOKS
80–81 Wimpole St, London W1G 9RE
www.hotkeybooks.com

A CIP catalogue record for this book is available from the British Library.

ISBN: 9781471408250
also available as an ebook

1

This book is typeset using Atomik ePublisher
Printed and bound in Great Britain by Clays Ltd, Elcograf S.p.A.

Hot Key Books is an imprint of Bonnier Books UK
www.bonnierbooks.co.uk

PROLOGUE

It was easier, she'd been told, if you kept a tune in your head.

Clementine sat as still as she could at the claw-foot vanity, searching her memory for any of the songs she'd learned on the piano in the parlor. But her mind had been blank ever since the auction, leaving only a wordless wail of fear like the keening of the dead. Behind her, mumbling around a mouth full of hairpins, Mother Fleur crowed over what an honor it was for Clementine to have fetched such a high bid, and how proud of her she was. The housemistress had spent the last hour preparing Clementine for her Lucky Night, lacing up her frothy white dress, rouging her cheeks, and shadowing her eyes with soot.

"You ought to be proud of yourself, too," the older woman went on. She brushed Clementine's woolly black hair away from her face and pinned it up in an elegant knot. A weary sigh tickled the nape of Clementine's neck. "Sixteen years old, finally a woman proper. I remember when you were just a cricket—you and your sister both. But she did fine, Clementine, and you will, too."

Clementine found no comfort in the words. Mother Fleur was well past working age herself. Her favor, a carnation, had begun to wither on her wrinkled white cheek, the cursed ink long since faded to gray. Clementine wondered how much she even remembered of her Lucky Night. Had she been this frightened? Had anyone? Sundown girls were discouraged from talking to daybreak girls about the business. They'd only told Clementine the essentials. Not whether these last minutes were supposed to stretch out like the held breath between lightning and thunder, or whether her stomach was supposed to drop like she was falling down a gorge. Even Clementine's sister, Aster, had never given any details about her Lucky Night.

It had been Aster's suggestion, though, to keep a tune in her head. *It doesn't have to be your favorite song,* she'd said. *In fact, it's better if it isn't. Just pick one you know in your bones, and think of nothing else.*

Aster had also insisted that Clementine didn't take any Sweet Thistle, the soothing tincture sundown girls were required to use to settle their nerves. She'd even gone as far as to tell Clementine to lie to Mother Fleur about taking her dose. Clementine hadn't asked why, even though she'd been surprised. She trusted Aster in everything.

Now, though, she wondered if a drop of Sweet Thistle might not have been a bad idea.

Mother Fleur finished fussing with her hair, sticking the last pin in place. "Almost done," she muttered. Clementine tried to relax and let herself enjoy being pampered. In her six years at the Green Creek welcome house, this was surely the kindest Mother Fleur had ever been to her. She'd never been prettied up like this before, and it was a welcome distraction from the duty that lay ahead.

2

Clementine cleared her throat. "I love the look of it," she managed to say.

"*You're* not the one we're trying to impress tonight," Mother Fleur said with a dry laugh. "But I'm glad you like it all the same. Gives a girl confidence when she knows she looks good."

Mother Fleur picked up a crystal bottle of perfume next. Clementine offered up the left side of her throat, where her own favor shone black against her dark brown skin: a clementine flower, her namesake, its starlike petals fluttering occasionally as if from a gentle breeze. It suited her, she liked to think. She'd gotten it when she was ten years old. The tattoo man had carefully prepared the ink, mixing it with the unsavory ingredients that gave it its power. A dead man's blood. Powdered bone. Venom from a black-fanged skink. Then he'd burrowed the needle into the hollow above her collarbone, sharp as a catamount's claw. The favor would mark Clementine as property of the welcome house for the rest of her days.

At first, the clementine flower had been just a seedling—two teardrop leaves, a curl of a stem. But it had grown slowly with each passing year, ink unfurling up the crescent of her neck, until this morning, finally, she had woken up to find it fully blossomed just above her jaw.

Her skin prickled at the cool kiss of the perfume. Mother Fleur returned the bottle to its place.

"There," the housemistress said, resting her hands on Clementine's shoulders. Her voice rang with finality. Clementine's heart leapt in her chest. She met Mother Fleur's eyes in the mirror, questions gathering at the top of her throat.

3

"Now, remember," Mother Fleur said, "you're not just representing yourself tonight. You're representing the whole of the Green Creek welcome house." A familiar hint of warning crept into her words. "But we all know how special you are, and so does the brag. That's why he paid such a fine fortune. You prove to him that it was worth every copper, and then we'll celebrate, hear?"

She didn't need to say what would happen if Clementine failed. The raveners, the welcome house's muscle, had ways of punishing a girl without leaving a mark on her body, of ripping into her mind and tricking it into a place of pain or fear. Clementine had been subjected to their bewitchment before. They all had, at least once. Every girl had to be conditioned when she first came to the welcome house, had to learn to fear the raveners' wrath. Some of them never recovered from the experience—girls who were thrown, gibbering mad, into the streets to die.

The veiled threat was enough to finally loosen Clementine's tongue.

"Mother Fleur—" She faltered. "It's only— Is it normal, to be this nervous? My stomach feels a touch unsettled."

"Those are just moon moths, Clementine. Every girl gets them. They're from excitement as much as anything. And why shouldn't you be excited?" She winked. "Flattered, too. It's not every girl who catches the fancy of such a respected young man."

"Who is he, though?" Clementine dared to ask. A politician maybe, or a slick businessman, or a world-class gambleman with winnings hot in his pocket—

"If I tell you you're just going to get yourself even more worked up," Mother Fleur replied. "He'll be good to you. That's all you need to know."

Clementine relented, afraid to push any further. And in the end, it didn't matter, did it? Her whole life at Green Creek had been leading up to this moment. There'd be no more maid work after tonight, no more scrubbing dishes until her hands were raw or sweating over the stove. She was excited to wear fine dresses and laze around the parlor rooms with the other sundown girls—including Aster, whom she'd hardly seen this past year. Spending time with her sister again . . . that would be the best part of all of this, Clementine knew.

She only had to get through tonight.

"You ready for me to send him up?" Mother Fleur asked.

"Yes," Clementine said, and she meant it.

"Good." She gave Clementine's shoulder another squeeze, nails biting into skin. "Don't disappoint, Clementine."

Mother Fleur swept away, turning out the gas-lit chandelier overhead as she went. The room was left with the rosy glow of a slag-glass lamp, as if blushing. The door clicked shut behind her.

For several heartbeats, Clementine remained seated at the vanity, her reflection an exaggeration of shadows. The brag would be up here any moment. Should she stand to greet him? Lie waiting on the bed? She'd had all day to plan for this. She'd had years.

Then she heard it. The heavy creak of footsteps on the stairs.

Think of a song, she told herself. *Aster's right downstairs. Just think of a song.*

The door opened.

The man behind it was more brutish than Clementine expected, a broad-shouldered ox stuffed in a suit. His fine black coat fell down to his knees, while his derby hat hung low over a shovel-shaped face framed by an auburn beard. Nothing about his outward appearance gave away who he might be, but his wealth was evident from the glint of the theomite ring on his thumb. The dark gemstone was large enough to buy the whole welcome house.

The brag paused in the doorway as he took stock of his suite: the plum-colored walls and their paintings of Arketta's red-rock mountains, the ornate imported rug underfoot, the plush couch against the wall, the decanter of wine at its table. And, of course, the royal bed in the center of the room, its pillows piled high against a gilded headboard. At last the brag's gaze landed on Clementine herself, who held up her chin. He ran his tongue over his thin lips and grinned. Clementine recoiled, then scolded herself for it. This was a welcome house. She would make him feel welcome.

The brag swung the door shut, the latch loud as a gunshot. He tossed his coat and hat on the hook. His thick shoulders strained against his white dress shirt, but Clementine could see now that he was younger than she'd first thought. Nineteen, maybe twenty, with ice blue eyes. She took a tentative step forward.

"Let me get that for you," she said, stepping in to unbutton his vest. "You must be glad to get off the road."

The scripted words felt unnatural to her, but the brag held out his arms cooperatively as she pulled the vest free and loosened his tie.

"And what would a girl like you know about the road? Or anything outside this fine establishment?" he drawled.

Clementine's memory flickered, sunlight on water. "Enough," she replied.

He licked his lips again, stepping in to study her more closely. He ran a thumb over her favor. "Skin like silk," he murmured. "They did a good job with you."

She was surprised by the roughness of his hands, the warmth of his touch. The only other man outside of kin who had touched her at all was the welcome house doctor, who always wore cold rubber gloves. She brought her own hand up to cover the brag's and wound their fingers together.

"Glad you like what you see," she said, summoning her courage. "Let's find out what else you like."

It must have been the right thing to say, or near enough, because he lifted his brow and led her to the bed, his bear paw of a hand still wrapped around hers. Clementine's stomach gave another flip. *Just the moon moths*, she told herself, and a moment later they were sitting side by side on the edge of the mattress. The brag leaned down to unlace his boots. Clementine struggled for some way to fill the silence. Her cheeks began to burn. She wasn't allowed to make idle conversation, wasn't allowed to ask his name or where he'd come from. Those secrets were a man's to give or keep as he saw fit.

Then he started unbuttoning his shirt. Clementine gripped the duvet.

"Quiet one, are you?" he asked.

She let out a nervous laugh. "I guess you might say that."

"Seems y'all are always quiet the first time," he said

matter-of-factly. "Just as well. All that cooked-up banter some of the girls throw around just wastes time. I'd rather get my shine's worth out of every minute."

Clementine's heart dropped. Her breaths grew sharp and short. "Looks to me like you're the kind of man with plenty of shine to spare," she replied. She had to keep him talking.

"Well, it's my father's money, for now." He stood and shrugged off his shirt, revealing a thickset chest matted with red hair. "You know who my father is?"

Clementine shook her head.

"Just as well," he said again. "I'll be running things soon enough. And once I am, I'll come back sometime and bring you something pretty, hear?" He tilted her chin up, meeting her eyes for the first time. His grin cut like a blade. "If you treat me right, that is."

Then, before Clementine could stall him any longer, he scooped her up and laid her down on the middle of the bed, crawling over her, trapping her between his arms. His breath was sour with the smell of whiskey. Clementine's stomach rolled as his gaze traced the v of her neckline. There was no more mistaking this queasiness for a few harmless moon moths. She was going to be sick.

I have to stop this—

The brag leaned in and began kissing her throat.

Clementine drew a startled breath and held it. Tensed, shut her eyes. His cracked lips scraped across her skin. His blunt teeth tugged at her with clumsy need. After a moment, though, she slowly opened her eyes. This wasn't so bad, she told herself. The kissing may be a little messy, but it wasn't so bad.

8

Then he relaxed, settling his full weight on top of her as he began to work way down her neckline, tracing her favor. Clementine squirmed underneath the suffocating pressure.

"Wait," she managed. He ignored her. She began to struggle, raising her voice. "Wait, please—"

"You said you'd be quiet," he said roughly. His hand slid up her leg, slipping under her dress, resting on her bare knee. Her heart beat hard as a horse kick. *Think of a song, think of a song.*

His hand moved higher.

"*Wait*, please, I'm not ready—"

He braced a forearm against her throat. To quiet her, Clementine was sure. She swallowed around a knot of pain. Lightheadedness washed over her.

She couldn't *breathe*.

It was enough to unleash the fear that had been mounting in her since that morning, spurring it into a red-blooded panic. She didn't want this, she wasn't ready for this, she couldn't breathe—

"Stop!" she cried out, pushing against his chest with all her strength. It was the last word she was able to choke out. He only pressed his arm down more firmly. Her vision swam, eyes watering. Her lungs grew tight. She reached out blindly for the side table, searching for something, anything. Her fingers found the lamp. Grasped it by its neck.

And swung its heavy base towards his head.

The man roared, reeling back, pressing his hand where the lamp had connected.

"*Damn you!*" he cried, eyes flashing with rage. "I'll *kill* you for that—"

9

Clementine hit him again, harder. This time his body went slack and he collapsed on top of her. She sucked in a gasping breath at the sudden, crushing pressure. She heaved him off of her and rolled away, leaping up and backing herself into the corner of the darkened room, her spine pressed against the wall. She coughed so much she feared she'd retch, forcing out the tears that had pricked at her eyes. She'd done it now. Now he was going to be even more furious, and he'd come for her again, and he—and he—

And he wasn't getting up. Clementine went still, listening for the sound of his breath. Looking for the slightest movement.

Nothing.

Slowly, she crept back towards the bed. She could just make out the shape of his body in the dark. She laid a hand to his head and snatched it back the moment she felt the bloody dent in his skull, warm and wet.

Shock washed over her, followed by a relief so pure it buckled her knees. A song finally floated up from her memory, its last three chords ringing in her ears.

Eliza Little with her hair so red,
Her first husband took another woman to his bed,
She found him out and listened to him beg,
Then she took her rifle and she killed—him—dead.

Aster uncurled her fingers.

"Beg pardon, Mother Fleur," she murmured. "Clem's right. I just haven't been up this early in a while."

Mother Fleur gave her a cold, knowing look, but she let it go. "Well, those lazy mornings are one of the many privileges of being a sundown girl that Clementine can look forward to," she said, with a forced breeziness. "Now, I'm needed downstairs to open the house. But I trust you can finish getting your sister settled in?"

"It'd be my pleasure."

Mother Fleur held her glare for a moment longer, then turned and flashed Clementine a bright smile.

"Well, then, happy birthday, Clementine," she said grandly. "I will see you both at breakfast."

She left them.

As soon as Mother Fleur was out of sight, Clementine let out a whoop and jumped backwards onto the bed, the skirt of her yellow day dress flaring around her like a bell.

"By the Veil! This room is fit for a princess. I reckon it's even bigger than yours."

Aster grinned despite her misgivings. She crossed her arms. "Yeah? I don't see any windows like mine's got. Bet you're right this room's bigger, though. Spoiled."

In truth, Aster would have taken even the smallest room if it'd meant she got to keep her window. She loved watching the sun rise over the mountains in the morning, light spilling like liquid gold into the valley where Green Creek slept. The welcome house was near the center of town, which gave Aster a view of just about everything, from the tidy shops that lined

13

Main Street to the deadwall that surrounded the town, its mortar mixed with theomite dust to keep vengeful spirits away.

That view was an escape, the only one she had.

"Spoiled, my hide," Clementine went on. "I worked hard for this room. And this *bed*. Look, even the pillows have pillows."

"Better than those piss-smelling cots upstairs?" Aster said.

"Much better." Clementine sat up, a shadow passing over her face. "But then, I guess it'd have to be."

A cold, slippery feeling trickled through Aster's gut. "Never mind all that for now," she said, pulling Clem back to her feet. "Let's go get all your stuff, make this place feel like home."

Clementine's excitement returned. "Right, if we hurry we can catch the others before they have to get to the kitchen."

The "others" were Tansy and Mallow, Clementine's two closest friends. They still lived up in the attic along with all the other girls who hadn't yet turned sixteen. Until today, Clementine had been on the kitchen crew with them.

"Does it feel strange not have any chores to do?" Aster asked as they made their way down the hall.

"Well, I sure don't miss it, if that's what you mean," Clementine snorted. Her smile faded. "I will miss Tanz and Mal, though."

"They turn sixteen in, what, three and four months? They'll be sundown girls soon enough," Aster reassured her.

"Right. And I'll still see them around some, so there's that," Clementine added.

Aster paused. "Right, there's that."

But, of course, it wouldn't be the same, not at all. Sundown girls and daybreak girls lived separate lives, and when they did cross paths, there was an unspoken barrier between them, like the Veil between the living and the dead. Clementine wouldn't be allowed to talk about the work with the daybreak girls—but for the sundown girls, the work was all there was.

Aster had been told, many times, to be grateful for that work. Good Luck Girls never went hungry, always had a roof over their heads, saw the doctor and the dentist twice a year. Entertaining the brags meant they got to wear the kind of clothes other girls could only dream of, too, and enjoy an endless supply of Sweet Thistle.

It was far more than most folks could expect in Arketta, especially out in the Scab, the ragged line of mountains that cut through the middle of the country. Its wind-torn wilderness was where, in the long-gone days of the old Empire, anyone the Empire deemed criminal had been banished to work in the mines. Some had been captured in Arketta on the battlefields where they'd fought against the Empire's onslaught. Others had been sent to Arketta on reeking prison ships from the colonies. Dustbloods, they were called. They looked just the same as ordinary, fairblood folks, except that they couldn't cast a shadow. The first dustbloods had had their shadows ripped away as part of their punishment, and their children had been born without them. A dustblood's debt could never truly be paid. If at first you owed ten eagles for stealing, then by the end of the year you'd owe ten thousand, for everything from the moldy bread you were rationed to the leaking roof over your head.

Now, some two centuries after the Empire's fall, there were more dustbloods living in the Scab than ever. Enterprising businessmen had bought up the land and taken on the dustbloods' debt in return for their labor—an arrangement that became known as the Reckoning. The Reckoning promised fairbloods the opportunity to become wealthy landmasters and live among Arketta's elite, while it promised dustbloods the opportunity to work away generations of debt and finally earn their freedom from the Scab. And it had worked out well enough for the landmasters, but the miners never ended up with anything to show for it but broken bodies and empty bellies. Disease took them, or they disappeared down the gullet of a mountain, or a vengeant ripped them open with its invisible claws. There was no escaping the Reckoning, the law had made sure of that—Arketta's border with its industrial neighbor to the north, Ferron, was protected by its finest armymen, and no one without a shadow got out.

That was how the welcome houses got girls to work for them in the first place. Scouts found desperate families with young daughters and offered to take them away for a modest compensation. Girls worked as the help until they turned sixteen, then serviced guests until they aged out at forty. They didn't have to pay for anything, but they didn't earn any wages, either. It was a bitter compromise, and everyone knew it. But when there were one too many mouths at home to feed, when an accident underground left parents unable to work, when the alternative for a girl was a life of suffering cut brutally short, the welcome house remained the only option. At least her belly would be full at night. At least her medical needs would be seen to. Indeed, the landmasters argued, these girls were lucky to live such pampered lives.

The only problem was, Aster had never chosen this life.

None of them had. And none could ever truly leave it. Not when their favors marked them for what they were even after they'd aged out. As much as the brags liked to talk about how great the Good Luck Girls had it, they never seemed to mention how most girls died on the streets, as beggars. On the extremely rare occasion, a wealthy brag would buy a girl from a house, to have for his exclusive use. But this was hardly preferable: once purchased, she never aged out at all—she was the brag's property for life.

Aster's hand wandered up to the side of her throat, where a chain of thin-petaled flowers mottled her skin like bright black starbursts. She had thought about running away. It was impossible not to. But a favor didn't just mark someone as property of a welcome house—it was bewitched, too. If a girl covered hers up, with makeup or a dustkerchief or anything else, the ink would heat and glow like iron in a fire. Red, first, then orange, then yellow, then white. The pain was enough to bear for a few minutes, but eventually it would bring even the strongest to her knees, and it took hours to fully subside.

They couldn't hide their favors, couldn't remove them. They couldn't even get past the front *door*. Dex stood guard in the foyer, watching all the comings and goings with eyes the color of rust. He was supposed to be there for their protection, but everyone knew any girl who tried to slip past him would be hunted down and dragged back for a prolonged execution.

Aster used to think she would become accustomed to the welcome house eventually, maybe even learn to see the glamor of it all, the way many girls did. The delusion probably made

17

it more bearable for them. But for Aster, no amount of time was going to turn this barrel of piss into wine. The only good luck she could see was that she and Clementine still had each other. Most of the girls never saw their families again.

Ahead of her, Clementine reached the stairs at the end of the hall and took the steps two at a time, swift and silent. Aster followed, muscle memory guiding her over the creaks beneath the carpet. They rounded the corner and passed the third floor, home to Mother Fleur's private rooms, and continued upstairs to the unfinished attic.

"Happy Lucky Night, Clementine!" a younger girl chirped as she passed them on her way down. Two other girls followed, nearly knocking Aster over in their hurry.

"Oh—sorry, Miss Aster," one of them stammered. She probably hadn't been expecting to see an older girl up here. Aster winced at the deference in her voice, as if she herself hadn't been one of them just a year ago.

"It's fine," she mumbled. *And don't call me "Miss,"* she wanted to add. But of course they were just doing as they were told. Aster eased by them.

The attic served as a makeshift bunkroom, and it had none of the luxury of the rest of the welcome house, bare floors bristling with crooked nails and cold morning air seeping through the walls. A string of mining lanterns offered sickly, flickering light. A dead scorpion nestled on the windowsill. At night, when all was still, you would hear a creak in the rafters where a girl had hanged herself with her bedsheets thirty years ago, and if you were fool enough to open your eyes you would see her moon-pale remnant, too.

But it was morning now, loud and full of life, and some two dozen daybreak girls bustled back and forth, getting ready to go to work. They hurried their friends along, made their beds, and changed into their maids' dresses—stiff green linen under a crisp white apron. Though they all wore the same uniforms, their bodies came in every size, shape, and color. It was common knowledge that a welcome house that offered a variety would get more customers.

Aster felt a swell of sympathy as she passed between the cots. Most Good Luck Girls were dustbloods like her and Clem, and they came to the welcome house hollowed out and hungry, without even their own shadow to keep them company. The youngest, only ten, still had that lean look about them. As they got older, though, they grew fuller and sleeker with health. But they were all hogs being fattened for a slaughter, and most of them didn't even realize it yet.

Don't think about that, Aster reminded herself. *Smile. For Clementine.* She exhaled and relaxed. She angled towards the lone mirror in the corner, where Clementine was showing off her outfit to Tansy and Mallow. The inseparable pair had always been opposites—Tansy with her wild, sandy hair and white, freckled skin; Mallow with her warm, brown skin and straight, cropped black hair. At fifteen, they were among the oldest in the attic—both of their favors nearing full bloom. Clusters of round flowers dotted Tansy's neck like tufts of cotton. Mallow's favor was as dainty as she was coarse, each flower unfurling into five heart-shaped petals.

"This isn't what I'll be wearing tonight, of course," Clementine was saying as Aster approached. "I'll get changed after the auction. But my wardrobe is already full of new delights like this."

"Are you nervous?" Tansy asked, fretting with the end of her fraying pigtail.

Clementine hesitated, the answer plain on her face, but then Mallow gave her an encouraging shoulder-shove.

"Of course she's not, she's about to get out of this shithole for good," Mallow said, glancing around the bunkroom. Clementine flashed her a look of relief.

"Yeah, whatever happens tonight, I figure it'll be worth it to start living like a sundown girl," Clem said.

Aster hung back, watching them, a tug in her chest. Unlike Clementine, she had never gotten close with any of the other girls. It was better that way. She couldn't lose people she didn't have.

Could've used a friendly face or two after my Lucky Night, though, Aster thought. Clementine and the others seemed to think things would be better after they came of age. Aster couldn't bring herself to tell them it would be far worse.

Instead, she summoned her smile and joined them. "Come on, Clem, we have to be downstairs for your breakfast banquet in a few minutes."

"Oh, hey, nice to see you, too, *Miss* Aster," Mallow said, with none of the reverence of the girls on the stairs.

Tansy snickered. "Promise you won't get too good to say hello to us, Clem."

"*Miss* Clem," Clementine sniffed.

Aster huffed. "Listen, I'm just here to tell you all that being grown won't stop Mother Fleur from giving you hell if you don't do what she says. And she said to get settled in your new room before breakfast. Now where's your stuff?"

Clementine sighed dramatically, but she led them over to her cot. A simple trunk stood at the end of it. She wouldn't be needing the old clothes anymore, so they only salvaged her more precious possessions. Notes and drawings she'd collected from other girls over the years, a jar of rock candy leftover from Reckoning Day, a dusky red feather she'd once found while sweeping a chimney.

"And what about . . . ?" Tansy asked at last, holding up Clementine's rag doll.

Aster glanced at Clementine, whose expression broke for a brief instant. But then she set her mouth and shook her head.

"A fine fool I'd look explaining that old thing to some brag," Clementine said. "The last girl who had this cot left that doll here for me. I'll do the same and let the next girl have her."

The next girl, Aster thought grimly.

Always a next girl.

CHAPTER TWO

The dining room was one of the finest rooms in the welcome house, from its gleaming marble floors to its gold tile ceiling. Every plate had been piled high with food: corncakes topped with whipped cream and jam, spiced hog sausage, scrambled eggs and skillet potatoes, fresh fruit carved into flowers. While daybreak girls ate yesterday's leftovers in the kitchen, sundown girls, along with any brags who stayed for breakfast, enjoyed a meal fit for a timberman. Idle chatter flowed between the tables like the murmuring of a creek.

Aster sat with Clementine and four other sundown girls, none of them older than twenty. Lily, Marigold, and Sage were all acquaintances Clem would remember from growing up together—Good Luck Girls tended to stick with people near their own age. To Aster's great annoyance, this meant that their group also included Violet, Mother Fleur's apprentice and favorite little pet. Unlike the rest of them, Violet had been *born* in the welcome house to one of its former sundown girls, which she seemed to think made her a damn princess. Even now, somehow, she had managed to make herself the head of the table, despite the fact that it was a circle.

"The brags have until noon to clear out of here," she was saying to Clementine. Violet was the only fairblood girl in the welcome house, her shadow trailing out behind her like the train of a dress. She always spoke with a superior tone that grated against Aster's ears. "Most men can't afford much more than an hour or two with us," she went on, "but if you get an overnighter, it's your duty to keep him company in the morning. Then, from noon to four, you'll be expected to bathe, groom yourself, tidy your room, and so on. I have a list of the expected duties, and while they're certainly more of a treat than the maid work, they're no less important: Green Creek represents the height of polish and professionalism. *Then*, at four, we open house again for the next round of guests—"

Aster curled her lip. "By the dead, Violet, will you let Clem enjoy her corncakes?"

Violet turned to her, narrowing her cold blue eyes and tucking a stray lock of black hair behind her ear. Her favor, with its elegant, teardrop-shaped petals, had the dark iridescence of a raven's wing. "I just want your sister to be successful, Aster," she said. "Don't you?"

"*I* just want her to finish her ripping food before it gets too cold."

"Foul language is strictly forbidden during work hours," Violet added to Clementine.

Aster gritted her teeth. Usually she was better at holding her tongue, but she didn't know how long she could take this *celebration* of what would happen tonight. It reminded her of how she always felt on Reckoning Day, the Arkettan holiday when dustbloods were supposed to celebrate their "good

23

fortune" and landmasters were celebrated for their supposed beneficence. The holiday always made Aster sick. Today was even worse.

Breathe. Smile.

Next to her, Clementine had begun busily drinking down her milk to avoid talking to either of them.

Lily laughed. "Come on, Violet. Aster's right. It's a lot to take in at once. What questions do you have for *us*, Clementine?"

Clementine finally set her glass down and licked the milk moustache off her lip. She glanced at Aster. "Well, um—I guess—what's the auction like? Do I really only stand there for a few seconds?"

Aster's grip tightened around her fork.

"Oh, don't worry yourself over that," Marigold jumped in. "It's quick, quiet. The brags aren't allowed to talk. Like Violet said, Green Creek's a nice place. None of the nastiness they get at some welcome houses."

"You'll be blindfolded, too," Lily explained. "It's tradition. Bad luck to see the brag before sundown. So you just stand there and look pretty, really. Nothing to it."

Aster didn't trust herself to look at Clementine, afraid her sister would see the truth in her eyes. Green Creek was not a "nice place." Its "traditions" existed to keep them all under control. But she knew Lily and Marigold were acting sunny for her sister's sake, as a kindness, and Aster let them. The auction would be the least of Clem's worries, anyway.

Clementine asked a few more questions, but they were all met with the same vague answers and false glamor. It was, Aster realized dryly, a perfect introduction to the sundown girl's

24

world. Shining on the outside with the promise of sweetness while the inside went soft with rot.

Aster picked at her food. Even after seven years at the welcome house, she never took a meal for granted, but this morning she had no appetite.

At last, some of the daybreak girls came by and cleared their dishes away. One of them let a glass slip from her hand. It shattered crisply on the floor.

"Beg your pardon," the girl said quickly, eyes lowered as she hurried to clean up the mess. But Violet caught her by the wrist before she could get started.

"You *fool*. Leave it for now," she ordered, showing teeth. "You'll only make more of a mess. Rest assured Mother Fleur will hear about this."

"But—"

Violet's brow arched. "Talking back, too, are we?"

The girl scampered off before she could make more trouble for herself. Violet turned back to Clementine, all smiles once more.

"Now, Clementine, it *is* your birthday, after all, so the girls and I each got you a little something. Aster, why don't you go first?" she said, businesslike.

Aster dragged her gaze up from the broken glass at her feet. This was the one part of the morning she actually had been looking forward to. She'd spent the past week working on a bracelet for her sister. She'd used spare thread from her sewing kit and a hairpin for the clasp. The bracelet had the same brown-black-white pattern of a diamondback rattletail.

"Look familiar?" Aster asked, pulling the bracelet out of her pocket. For the first time that day, her smile felt real.

25

Clementine's eyes lit up with recognition. "You know it does! I'll never forget those colors as long as I live."

"Wait . . ." Sage began uncertainly. "I remember you telling us once that you got bit by a snake when you were little, Clementine, right? Is that what this is about?"

Aster nodded. It was ten years ago, long before they'd come to the welcome house. When they'd still lived in the tenant miners' camp. Death had prowled from house to house like a coyote on the hunt, and some nights Aster's hunger had been so vicious she'd chewed on the collar of her nightgown for relief. But at least, then, she and Clementine had been free.

One evening they'd been sitting outside while their mother swept the porch, and Clementine, who'd wandered into the grass to play, had disturbed a rattletail in the brush. It sank its fangs into her ankle—but, somehow, thank the dead, she had survived.

"You weren't supposed to survive that," Aster said. "But you did, and you're here—" She swallowed. She hadn't planned this. "And that means everything to me." She clasped the bracelet around Clementine's wrist, hands shaking, then kissed her forehead. "You survive something like that, you can survive anything, hear?"

Violet cleared her throat. Probably she was upset that Aster hadn't kept to the script.

Too damn bad, Aster thought. Someone had to be honest with Clementine. This work wasn't to be enjoyed. It was to be endured.

Sage shifted uncomfortably in her seat. "Well, I got one of my friends on the kitchen crew to bake up a batch of sweet potato cookies," she said. "I know they're your favorite, so . . ." She handed over a lumpy bundle wrapped in old newspaper. Marigold and Lily went next, Marigold offering a sketch of Clementine with Aster, while Lily gave her a broken pocket watch a brag had once left behind. Clementine thanked them all, her face split with a grin. It was the most she'd ever gotten for any birthday. Every so often she glanced down at her bracelet, though, her smile slipping, and Aster wondered if it had been a mistake not to play along like the others.

Then it was Violet's turn.

"My present comes on behalf of Mother Fleur," she said, and she handed Clementine a small brown bottle. "Sweet Thistle."

Now all the girls were smiling. "That's the *real* gift," Marigold murmured.

"Liquid gold," Lily said, nodding along with her.

Aster said nothing, though her neck burned.

"I'm sure you've heard us all talk about Sweet Thistle before, Clementine," Violet continued, "but words don't really do justice to the feeling it gives you. It's like letting your mind sink into a warm bath. Outside the welcome house there're people clawing at each other for just a taste, but now that you're a sundown girl you'll get it every night. The cap is an eyedropper, see? One drop under the tongue will do. Mother Fleur will refill it for you every week."

Aster had only ever used her Sweet Thistle once, on her Lucky Night. She could understand why some girls liked it, but it left her limbs sluggish and her mind foggy in a way that had only made her feel more helpless, and the crushing hollowness it left the next morning had been worse than any natural hunger. Another dose would have sated it, but Aster knew that if she gave in, she'd be lost to Sweet Thistle for good. Even girls like Violet, who had only been taking it for a year, became fatigued and forgetful from its influence, and many of the older girls' minds had melted away completely.

Aster hated the thought of Clementine ending up like that.

"Thank you, Violet," Clementine said quietly. "Really—thank you *all*. This has been my best day at Green Creek, and if every day as a sundown girl goes something like this . . . *lucky* really is the right word."

She unscrewed the top of the bottle, running it under her nose.

"Oh, not yet," Violet said. "Save it for tonight."

"Oh—sorry."

"Don't apologize. We're all happy for you. Aren't we, Aster?" Violet asked.

Aster let out a breath through her teeth. "Delighted."

After breakfast Aster and Clementine took the presents up to Clementine's bedroom. Clem carefully laid the cookies and sketch on the bureau, and put the pocket watch in her jewelry box alongside all the glinting necklaces and earrings Mother Fleur had given her. Now that they were alone, it was as if Clementine let a mask slip away. Her smile was genuine, but it was tired. She ran her finger over the bracelet Aster had given her.

"Thanks again," she said. "You know, it means everything to me to have you here, too." Then she paused. "What should I expect tonight? Really? I know you're not allowed to talk about it, and you don't have to now, but I just—I want to know."

Aster looked over her shoulder, making sure the door was closed behind them. But still she hesitated. She'd never seen the good in planting fear in the Clementine's mind. Not when she could do nothing to help her. Aster wondered, again, if Violet had the right of it.

But Violet lied. Mother Fleur lied.

Everyone lied. That was how girls ended up in welcome houses to begin with, sent there by parents who'd been desperate enough to believe it would be better than the life they could provide.

Aster finally met Clementine's eye. "None of us can really know what to expect on any given night," she said. "That's just as true for me now as it was when I turned sixteen. But listen, I meant what I said, Clem. You've always been stronger than anything they've thrown at us. Stronger than me, too, because you still find a way to be your same sunny self no matter what." Aster managed a smile, even though she felt dangerously close to tears. "So if you feel yourself getting scared . . . just think of a song, hear? It doesn't have to be your favorite song. In fact, it's better if it isn't. Just pick one you know in your bones, and think of nothing else. That's what I do."

Clementine nodded. "Okay. Right, okay." She exhaled and wrapped Aster in a hug. "Thanks."

Aster squeezed her tightly. "I'll be just downstairs the whole time."

"Okay."

Clementine let go, laughing a little self-consciously. "Anyway, I better get down to the reception room for the auction. Wander

29

well."

"Wander well," Aster replied solemnly. She followed her sister out of the bedroom and into the hallway, where they would part ways. Aster had to head back to her own bedroom to prepare it for the next brag. The next time she saw Clementine, the worst of this night would be behind them.

And then we'll be on the same side of things again, Aster thought.

She wouldn't have to keep secrets from Clementine anymore, wouldn't be separated from her. They could talk like they used to. Find things to laugh about. Steal their happiness where they could. That was how they won.

Unless . . .

Aster spun around. "Clem?" she called, cold at the sudden image of Clementine as empty-eyed as the oldest Good Luck Girls, the girls whose only remaining happiness came in a little brown bottle.

Clementine turned. "Yeah?"

"Don't—don't take the Sweet Thistle, okay?" Aster pleaded. "Lie to Mother Fleur if she asks you about it. Your body may belong to them, but your mind doesn't have to. We can keep each other brave. Same as always."

Clementine's brows furrowed in confusion. "But, Violet . . ."

"Promise me, Clem."

She swallowed and nodded. "I promise."

CHAPTER THREE

Evening had fallen on the Green Creek welcome house, and the sundown girls, true to their names, came alive as they worked the growing nighttime crowd.

Aster was far too worried for Clementine to put any effort into flattering the puffed-up men around her. Instead she clung to the shadows of the reception room, watching as the other girls draped themselves over the parlor furniture and flirted with practiced ease. The mirrored walls reflected the chandelier light infinitely, creating the illusion of stars in a sky, while the deep rugs underfoot dampened all sound to an intimate hush. Iris, one of the oldest women at the welcome house, leaned into the grand piano that dominated the southwest corner of the room and began to play a slinking melody. Aster remembered when they'd first arrived at the welcome house, and how nine-year-old Clementine had been caught sneaking out of bed to try to pick out a lullaby on the creamy white keys. The raveners scoured her mind so viciously that she hadn't spoken for three days. But then kindly Iris had taken her under her wing. *It's about time I started training one of you to take over this old beast for me*, Iris had said. *I know it looks like it has teeth, but I promise it won't bite.*

Right about now, Clementine would be greeting whichever brag had bought her at the auction.

Aster fought a fresh wave of queasiness. The air in the room was stifling, adding more heat to her temper. The men must have sensed it because for once, they left her alone. Some of them were connoisseurs of the business, come to see if the Green Creek welcome house lived up to its reputation. Others were wealthy but road-weary travelers just looking for a rack and a roll for the night. And almost all of them had come to the Scab from one of Arketta's fattened cities along the borders—where they belonged. The Scab had a way of making even big men feel small, what with its towering mountains and its restless dead. Good Luck Girls made them feel big again.

Or at least, they were supposed to.

Aster continued pacing along the edge of the room, tugging up the front of her corset. Her dress, cobalt blue with black lace, barely reached midthigh, leaving her legs to sweat under too-tight fishnet stockings. Her hair frizzed around her silk headband like a thunderhead. Mother Fleur frowned at Aster from her favorite chair, but, mercifully, the housemistress decided not to try her tonight, either.

A particularly loud chord rang out from the piano, and Aster jumped, nerves strung near to breaking point. Violet, who sat on the nearest couch, cocked her eyebrow up at the brag whose lap she was perched on.

"You look tense, Aster," she said lazily. "No need to worry. Your sister is just fine."

"And how would you know that?" Aster asked.

"I got a good look at the brag with her. He's big as a house. I suspect she's having a Luckier Night than most."

"*Excuse* me?" Aster took a step towards her, fist clenched. Violet's smile fell clean off her face. But before Aster could say anything more, someone grabbed her wrist from behind with a deathly grip. A feverish chill shot up her arm and spread through her whole body, followed by sudden, crushing dread.

Ravener.

"That'll do," he said, his voice slipping down the back of her neck like cold water.

She turned and faced a lean, smartly dressed man, his forest green vest marking him as welcome house help. Aster recognized him as Amos. Like all raveners, his eyes were an ember-orange, set deep in his hawkish face. Meeting his stare only intensified the effect of his bewitchment. Aster's knees crumpled beneath her. Pain blossomed in her chest. And the fear roared in her skull, building to a scream—

Amos released her mind. A moment later, he released her wrist, too. He had only trapped her for a few seconds, but having your mind ravened was akin to holding your hand to an open flame: a few seconds was more than enough.

"Don't let me catch you skulking again," Amos hissed in her ear. "Find a brag, or you'll get worse."

His work done, he retreated to his post in the corner of the parlor. There were others like him scattered throughout the house. Raveners drew their power from beyond the Veil, and it made them half like the dead themselves—indifferent to cold or hunger, fatigue or pain. It was said that all men who became raveners lost their souls to that power over time, though Aster suspected anyone drawn to raveners' work didn't have much of a soul to begin with. *They're necessary to keep the peace,* Violet would've said.

The little bootlick was smirking at Aster now. Probably she thought Aster had had this coming. Aster curled her lip and stalked off. She was still shaky, sweating. She needed to clear her head.

The reception room was flanked on either side by two smaller parlors, a gambleman's room and a saloon that doubled as a dance hall. Aster made the rounds through both, careful to avoid further attention. The walking did little to calm her. Amos might have dredged up an ancient, animal fear, but it had already been just below the surface. It'd been mounting all night.

Aster had always known it was her job to protect Clementine, had always known that meant playing by the rules as best she could and avoiding Mother Fleur's deadly temper.

So why did she feel like she had failed Clementine completely?

Soon enough, Aster found herself back in the reception room, which was now livelier than ever. She angled towards one of the windows, where it was quieter. She could see nothing in the black square of night, but the pocket of cool air was a welcome relief. The worst of the ravening began to wear off.

Then, just as Aster was about to drag herself back into the crowd, she saw it: one window over, by the foot of the stairs, the velvet curtains jumped.

Far too sharp a movement to be a draft.

Aster narrowed her eyes. The welcome house had its dead, of

course. The Veil was always thinner in places of great suffering. But a hallower came through once a month to cast out what spirits he could; there hadn't been a serious disturbance in years.

Another rustle, more exaggerated this time. No one else seemed to have noticed yet. Aster steeled herself and wandered over to investigate, if only to give herself a distraction from this never-ending night. When she pulled the curtains back, she swallowed a gasp.

Clementine.

Her hair had come undone, and her eyes were wide with panic. She shook feverishly. Aster's shock robbed her of her words. Clementine pulled the curtains closed before anyone else could see her. Aster turned around quickly, making it look as if she were just leaning against the wall.

"What *happened* to you?" Aster whispered out of the side of her mouth, looking around them anxiously. She hadn't even noticed Clem coming down the stairs, but someone else might have. Some of the daybreak girls working the floor were sure to be spies, selling others out in return for Mother Fleur's goodwill. And a ravener could sense fear just as well as he could control it.

"Aster, the brag I was with—um—he's—" Aster could barely catch Clem's voice. "I think I—" Her voice faded entirely.

"What?"

"I said I—I think I killed him."

Killed? No. Clementine wasn't capable of such a thing. The brag must have passed out drunk. He could wake at any minute and come looking for her.

Aster started to tell her as much, but Clementine's words

poured out in a rush. "I didn't mean to do it, Aster, I swear. I hit him over the head with the lamp. He was choking me and I wasn't thinking, I just wanted him to stop, but now there's all this blood—"

By the Veil.

"Okay," Aster said. "*Shh*, Clem, it's going to be fine. Just stay quiet for now."

In fact, her own heart had begun to hammer in her chest. She took another look around through the haze of cigar smoke. Mother Fleur wasn't paying her any mind, but Violet was watching her with obvious suspicion. Aster had already challenged her twice today. Violet would be dying for an excuse to rat her out.

Look away, Aster pleaded. *Just this once, Violet, please, mind your own business.*

Violet's brag took her by the chin and brought her down for a kiss. Violet closed her eyes.

"We have to go," Aster whispered immediately. "Now."

They left the window and slipped up the stairs, Clementine sticking close to the shadowed wall. Aster forced herself to remain calm and keep her pace measured, squeezing Clementine's hand to quell her fear, too. It was only once they reached the hallway that they began to run.

Clementine stopped a few feet away from her door, clearly unwilling to take another step. Praying that her sister had misjudged the situation, Aster opened the door herself.

The room was dark except for the rectangle of light pouring in from the hallway. But even so, Aster could see the body on the bed. The man was massive, naked from the waist up, and sprawled on his stomach with thick limbs spread in an X. His skull glistened with blood, a rotten melon that had been kicked in. The broken glass of the lamp glittered on the floor.

Aster stared, as if waiting for him to get back up.

"It was an accident," Clementine whispered again, almost pleading. "That's what we'll tell them, right? That it was an accident?"

Aster pulled Clementine inside and closed the door behind them, leaning against it, giving herself a heartbeat to think. It wouldn't matter that it had been an accident. There would be no forgiveness for this.

"Clementine—" Aster's mouth had gone dry. "We can't tell anyone. If Mother Fleur finds out . . ."

She trailed off. Clementine had turned on the gasolier overhead, twisting the knob to full brightness. Horror pooled in Aster's belly at the sight before her, the empty shine of the brag's eyes and the silent scream of his slack mouth. There wasn't a night that went by that she hadn't fantasized about killing the men that came into her bed. A pistol kissed against their temples. Her hands wrapped around their throats. But they were just that—fantasies. The real thing left her sickened and stunned.

Still, she would rather Clementine kill this man a thousand times than risk him doing the same to her. It wouldn't have been the first time a Good Luck Girl had gotten killed on the job because a brag got too rough.

Thank the dead I told her not to take the Sweet Thistle, Aster thought suddenly. Clementine never would have had the strength to defend herself if she'd been drugged.

For the briefest instant, Aster was almost proud. Her sister had shown the kind of courage Aster wasn't sure she had anymore.

"I'm so sorry," Clementine said at last, wiping her tears.

"*Don't be*," Aster said. "Don't apologize, Clem. I'd rather it was him."

Clementine sucked in a deep breath. "What do we do?"

Aster silently ran over their options. If anyone found out about this, Clementine would be put to death. That was for certain. Murderers in the Scab were hung high in a gibbet and left to the mercy of the vengeants, the most ruthless spirits this side of the Veil. A man might languish in that gibbet for days before the vengeants were drawn, irresistibly, to his suffering . . . but sooner or later they would always have him, splitting his belly with invisible claws and savaging his throat with unseen teeth. The crows would pick at the ruined body until the bones fell to the ground.

Aster would die herself before she let that happen to Clementine.

"All right," she said, straightening. "All right, first we hide the body. Mother Fleur likes to check up on the new girls, make sure they're doing right by their men. We can't have her coming in and seeing yours like this."

"And then what?"

"I don't know!" Aster snapped. She shot Clementine an apologetic look. "Sorry—I'm just—I'm working on it. But all I know for sure is that we need to get rid of this body." She scanned the room. "The wardrobe," she said. It was the best hiding space available.

After opening the wardrobe doors and shoving aside dresses to make room, they moved quickly, Clementine grabbing the brag's ankles, Aster taking his wrists. But as they started to drag him, it became clear he was too heavy. Even if they could get him all the way off the mattress, they could never hold him up. His body would crash down on the floor and bring someone running. Clementine suggested they get Tansy and Mallow to help. Aster didn't trust them with this secret. Clementine insisted she could. Aster finally gave in, all too aware of the time they were wasting arguing.

With as much composure as she could muster, Aster hurried to the attic. Clementine stayed behind to keep talking as if the brag were still alive, in case Mother Fleur listened at the door, like she was known to.

The attic was relatively empty—it was the busiest time of the night, and most of the daybreak girls would be needed on the floor. But Tansy and Mallow had finished their last shift after supper. They were both relaxing on Mallow's cot, still in their livery, Mallow lying down with her head on Tansy's knee. Tansy giggled over something Mallow said.

Aster marched over.

"Tansy! Mallow!" she barked. "You're wanted downstairs."

"And just what the hell for?" Mallow demanded.

"Just come with me," Aster ordered. Then she leaned in and said softly, "Clem's in trouble."

Tansy and Mallow sobered immediately. They got up from the bed and followed Aster downstairs, through dimly lit hallways. Aster explained the situation in a whispered rush, stopping and forcing a smile the couple times they passed another girl.

Before opening the door to Clementine's room, she paused a moment and glanced both ways to make sure no one was coming. "Listen," she said. "If you want to turn back, now's the time." She held each of their gazes, one after the other. "I'll understand if you don't want to be a part of this. So will Clem."

A look passed between them. "We're not going anywhere," Mallow said first, turning back to Aster. "We can't leave you alone with this."

Tansy nodded. "She'd do it for us."

Aster gave a quick, grateful nod back. Then she opened the door.

"Oh," Tansy said softly, covering her mouth with her hand.

"Well, shit, Clem," Mallow said under her breath, though she sounded more impressed than anything. "Remind me never to cross you."

"It was an accident—" Clementine began.

"Never mind what it was," Aster interrupted before her sister could get going again. She closed the door behind them. "Everybody grab a limb. We're stuffing him in the wardrobe."

Mallow rolled up her sleeves, exposing farm-strong forearms, while Tansy tugged her sleeves down over her hands, presumably to keep them clean. They grabbed the legs while Clementine and Aster grabbed the arms. Even with all of them working together, the body was still heavy and awkward to handle. They shuffled over towards the wardrobe. Luckily, it stood against the front wall, out of the line of sight from the doorway. So when the inevitable moment came and Mother Fleur opened the door—

"What's the plan after this?" Mallow whispered, as if reading Aster's thoughts. "They're sure as hell going to notice when he doesn't come downstairs."

Aster had been thinking of nothing else. She still didn't have any idea. Clem couldn't stay here—not if she wanted to live—but there was no way to get her out of the welcome house, either, with Dex at the door. The only people let in and out of that door were paid customers.

The brags.

Like the one right here.

"Well?" Mallow prodded, her voice tight with effort.

Adrenaline surged through Aster's body as an idea sparked through her. "Hold on, I'm thinking," she said. "Rest him here for a second."

The girls set the body down gently on the floor. Aster stared at the brag's hand, coming out of his shirt cuff near where she'd gripped his arm. Like all guests, he'd gotten a temporary favor on the back of his hand on his way in—the welcome house emblem, a skull with roses growing through it. He'd have to show his hand to Dex on his way out. Proof that he'd paid for his pleasure. Then he was free to go.

"We're going to run," Aster said, with more confidence than she felt. "Me and Clem. We're getting the hell out of here." The brag's favor would disappear once the time he'd paid for ran out. And, for all Aster knew, it might fade away any minute now that he was dead, too. But if they hurried . . .

Clem stared at her, eyes wide. "We are?"

"You can't be serious," Tansy said. "You can't get past Dex."

Aster didn't have the details all worked out yet. But she

knew they had the most important thing they needed. "Yes, we can. Give me a minute to figure it out," she said. "Clem, get your things. We're bolting. No way you'll survive if we don't."

"How?" Clementine said. "Where?"

"*Out of the damn house*," Aster barked, breaking her whisper. She swallowed hard. "For now, just get ready."

After one more moment of shock, Clem hurried over to her trunk.

Aster stood staring at the brag, desperately trying to puzzle out the rest of her plan. Mallow fished out a knife tucked in the brag's boot, giving it an expert flourish. "I hope you don't need this, but I'll feel better if you have it," she muttered. "Though I still don't see what you're thinking."

"And you're definitely going to need some shine," Tansy added, pulling his theomite thumb ring free. "This ought to fetch you plenty."

"How can we—" Clementine started.

But before anyone could say anything else, the doorknob turned with a soft rattle.

They'd been discovered.

CHAPTER FOUR

Violet stood in the doorway with her arms crossed.

"I swear I knew you were up to something, Aster," she said. "What the hell is going on here?"

Aster let out a low curse. *Of all people.* Violet, the one girl guaranteed to turn them in.

They had to get rid of her.

"Nothing that concerns you," Aster said. "I'll see you back downstairs in a minute."

"Mallow? Tansy?" Violet continued, ignoring Aster. Her face reddened. "One of you better answer me. Clementine, where's your brag?"

Clementine glanced at Aster, her desperation plain.

"He took off early," Aster said evenly. They crowded the doorway enough that Violet wouldn't see the body unless she looked past them. Aster couldn't give her any reason to. "Went on over to Clooney's," she added. The gambling hall across the street. It was plausible enough. Not every man stayed the night.

"That's right," Clementine jumped in. "And after he left I decided I might as well go get my friends to . . . you know . . . just to have someone to talk to . . ."

Violet narrowed her eyes. "You mean your brag paid for a Lucky Night and left after twenty minutes? Was he that unsatisfied?" She took a step towards Clementine. "If you lost us that patron, Mother Fleur will have your hide—"

"Hey, easy," Mallow said in a low warning.

"And *you* better get back upstairs before I let Mother Fleur know you're wandering around without permission," Violet added, rounding on her. "You, too," she said to Tansy. "And look at the two of you, all a mess. Is this how you present yourselves?" Her eyes caught on something. "Tansy, what's on your sleeve? It's stained." She stepped forward.

Aster now saw that a dark red splotch marred Tansy's cuff.

"Nothing," Tansy said, quickly moving her hands behind her.

"On Mother Fleur's behalf, I demand—" Violet came in even closer as she spoke. Heart racing, Aster stepped forward to block her. But it was too late. Violet's face shifted, wide eyes finding the blood on the bed and tracking it to its source. "What the—"

Aster's hand shot out before she could even question herself, grabbing hold of Violet by the wrist. She yanked her inside and kicked the door shut. Violet let out a short, sharp cry as Aster held her pinned against it.

"*What did you do to that brag?*" Violet screeched. "*Let me GO!*"

"Quiet!" Aster said. She looked back over her shoulder, holding Violet's upper arm against the door with one hand. "Mallow, the knife." She held her free hand out for the weapon.

"Aster," Clementine began.

"*The knife.*"

Mallow surrendered it wordlessly.

So this is what it feels like, Aster thought as she took the knife, the leather smooth beneath her fingers, the blade heavy in her hand. Something about it immediately stilled her frenzied mind.

Finally, she wasn't helpless.

Violet stopped struggling and went quiet at the sight of the weapon. She desperately scanned the room. "What happened?" she asked again, softer.

No turning back now.

Aster held the knife up to Violet's throat, pressing the flat of the blade against her skin.

"The brag is dead," Aster said slowly, quietly. Her voice shook, but her hand was steady. "I killed him. It was an accident. Now me and Clem have to make a run for it."

Clementine began to speak, but Aster shot her a warning glance. *Let me handle this.* If all else failed, at least Aster could take the blame.

"You expect me to believe that?" Violet choked out. "Clementine's the one who was with him this whole time. And she looks a damn sight more rattled than you do."

"Believe what you want. I don't have time to convince you. But if you can't convince *me* you'll keep your mouth shut, I'll carve your tongue out before we go."

Aster sensed the others shifting uncomfortably. Violet met Aster's dark stare. Weighed her words. When she answered, her voice was just above a whisper.

"You're bluffing."

"Am I?" Aster snarled, pressing the knife deeper. She spoke roughly in hopes of hiding the fact that, in truth, she *wasn't* sure she had the stomach to follow through on her threat.

But she had to. Or Clementine would be killed.

She drew a jeweled bead of blood just below Violet's favor.

"All right, all right, stop!" Violet hissed.

"Quiet," Aster reminded her.

"You're serious about leaving?"

"As the dead."

"You take me for a fool? If there was a way to run, don't you think I'd know? Don't you think other girls would run all the time?"

"Other girls don't have what we have."

"A death wish?" Even now, up against the wall with a knife to her throat, that condescending tone never quite left her voice.

Aster hesitated. It felt wrong to tell Violet anything about their plan. But, at this point, it didn't really matter.

"The brag's hand. We can cut it off, use it to get past Dex."

The dead body was the only answer to the problem it had created for them.

"Ripping hell," Mallow muttered after a moment. "You're right."

Violet's brow furrowed. "That . . . might actually work . . ."

Aster drew a breath and backed up a step. "Go on and sit on the bed," she said to Violet, gesturing with the knife. "I think you know you're not leaving this room until you convince us we can trust you."

Violet walked to the bed as straight and proper as ever. She perched on the edge.

"I'm still working out the details," Aster said, looking at Clementine, Mallow, and Tansy, who were all staring at her.

"But that's the basic idea: Clem and I use the hand to get out."

Mallow looked at Tansy. A wordless question passed between them. Tansy gave her a subtle nod and turned to Aster.

"Take us with you."

"No *way*," Clementine jumped in before Aster could reply. "I won't have you all killed because of us. Bad enough we asked this much of you."

"She's right," Aster agreed, relieved they felt the same. "We have no idea what to expect out there, and the law's going to be on our tail the whole time. We're only running because we have to. But no one else knows you all are involved—you can still walk away from this."

Mallow scowled. "So, what, me and Tanz stay here, give up our one shot of getting out of this place?" she asked. "I don't think so. I'd rather die on the outside tomorrow than live out the rest of my days in here."

"I feel the same," Tansy said quietly.

Violet shifted. Aster immediately raised the knife. But Violet held up her hands in surrender.

"Take me with you," she breathed. "I want to run, too."

Aster laughed. "Right."

"Take me with you!" Violet repeated desperately.

"And why in the hell should we? After all your years of bullshit?"

"*Please.*"

Violet had never said "please" to any of them. *What's she playing at?* Aster looked at the others, but Clementine, Tansy, and Mallow seemed just as mistrustful.

"Some sort of trick," Tansy muttered.

47

"It's not a trick!" Violet insisted. "I want out." Then she set her mouth. "Either you take me with you, or I tell Mother Fleur everything."

"*Or* I cut your throat," Aster reminded her.

"Better than living like this."

Aster felt a flicker of doubt. If it had been anyone else, Aster would've believed them, no question. But Violet? Mother Fleur's favorite girl? The one who never shut up about how much she *loved* Green Creek? No, something wasn't right.

By the Veil, we don't have time for this—

"Besides, you need me," Violet continued.

"For what, exactly?" Clementine asked, sounding equally unconvinced.

"I *know* things, things Mother Fleur doesn't tell the rest of you."

"You'd only slow us down," Mallow spat. "Pampered little princess—"

Violet showed her teeth. "Dustblood scum—"

"*Shut up.* All of you," Aster broke in. She didn't trust Violet any more than the others did, but they couldn't keep arguing. Mother Fleur could be here any second. And even if cutting Violet's throat was clearly the only sure way of keeping her quiet, Aster still felt sick at the idea of it. Unlike the brag, Violet was an innocent—an insufferable, selfish shrew, yes, but an innocent.

She had to make a decision.

Aster dropped her voice to a low warning and raised the knife once more. "You do anything to try to sabotage us, and I *will* make you sorry."

* * *

Once again, Aster circled the reception room. This time, though, she was the hunter, not the prey. She needed to find a guest who was still unattended, and she needed to do it quickly, before Violet came downstairs disguised as Clementine's brag.

The idea was for Violet to slip outside, find a hay cart in the livery stable, and wheel it around underneath Aster's bedroom window so the rest of them could jump out. But in order to get past Dex, she'd have to hold out the severed hand from the end of the coat sleeve as if it were her own. Aster hated trusting the most important part of the plan to Violet, but she was the only one tall enough to wear the big brag's clothes.

Mallow and Tansy had agreed to see to the grisly business of cutting the hand off with the brag's knife. It was Aster's job to create a distraction in the reception room so Dex wouldn't look at Violet too closely when she tried to leave.

Aster's neck prickled with frustration as she continued to scan the crowd, her every heartbeat like the ticking of a timer. They had no idea how long the brag's favor would last. And if it disappeared before Violet got out? They were dead.

A skinny brag in a long brown coat stood by himself at the bar, looking down at an untouched drink. He was one of the youngest men here. Aster was just about to approach him when another girl reached him first, leaning easy against the counter.

Damn it.

Aster turned away, searching desperately for someone else she could corner. Then, she spotted him: a man hovering alone by the piano, near enough the front door that Dex was sure to come running at her distraction. The brag wore the faded gray uniform of the Arkettan forces. *Glory to the Reckoning,* the words beneath his stripes said—the national motto. Like lawmen, armymen were offered a reduced price at welcome houses. They were always eager to find someone to listen to their stories about the dustblood rebels they'd helped capture.

Aster started towards him, slicing through the crowd.

"Looks like you could use some company," she said, slipping in at his side and trailing her fingers along his arm. Aster was never usually this forward, and for the first time she found herself wishing she had Violet's skill in effortless flirting.

The armyman squared up, his eyes glassy and unfocused from too much drink. "And what's your name, miss?" he asked thickly.

"I'm called Aster. See?" she teased, turning to show off her favor. She managed a sweeping glance of the room as she did so, but there was still no sign of Violet. She swallowed around the knot in her throat.

"Well, Lieutenant Carney, at your service, Aster," the armyman introduced himself, clumsily tipping his slouch hat. He eyed her up and down slowly, a half grin spreading across his face. A daybreak girl passed by with a tray of bright cocktails. He swiped two.

"Sweet drink for a sweet girl?" he asked.

Aster thanked him demurely, taking the glass. She looked past him to the stairs. *Where* was Violet?

And then Aster spotted her, swaggering down the steps with surprising confidence. Her long hair had been tucked away underneath the brag's hat, her feminine figure hidden by his knee-length coat. She'd wrapped his silk dustkerchief around the bottom half of her face. But it wasn't these things that made her look the part. It was the way she carried herself, the natural authority and obvious sense of entitlement. She showed none of the fear that she surely felt.

Aster's blood raced. She wet her lips.

"Wander well," Carney said to her cheerfully, raising his glass in a toast.

She turned to the armyman, fighting to keep her calm. "Wander well," she replied with a forced smile, and she drained her drink in three swallows.

The alcohol lit a fire down her throat, sticky sweetness burning on her tongue. She coughed violently. Braced herself against Carney's shoulder as her head spun.

Carney rubbed her back, laughing. Her skin crawled at his touch.

"Easy!" he said with disbelief. "You dustblood girls really are tough as drygrass."

"Well, we aim to impress, Lieutenant," she replied airily. "Though I'll confess I'm feeling a bit faint now." She straightened up but let herself sway where she stood.

"Nothing a chaser won't fix," Carney said with too much eagerness.

Aster looked past him again. Violet had made it to the foyer. She was next in line to leave.

Carney persisted. "Here, I'll take you to the bar—"

"Don't trouble yourself," Aster said quickly. "I just need to sit for a spell." She took a few wobbly steps, let out a dramatic wail, and collapsed to the floor. The piano music cut off. A collective gasp went up around the room.

Aster remained on the floor, eyes closed, as chaos erupted around her. A jumble of voices filled the air: girls calling her name, a man calling for help. The floor vibrated under her cheek with the thumps of footsteps as a crowd gathered. She could hear Mother Fleur pushing through them and apologizing for the disturbance. The smell of cigar smoke in the rug turned her stomach.

"Keep back, she's with me," Carney ordered.

Aster fluttered her eyes open. A tangle of legs stood between her and the front door, but she could just make out Violet, striding outside. Dex was lumbering towards the growing crowd, forcing calm upon the guests with his mental influence. Aster's relief, however, was her own.

Violet had made it out.

Then a cold realization trickled down Aster's spine, chilling her brief rush of triumph: what if Violet simply ran away? What if she didn't wheel the cart around for the rest of them, just used the brag's hand to make her escape and leave them for dead? Maybe she'd only wanted to use them, maybe that had been her plan all along.

No choice now but to see this through.

Aster looked up at Dex, whose lip curled to reveal yellowed teeth, and Mother Fleur, whose mouth smiled but whose eyes flashed with fury. Aster's sloppy behavior would reflect poorly on the welcome house. Normally that would mean she'd spend tomorrow having her mind pulled apart by one of the raveners.

But by this time tomorrow, Aster would either be free or dead.

"Are you all right, Aster?" Mother Fleur asked, her voice dripping with false concern.

Aster took Carney's hand and stood up slowly. "I'm fine now, ma'am. Just got a little lightheaded. Sorry for causing a stir." She didn't have to fake the quaver in her voice. "I think I had better retire for the night, though, with your permission."

"Of course," Mother Fleur replied. "And the Lieutenant here would like to come along and make sure you're okay, and spend a little time with you." She turned towards the brag and smiled. "The Aster Room is at the end of the hall on the right."

Carney stepped in closer as the rest of the crowd began to dissipate. Aster's panic doubled.

"Actually, I'm not sure—" she began.

"Don't worry, I'll look after you," he promised. He draped his arm around her and guided her towards the stairs.

Aster's heart thudded against her ribcage. This wasn't part of the plan. She couldn't bring him into her room. Clementine and the others were probably climbing out of the window right now. Or, if Violet had abandoned them, they were trapped there with no escape.

She made herself stumble on the first step.

"Careful, now," Carney said. "Don't want you taking another nasty tumble."

"Seems I'm too weak to go upstairs just yet," Aster demurred. She'd hoped to stall for a moment, give everyone time to get out, but Carney simply scooped her up and started up the stairs.

"No problem at all," he said gallantly.

Aster mouthed a curse. Of course acting helpless would only encourage him.

He smiled down at her as he continued to talk, and Aster

began to feel ill in earnest. And then there was the usual fear, too, the one that took hold of Aster every time she climbed these stairs with a brag. Bone-cold dread rose up to drown her. It didn't matter that Carney seemed to think himself chivalrous. The end result was always the same.

They reached the top of the stairs. Carney set her down. Aster made a slow gallows walk to the end of the hall. She drew in a tight breath as she wrapped her hand around the knob.

Please, by the Veil, don't let me find anyone behind this door. Let them have escaped. Please.

She opened the door.

And exhaled. The room was empty, the window open. She strolled over to it, pretending to simply close the curtains. She glanced down and saw the hay cart waiting below.

Clementine had gotten out. They'd all gotten out.

Then Carney closed the door behind him with a thud, dropping Aster's heart. She couldn't jump with him standing there right behind her.

You'll just have to fight him. Knock him out.

A trained soldier? She didn't like her chances.

"Well, then, where should we start?" Carney asked, his words slurring slightly. He stepped in behind her and circled her waist with his meaty hands.

Aster's throat swelled. Her eyes burned. She could already feel herself sliding into that place of numb detachment where she went every night, her mind floating farther and farther away and leaving her body to fend for itself. Her breath was overloud in her ears, and her limbs grew so heavy she might as well have swallowed a whole week's worth of Sweet Thistle.

Sweet Thistle.

That's it.

"Let's get you out of that dress. Help you breathe a little easier," Carney said. She spun around to face him, still in his grasp.

"There's something I've been wanting to try for a while," she murmured into his ear. "But I'm not sure you're up for it."

"Oh?"

"Let me see if I can find it."

Aster disentangled herself and retreated to her vanity, where her bottle of Sweet Thistle sat nestled among the jewelry and hairbrushes.

She wet her lips, a flare of anger burning through the fog filling her mind. Every week, Mother Fleur had expected her to be grateful for this Sweet Thistle. Her parents had expected her to be grateful for this home. Lieutenant Carney probably expected her to be grateful for his restraint. As if any of those things changed what this place was, what it had almost done to Clementine. What it had already done to Aster.

"You're beautiful, you know," Carney said idly. "Most of these dustblood girls . . ." He just shook his head. "But what else can a man expect from the Scab? Glad I found some good luck here after all."

I should crack a mirror over his head.

Slit his throat with a shard of the glass.

Let him bleed like a pig.

But no, she couldn't. She had to control her anger just as she controlled her fear. It was the only way she would make it out of here alive.

"What've you got there?" Carney continued. He had snuck up behind her, surprisingly light-footed.

She swallowed and showed him the bottle of Sweet Thistle. "Just a little pick-me-up leftover from a former guest," she said brightly. "Interested?

Carney raised an eyebrow. "What exactly does this pick-me-up do?"

"It's an extract of a rare flower from the peaks of the mountains," Aster lied. "Said to open your mind and senses and unlock your deepest potential for pleasure."

"That so?"

She nodded. "Just a drop under your tongue. And the more you use, the stronger the effect. Not every man can handle it, though. Most can't manage more than a dose or two. But an armyman such as yourself . . ."

"Hand it over," Carney said roughly. Aster obliged, watching, tensed, as he unscrewed the cap and ran the bottle under his nose. If he recognized the scent of Sweet Thistle, he would know Aster was playing him. But he just filled the dropper all the way to the top, opened his mouth, and emptied the liquid under his tongue.

"See? No problem," Carney said, his slur growing even more pronounced, the drug beginning to work its magic. "Now you just come over here and we can—we can—"

He sat heavily on the bed, muttered a low curse, and fell back. Aster hurried to his side. His eyes were half open but unseeing, his words faint and incomprehensible. If he wasn't already asleep, he would be soon.

Aster moved quickly.

She ran back to the window. The hay cart was still there, mercifully. And the sluggishness that had taken over her limbs just moments ago had lifted completely. Aster brimmed with energy, equal parts fear and anticipation. How many nights had she imagined an escape? It was finally happening.

But not if she didn't hurry. Every second she wasted was a second the other girls might be discovered in the stables.

She lifted first one leg then the next out the window, the iron sill biting into her palms. She was certain that if she lingered even a moment, someone, something would come to stop her. A heartbeat later, she sat on the window ledge, legs dangling over open air. The distance between her feet and the hay cart seemed to yawn wider, now that the moment to jump was here. *Go*, she told herself. *Jump*.

But instead Aster turned and looked over her shoulder—at the room that had been her prison for so long, at the man who would have used her like so many others already had. Nothing short of the death of a brag had given her this chance to escape, and she knew it was a chance that would come only this once.

Aster made a decision right then. Even if it meant her life, she would never come back to this place or any place like it.

She would never be a Good Luck Girl again.

CHAPTER FIVE

Aster pushed off the ledge, and then for a moment, just a moment, she felt like she was flying.

When Aster was seven years old, she had jumped from the high branch of a half-dead evergreen behind their rundown house in the tenant camp. She'd thought if she climbed high enough and jumped far enough, the wind would carry her and she would soar over the mountains and out of the Scab.

Instead, she'd crashed to the ground and twisted her ankle, which swelled up to the size of a crab apple. But it had been worth it, for that fleeting moment of flight and the promise of freedom.

This time, Aster knew the wind wouldn't carry her anywhere—but as she fell, the night air whispering around her, anything felt possible.

She hit the cart feet first, pain shooting through her shins despite the cushion of the hay. She couldn't help a startled cry. The crack of the wood seemed loud as a gunshot. She shook off the sting as best she could and clambered over the side slats, stumbling away into the night before one of the raveners came to investigate.

Aster hugged the white wood siding of the welcome house, picking her way through low bushes that snagged on her stockings, crouching every time she passed the glow of a window. Part of her was desperate to break into a run, but another part of her knew she had to stay careful and quiet. There were too many people milling around the veranda outside the welcome house. The livery stables were right next door, but the distance felt endless.

Aster couldn't even remember the last time she'd been out after dark. Mother Fleur made the younger girls tend to the outside of the welcome house, washing the windows and sweeping the porch, but that had always been during the blistering heat of day. This night was refreshingly brisk in comparison, a cold compress held to a feverish forehead. Aster took a deep breath, unable even in her desperation to help but savor the sweetness of the air, the taste of the mountains on her tongue.

Finally, she reached the end of the building. She paused, checking around the corner to make sure no one was lurking in the side yard between the welcome house and the stables, then dashed across the gap and ducked through the stable entrance. The thick, grassy smell of manure and hay filled her nose.

She kept low and scanned the dark for any sign of Augie, the nighttime stableman. It was a well-known fact that, on slower weeknights like this, Augie could usually be found across the street at Clooney's, gambling his meager earnings until he could afford to treat himself to the girls' company. He liked to joke it was his job to take care of them, same as the horses. His habits were now welcome: he was nowhere in sight.

Still, at least one stableboy would have been left alone to mind the horses and muck the stalls. It had been Violet's job to subdue him discreetly somehow. He'd be young and unarmed, Aster had reassured her—but then, so was Violet.

Aster crept further into the building, searching for the others. Most of the horses slept where they stood, but a few whickered softly as Aster checked their stalls, their eyes black and shiny as wet ink and the air thick with their scent. The stable was open on both ends, and the opposite entrance faced Main Street, where groups of men ambled by on their way from saloon to saloon, silhouetted in the lamplight. Their laughter crackled through the dark. Aster knew there would only be more of them as the night wore on.

She had to find her sister, now.

Aster neared the end of the aisle. Dread ate away at her from the inside. *Maybe they already left.*

Or maybe they'd been caught.

Then she heard tight whispers not far up ahead. She followed them, mouthing a prayer.

And then there they were: Clementine, Mallow, Tansy, and Violet, all four huddled together in the dark corner of an empty stall. The shaggy-haired stableboy lay next to them, hurriedly bound and gagged.

Aster let out a ragged breath, her body flooding with relief so strong it left her lightheaded. She put her hand against the rough wooden wall to steady herself. And then sank down to the hard earth.

"You made it," Tansy said, her voice an excited whisper.

Clementine crawled over and wrapped Aster in a fierce hug.

"What the hell took you so long?" Violet demanded.

Aster sighed and released Clementine.

"Ran into a spot of trouble," she said shortly. "Took care of it, but someone's sure to notice that cart soon. How'd you handle the stableboy?"

"Came in here pretending to be a customer and cracked him over the head with a pitchfork as soon as he turned his back."

"*What?* I told you to handle him *discreetly*," Aster hissed. "The last thing we need is another body to hide—"

"Calm down, I didn't hit him that hard. We're not all murderers like your sister here."

Aster's face grew hot. "Listen—"

Clem grabbed Aster's wrist, shaking her head and pointing towards the stable entrance. Two men stood in the wide opening.

Augie. He held his lantern high, and a gun hung easy at his hip.

Aster's heart hammered painfully in her chest as she crouched lower in the hay. She and Clem began crawling, as silently as possible, back into the corner where the others were huddled, alarm plain on all their faces.

"You ever known me to lie, Rich?" Augie asked. "Honest to the dead, Baxter McClennon was at the tables with me, and I won twenty eagles off him."

"As if McClennon would plant his pampered ass at a table you were reeking up."

"Hey, any man that don't reek by the end of the day is hardly a man at all," Augie argued.

Aster pressed up against the stall's wall. She held her breath as the men's voices got closer. Everyone stilled. The light of the lantern swept across the floor.

Clementine gripped Aster's arm, her fingernails digging into Aster's flesh.

"You just count your blessings it wasn't Derrick you were playing," Rich went on. "Everyone knows he's the *smart* brother. Off at some fancy boarding school overseas—"

Closer, closer . . . Maybe four steps away now. Three, two. Aster tensed, forming a fist, prepared to strike.

"—too busy with his studies to give you the drubbing you deserve," Rich finished, passing their stall without stopping.

Their voices receded. Rich found his horse a moment later, and Augie led him back out. The girls watched the stableman hurry back across the street to Clooney's.

Aster exhaled.

"That was way too close," Clementine whispered.

"And he could be back any minute," Aster agreed. "We need to get out of here—"

"We *need* to do exactly as I say," Violet interrupted. "I have a plan."

Aster turned to her, biting back frustration. "Whatever it is, I'm sure it can wait until we've put Green Creek behind us."

"You don't even know which way you're going. You barely made it out of the house. But follow me and we can get rid of these favors for good."

"What the hell are you talking about?" Aster asked, bewildered. Favors were impossible to hide and impossible to remove. *Everyone* knew this. Aster turned to the others and asked again: "What the hell is she talking about?"

"She explained the whole thing to us while we were waiting for you," Clementine said. "I think it's maybe worth listening to her. It might actually work."

"See?" Violet spat. "I told you. I know things."

Aster had completely forgotten about Violet's wild promises of privileged information. She'd thought then that Violet was bluffing, trying to get them to let her come along.

It was clear now that she was just the world's best fool. But Aster would hear her out, if only because Clementine insisted.

Aster gritted her teeth.

"All right, then, how do we get rid of our favors?"

Violet paused. "We're going to find Lady Ghost," she said. "I know where she lives."

For a moment, no one said anything. Aster felt something bubbling up inside her. A laugh. It came out of her mouth, harsh and sharp.

"Lady *Ghost*?" Aster demanded in a whispered snarl. "*That's* your brilliant idea?"

The other girls were silent.

"She's real," Violet said coldly.

"She's a *bedtime story*. If I wanted horseshit, Violet, I could just stay in this stable."

Lady Ghost was just a tall tale the youngest Good Luck Girls told themselves, a mysterious housemistress with the power to magic favors away. Some said she was called "Ghost" because of the way she made the tattoos disappear. Others said it was because she was so elusive herself.

Nobody over the age of twelve believed in her. Aster never had.

"It can't hurt to try, can it?" Tansy asked. "We have nowhere else to go. If we try to find our families, we'll just put them in danger, too."

Tansy. Probably the cleverest among them, and here she was swallowing this false hope. Aster squared her gaze on Violet. "Listen, I get how you might be able to come up really believing Lady Ghost was out there," she said slowly. "You've lived your whole life in this world. But we're in the real world, now, so you're just going to have to trust me on this, hear? She doesn't exist."

Violet curled her lip. "I'm done explaining myself. I already told you. I know things."

"So where *is* Lady Ghost, then?" Aster asked.

"I wasn't born yesterday. I know if I tell, you all will just abandon me. You're stuck with me because you don't know where you're going, and I'm stuck with you because I know better than to travel in Arketta alone. And don't give me that bit about cutting my throat. If you were going to hurt me, you'd have done it already."

Aster stood up and began to pace. She wished to the dead that Violet had never discovered them. But there was no use in arguing with her now, and Aster didn't want to give Violet any reason to cross them later. And if there was the tiniest hint of a chance . . . No. Of course there wasn't.

But what if?

Aster turned to the others. "Do you honestly believe her? Do you believe what she says?"

"It's possible, isn't it?" Clementine asked. Her voice was pleading. Aster had no response. She knew the others were right about one thing—they had nowhere else to go. There was no telling where their families lived now; landmasters traded dustbloods between one another like collectibles. And their parents certainly couldn't protect them.

Aster never would have wanted to crawl back to the ones who had abandoned her in the first place, anyway. She couldn't go home.

Violet seemed to take Aster's silence as a surrender. She flashed a self-satisfied grin. "Right, now that that's settled. All you need to know for now is that we're heading towards Killbank. Just do as I say."

Killbank. A decent-sized town a day's ride north. Just the thought of crossing the Scab made Aster's skin crawl. No one traveled far without hiring a rangeman. Not only because of the living things that hunted in the woods, but because of the dead things, too. The predators that couldn't be seen or heard.

The vengeants.

But we don't have a choice. We have to get out of Green Creek.

"Unless you have a better option?" Violet said, a smug challenge in her voice.

Mallow and Tansy were staring at Aster.

"We have to go in some direction," Mallow said. "Might as well be that one."

Aster turned to Clementine. *Okay?* she asked with a look.

Clementine gave her a single nod. And while their eyes were still locked, she leaned in, brushed a hand against her own favor and whispered, "Aster, I want to try."

Aster turned to Tansy and Mallow next. They were already helping each other up, checking to make sure the coast was clear. Like Aster, they probably just wanted to leave as soon

65

as possible.

It was decided.

Aster turned back to Violet.

"All right," she said. "But you remember what I told you, Violet. You don't get a second chance."

"I won't need one," Violet said. There was an expression of steely certainty on her face.

They didn't waste any more time. They ransacked the stable for what little supplies they could find—blankets, a bit of food and a canteen of water, spare men's clothes from Augie's living quarters. They quickly changed into the trousers and shirts, stashing their dresses under hay bales, then picked three horses and tacked up: a bay for Aster and Clementine, a piebald for Tansy and Mallow, and a black mare for Violet. It had been a lifetime since Aster had last saddled a horse, but her hands remembered how, and the ritual of it reassured her. Aster took the reins and Clementine slid in behind her, wrapping her arms around Aster's middle. And with a crack of the reins, they began to ride.

Aster led them down Green Creek's beaten dirt roads, angling north. The heart of town pulsed with wild energy, men pouring out of saloons and shouting to one another across the street. Nearer the edge of town, most of the shops were darkened on the street level, lamplight glowing from their upper levels where the shopkeepers had retired. They rode by the dress shop where all girls from the welcome house were taken, supervised by raveners, to be fitted for their new wardrobes when they became sundown girls. Aster cast her gaze to the mountains

66

that loomed black against the night sky. A girl could lose her way in those mountains, easy. But so could anyone on her tail.

She just had to get there.

None of them spoke, though their tension hummed in the air. They'd wrapped dustkerchiefs around their faces to cover their favors. That in itself wouldn't arouse suspicion, Aster hoped—plenty of folks covered their faces in the Scab on account of all the mining dust in the air—but it wouldn't take but a few minutes before their favors started to glow, giving them away. Not to mention the pain.

Still, they moved at a painstaking pace so as not to attract attention. Aster kept listening for any sound, near or far, that indicated the brag's body had been found, that the alarm had been raised, or that the welcome house raveners were on their tail. But there was only the fading sound of the revelry they'd left behind. They reached the ragged outskirts of town. It was as far as Aster had been from the welcome house since becoming a Good Luck Girl.

But it wasn't until they crossed the threshold of the deadwall and dove into the woods that something in Aster released, a loosening of the blood in her veins.

"Come on!" she called back to the others, surprising herself with a laugh. They pulled their dustkerchiefs off, and Aster saw her grin reflected on all their faces. Even Violet's mask of lofty indifference had slipped. Aster broke into a gallop, racing away from Green Creek and up into the foothills. She hadn't felt this fast since she was ten years old. The way the air rushed against her cheeks, the way her heart beat fast with joy, not fear—there was something indescribably *right* about the rhythm of a horse's hoofbeats, the creak of the leather saddle, the earthy, animal musk. Another laugh tore out of Aster. Clementine raised her hands to the sky.

Aster didn't know if Mother Fleur had found the body yet. She didn't know if Violet was full of shit. She didn't know where they would sleep tonight, or where their next meal would come from, or whether or not the iron of the horseshoes would be enough to keep the dead at bay.

But the welcome house was shrinking in the distance, its light no bigger than a candle flame, and just then, that was enough. She savored the unfamiliar feeling of freedom. Grew full from it. Until . . .

"Thank you, Aster," Clementine said from behind. Her relief was near a solid thing. "Thank you for getting us out of there."

And with that, Aster's happiness fractured, letting in a trickle of fear of what lay ahead. At the welcome house, she'd learned what kind of dangers to expect. Out here, she could only guess. What if she'd gotten Clementine out of one hell just to drag her into another?

Nothing could be worse than what they'd left behind, Aster told herself. Still, even as she squeezed her sister's hand in reassurance, all she could think was: *Don't thank me yet.*

CHAPTER SIX

It wasn't long before the darkness of the forest swallowed them entirely. Aster squinted into it, urging her horse along the steep, rocky deer path and ducking her head underneath overgrown branches. She and Clementine led the way, while Tansy and Mallow followed them and Violet brought up the rear. Violet lagged a bit behind the rest of group, seeming to struggle with her mare, though whether that was because the horse was just as hardheaded as she was or because the path was so damned treacherous, Aster couldn't say.

Aster had considered sparing them the trouble by taking the relatively level main road that cut through the Scab. The Bone Road, folks called it, on account of how many unmarked graves sprouted up along its banks. Most travelers died from heat sickness or exposure. Some were killed by highwaymen. Others just had the bad luck to stir up a scorpion. But deadly as it was, The Bone Road still made for the safest traveling in the mountains. It was lined with iron wardants to discourage vengeants, and it was crawling with lawmen to discourage criminals—which now included all five of them. And so rather than chancing discovery on the Bone Road, Aster had led their group into the trees instead. The law would have trouble following them through the woods, even if Mother Fleur's raveners would not.

And the dead, of course, would be waiting to greet them.

There were three varieties of spirit this side of the Veil: seraphants, benevolent spirits of your ancestors that returned to the land of the living to guide you; remnants, spirits trapped in the land of the living because they weren't yet ready to move on; and vengeants, spirits born of the raw anger of a tortured soul, released at last upon death.

Seraphants were so rare Aster wasn't convinced they were even real—folks prayed to the dead for wisdom and luck, but Aster knew no one was coming to save her.

Remnants were more common. They could be frightening, but they were ultimately harmless, and a well-trained hallower could help most of them find their peace.

Vengeants, though, would rip into anyone unlucky enough to cross their path—and the Scab was overrun with them. Even now the vengeants' howls rose up around Aster and Clementine, human cries that had been twisted into something animal. The vengeants started up their keening every night come sundown, right along with the crickets and the bullfrogs. Aster was used to that.

But they'd never sounded this ripping close before.

If one of the vengeants attacked, Aster and the others would have no choice but to flee. They didn't have the weapons to defend themselves. But how could they escape from monsters they couldn't even see? Vengeants were only visible in the direct light of the moon, and it was pitch-black here under the trees.

As they rode, Aster's worry gathered speed. Maybe they

hadn't had much time to come up with a plan, but anything, surely, was better than diving recklessly into the dark like this. Every thud of the horse hooves sounded like a nail in her coffin.

"Clem? You still awake?" Aster asked softly. Clem had gone quiet behind her, though her grip around Aster's waist was tight as ever.

Clem stirred. "I don't feel like I'll ever be able to sleep again," she murmured. "I can't stop thinking about it."

It was clear the glow of freedom from their escape had begun to fade, and the truth of what Clem had done had begun to sink in for her. Aster swallowed, wishing she had any idea what to say. She knew all too well what it felt like to be trapped in a bad memory, reliving every moment over and over until your guts turned to water and your chest was fit to burst. But if there was any way to free yourself from those memories, Aster hadn't discovered it yet. You just had to wait for the storm to pass.

"Try your best not to think about it," Aster managed finally. "You didn't do a thing wrong."

"But Aster, what if I've damned myself?" Clementine went on. "What if—"

"No! Come on, now. Don't even talk like that."

"It's right there in the Hallowed Book. *To take the life of your fellow man on Earth is to forfeit paradise beyond the Veil*—"

"That means *murder*, Clementine. Everyone knows that. It's not murder if you're defending yourself."

"But *murder* is what people will call it."

Well, Aster couldn't deny that. But she also couldn't bear

71

for Clem, of all people, to start losing hope. Aster was quiet for a moment, her breath feathering in front of her. It could grow bitterly cold in the Scab at night, and Augie's thin work shirt did little to warm her. A chill had already begun to settle beneath her skin.

"You know the dead better than anyone," Aster tried again. She reached for Clem's hand and tugged gently on her rattletail-patterned bracelet. Ever since Clementine had nearly died herself, she'd been sensitive to ghosts—could see a vengeant even without moonlight, could sense the bent of a remnant's thoughts and sometimes even communicate with it. "Trust that they'll understand why you had to do what you did, and that they'll judge you fairly in the end." Aster glanced over her shoulder. "Speaking of the dead, are any of these vengeants are getting too close?"

"I don't think so," Clementine said, shifting in the saddle. "I've never seen this many before, though. And my skin's crawling like we're in the middle of a lightning storm. But they seem to be avoiding us for some reason—"

Then, suddenly, a swift shadowed *something* dashed across the path in front of them, close enough for Aster to smell the rot left in its wake. Panic spiked through her blood. The vengeant's howl pierced the air an instant later, filled with unspeakable agony. Clementine screamed. Their horse reared up, nearly throwing them.

"What the hell was that?" Mallow cried out, her voice taut with fear, while Tansy let out a rare curse.

"Vengeant, but it's already gone," Aster said quickly, if only to quiet everyone. But in truth, her own heart threatened to leap out of her chest. She searched the thicket of trees helplessly. Nothing but darkness. Then she saw the vengeant for an instant as it cut across a pool of moonlight, silvered and skeletal and feline, lunging for them swift as the wind. Its eyes glowed red-black. Its batlike wings spread wide. Its skull bristled with a crown of antlers and a mouthful of wolfish fangs. Then it passed out of the moonlight and became invisible once more, leaves hissing beneath feet as it rushed towards them.

Primal fear seized Aster by the throat. She spurred the bay forward. "Come on, we need to move, it's coming back around!"

"Wait, I dropped something!" Violet cut in.

"Ripping hell, just *leave* it," Aster cried. But she turned back to see that Violet had already dismounted. This girl was clueless. She was going to get them all killed. "We're not waiting!"

"Just give me a second!"

Aster ignored her, snapping the reins, urging the bay faster than ever. *She wants to sacrifice her life for a lost earring or something, that's fine by me*, she thought.

But Violet wasn't taking the rest of them down with her.

They rode off without her. Tansy said something to Mallow that Aster couldn't make out, though she could guess well enough that they didn't feel right leaving Violet behind.

But Violet had been more than happy to sell them out whenever it suited her back at the welcome house. She'd even seemed to enjoy it. Why should they stick their necks out for her now?

She's grown, Aster told herself fiercely. *She'll be fine.*

Aster felt like she'd swallowed a stone. Indecision burned in her chest. She gripped the reins, prepared to turn around.

73

Waited in agony for the sound of stricken scream. A moment later, though, Violet caught up.

Aster said nothing, but her chest loosened with relief.

It wasn't until the sky began to lighten that Aster realized, with a dull, sickening shock, that she hadn't been certain she would see another sunrise. She was too nauseous with exhaustion to feel any relief, but she clung to a stubborn sort of pride.

They had made it through their first night on the outside.

"Is that daylight?" Clementine croaked. She had been dozing for the past couple hours.

"Seems to be," Aster said softly. The others were straightening up in their saddles, each of them looking as tired as she felt. The dead had begun to quiet around them with the coming of morning—it was the living they'd have to worry about today. Aster had no doubt the welcome house raveners had been sent into the woods after them by now.

Still, their group had put Green Creek further behind them than Aster had dared to hope. They were in the forest proper now, passing between ancient evergreens with flaking red bark and matted branches that cut the sunlight into golden columns. The ground was still rocky and uneven underfoot, dotted with snarls of drygrass, but the space between the trees had opened up considerably. Violet pulled her horse up on Aster's left, Tansy and Mallow on her right. Augie's ill-fitting work shirts and pants hung loose on their frames, the ratty fabric torn from their flight through the underbrush. Violet was hardly much better in the clothes she'd stolen from the brag, the knees of her fine dress pants stained with mud from

74

her desperate search for whatever she'd dropped last night. They had all worn their own shoes out of the welcome house, but the thin, ankle-high boots hadn't been made for riding, and the balls of Aster's feet were already tender with blisters.

"How in the hell did we survive last night?" Mallow growled.

Aster only shook her head. That they had managed to keep ahead of any raveners was blessing enough, but to have avoided the vengeants—that seemed nigh on miraculous. There were only a few things known to keep them at bay—iron, if you had enough of it; grayleaf, if you burned it; and pure—

Theomite.

"The brag's ring!" Tansy said suddenly, seizing on the same realization. "It must have held the vengeants off."

"I bet you're right," Aster agreed. She pulled the gold band out of her pocket, turning it over so the theomite caught the light. "I bet that's what it's for, even. Rich boy like him, no way he'd be traveling through the Scab without some kind of protection."

"Well, *obviously*. All the rich folks do that. You might have *told* me we had a stash of theomite on hand this whole time." Violet, looking pinched and pale, sounded more peevish than ever.

"Looks like we owe you our hides, Clem," Mallow said, ignoring Violet. Aster glanced back at her sister, all too aware that Clementine hadn't been feeling at all the hero last night. But Mallow's praise had managed to pull a smile out of her.

The tightness in Aster's shoulders eased, just a bit.

"Think I hear a creek up ahead," she said. "Let's stop there for a minute, water the horses, catch our breath."

It certainly would be a relief to rest. They had been awake for twenty-four hours now, and the last third of that had been spent on the run. Aster's thighs ached so bad she could barely grip the horse at all anymore. She wondered how much further they'd have to go before they were out of the raveners' reach entirely. Unlike lawmen, who were public servants, raveners were privately hired, and the welcome house's pockets were only so deep. And besides, Mother Fleur wouldn't want to spare so many raveners for the search that there weren't enough left to keep the other girls under control. They wouldn't chase the runaways past Killbank, Aster convinced herself. And the lawmen, at least, were tethered to their towns.

We're almost past the worst of it.

The creek slipped into view a moment later. Aster pulled her horse up short. Her brief glow of confidence was snuffed dark.

A young man crouched at the creek's edge, splashing his face and the back of his neck. Water shimmered in his black cottony hair. His shirt hung drying from a nearby branch, and his bare brown back flexed with muscle. He was built lean and sharp as a jackknife, and he was just as sure to cut them.

"Who's that?" Clementine whispered.

"No one we want to see us—" Aster hissed, urging their horse around. But it was too late. The boy turned at the soft snap of a twig. Saw their faces.

Their favors.

Aster spurred her horse hard, no longer concerned about keeping quiet.

"Come on!" she shouted back to the others.

"*Stop!*" the boy ordered. She looked over her shoulder. He

was running for his horse. Aster cursed, her head spinning with a rush of blood. They rode off as fast as possible, begging the horses for one last burst of speed. Was he a ravener? Aster hadn't gotten a good look at his eyes. But what else would he be doing out here? Who else would travel the Scab alone?

He's probably not alone, though.

There are probably others nearby.

And now they have your trail.

"Ripping hell," Mallow swore.

Aster couldn't help but agree.

By late afternoon, there was no sign that the stranger by the stream was on their trail—though maybe that just meant he'd gone off to report them instead, in which case, they'd have to hurry to maintain what little head start they had. But after a full day of riding, the animals were worn out, as were the girls. Worn out, sweaty, saddle-sore, and starved. They had to find somewhere to stop for the night or else collapse in their saddles.

Killbank still had to be at least an hour away, though. And Aster was determined to reach it.

"Aster," Violet murmured, so softly Aster almost didn't catch it. She had been uncharacteristically quiet all day. Aster assumed that she, like Clementine and the rest of them, was simply too tired or anxious to make conversation anymore. But now Aster saw, with alarm, that Violet looked dangerously washed out, her blue eyes bloodshot, her lustrous black hair limp.

"What is it?" Aster asked, her tone losing its usual edge.

Violet's reply was unintelligible.

Aster furrowed her brow and leaned over a bit closer. They were riding side by side now, at a slower pace. "What?"

"She asked if she could have a dose of Sweet Thistle," Clementine said quietly.

"That's what I dropped back in the woods last night," Violet said, a little stronger now. "I tried to find it, but it was too dark, and I was afraid to fall behind."

"Oh." Aster felt a surprising pang of sympathy. "I'm sorry, I don't have any."

"You don't—" Violet stared at her in confusion. "But—but you must have taken some since we left. Otherwise you'd be . . ." She wet her lips. "Please, I only need a little."

"I don't take it. I never have. I only pretended to so Mother Fleur wouldn't have me punished." Violet's expression seemed to shatter. "I'm sorry, Violet," Aster said again. "Truly. Just try to take it easy, hear? We're almost there."

Violet's face settled back into smooth indifference, but it still had that dull, waxen sheen. She retreated into herself.

"Maybe it's a blessing we don't have any Sweet Thistle," Clementine whispered. "Now she can be free of it."

"Maybe," Aster said, though she was less sure. Could folks just stop taking Sweet Thistle without terrible consequences? Back at the welcome house, no one ever stopped once they'd started. She'd heard rumors here and there among the sundown girls about women who'd aged out of the house and were no longer supplied with the drug, rumors about the desperate things some did for a couple of drops.

The silence between them grew strained, all of them watching Violet carefully, but none of them wanting to let on to their worry. And Violet, of course, was too proud to say another word. She managed to make it another half hour before her eyelids fluttered, her head lolled forward, and she slumped over and fell to the dirt with a *thump*.

"Violet!" Aster called out. She and Clem dismounted quickly, her aching legs almost buckling as she hurried over to Violet's side. This was a bad place to be stuck, just outside Killbank now. They might well be within range of any lawmen on patrol. The others dismounted too, forming a circle around Violet, whose eyes were open but unseeing. "Violet, can you hear me?"

Tansy knelt beside her and felt her forehead. "She has a dangerously high fever. She's probably delirious. Did she hurt herself earlier, do you know? Something that might've gotten infected?"

Violet shivered violently. Aster looked over at Tansy, her calm words seeming to come from far away.

"Hurt herself? No . . . she . . . she needs Sweet Thistle," Aster explained. "She asked me for some about half an hour ago."

"Withdrawal," Tansy said grimly.

"I mean, she's been looking like hell all day, but I just figured, you know, she's not used to roughing it like we are," Mallow said. She stood, looking around them with growing panic. "What do we do, Aster? We can't stop here."

"We have to get her another dose tonight, or she'll die," Tansy answered for her. "You can't just stop suddenly with Sweet Thistle, you have to ease off."

Aster shook her head. "But none of us have any."

"There'll be an apothecary in Killbank," Tansy continued in her calming way. "We can get some Sweet Thistle there."

79

"Well it's not as if we can just walk in and *buy* it," Clementine said. "And besides, I thought we were going around Killbank, not through."

"We are," Aster said firmly. "The place will be crawling with lawmen."

"Please," Violet begged, her voice brittle. "Please help me. I'll do anything. I'll tell you where Lady Ghost is."

"Definitely delirious," Mallow muttered.

But all of Violet's posturing was gone now, and something about that frightened Aster more than anything else that had happened since they'd lit out.

"Please . . . I don't want to die before I get there," Violet continued, her gaze squaring with Aster's now.

Aster swallowed. She still couldn't let herself believe in Lady Ghost—not after so many years of being sure she was a myth—but if Violet, of all people, had been willing to run away from the welcome house and risk her life for this, then maybe there was a kernel of truth to the story. Something, someone out there, worth finding.

Aster squeezed Violet's hand. Told her what she needed to hear.

"We'll get you that Sweet Thistle, Violet," Aster said. "I promise—we won't let you die before you get there."

CHAPTER SEVEN

Aster and the others found an abandoned mine just outside Killbank where Violet could rest while they worked out their plan to steal the Sweet Thistle. It was said you could cross the whole length of the Scab through its mazework of mines, though no one in their right mind would dare try. If you didn't lose your way and starve to death, you'd be buried alive by a cave-in or poisoned by bad air. The very earth was steeped in the suffering of generations of dustblood miners, and abandoned mines like this one were often overrun with vengeants. There was a remnant near the entrance as well, faint and foggy—a barefoot little boy sitting balled up, his bony knees pulled to his chest. His childlike terror hung in the air like a sharp scent.

And yet, if Aster had had a choice between staying here in the mine or venturing back out to Killbank, risking a run-in with the law, she would have picked the mine every time.

"I'll admit the name does not inspire confidence," Mallow said idly, tying her horse to one of the rotting timbers supporting the tunnel. "*Kill*bank. If I didn't know better, I'd say they were trying to scare us off."

She was joking with Tansy, but Tansy seemed too distracted

to respond. She had volunteered to go into Killbank with Aster, saying she might recognize other supplies at the apothecary that they could use. It was too valuable an opportunity to pass up. But Aster could see Tansy was already anxious at the thought of a run-in with the law. She twisted the end of her braid, staring out into the quickening dark with furrowed brows.

"Hey." Mallow touched her arm. "Honest, now, you sure you don't want me to go with you?"

"You can't," Aster answered for her, not unkindly. "If all three of us go into town, then Clementine's as good as on her own, since Violet's in no shape to fight."

"And I *have* to be the one to go with Aster," Tansy agreed, forcing a smile. "Seeing as the rest of you wouldn't know snakeroot from snake oil."

Mallow grumbled something unintelligible, but she relented, turning to where Clementine crouched beside Violet, who shivered beneath the rough blanket she'd folded herself into.

"And Her Highness? How should we tend to her while you're gone?" Mallow asked.

Tansy's smile faded. "Just manage that fever as best you can. There's not much you can do until we get back."

"But we'll hurry," Aster promised.

They were ready to go a moment later, mounting up on Violet's horse. Tansy tucked her pigtails away under her hat. Aster held out the theomite ring to Mallow.

"You all better take this. You can be damned sure there's vengeants in this place."

"There'll be vengeants out there, too," Clementine said, standing now, her arms crossed.

"There will. But at least *we'll* be on the move. I don't much like the idea of you all trapped here with no protection."

Mallow took the ring, the gemstone glinting darkly in the half-light. She looked back up at Tansy. "Be careful," she said, all trace of humor gone now.

Tansy gave a single nod. "Always am."

Aster leaned down to kiss Clementine on the crown of her head, and then they rode off, Aster guiding the horse towards the Bone Road. The last rays of sunlight filtered through the branches above, the wind sighing through the trees as they settled for the night with their old man groans. A shower of dead pine needles rained down on Aster and Tansy, and Aster shook them free of the brim of her hat.

Tansy sat quiet in the back of the saddle. Aster was grateful for the silence so she could think through their plan one last time. The girls had agreed that by the time they got to Killbank, the apothecary would probably be closed—all they'd have to do was break a window and sneak in. As long as they were careful, quick, and quiet about it, they shouldn't draw any attention to themselves.

A dark current of excitement coursed through Aster as she imagined it all, setting her stomach fluttering. And her newfound freedom still buzzed in her blood. This would be dangerous, yes—but for once it was a danger she had chosen.

"You know, I've never actually been to an apothecary," Tansy said after a moment. There was nervous excitement in her voice, too.

Aster glanced over her shoulder in surprise. "How do you know so much about medicine, then? You talk like a damned textbook."

Tansy laughed a little, though she hesitated before answering. Aster realized, too late, that it might have been wrong to ask. There was an unspoken rule among Good Luck Girls never to mention their lives before the welcome house, and Tansy was even more withdrawn than most.

"My mama was a nurse," Tansy said at last. "A doctor came through our camp once a season to take care of the miners, but every other day of the year, it was up to her."

"One woman was expected to be responsible for the lives dozens of men?"

"Well, she had help," Tansy admitted. "There were other nurses at the camp. But she'd been at it the longest. Most of the others were girls not much older than us. They looked up to her." Tansy paused. "So did I."

Aster waited to see if she'd say any more, and after a moment, Tansy went on.

"She used to let me shadow her. Dust lung was the most common ailment we saw. Just about everyone in the Scab has a touch of it, but it's usually only deadly to the very young and the very old. Then there were the broken bones, the torn muscles, the burns, the busted eardrums . . . things that could make a man miserable, but they would heal in time. And then there were the—the catastrophes. One group of men had been forced to work in standing water for so long that the flesh on their feet had begun to rot off the bone. Another man survived an explosion that melted away all the skin on his back. My mama didn't spare me any of it—that was how she had learned, and that was how I would take her place one day."

84

"By the dead," Aster said, feeling sick.

"I got used to it." There was a shrug in Tansy's voice. "I even enjoyed it. I liked knowing I was making my mama proud. But then some fool stove her head in with a branding iron one night because she refused a dance with him. My family sold me to the welcome house a week later. They couldn't afford not to."

Aster swallowed, at a loss for words. It was both a uniquely horrifying story and all too common, something that might have happened to anyone she grew up with. The Scab was known for such reckless violence.

"I'm sorry, Tansy," Aster said at last.

"She'd be glad to see what we're doing for Violet. But I don't mind telling you, Aster, I don't like hurting folks. It's helping folks that I always wanted to do. So if this comes down to a fight . . ."

"It won't," Aster promised, hoping she sounded more convincing than she felt. "If it looks bad, we'll just run, all right?" She wanted to help Violet, too, but she wasn't about to die for her.

A moment later they reached the edge of the Bone Road, winding its way down to the valley where Killbank slept behind its stone deadwall. Iron wardants stood every fifty feet on the sides of the road, worked into the shapes of sad-eyed children holding lamps that lit the way. Aster's hackles raised at their unblinking stare. She wet her lips and turned to back to Tansy.

"You ready?" she asked. The moment they stepped out onto the road, into the open, they risked discovery.

Tansy sucked in a breath. "If I have to be."

Aster nodded and pulled the black fabric of her dustkerchief over the bottom half of her face, covering up the cursed ink that would give them away as Good Luck Girls.

You're the one in control now, she reminded herself, trying to still the panic stirring in her belly.

They *are afraid of* us.

"I've never made it longer than twenty minutes, Aster," Tansy warned as she covered her own face.

Aster lowered the brim of her hat. Twenty minutes—that was pretty standard. Every Good Luck Girl, when they were little, tried to see how long she could stand to keep her favor covered up before the pain became unbearable. Aster's record was twenty-four minutes. The Green Creek record, legend had it, was thirty-three.

An uncomfortable prickle had already started up under Aster's skin. "We'll be done in fifteen," she promised.

They rode into town.

Killbank reminded Aster a good deal of Green Creek—a vibrant oasis for the well-heeled Arkettans living in or traveling through the Scab. She searched for the apothecary among the tidy shops that stood shoulder-to-shoulder with raucous saloons. The street was filled with men in patterned waistcoats and cocked derby hats, shouting at one another over bottles of beer. There would be precious few dustbloods here, outside the Good Luck Girls in the welcome house, and there would be plenty of lawmen with guns at their belts to keep it that way. Aster held her breath as they passed two officers standing guard outside the bank, watching them from beneath flat-brimmed hats. Had word of the girls' escape spread beyond Green Creek already?

One of the lawmen narrowed his eyes, reached for his sidearm. Aster tensed, gripping the reins, preparing to bolt.

Crack! Aster's heart leapt to her throat. The lawman had drawn his gun, fired. But not at them—at a rat scuttling in front of their horse's hooves. The horse took off skittishly. Aster's vision swam as she struggled to fight back the terror that had seized her.

"*Bastard*," she muttered. "Are you okay, Tanz?"

"I think so," Tansy whispered, but she was shaking.

Main Street grew quieter as they neared the end of the road, which was left to smaller businesses that had closed by sundown. Aster scratched at her favor. If Killbank didn't have an apothecary . . .

But then, finally, they came upon the drug store's darkened storefront. LISTON'S APOTHECARY, giant red-and-gold letters proclaimed from the front window. Aster slid down from the saddle and hurried to tie the horse up, looking around them to make sure no one was nearby. A few folks milled around outside a nearby inn, but otherwise they were alone.

Aster's favor had begun to burn now, fire ants under her skin.

"In and out," Aster promised Tansy, whose eyes were wide and shining. "You just point out what we need, and I'll grab it. And remember, our priority is the Sweet Thistle."

Tansy nodded, sliding down after her. Aster tried the front door, but, unsurprisingly, it was locked. The window was much too big to break without causing a commotion. She swore under her breath. They had to come up with something else.

After stealing another glance to make sure no one had wandered down this way, Aster picked up a stone, bashed the doorknob until it broke, and kicked the door open.

And came face-to-face with an old man pointing a rifle at them.

"That's far enough!" he said hoarsely. "Get back or I'll shoot, I swear I will!"

Shock hit Aster like a punch to the gut. She took stock of the man in the space of half a second—gray hair wisping out from underneath a wilting nightcap; threadbare nightclothes hanging loose from a bony frame; small, round spectacles flashing in the light of a candle on the table behind him. *Liston himself?* The sound of their break-in must have brought him running from his bedroom.

"I said *get*—"

Aster didn't give herself time to think. She lunged forward, shoving the barrel of the rifle upwards with her left forearm. She struck Liston in the chest with the heel of her right hand, knocking the wind out of him before he could call for help.

The old man staggered backwards, gasping. Lost his footing and fell to the ground. Aster yanked the gun out of his loosened grasp and turned it on him. She had no idea how to work it, but Liston didn't know that.

He coughed and spat, looking up at her balefully. His eyes narrowed as he realized they had no shadows at their feet.

"Damned *dustbloods*. What do you want from me?"

"Not another word," Aster warned, her voice low. She pressed the muzzle of the gun to the hollow of his bobbing throat, sickened by the fear that lit up in his eyes. First Violet, now this old man. Who was she becoming?

Whoever I have to be to keep us alive, she thought, steeling her resolve.

"Sweet Thistle," she ordered. "And whatever else my friend here wants."

She handed Tansy a riding satchel they'd stolen from the stables. Tansy took it, her face flushed under a sheen of sweat—though whether that was from fear or the mounting pain of her favor, Aster couldn't be sure.

Almost done, Aster said with her eyes. She turned back to Liston and jerked her head towards the counter in front of the medicine shelves. "Go on," she said, lowering the gun. "Make it quick."

Liston hesitated. Aster didn't like the look of recognition in the shopkeeper's expression.

"Sweet Thistle?" he repeated.

"*Now*," Aster snarled.

He climbed back to his feet slowly, still trembling, then hurried over to the shelves. Tansy followed, satchel held open.

"Burdock . . . laudanum . . . calamine . . . ghostweed," she muttered, her voice soft with apology. Aster watched warily, scratching at the side of her neck. The pain was beginning to make her sweat, too, and soon her favor would be glowing brightly enough for Liston to see. She gripped the barrel of the gun tighter, turning to make sure no one was else was approaching the shop. So far, nothing. But as her eyes swept the room, they caught on several signs posted on the wall, each one bearing the same message in blocky black letters.

WANTED

Aster swallowed, dread crawling down her neck. She stepped closer, praying to the dead she wouldn't recognize the faces on the posters.

But Aster would have recognized her sister's face anywhere. There were five posters in a row, one for each of them, their faces sketched out by an expert hand. Their favors in particular had been rendered in stunning detail, identical to the ones burning so brightly now that Aster could barely bring herself to focus on the words in front of her.

. . . Good Luck Girls from Green Creek . . .

. . . the vicious murder of Baxter McClennon . . .

. . . stolen property . . . theomite ring . . . three horses . . .

. . . Reward of 50,000 eagles . . .

. . . WANTED ALIVE . . .

Baxter McClennon.

Clementine had killed Baxter McClennon.

Heir to the McClennon mining empire. Son of the most powerful landmaster in the Scab. The realizations hit Aster one after another. His family would tear down the mountains to find them. They would set every ravener in Arketta on their trail.

Aster felt her gorge rise.

"Not a bad likeness," Liston said suddenly.

Aster couldn't help a desperate sob as she whirled around, gun raised. But the shopkeeper held up his hands in surrender. Tansy stood behind him, busily buckling the satchel shut. Her hands slowed as she looked past Aster and read the signs for herself.

"If the Sweet Thistle didn't give you away, the way you're looking at those posters surely does," Liston went on, a sneer curling his lip.

Aster flicked her eyes at Tansy. They had no choice. She rammed the muzzle of the gun into his chest, forcing him

90

backwards until his tailbone hit the counter with a rattle of glass. Her finger closed over the trigger.

"Go get the rope from outside to tie him up with," Aster told Tansy. "*Now*," she added when Tansy hesitated.

Tansy dashed off. Fresh pain spiked through Aster's favor. She tried to hold the rifle steady in her slick grip. Pinned Liston with a warning glare, praying to the dead he wouldn't call her bluff. The corner of his mouth twitched, but he didn't dare speak.

Tansy returned with rope in hand.

"Tie him up," Aster ordered without dropping her gaze.

No hesitation this time. Tansy bound Liston's wrists and ankles in a hogtie, her favor beginning to glow beneath her dustkerchief as she worked. The moment she was done, Aster lowered the gun, relieved that she hadn't had to use it.

"Come on," Aster said. They ran over to the wall and ripped the wanted posters down, then hurried back towards the door.

"Dirty Luckers!" Liston shouted after them, finally free of the gun's muzzle. "You don't know how good you had it in that house! I can't wait to see what the McClennons do to you—"

Rage surging through her, Aster turned back around. She rushed over and gagged him with his nightcap, her blistering anger urging her to do worse.

"Aster, hurry, *please*," Tansy begged. Her favor burned red-orange now, minutes away from white heat.

Aster swallowed and nodded. "We're done here," she said. "Let's go." She made her way towards the door and Tansy followed. Outside, they mounted their horse, the shopkeeper's words still ringing in Aster's ears as they left the apothecary behind.

* * *

By the time Aster and Tansy returned to the mine, Violet had passed out. Tansy quickly dismounted and went to her side. Aster followed more slowly, still shaken by what they'd discovered. Clementine ran forward and wrapped her in a hug.

"You made it," Mallow said, her whole frame relaxing with relief. "Thank the dead."

"Ran into some trouble," Aster admitted. *An understatement.* The pain of her favor was only just now beginning to subside. "Did you have any problems here?"

Clementine released her and shook her head. "You can hear the vengeants started up. It's a good thing we had the ring."

The ring.

Baxter McClennon's ring.

Tansy squeezed a drop of Sweet Thistle under Violet's tongue and stood, exhaling. "Good news—Violet ought to come back around in a few hours' time." She looked at Aster levelly. "You want to tell them the bad news?"

It wasn't as if waiting would make it any better. Aster wet her lips, turned back to Clementine.

"We saw wanted posters in Killbank. One for each of us. The brag you killed . . . it was Baxter McClennon."

For a moment, Clementine said nothing, her expression working its way from surprise to fear. "*McClennon?*" she repeated in a whisper. "Are you sure?"

"See for yourself," Aster said grimly, pulling out the posters from her pocket.

"Wait, wait, somebody tell me what I'm looking at," Mallow interrupted as Clementine slowly unfolded the posters. "Who's

Baxter McClennon, and why should I give a damn that he's dead?"

"McClennon—you know, like *Mount* McClennon?" Tansy replied. "His father Henry owns half the Scab, and his uncle Jerrod is running for governor. I grew up in one of their family's mining camps."

"Oh." Mallow eyes widened. "*Oh*."

"Exactly," Aster said. "I thought it was just the welcome house raveners we had to worry about. But the McClennons will be able to hire enough of them to chase us off the edge of the map."

"And the law will be in their pocket, too," Tansy warned. "Every badge in Arketta is going to be after us now, if they weren't already."

"So let's keep riding," Clementine said, finally finding her voice again. "There's no time to lose. One of us can hold Violet on our horse. Once we find Lady Ghost—"

"We don't have any idea where Lady Ghost *is*," Aster reminded her. "We can't go anywhere until Violet wakes up and tells us which way to go."

She didn't add what she was truly thinking—that Lady Ghost probably wasn't even real, and if they couldn't get rid of their favors, they were as good as dead. Any other criminal could change their appearance, run away, lie low, and hope to disappear into a new life. But with these favors marking them not just as escaped Good Luck Girls, but as Baxter McClennon's murderers . . .

"For all we know, Lady Ghost could be somewhere right around here," Tansy said hopefully, glancing at Violet. "We might not need to run anywhere."

Aster could see Clementine didn't like staying put, but they had no choice.

"Just go on and get some rest for now," Aster told her, more quietly. "We'll figure this out. I promise."

Tansy and Mallow agreed to take the first watch together. Aster lay down on the hard strip of ground beside the rusted red minecart tracks, wrapping her hair for the night with the dustkerchief. The blanket she'd folded herself into did a poor job of protecting her from the chill leaching out from the stones. Clementine settled down next to her, and without a word, they curled into each other for warmth, just as they'd done when they were little. Before Green Creek. Before all of this.

For a moment they just lay there, listening to the longing cries of the vengeants that echoed up from the dark. It was never words in any living language, just raw vowels that bled into each other, endlessly, helplessly. And yet Aster always felt as if she were on the cusp of understanding the vengeants—as if she could answer them, if she chose to. And this was somehow the most frightening thing about them.

Clementine seemed to crackle with tension, as if she, too, were holding in a scream.

"I know what you're thinking," Aster whispered at length. "Don't be."

"Don't be what?"

"Don't be sorry."

"You're all going to die because of me. At least in the welcome house we were safe. But the McClennons—"

"We weren't safe. We were never safe there."

94

"Violet almost got ripped apart by those vengeants. And you and Tansy almost got caught in Killbank. And that ravener by the creek—"

"And none of it was your fault. Listen to me: if the McClennons kill us, then the McClennons are to blame. It's as simple as that. Back at Green Creek, we didn't have a fighting chance against the people who wanted to hurt us. Now we do. *You* gave that to us. You have nothing to apologize for."

Clementine was silent.

"Promise me you understand, Grace."

Clementine's true name—the name she had answered to before the welcome house, the name she'd been forced to forget. It was easier that way, even, some girls found. Easier to pretend it was some stranger suffering, and not the real you.

But maybe they wouldn't have to be those people anymore.

"I promise," Clementine said at last.

And then, finally, Aster allowed herself to fall asleep.

Violet was the last to wake in the morning. While Aster and the others started tacking up their horses, Violet remained curled underneath her blanket, hands pillowed delicately beneath her head. The sickly pallor that had stolen over her yesterday was gone now, and her breathing once again sounded slow and even. Her hair was still damp from her fever sweat, and her face was still grubby with dirt, but even so, she looked as peaceful as Aster had ever seen her.

Mallow poked her in the ribs with a stick.

"Mal," Tansy scolded.

"What? She needs to get up."

"She needs to *rest*. She's been through a lot."

"So have we all. She looks fine to me."

"Let her have another fifteen minutes," Aster said, biting into a half-rotted carrot—the last of the food they'd stolen from the stables. She shared Mallow's impatience, and she didn't want to let a minute of the day go to waste. But there was no point in leaving if Violet was just going to collapse again. Fortunately, though, Violet woke up on her own a moment later. Perhaps her ears had been burning.

Aster guessed from the look on Violet's face that she'd forgotten she wasn't back at the welcome house. If so, she was in for a surprise.

"What the hell is going on?" Violet asked. She sat up and looked around with a wary eye. Then it seemed to come back to her. "Oh, *rip* me."

"Welcome to Killbank," Aster said dryly. "Or at least, welcome to this cursed mine a couple miles outside Killbank. We stopped to get you the Sweet Thistle—do you remember?"

"Well enough," Violet muttered. She swore again as she tried to stand and fell back to the ground.

"Easy," Clementine warned.

"I'm all right," she insisted. "I just need some water."

"And I'll go get you some," said Aster. "But first, I've got something to tell you, and something to ask."

Violet flashed her a haughty look. It was as good a sign as any that she really was starting to feel like herself again.

"Get on with it, then."

You're going to want to sit for this anyway, Aster thought. And then she told Violet about the wanted posters they'd discovered last night. Violet's face remained carefully set as she listened.

"You don't seem all that worried about the McClennons," Clementine observed.

"What's the use in worrying? What's done is done." She ran her tongue over her lips. "I'll take that water now."

"In a minute," Aster promised. "We still have something to ask—you said if we got you the Sweet Thistle, you'd tell us where we could find Lady Ghost, remember? So, where is she?"

Violet's gaze hardened. "Swear you'll still take me with you?"

"For the love of the dead, *yes*, just tell us where we're going," Aster said, exasperated.

"You *did* save my life," Violet admitted. "I would thank you, but it's your fault for abandoning me when I dropped the Sweet Thistle in the first place. So. I guess we're square now."

"All right, you know what—"

"Northrock," Violet said finally. "That's where I'll find—that's where *we'll* find Lady Ghost."

For a moment there was silence. A swell of anger rose in Aster's chest, as if she'd been betrayed. Northrock was at least a month away on horseback, near the border of Ferron. Well outside the Scab. Violet might as well have said Lady Ghost lived on the moon.

"*Northrock?*" Clementine echoed, before Aster could tamp down her anger enough to speak.

"But—but I thought you said we just had to get to Killbank," Tansy stammered.

"I said we had to go *towards* Killbank," Violet corrected. "But we've got a long way to go yet."

"What else aren't you telling us?" Mallow demanded. "Will

her 'magic' work on anyone? Is there a cost for her services? I'm not skipping halfway across the country just to get turned away at her door."

Violet hesitated. "They say it's a thousand eagles a head to get a favor removed."

"Hold on," Aster snapped, her tongue finally loosened, "so we have to make it all the way to Northrock, *and* we have to come up with five thousand eagles along the way?" Most miners would be lucky to see a thousand eagles in a year. "And what do you mean, '*They* say it's a thousand eagles'? Who the rip is *they*?"

"I said I'd tell you where she is, not how I know," Violet said.

"If we're going to base all our damn plans on your supposed information, I'd think we'd have a right to know the source." Aster crossed her arms.

"Fine." Violet sniffed. "If you don't believe me, don't worry about the money. Just show up and take your chances."

It was clear from the worried looks the others were giving Aster that they believed Violet. Both about where Lady Ghost was and about the fee. In spite of her anger, Aster had to admit that, in some way, the thousand eagles made Lady Ghost feel just a tiny bit more real—not a mythical savior, but a woman charging for a service. Still, that didn't begin to solve the problem of where to get it. Or how to get to Northrock.

"We have the ring," Tansy began, clearly sensing the shift in Aster's mind. "We could sell it—"

"To who?" Aster interrupted. "This ring was on the wanted posters. Anyone who recognizes it is going to turn us in."

"Lady Ghost might not. Maybe she'll accept it as payment,"

Clementine said.

Might. Maybe. Aster felt the beginnings of hysteria creeping in. They would never make it to Northrock. It would be suicide to try. But there was also no hope of surviving if they stayed here, not with the McClennons after them. Chasing down Violet's fantasies was just about the only option they had.

Dirty Luckers. You don't know how good you had it in that house. Aster's mind echoed with the apothecary's words. "I need a minute," she muttered, forcing herself to her feet.

"Wait, Aster, we shouldn't any of us wander out alone—" Tansy fretted.

"I'll only be a minute," Aster said firmly. "I'm going to refill the canteen. I'll be back." She met Clementine's eyes. "Promise."

Aster slung the canteen over her shoulder and stumbled outside, blinking in the now-bright sunlight. It was a completely different forest from the one they'd braved last night. Songbirds called out to each other from tree to tree. A little lizard sunbathed on a rock.

She began to feel a little steadier. It wasn't all bad, after all.

After a brief walk, Aster reached the creek. Even after their run-in with the stranger earlier, they'd been afraid to stray too far from it. Fresh water could be hard to find in the Scab. She angled carefully down the muddy bank. Knelt to fill the canteen.

A sudden rustle from above jerked her gaze to the branches overhead. A man's shout punctured the air. Aster reached for her knife.

Before she could grab it, she was shoved to the ground.

CHAPTER EIGHT

Aster's chest exploded with pain as the wind was knocked out of her. Her muscles seized with the familiar fear of being at a man's mercy. She rolled over, regained her feet, grabbed her knife, and slashed out at the attacker in front of her with a desperate cry. He dodged the blade and pushed her down again.

"Be still!" he hissed. "I can't fight both of you at once."

Both?

He'd knocked the knife out of her hand. By the time she scanned the ground and reached out for it, the young man was already several feet away, his back turned to her, his own knife held out in front of him.

At the snarling catamount circling them.

Aster's breath caught. She had never seen a catamount up close, though she'd sometimes heard their yowling in the distance. This one was even bigger than she'd imagined, twice the size of a man, muscular shoulders rolling beneath its sandy brown coat as it approached them with fangs bared.

It was bleeding from its chest, though. A long, shallow cut. The young man had already managed to get a lick in somehow.

He saved me, Aster realized. Her heart hammered as she

climbed to her feet once again. The catamount must have been stalking her and the stranger had pushed her out of its way just in time. He was bleeding, too, from where the cat had raked his arm.

Doesn't make him your ally, though, a voice in the back of Aster's mind warned. The dead only knew what *he* wanted with her.

But if she didn't help him, the catamount would kill them both.

Aster wet her lips and gripped her knife tighter. The stranger feinted at the cat. As soon as it lunged towards him, Aster darted in and nicked its side. It let out an earsplitting screech. She leapt back quickly as the cat turned towards her. Then the stranger attacked it again, grazing its haunch. The cat wheeled around. Threw a heavy paw. The stranger ducked a swipe that would have crushed his ribs. Rolled away. The cat peeled back its black lips and lowered into a predatory crouch, preparing to pounce on him before he could recover.

Aster didn't think. Her body was moving before her mind could stop it. She sprinted to the catamount, raised her knife, and brought it down, hard, between the beast's shoulder blades. It let out an almost humanlike yelp, writhing in pain. Terror ripped through her. She yanked the knife free and backpedaled quickly, expecting it to face her with renewed fury. But the catamount had had enough. It snarled at them as it retreated, disappearing into the underbrush as suddenly as it'd come.

The forest grew still. Aster was breathing hard, her hands shaking and her insides loose. She summoned her courage. Now to deal with the stranger. She hadn't been alone with a man since Green Creek—but things would go differently this time. Better to have died by the catamount's claws than to let him have his way with her. She would carve *him* up, too, if she had to. She raised her knife again, approaching him from behind, as he stood watching the spot where the catamount had disappeared.

"You're not supposed to show fear around these mountain cats," he said, "but I'll tell you what, I damn near pissed my pants just now." He let out an easy laugh, sheathed his knife, and turned to face her. Aster flinched back in surprise.

The stranger by the creek.

She was close enough now to see he wasn't a ravener. His light brown eyes were a mortal man's, and there was none of that dreadful, draining energy about him. He had no shadow at his feet, either, which meant he was a fellow dustblood—usually a good sign. In fact, Aster was almost certain she'd seen his face somewhere before. But still—

"You've been tracking us," Aster snarled. She pressed the point of the blade to his chest.

He held his hands up, his face a mirror of her own alarm. "Hey, easy—"

"Who are you? What do you want?"

"*Easy*, I said. You'll want to put that knife down. My name's Zee. I'm a rangeman. I can help you."

A rangeman—a Scab guide. From what Aster knew of them, he fit the bill. He wore a long brown duster coat over a simple work vest. Dark denims, piss-free, as promised. Riding boots. A wide-brimmed hat. And, of course, he was seemingly traveling the Scab alone. That was what rangemen did: they tamed the wilderness, they explored the unknown, they protected the weak and helpless from all the wicked things in the mountains.

Still, any asshole could put on a hero hat and ride into the hills. Was the whole thing just an act to lure them to the McClennons? Aster thought it more than likely.

"We'll be fine," she said stonily.

"It's hard to be 'fine' out here, even for someone like me," Zee argued. "There's worse than catamounts in these woods." His eyes dropped back down to the knife, pleadingly, but Aster refused to lower it.

"Even so. We don't have the shine to pay you," she said. And they certainly weren't going to pay him any other way, if that was what he was expecting from a bunch of Good-Luck Girls. She would cut his throat first.

"I don't want your shine. I want McClennon's ring," Zee said. He slowly pulled one of Clementine's wanted posters out from his inside pocket, keeping his other hand held up in a gesture of peace. "It says here that you all stole it. A ring like that's priceless for a man in my line of work."

Aster's face burned with anger. "So you're blackmailing us, is that it? Hand over the theomite ring or you'll turn us in?"

"No! Ripping hell—"

Before Aster could respond, the brush rustled behind them. She spun, fearing the catamount had come back. But it was only the rest of her group. Aster sheathed the knife with relief. The five of them together could surely overpower this boy, if it came to that.

"Aster!" Clementine cried. "We thought we heard a catamount—"

They stopped short.

"Who the hell are you?" Violet demanded.

"It's that stranger we saw yesterday. He claims he's a rangeman, wants to help us get where we're going," Aster explained, her voice heavy with skepticism. "He tracked us."

"He *is* a rangeman, and his name is Zee," Zee said. He clutched at his still-bleeding arm. "Listen, I'd rather tend to this injury sooner than later. What's it going to take to convince you all? I've been following you since Green Creek—I've had plenty of time to turn you in. And I don't know what happened between you and McClennon, but I don't particularly care, either. I'll always side with Good Luck Girls, especially over those landmaster bastards. Always."

Aster clenched her jaw. "Is that so?" Aster looked Zee straight in the eye. Her time at the welcome house had taught her the many ways men lied. To themselves and to one another. To feel more powerful or to hide something shameful. She was no stranger to men who promised you could trust them and a half second later showed you that you sure as hell better not. They had an oily, shifty look about them, she could always spot it. And Aster had to admit she saw none of that in this boy—but she didn't know if she could trust her own self to notice now, not in this moment, exhausted and desperate as she was. "I trust you'll stay put while we talk it over, then."

She motioned for the others to follow her a short distance away—close enough to keep an eye on him, but far enough that he wouldn't be able to overhear them. Once they were huddled in a circle, Aster filled them in on everything they'd missed. Zee had saved her from the catamount, true. But,

Aster added, he was expecting payment for helping them further. He wanted the ring—which they ought to be saving for Lady Ghost.

"Maybe we can come up with the shine for Lady Ghost along the way somehow," Tansy suggested. "We're going to need help to cross the whole Scab, Aster. We barely got away with the medicine last night, and we're almost out of food."

"Yeah, and if he was going to turn us in, he would've done it yesterday. He knew where we were camped," Clementine pointed out.

"And we're more than enough to handle him," Mallow said, echoing Aster's earlier thought. "If he wants to betray us, he's not going to have an easy time of it."

"*And* he saved you from the catamount," Clementine continued.

"Because I'm worth more alive than dead," Aster said, exasperated. "We *all* are—"

"Look, I have no idea what he's up to, and I won't pretend to," Violet interrupted. "But Northrock is hundreds and hundreds of miles away from here. We're sure as hell going to need some kind of help to get there in one piece. And right now I think he's our best option. Forgive me if I don't trust *you* to do it."

"You don't find it a little *convenient*, though, that as soon as we decide to go to Northrock a rangeman shows up to escort us?" Aster asked, crossing her arms. "I'm sorry, but this whole thing smells sour."

The others were silent for a moment. "I just have . . . a good feeling about him," Clementine said finally, not quite meeting Aster's eye.

Oh, well, Clem has a good feeling, *so I guess that settles it then,* Aster thought, exasperated. But Aster knew her sister's feelings had a funny way of turning out right, more often than not, and the others had made convincing arguments, too. And, as Aster looked around their circle, she couldn't help but wonder if they had a point. She was suddenly aware of how run down they all were: Violet still shaky from her ordeal, Tansy rubbing at a nasty sunburn at the back of her neck, all of them dirty and dehydrated and exhausted. And she herself would be dead right now if Zee hadn't been there . . . As much as Violet's words had bristled her, Aster feared she was right—they needed help.

"All right," Aster conceded at last. "We'll let him ride with us *today*. See how it goes. Feel it out. Let's bring him back to the camp for now, get him patched up."

But if Zee crossed them, Aster thought, she wasn't going to hesitate to cut him right back open.

Whatever else Zee's intentions, it became clear within the first few hours that he was at least, legitimately, a rangeman. He rode a pretty palomino mare named Nugget, and her saddlebags were loaded with supplies to survive on the trail. Flint and matches. Dried fruit and salted meat. A compass and a cook-kit. A rifle and a shotgun.

"Why do you need a rifle *and* a shotgun?" Mallow asked as they rode single file along a game trail. It was particularly windy today, red dust swirling up into the air in a haze that left Aster's eyes watering and her throat coated with grit. Every so often one of them would be seized by a coughing fit, and Tansy would pass them a soothing honey drop from her bag of stolen medical supplies. Aster was working on one now.

"Well, the rifle's just for hunting," Zee explained. "But the shotgun's for vengeants."

"Does it kill them?" Violet piped up from the back.

"Of course not," Aster answered for Zee. She was always astounded by Violet's ignorance of the kind of basic knowledge every dustblood child had to learn by the time they were five. Ghosts were like stains, fading slowly over time. Some were more persistent than others. Vengeants, extremely so. The best you could do was weaken them.

"I'm sorry, Aster, was I talking to you?" Violet snapped back.

"The shotgun's just a deterrent," Zee said from the front, a little hastily. "I use iron pellets instead of lead. Drives the dead away."

"Like the iron wardant we had outside our house growing up," Tansy offered.

"Exactly," Zee confirmed. "Most people carry a small piece of iron on their person for protection, too. But a lucky horseshoe won't scare off a vengeant any more than a lit match will scare off a hungry wolf. You need a *lot* of iron, more than is practical to carry around. That's why I prefer the shotgun. A little iron goes a long way when it hits a vengeant directly. Sends them running before they even get close." Zee slowed down so he was beside them and passed the shotgun to Clementine for inspection. It was a handsomely made piece, even Aster could admit that, with a polished cherry-wood stock and fine gold inlays.

"You ever fired one of these before?" Zee asked, glancing over his shoulder.

"Oh, of course, you know, back before the welcome house,"

Clementine said. This was barely true, Aster knew—she'd fired a six-shooter, once, on a dare. Boys in the Scab started handling guns as soon as they could walk, but girls were considered too delicate.

"That so?" Zee asked, sounding impressed. "Well, here I was hoping for the honor of teaching you a thing or two. But I see that won't be necessary."

"Well, it's not as if I had a rangeman helping me last time. So I'm sure you can teach me one thing. I wouldn't bet on two."

"All right, go on and give it back to him, Clem, it's not a toy," Aster said, strained.

Zee went on to tell them that he also had an emergency stash of grayleaf to burn, as vengeants couldn't abide the stench. It was the same herb hallowers used when blessing holy spaces. But theomite was the best protection of all, he said. It was made from the blackened bones of the great beasts that had existed when the world was young and the Veil was thin, and it still pulsed with their ancient energy, repelling malevolent spirits the same way alike magnets repelled each other.

"No vengeant's going to come within a stone's throw of a theomite ring like yours," Zee concluded. "It's no wonder folks are driving themselves wild trying to mine the stuff up."

He certainly likes to hear himself talk, Aster thought. But at least it was keeping everyone distracted.

It was around midday that Zee insisted they stop. Aster bristled as he dismounted.

"We ought to keep going until dark," she said. "We rode through the day yesterday without stopping at all."

"It won't do us any good to wear the horses out," Zee said

patiently. "Then they won't be able to run when you really need them to. Let them rest and graze for a minute. I promise we're safe here."

Aster had no intention of taking orders from some fool they'd just met. This particular patch of woodland didn't look any safer than anywhere else they'd been. But then Zee made a sweeping gesture to their surroundings.

"We have the high ground," he explained—and sure enough, their backs were to a cliff face while the forest around them sloped down gently into the distance. "And the trees are thinner here, too. So we'll be able to see anyone coming from any direction."

Zee had already made several adjustments to make it harder for the raveners to follow them, wrapping the horses' hooves in cloth to hide their tracks and traveling downwind to mask their scent. They'd stuck to hard-packed game trails whenever they could, and whenever they couldn't, they'd left false trails before doubling back. Their pace had slowed down to what felt like a painstaking crawl to Aster, especially compared to the full-tilt flight they'd made out of Green Creek. And now Zee wanted them to stop altogether? No, she didn't like it, high ground or not.

But what if he's right? What if this is the only way to stay ahead of the people after us?

Aster ground her teeth. She hated how little she knew about all of this, how vulnerable it made her. Zee could be setting them up for a slaughter and they would be none the wiser.

"Have we lost the raveners yet, do you think?" Tansy asked,

taking off her hat and wiping away the band of sweat it left behind.

Zee shook his head grimly. "You can't ever expect a tracker to lose you completely, especially when it comes to raveners. You just try to slow them down as best you can. I saw signs of at least two hunting parties tracking you out of Green Creek. I did what I could to cover your trail, but we have to assume they'll pick it up again."

"Two?" Aster nearly choked on her honey drop. She'd known, of course, that someone would come after them, but still—

"Could you tell who they were with?" she asked, trying not to let her voice betray her alarm.

"One of them was a group of raveners from the welcome house. The others, I'd guess, were working for McClennon," Zee said.

And we can be sure they won't be taking any breaks, Aster thought, watching with disbelief as the others dismounted and took long pulls from the canteen. It was clear they were all too happy to take Zee's advice. While they were stopped he also showed them how to tap fresh water from a tree trunk with a spile, which plants in the area were edible and which were poisonous, and how to spot signs of dangerous wildlife. It wasn't just the coyotes and the catamounts you had to watch out for, he claimed. There were tarantulas the size of a wagon wheel and bats big enough to carry off a baby goat. Rattletails. Copperheads. Black-fanged skinks.

"Clementine survived a rattletail bite," Mallow piped up. Aster shot her a dirty look.

"That so?" Zee said again. "Well, it might not have been

110

a rattletail, you know. Most snakes are actually harmless—"

"You calling me a liar?" Clementine asked, a smile playing at her lips. She fiddled with the bracelet Aster had made her.

"Course not!" he backtracked quickly.

"Then a fool."

He seemed flustered. "I'd never—"

"Clem," Aster growled. She beckoned. "A word."

She led her sister aside, back into the shade of the trees. Clementine was still flushed and grinning.

"You need to stop," Aster said under her breath.

"Stop what?"

"Joking around with him like that. He's not our friend."

A line formed between Clementine's brows. "Not *yet*," she said. "That's the point. I'm trying to *make* a friend of him. We need help, Aster."

"Well, you need to be more careful. Everything you tell him about yourself is something he can use against you later."

"But I've hardly told him anything!"

Not in words, maybe. But there were some things a man could read in your face, in your voice. In the way you looked at him, or didn't. Clementine had not yet learned to control herself, not the ways she would need to survive.

"Just . . . keep to yourself for now, all right?" Aster urged. "Zee hasn't earned our trust, not by a long shot. If he seems nice, it's because he wants something."

Clementine was quiet for a moment. She crossed her arms and squinted up at the sun. After two days on the road the brown of her skin had deepened to a shade Aster hadn't seen since they were young children, lying belly-down in the dirt and watching ants creep up an old stump. A fierce protectiveness rose up in Aster's throat.

"All right," Clementine agreed at last, and Aster let out a low breath.

They rode on.

It wasn't until late afternoon that the knot of anxiety in Aster's gut finally began to ease just the tiniest a bit. They were about a half mile outside of the next big town, Drywell. They'd made good time, even with Zee's extra precautions, and every hour of it had been without major incident. There was no denying that Zee's first day with them had been a success.

Zee found a little hollow where they could shelter for the night, a patch of dirt beneath an overhanging outcrop of rock. While everyone else hiked to a nearby stream to water the horses and wash up, Aster stayed to help Zee as he set up camp. Someone had to keep an eye on him.

They began unpacking the saddlebags. Zee watched her from the corner of his eye. "You did good today," he said after a moment. "I see why the others follow you."

Aster grunted noncommittally.

"I'm not here to take that away from you, you know," Zee persisted. "I've been trying all day to figure out how to tell you . . . I'm not looking to be you all's new leader. You don't need that, and I don't want it. I just want to help."

"So you've mentioned once or twice."

"By the *dead*, it's like talking to a brick wall."

"I'll bet you've tried."

Zee muttered a curse and left her alone. They worked in

silence for a few moments more. Aster moved on to clearing away some of the brush to make room for them to sleep later. The muscles in her legs and back were strung tight from riding all day, and the simple act of bending over to pick up loose branches and stones seemed to double her soreness. Sweat cut through the film of dust on her face. Her mouth tasted like dirt. She winced as she reached for the final stone—

—and gasped when she realized what it was.

Aster's stomach flipped. She dropped the bundle of branches in her hands.

"What's going on?" Zee asked, hurrying over. Aster pointed to the human skull, to the cracked gray cap covered in earth, to the empty eyes and the broken teeth. She thought of the Green Creek welcome house emblem, stamped on the back of every brag's hand. A skull and roses.

She couldn't seem to make her mouth work.

Zee dropped his shoulders and sighed. "Oh. Poor bastard." He picked the skull up, brushed it off. "I wish I could say I'm surprised, but this kind of thing is common out here. A lot of folks try to leave the Scab, and some desperate fools even think they have a shot at making it to Ferron, where there are no dustblood debts. But the mountains are their own death sentence." Zee shook his head. "Maybe a better way to go than being killed at the border, though."

Aster had known that much, but still, to actually see the bones . . .

"Why don't more rangemen help them?" she asked.

"Well, it's illegal to help anyone trying to escape the Reckoning, for one. And two, most of them can't pay for our

113

services. It's fairbloods who hire us, mostly."

Aster leveled her gaze on Zee, who carefully placed the skull up on the outcropping of rock, out of harm's way.

"And would *you* be helping *us*, if we didn't have that big chunk of theomite to pay you with?"

Zee furrowed his brow. "Aster, I'm not just doing this for the shine. I . . ." But before he could finish, the others returned. Zee dismissed himself from the conversation with obvious relief, going to greet them. Aster watched him with hawklike scrutiny.

Once they finished setting up the camp, they settled in to eat their supper—biscuits and beans. Zee showed them how to dig a smokeless fire pit that would provide them with meager heat, and they cloaked their blankets around them to protect them from the wind.

Zee was quiet for once. While everyone else talked over their food, he only stared silently into the fire. Maybe he was still upset that Aster had questioned his integrity? Maybe there was some danger lying ahead that he had yet to tell them about? Or maybe he was just tired, as they all were—Aster had no patience to try to divine this boy's moods. And yet she couldn't relax without knowing why he was so tense.

Finally Zee stood, brushing the dust off the seat of his denims. "If you all are good for now, I'm going to make a stop in town. We'll be needing a lot more supplies than what I usually carry around. Spare canteens, horse feed, some clothes that'll actually fit you all . . . it'll take a while, and I want to be back before dark."

"You have the shine for all that?" Violet asked, looking him up and down as if she sincerely doubted it.

"My father was a gambleman, left me a bit of gold when he

passed. I've been saving it for an emergency." He flashed an uneasy smile. "I expect he'd agree this counts."

How lucky for us, Aster thought dryly. This all seemed far too good to be true.

"We can't accept your charity, Zee," Clementine said.

"It's not charity," Zee promised. "The theomite ring will more than cover these expenses. Every job requires supplies. It's built into the asking price." He smiled again. "So you all just relax until I get back, all right? You've earned it."

Aster watched Zee carefully as he readied his horse. And though Zee's words seemed honest enough, something in his shifty manner told Aster that he was lying now. She could feel it in the nape of her neck. But lying about what?

Maybe he's going into town to turn us in, she thought. Aster looked around the circle. She had to tell someone. Clementine would only defend him. Mallow might do something reckless. Tansy would overthink it. But Violet . . .

Aster waited until Zee left, sweating even though the cool air had raised a chill on her skin. As soon as the sound of his retreat faded, Aster hurried over to Violet, who was busy brushing out her hair with Zee's boar-bristle brush.

"Violet."

"By the dead, what *now*?"

"I have to talk to you." Aster pulled Violet aside despite her protests and explained her suspicions about Zee. Violet scowled at the idea.

"I don't know, Aster, why would he have waited until now?"

Aster burned with frustration. "The hell would I know? I think I'm going to follow him. I just need to be sure. If I find out I'm right, I'll come back and we can get a head start leaving. And if I don't come back, I need you to get them out of here. But for now, just tell them I went after Zee because . . . because I thought of something else we needed him to pick up. I don't want to worry them unnecessarily."

"They'll say you're a fool for going off on your own," Violet sighed. "And they'll be right."

"Maybe." But if she did nothing, and Zee brought the law down on them, she would never forgive herself. "Just look after them."

Violet finally conceded, and as she returned to the camp, Aster slipped away. She untied her horse, mounted up, and followed Zee's trail. She'd wanted to wait long enough that he wouldn't know she was following him, but she was also terrified of falling too far behind. Every second counted.

Still, she paused and tied the dustkerchief around her face once she drew near the Bone Road, her hands shaking as she did so. Everyone would be looking for her now. Even folks who might normally be sympathetic would see McClennon's reward and think twice.

Sudden doubt seized her. Maybe she should just go back to the girls and tell them they had to run . . .

But no, they would want proof. If she was going to make them abandon the first person to offer them hope, they would demand it.

Aster realized then, to her surprise, that she'd allowed herself to hope, too. It wasn't much, but it was there. Like finding a copper in your pocket.

Please, Zee, Aster thought. *Let me be wrong about you.*

She clicked at her horse and guided him out onto the Bone

116

Road. Sweat trickled down her spine. She rounded a bend and spotted two lawmen standing guard at the edge of town. That wasn't unusual, Aster told herself. Bandits were common in these parts. These badges were just here to keep an eye out.

So why had they stopped the two men on horseback ahead of her?

Aster tensed, gripped her reins. But it was too late. One of the lawman had seen her and was waving her forward. His partner sent the two men on into Drywell.

Aster's favor prickled. She took a deep breath and trotted ahead. She was still wearing Augie's loose stableman's clothing, and with her hair hidden in her hat and her face covered up, she might just be able to pass for a young man in the fading light. But even so, dustbloods were often turned away from deadwalled towns if they didn't have papers from their landmaster stating their business.

And Aster certainly couldn't pass for a fairblood.

"Evening, sir," the first lawman said as she stopped beneath the shade of a tree. His mouth was a hard line beneath his bristling blond moustache. He held up a large wanted poster with Clementine's face on it. "Have you seen this girl?"

Aster shook her head slowly, not daring to speak, praying they wouldn't ask her to come into the light.

"What about these?"

He held up the other posters one by one. She shook her head again. Her insides crawled. When he showed Aster her own face, a spike of terror ran through her, sweat breaking out beneath the fabric of her dustkerchief.

"All right, well, you keep an eye out, hear?" the other

lawman said. His eyes were black as coal. "They killed a man. They're dangerous. And we have reason to believe they're in the area."

Aster touched the brim of her hat, and they let her through the gates. She didn't dare exhale until they were out of sight. If her favor had burned through the dustkerchief . . . if the shade hadn't hidden her own lack of a shadow . . . if either of the lawmen had demanded that she state her business . . .

Never mind that. Just find Zee and get the rip out of here.

Aster urged her horse down Main Street at a hurried pace, trying to steady her own breathing. Drywell seemed to be a quieter town than Killbank. Most of the shops were still open. A handful of fairblood women outside the general store gossiped to each other over their purchases. Two dustblood men hammered away at the roof of the inn, shirtless and sweating in the late sun.

There was no sign of Zee. If he was going to turn them in, surely he would have done it when the lawmen stopped him? Had he been telling the truth after all? She hadn't seen him in any of the shops—but then, she hadn't been looking.

Aster finally reached the lawmaster's office, but Zee's mare, Nugget, wasn't tied to the post outside. He wasn't there.

She hesitated. Her favor had begun to burn with true pain now, enough to make her head swim. It would begin showing through her dustkerchief soon. She had to go back. Even if she had no proof that Zee meant them harm.

But then, as Aster turned to make her retreat, she saw it: the Drywell welcome house.

Aster recoiled as if she'd been slapped. The stately mansion loomed over the other buildings, all dark brick and towering gables. A ravener leaned easily against the doorframe. Every cell in Aster's body screamed at her to run, but she couldn't seem to work her own limbs. When she'd escaped Green Creek, she'd meant to leave all her memories behind with it. Now they came rushing back, choking her, drowning her.

She would die here. These men would kill her, as they'd always been meant to. Even now the ravener turned his rust-colored eyes towards her. She swallowed, and it cut like a dagger.

That was when Aster finally saw Zee. His rangeman's hat; his lean, shrewd face; his easy, gliding gait as he went to untie his horse. The sight of him was enough to shock her out of her terror—and turn it to rage.

He was walking out of the welcome house.

CHAPTER NINE

Aster's anger burned hot as her hidden favor. She'd known Zee was up to something, but she hadn't ever imagined this. Her hand went to the hilt of her knife. She would gut him like a pig.

But no, that would be suicide. Aster swung her horse around before Zee could see her. She had to get back to camp and warn the others.

She rode off without looking back.

Aster broke out in a sweat from the pain of her favor as she made her way up Main Street. It was as if a white-hot iron had been pressed to her skin. She gritted her teeth against the scream building in her throat. She'd waited too long. There was no way she'd be able to get past the checkpoint at the gates now. She pulled the collar of her coat up, hoping to buy herself a few extra minutes, and took a sharp turn down a side street, angling for the far edge of town. She approached the deadwall, head bowed, heart pounding, eyes trained on the lawmen ahead.

Please don't stop me, please don't stop me, please don't—

And whether there was someone beyond the Veil looking out for her, or whether it was just luck, Aster didn't know. But whatever it was, she rode by them unchecked.

She released a breath. The sky was beginning to darken, blue-purple as a bruise, by the time Aster finally reached the woods. She clawed her dustkerchief away, gasping at the pain, and spurred her horse into a sprint. She had to make it back to camp before nightfall brought out the vengeants. The wind pulled at her skin as she galloped towards the outcrop.

All the girls looked surprised by Aster's sudden return—except for Violet, whose face was taut with anticipation in the lantern light. Aster slid down from the saddle.

"Pack up the camp," Aster said, answering the silent question in Violet's eyes. "We need to get out of here."

"Why?" Clementine asked, alarmed. The others leapt to their feet and got to work.

"Zee." Aster made his name a curse. "When I went into town, I saw him at the welcome house."

Mallow's eyes flashed with anger. "Hold up, are you *sure*?"

"Yes. It was him. He was on his way out. He can't have afforded to stay long." Aster felt sick. Zee was no better than Lieutenant Carney, or any of the rest of them. He'd probably think himself one of the good ones just because he wasn't as openly cruel as the likes of Baxter McClennon.

But there was no such thing as a good brag. Every last one of them knew the girls they paid for were prisoners.

And the fact that Zee had smiled and promised to help them escape, only to turn around and subject some other girl to the same evils they were all running from . . .

"It's damned twisted," Violet said darkly.

"Ripping hell, they're all the same," Mallow swore.

"But he's a *dustblood*," Tansy said. "He's one of *us*. I would've thought that meant—"

"It doesn't mean a thing," Aster spat. She'd once been innocent enough to believe otherwise, too. But, if anything, some of Aster's most hateful customers had been dustbloods—bitter, broken men who'd been rewarded by their landmaster with a trip to the welcome house. It was the kind of privilege they could earn for warning their overseers about a strike or an escape attempt.

You couldn't trust anyone.

"Come on, let's go," Aster urged, kneeling to roll up a blanket. "We need to be gone before he gets back."

"Wait." Clementine spoke for the first time since hearing the news. She was still sitting cross-legged on the ground. She struggled to keep her voice steady, but Aster could hear the hurt in it. "I . . . I want to wait for him. We deserve the chance to have it out with that snake in the grass for lying to us."

For a moment, Aster saw her own burning shame and anger in her sister's face, and if Zee were with them now, Aster could have cheerfully broken his jaw across her fist. She knew all too well the need to confront those who had done you harm, and she knew the pain only doubled when you never got the chance. Unsaid words dissolved to poison in the veins.

But that poison was still a slower death than one at the hands of dangerous men—and Zee was dangerous. There was no doubting that now.

Aster was about to say as much when Mallow spoke first.

"Actually, Clem might have a point. If we wait for Zee to get back, we can rob him for everything he's got," she said. "He clearly has shine to spare, if he can afford to be going to the welcome house."

"Then we tie him up to make sure he can't follow us again," Violet said. "Honestly, we ought to do that anyway."

They all fell silent for a moment, seeming to consider it. The vengeants' cries rose up around them, blending with the wailing of the wind through the trees.

"We need the shine," Aster said finally. "We need it to resupply at the next town. We'll never make it to Northrock if we don't. Zee was telling the truth about that much."

"And I'd much rather steal shine from a brag like him than steal supplies outright from some innocent storeowner," Tansy added.

"And Zee?" Clementine asked. "What do we do with him?"

Aster hesitated. "We won't hurt him. Say we owe him that much for getting us to Drywell. But we'll tie him up before we go, like Violet said. And the dead help him if he decides to come after us again."

Mallow nodded, rolling up her cuffs. "It'll be better to ambush him from the road. He won't be expecting us there."

"All right," Aster agreed, "but not too close to town. There are lawmen around the deadwall."

They hurried towards the Bone Road on foot, the better to navigate the thick undergrowth quickly. Brittle brown pine needles crunched softly beneath their steps; stars jeweled the sky above. Aster led the way with the theomite ring hung from a loop of twine around her neck. A chill had crept into the air, and not just from nightfall: the dead were waking, and they would be on the hunt, too.

When the five of them reached the edge of the road, just before the bend, they crouched beneath the cover of the brush as best they could. They positioned themselves in the gap of darkness between two of the iron wardants whose lamplight lit the road. It didn't take long for someone to come along, though it wasn't Zee.

First there was a loud party of well-dressed gamblemen in a large, open coach, none of them older than thirty. They were probably coming to town from some landmaster's manor in the hills. Aster had no doubt one or all of them was on their way to the welcome house, and her nails dragged furrows into the dust as her anger grew. But she and the others were no match for such a large group.

Then came a pair of mounted lawmen on patrol. Aster counted her heartbeats until they passed.

Then came a middle-aged man traveling alone in a slow-rolling open coach. He peered into the dark of the forest uneasily, and he took a furtive sip from a flask to shore up his courage as a vengeant wailed somewhere in the near distance.

"I recognize him," Violet whispered harshly. "He's a statesman, stops by the welcome house every year during election season to talk up the other customers. And have his *fun*, too, of course."

"He's probably on his way to the welcome house *now*," Clementine said. "A hardworking man *deserves* a little rest. Isn't that what they say? Aster . . ." She gritted her teeth, her jaw twitching. "Aster, we have to stop him."

"Zee," Aster reminded her.

"To hell with Zee," Mallow snarled. "To hell with all of them. Now's our chance to gut one of these shitheels. I'm not letting it go." She was already rising to her feet, hands clenching into fists.

"*Wait*," Aster ordered, grabbing Mal's wrist. She understood what the others were feeling. She felt it, too. Her mind worked quickly. "Maybe Zee's not the only brag we can rob . . ." The statesman was only a couple lengths away. "Look—his hat alone is worth two hundred eagles. He'll have more shine on him than any rangeman." They could still deal with Zee afterwards, but Mallow was right—they couldn't let this opportunity go.

"But how do we do it?" Tansy asked.

"I know his type," Violet murmured. "Let me lure him to you all quietly. We don't want to draw attention to ourselves."

She crept out from under the bushes and onto the road before anyone could argue with her. Aster swore, tempted to follow her. Violet wasn't even armed. But it was already too late. The coach was right in front of them, and Violet stumbled into its path. She still wore Baxter McClennon's clothes, but she had removed the hat and let her hair down. She waved her arms desperately over her head.

"Oh, thank the dead!" she said in a choking half sob as the driver brought the coach to a stop. She ran to its side and clutched at the door. The statesman looked down at her, bewildered.

"Easy, now, miss," he said. "What are you doing out here all on your own? And dressed like a rough?" He narrowed his eyes as he noticed her favor. His tone grew considerably colder. "Are you a runaway? You ought to know you won't get any help from me. I'm a man of the law, hear? I'll be reporting you the moment we get into town."

"Yes, please, take me with you," Violet begged. "I'm from the Drywell welcome house. I've been kidnapped. The brag I was with, he and his friends—they didn't want to pay, so they attacked the ravener at the door and ran off with me."

"*What?*"

"Yes! And they made me wear these clothes so they could smuggle me out of town. I managed to give them the slip just now, but they still have another girl with them back at their camp. Please, sir, you have to do something. We only want to go home."

The brag was silent. Aster watched him carefully, leaning forward on her haunches, preparing to spring. If he had seen their wanted posters already, he would recognize Violet at any moment. They'd have to fight him and his driver both.

But he just mopped his forehead with his silk dustkerchief, his face drawn with distress but not disbelief. "I'm sorry," he said at last. "I have a charity event to attend. But I can drop you off at the lawmaster's office, let them handle this—"

"There isn't time! These men, they'll kill my friend when they're done with her. I heard them say so. But they're cowards, I know it. They'll scatter like cockroaches when they see *you*."

"Well—"

"The welcome house will be forever in your debt if you help us, sir." Violet stepped in closer, resting a hand on his wrist. "And so will I."

That seemed to decide him. He sighed. "Is it far?"

"Not at all, just follow me . . ."

Aster couldn't help a grudging respect as she watched it all unfold. How *easily* Violet slipped into whatever character she needed to be for the given moment, how effortlessly she detached from her true self. Aster had always envied that about her—the ability to escape. As soon as Violet turned her back to the brag, her expression relaxed into its usual cool indifference, the barest hint of her disdainful smile at her lips.

But it was far too soon to celebrate. Aster drew her knife and nodded at the others to ready themselves. Violet led the brag by the hand to the woods.

"All right, on my mark," Aster whispered. She deepened her crouch. The sounds of the night grew overloud around her. She felt every pebble in the dry earth beneath the soles of her shoes. Violet and the brag broke through the bushes.

"*Now*," Aster ordered.

They all leapt up to tackle the brag. His eyes widened in panic, but he didn't have time to let out more than a strangled squawk before Mallow caught him with a straight punch to the nose. A crunch of bone, a gush of blood. He stumbled backwards, knees buckling, and Aster shoved him to the ground. Fell on him. The feel of her hands hitting flesh made her gorge rise. She'd been struck before. She knew where a body was most vulnerable. The throat. The groin. The dead center of the chest, where the heart beat just below the surface. She hit him as if doing so would frighten her own nightmares away. She hit him until her knuckles bled.

The others helped her. Their anger was a live thing, mindless and starved. He was not the one who had hurt them, but he would do. Clementine kicked his ribs. Tansy gagged him with his dustkerchief. When the coach driver ran into the bushes at the commotion, Mallow swung her fist across his jaw, leaving him dazed and moaning on the ground. Finally Aster pressed her knife to the brag's throat, daring him to move. He stared up at her with hate in his eyes.

"I'm not surprised you didn't recognize my friend," Aster said to him, her voice deathly quiet. "I know we're all the same to you. But *she* recognized *you*, Statesman. Said you've been to our welcome house many a time. We're only here to collect our due. Then we'll be on our way."

By now Tansy had found the heavy coin purse in his coat. She whispered urgently in Aster's ear. "The rope, Aster, we didn't bring any rope to tie him up with."

Aster faltered, the words breaking through her red haze. "Does he have any rope on him? Check his coach."

"No luck there," Violet said, running to Aster's side. "I went back to look through it for valuables, but there's nothing we can use."

A bead of sweat fell from Aster's brow. Her hands were trembling like an old woman's.

"Well, someone has to go back to camp and get some, then," she said finally.

"Let me go," Clementine offered. She was looking at Aster knowingly. "I'm the only one who might be able to make it without the ring. At least I can see the dead coming."

And yet the idea of Clementine running alone, through the woods, in the dark, with vengeants at her heels, was immediately unacceptable.

"Take the ring anyway," Aster said, unlooping it from her neck with her free hand. "We're by the Bone Road. We'll be fine."

Violet cleared her throat. "Listen to your sister, now, Aster, we need that ring here. They don't call it the Bone Road for nothing."

Aster spun away from the brag then, glaring at Violet. Why did she always choose the worst moments to be difficult? "I don't recall asking for your opinion," Aster snarled.

As soon as Aster turned, though, the brag broke free, yanking out his gag and stumbling towards the road.

"*Ripping hell!*"

"Grab him!"

Mallow tackled him around his legs just as he reached the edge of the road. They dragged him back into the dark. He cursed them, his voice cracking.

"You're *dead. All* of you. I was campaigning with Jerrod McClennon himself in Green Creek, and I know for a *fact* that he followed you out of there with his best raveners. They're coming for you Luckers. You'll see—"

"By the Veil, *shut him up*," Aster ordered. She felt on the edge of hysteria. Her throat burned with either laughter or tears. Clementine managed to gag the statesman again. His driver watched in wide-eyed silence, not having moved from the ground where Mallow knocked him down.

The girls were all breathing hard now, eyes glazing over with panic. Aster swallowed.

"Go on and get the rope, Clem," she said. "Take the ring. Hurry back."

Nobody argued. The rest of them each took hold of a limb to keep the brag from making another escape. They waited in silence for Clementine to return. Two more parties passed them by on the road, but, mercifully, none heard the brag's muffled struggling. It would only be a matter of time before someone stopped to have a look at his empty coach, though, and realized something was wrong.

Clementine emerged from the dark. She looked shaken but unhurt.

"You all right?" Aster asked. She was afraid to turn her back on the brag again.

129

Clementine nodded. "Here's the rope," she said, passing it over.

"Thank the dead," Violet muttered. They went to work propping the brag up against a tree trunk and tying him to it, then tying his driver next to him. The brag had resigned himself to his fate, it seemed, but he still glared at Aster with beady black eyes that shone like an insect's. His loathing was palpable.

Well, the feeling was mutual. Aster pressed the point of her knife to the softness of his chin. With her other hand, she plucked the gold pin from his lapel. It was the Arkettan seal.

"*Glory to the Reckoning*," Aster quoted softly. How many times had she seen those words? On the flag that had hung above the mining camp. On the sleeves of lawmen. On every coin that'd been exchanged to purchase her. A reminder that freedom in Arketta had to be earned.

As if it hadn't been her due from the moment she drew her first breath.

Aster sucked her teeth and pocketed the trinket. "I bet you'll be too ashamed to tell anyone it was a bunch of girls that did this to you, won't you, Statesman? A fine public servant like yourself can't afford to have that rumor going around. You'll seem *weak*."

The brag hesitated, then nodded once.

"Better stick to that, or we'll be back to finish the job," Aster warned.

She nodded to the others, and they retreated, leaving the brag to sweat in the dark until someone else found him. There could be no question of waiting to ambush Zee now, not after this. They had to get out of Drywell as soon as possible.

"Think he'll rat on us?" Clementine asked as they picked their way back to camp.

Aster just shook her head. "Can't see how it matters if he does. The McClennons already want us dead as it is."

They were silent for a few paces. Then Tansy spoke up, hesitantly. "I've never seen a man afraid of me like that before," she said. "It's always been *me* who's had to be afraid of *them*."

"Felt good," Mallow said, nodding.

No one else replied, but Aster could sense the others' unspoken agreement. And yet, none of them could quite seem to meet anyone else's eye. Aster didn't feel guilty in the least for what they'd done.

But she wondered if she ought to.

No. That dirty rip had it coming, she told herself fiercely. *Let him be at our mercy, for a change.*

But he'd almost gotten away. And if he had—

"We'll be more careful next time," Mallow went on, as if she'd heard Aster's thoughts. "There'll be a next time, won't there?"

They hadn't counted the shine yet, but Aster suspected it was enough to justify the risks they'd taken.

"There'll be a next time," she promised.

Some part of her looked forward to it.

When they got back to the camp, Zee was waiting for them, pacing back and forth like the catamount he'd driven off. Aster had known he might beat them back to camp, but the sight of him still sent a jolt of shock and nausea through her. She didn't want to get in another fight tonight, but she would if she had to. The others stopped short behind her, their sudden fear palpable. Though Aster's hand was sore and caked with dried blood, she clenched it into a fist, taking a step into the lantern light. A bitter wind twitched at her jacket as the song of the crickets rose and fell.

Zee's shoulders dropped with relief at the sight of them. "Thank the dead! I was afraid you'd been captured. Where the hell have you been?"

"Where the hell have *we* been?" Aster echoed slowly. "Where the hell have *you* been? Because last time I saw you, you were walking out of the welcome house."

It was too dark to read Zee's face clearly, but Aster could sense the guilt in his silence, sharp as turned milk.

"It's not what it looks like," he began.

"We don't want anything else to do with you," Clementine broke in. "If you ever had even a drop of respect for us, then you'll let us go our separate ways and forget we ever met."

He walked towards them, hands held up. "Please, just let me explain—"

"You'd best not take another step, if you don't want this to get unfriendly," Mallow warned.

"I was trying to find my sisters!" Zee shouted. He cursed and turned away from them. Took a moment to collect himself. Turned back around. When he spoke again, his voice was softer, but raw now, exposed.

"I have three younger sisters: Elizabeth, Elena, and Emily. I've been looking after them ever since our parents died two years back. That's why I started working as a rangeman—so I could provide for them like my father had. But eight months ago, while I was off on a job, they disappeared. There was no sign of them when I got home, no sign of where they might've gone, either. They were kidnapped, I'm sure of it. Sold into the system. I've been searching welcome houses ever since, trying to find them. That's why I was in Green Creek the night you all ran away."

And that's why he looks familiar, Aster realized, a chill creeping down her arms.

She'd seen Zee in the reception room. The young brag by the bar.

Zee stabbed an accusing finger at his own chest. "It was *my* responsibility to take care of my sisters," he continued. "It's *my* fault this happened. So I'm just trying to make things right, hear? Don't you *ever* accuse me of being like the men who would hurt them."

He let out a long breath, lacing his fingers over his head and crumpling his hat. "There, now you got me huffing and puffing like a hallower. Probably woke up half the damn Scab. Praise be to the dead, may they bless us with their wisdom."

A sarcastic slant had crept back into his voice, but Aster wasn't fooled. She recognized his pain as well as her own.

"Zee . . ." Clementine said softly. "Why didn't you tell us about your sisters before?"

Zee shrugged, sighing. "Seems to me like you all already have enough to worry about as it is."

Well, that was true enough. But Aster gave him a single nod, to show him that she understood.

Zee gave them a small smile in return. "All right, I told you all where *I've* been," he said. "Now where the rip were you?"

Aster glanced at Violet and started towards the horses. "We'd better tell you on the run."

CHAPTER TEN

They didn't stop riding until midday the next day, when Zee led them to rest under a tree that had been struck dead by lightning. Aster took the opportunity to finally count the shine they'd stolen, her hands clumsy from the cloth bandages Tansy had wrapped around her knuckles. The silver coins felt greasy in her fingers. The total came to a little over one hundred eagles.

Aster had to admit—she'd been hoping for a little more for her trouble.

"Well? How much did we get?" Clementine asked expectantly, looking over Aster's shoulder.

"One hundred and two eagles and a handful of coppers," Aster muttered. Clementine, Tansy, and Mallow let out a whoop, clinking their canteens like champagne glasses. Aster pinched her brow. It was more shine than any of them had seen at once, true, but it wouldn't cover the cost for even *one* of them to get their favors removed, if Violet's information was right. It was far too early to celebrate.

But the others had been in good spirits all morning. Zee had brought them back the fresh supplies he'd promised and proved himself loyal, at least in their eyes. They'd made it out of Drywell without being caught, and they were richer than they'd ever been. They looked prepared for anything in their crisp new rangemen's gear. And for now, they were free. Zee's eager grin was reflected on all their faces.

Aster chewed the inside of her cheek as she packed up the coin purse. Maybe there was something wrong with *her*, that she couldn't look at Zee without her gut churning with suspicion.

Or maybe she was right, and Zee was still hiding something.

Once again, Aster found herself tempted to confide in Violet, the only one who wouldn't rush to defend him. Violet didn't seem to share Aster's suspicion of Zee, but neither did she seem to want anything to do with him. Right now she was sitting up against a tree, silent and scowling, as if she couldn't be bothered with any of them.

Aster walked over and sat next to her anyway.

"Fine weather we got today," Aster said, trying her best to sound pleasant.

Violet cracked open her eyes and shot her a withering look. Tansy had warned them that Violet's withdrawal as she tapered off the Sweet Thistle would make her sensitive to light—and sweaty, and sickly, and even more irritable than usual. Today seemed to be a particularly bad day.

Well, if talking to Violet distracts her from her cravings, so much the better.

"You sure it's a thousand eagles a head for Lady Ghost to help us?" Aster began, leaning back against the blackened bark.

Violet took a drink from her canteen with trembling hands. "Well if you don't believe me, there's nothing I can do to prove it to you," she said sharply.

"No, it's not that, I just—" Aster shook her head. "It's going to be tough. If we're sticking with Zee for certain now, we'll have to pay him with the theomite ring at the end of all this, which means we won't be able to use it to pay Lady Ghost. What we did last night, it helped . . . but it's not enough." As she spoke, Aster realized she was talking about Lady Ghost as if it were a given the woman was real. She supposed she'd had to start thinking that way, since they were risking their lives on the promise of it being true. Easier than always fighting off the doubt, which she knew was hiding deep down in her gut, ready to come out if she let it.

"So we do it again," Violet said. "Arketta's not going to run out of brags for us to rob. They're all over the damn place."

"You don't think we ought to lie low, though?" It had all seemed like a good idea last night, when they were caught in the moment . . . but now, in daylight . . .

"Listen, if you're looking for someone to talk you out of it, it's not going to be me. As far as I'm concerned, these bastards owe us. They've been stealing from girls like us for years."

Aster couldn't disagree with that. Still, it was strange to hear *Violet* arguing for any kind of unlawfulness. *Her* blood wasn't tainted with the criminal instinct, as she'd always reminded anyone who would listen. Aster almost pointed this out, but she took another look at Violet's strained, sallow face and thought better of it.

"All right, then, but we'll have to try and hit every town between here and Northrock if we're going to get the shine in time."

"Mm," Violet said vaguely, and closed her eyes again.

She clearly wanted her to piss off, but Aster wasn't done yet. She glanced back up at Zee. He and the others were beginning to ready their horses to leave again, laughing as they did so.

Aster wet her lips and lowered her voice. "Listen, Violet, I don't want to trouble you—"

"Too late."

"—but I was wondering if I could ride with you this afternoon. There's something I wanted to talk to you about."

Violet finally met her eye. "And by *talk to*, are you sure you don't mean *nag, reprimand*, or *bully*? Because I'm not in the mood to butt heads with you today."

Well that's a relief, Aster thought sourly, considering Violet was the one who was always trying to start an argument. But she bit back that reply, too.

"No, I just want to talk about Zee. I can't seem to sort out how to feel about him, and I don't think any of the others would understand."

"Don't tell me you're sweet on him," Violet said with clear distaste.

Aster rolled her eyes. "No, actually, the opposite. I don't trust him. And I don't know if that's because there's truly something hateful about him, or if it's just . . . just that I can't help but see hatefulness in all of them now. The whole thing's making me sick." Aster let out a short breath through her teeth. "Rip it," she swore. "Never mind. Forget I said anything—"

"Wait," Violet sighed. "You can ride with me for a bit. But I won't hesitate to give you back to your sister the *minute* you begin to bother me."

Aster rolled her eyes, but on the inside, she was relieved. She ran back to Clementine to tell her she'd be with Violet for the rest of the day, then returned to help Violet start tacking up. The group set off a few moments later, with Zee and Clementine riding side by side at the front, Tansy and Mallow together in the middle, and Violet and Aster pulling up the rear.

For a moment they were silent, settling into the pace Zee had set. Aster felt in no hurry to fill the silence between them. In truth, she barely trusted Violet any more than she did Zee. Violet had ratted out girls to Mother Fleur for even minor offenses. She'd scolded girls for crying, taunted them for making mistakes, laughed at all their little humiliations. There were times when Aster had hated Violet as much as any brag.

But Violet has no power here, Aster reminded herself.

"I've never met a man that wasn't rotten," Violet said at last, breaking in on Aster's thoughts.

Aster looked up, surprised.

"Born in the welcome house," Violet reminded her. "The only men I ever knew were brags and raveners."

"Doc Barrow was kind enough," Aster offered, thinking of Tansy. The welcome house doctor had always let her follow him around like a lost little duck.

Violet let out a hollow laugh. "Kind enough to cut us from the inside so we can never have children? Kind enough to give us Sweet Thistle so we're too numb to fight back? That man collects his coin from the same people who kept us prisoner. He can take the next train to hell."

Aster flinched. She'd never looked at it that way. But it was true that Doc Barrow had been the first man from Green Creek to hurt any of them. All girls had to be "treated" before

138

going to live in a welcome house. Children like Violet, born to a Good Luck Girl, were rarer than rare, almost always the result of a botched procedure.

Aster swallowed down a sick feeling in her throat.

"So Zee must be rotten, too, is that what you're saying?" Aster asked.

"If he's not yet, he will be one day. Aster, the whole damn *world* is rotten. That's what it takes to survive. I learned that a long time ago."

"So that's your excuse, is it, for making the rest of our lives miserable all the time?" Aster muttered. She knew she'd promised to behave herself, but the words simply slipped out.

But Violet was unbothered. "What? You think I don't know how much you all hated me? You think I gave a wet shit? I was just looking out for myself. If you had any sense you'd have done the same."

The words hung in the air, a challenge. Their conversation was still too low for the others to hear, and Aster bit her tongue until she was confident she could speak without raising her voice in anger.

"I didn't have the *luxury* of looking out for myself," she said at last. "I was too busy looking out for Clem."

"And a fine job you did of it. She would have died if she hadn't killed McClennon—which is exactly my point. If you're not willing to play dirty, you've already lost."

Aster curled her lip, near ready to strangle Violet, but all of a sudden the fight went out of her.

Because Violet was right.

Violet understood.

It was foolish to trust anyone. To hope for the best. To play fair in an unfair world. The others might have felt ready to put their faith in Zee, but Aster was not yet ready to put her faith in anything. And she was clearly right not to do so.

Aster should have felt vindicated by Violet's answer, but instead she just felt empty. And exhausted beyond words.

Violet's manner seemed to soften, as if she'd felt the sudden shift in Aster's temper. She glanced back over her shoulder.

"For what it's worth, I *do* think Zee's telling the truth about his sisters," Violet said quietly.

"So do I," Aster admitted, but only because she'd seen him lie before and knew what it looked like.

"And he used his father's shine on the supplies for us, too," Violet went on, businesslike. "So, I suppose that counts for something."

"He knows he's going to earn it all back ten times over when we pay him, though."

"Just the same," Violet said. "My point is—you don't have to trust Zee, or anyone, for that matter, but you at least have to recognize when they're *useful*. Zee is useful to us because he knows how to get us to Northrock in one piece. And we're useful to him, too, because he clearly feels no end of guilt that he can't help his sisters, and helping us is the next best thing. Our boy wants to be able to sleep at night again. Works for me."

Violet's callous assessment of the situation threw Aster at first, a startling reminder of just how much Violet treated emotion as something to be exploited. But then she began to feel comforted by the clear-cut logic. Honor, justice, basic human decency—these were not things to stake your life on. But mutual usefulness was just about solid ground.

"Thanks, Violet," Aster said, sitting up straighter in the saddle. "I feel better . . . I think."

"Give it time, it'll pass."

They rode on, the sun beating on the back of Aster's neck. The trees sagged under the weight of the still, windless heat. The sky was bright blue marble streaked with white. Aster and Violet began discussing their next robbery, Aster all too aware that it had been Violet's quick thinking that had allowed them to pull the last one off. But even so, it had been a near disaster. The next brag might be better prepared. They had to be, too.

"We were right to bring the first brag into the woods," Aster said. "It was just in restraining him where we got sloppy. But it's hard tying up a man who's fighting you every step of the way."

Violet nodded. "Maybe if we held a gun on him next time? Zee has the hunting rifle."

"I can't shoot worth a damn," Aster muttered, thinking back to the apothecary robbery. She hadn't had any idea what to do with the gun in her hands. And that was only part of the problem—even if Aster knew what she was doing, she wasn't sure she was ready to cross that line. Holding a knife on a man was bad enough.

They never had a problem crossing lines when you were at their mercy, a little voice in the back of her mind whispered.

Aster forced herself to ignore it. "You might be onto something, though, asking Zee for help," she continued. "Making him . . . useful. He must know a thing or two about trapping—maybe there's a way to lure the brag into a snare . . ."

But Aster suspected she'd have a hard time convincing him

to help. He'd seemed upset enough when they told him they'd robbed the statesman. A few eagles weren't worth the risk, he'd said. But that air of guilt still clung to him as he spoke, and he hadn't argued the point long. Perhaps he'd blamed himself for their desperate actions.

Whatever—as long as he had their backs when it mattered.

Violet and Aster continued talking through their plans, but as the hours wore on, Aster couldn't help but be distracted by Clementine's peppering bursts of laughter from up ahead. Aster was too far away to hear what Zee was saying, but it was obvious enough that he was the one responsible for Clementine's good mood. A moment later he gave her a mouth harp that she struggled to play.

"And here you had me believing you played the piano," Zee cried indignantly, now loud enough for everyone to hear.

"I do! This is nothing like it."

"It's the same basic principle."

"What would you know about it?"

"It's not supposed to sound like a dying cat, I know that much."

"They better quiet down before they get us all killed," Violet said to Aster, sounding bored.

Aster didn't respond. She was too busy quelling her anger—at Clementine for letting her guard down, at Zee for talking to her in the first place.

But even if Zee were as good as everyone seemed to think he was, it didn't change the fact that the closer Clementine got to any man, the more power he'd have to hurt her. Half the girls at the welcome house spun themselves a fantasy of falling in love with a man who would take them out of the house for good. But in reality, men just used your weaknesses to manipulate you. That was just as true out here as it was on the inside. If she hadn't been convinced of that before talking to Violet, she certainly was now.

Aster hadn't gotten Clementine out of one prison just to watch her walk into another.

Take it easy. They're just joking around. It doesn't mean anything.

It had better not.

It was late afternoon when they stopped for the day. Zee led them to a narrow gully with a thin stream of water running through it that would help to hide their tracks and scent. Aster sidled up next to him as the others knelt gratefully to drink and wash their faces.

"Talk to you for a minute?" she asked, clearing her throat.

He turned, his easy smile still hanging loose on his face, his brown eyes bright as copper in the sunlight. Aster could see why her sister might be swept up by him. But it didn't change the way things were.

Zee brushed his hands together. "Sure thing."

They staggered up the side of the gully. Zee helped Aster over some of the rockier stretches, and she couldn't help but flinch away from his touch. Her skin crawled at the contact.

"So what's on your mind?" Zee asked, stuffing his hands in his pockets and leaning against the trunk of a tree.

Aster hesitated. Something in the gentleness of his voice almost convinced her to tell the truth. *I can't help but be afraid of you, Zee. I can't help but be afraid for my sister. But we need you right now, and I don't know what to do.*

But instead, she just said: "Violet and I've been planning out our next robbery. We'll need your help to pull it off."

Zee's face fell. "Another robbery? Why?"

"We need the shine for Lady Ghost. Otherwise the whole trip is a waste."

"We won't even *make* it to Lady Ghost if the law catches us. It's hard enough avoiding them as it is without advertising our location like that."

Aster crossed her arms. "Well, what would you have us do?"

"Not get killed, for a start," he said tiredly. "I don't know. I reckon you're right. But it's not just the law, Aster. It's the raveners I'm most worried about. You don't understand how dangerous they can be."

"Don't I?" Aster bristled at his arrogance. "You're not the one who grew up being tortured by them, last I checked."

Zee's expression darkened. Aster took a step back, fear spiking through her blood. She knew all too well the way anger twisted a man's face. Her skull buzzed as if with a swarm of hornets. Her throat tightened like a fist.

"You don't know a damn thing about *how* I grew up," Zee said, raising his voice and taking a step closer. "I know the raveners better than they know themselves."

Aster stepped back from him, panic seizing her. She stumbled in her retreat. Nearly fell. Zee's expression softened immediately, and he stepped back again.

"I'm sorry. I didn't mean to scare you."

"I'm not afraid of you." Aster's voice was strained, her heart kicking. *I'm not afraid of any of you. I'll kill you. I'll strike you dead.*

144

"Well, good. I promised I'd help you however I can, and I mean to," Zee said, exhaling. "What kind of rangeman would I be if I went back on my word?"

"A shit one, I'd think."

"Exactly." Zee lowered his hands slowly. "So . . . how can I help?"

Aster's eyes burned with tears. She blinked them away furiously. She hated when this happened to her.

"Aster—by the dead, I'm sorry, honest, let's talk about it—"

"Follow me," she muttered, starting back down the gully. "The others will need to hear the plan, too."

It wasn't as easy as it looked, rigging a trap.

The kind of snare you used to trap a squirrel wasn't near strong enough to trap a grown man, Zee had explained. But they could improvise using the same basic principles: fashion a lasso-like snare out of some rope, throw it over a sturdy tree branch, wait for the brag to step into the trap, then pull the rope tight and hoist him high by his ankles.

"A true snare is supposed to do all the work for you," Zee said. They were gathered underneath the tree in question, walking through the plan. "You come back later and collect the game. But since you all aren't going anywhere, you can do some of the work yourselves."

"And collect immediately," Mallow replied.

Zee grinned. "That's right."

The girls would lie in wait just outside the town of Whitethorn while Zee went to the welcome house to look for his sisters. Provided he didn't find them there, it'd then be his job to lurk outside the front and catch a man on his way into the house.

"Tell the brag you've got girls back at your camp that they can roll with for half the price," Aster instructed. "Then bring him back here."

Zee frowned. "Won't he know there's a catch?"

"If he asks, just say we're bad girls who got kicked out of the welcome house. They like that sort of thing."

"I don't know that I can lie that convincingly, Aster."

"Why not? You had no trouble lying to *us*." Aster still felt brittle after their tense exchange. Clementine shot her a dirty look, but Zee backed off.

"Fine. But what about the law? They'll have a checkpoint at the edge of town, just like in Drywell."

"Just walk with purpose. There's no reason for the law to stop two men on their way *out* of town," Violet said.

"I'm a dustblood," Zee reminded her, looking at her pointedly. "People assume I'm a criminal the second they see I don't have a shadow. It wouldn't be the first time the law stopped me for no reason."

"Oh, poor thing," she said with a sneer.

"Violet." Aster cut her off with a look, then turned back to Zee. "The brag you pick will be a fairblood. I doubt the law will give you too much trouble as long as you're together."

Zee's hands were on his hips. He looked at the ground, his face obscured by the brim of his hat.

"It's just, I've spent my whole life outrunning the idea that our people are criminals," he said finally. "I've spent my whole life trying to prove I'm a good man."

146

"You are a good man. You're doing a good thing, helping us," Aster replied. *Just tell him whatever he needs to hear.*

He nodded. Once, slowly, and then again, with more confidence.

"All right. All right, then. What kind of brag am I looking for?"

Aster and Violet taught him how to recognize the wealthiest brags. It wasn't always obvious, since most welcome houses had a dress code and even poorer men looked the part. But there were subtle tells. You could look at a man's hands to see if he worked with them, watch the way he walked to see if he expected folks to jump out of his way. Rich men liked to talk about the politicians they'd met or the business deals they'd struck. They had good teeth, too, and they always smelled sweet—too sweet, cloying, like overripe fruit.

Since Violet insisted she was too delicate to help them pull the rope, they used her as a stand-in for the brag instead. The undignified squawk she let out when they finally got the trap to work just about made up for her bullshit.

They ran several more practice runs until they were sure they had it down. Violet walked over stiffly to sit on a tree stump, "keeping a lookout," while Aster, Clementine, and Mallow held the rope, ready to yank it taut as soon as the brag walked by. Tansy made some final adjustments to the snare to make sure it was well hidden under the leaves and free of snags.

Aster tried to steady her breathing as they waited. That rush was in her blood again—the same one she'd felt when she jumped out of the welcome house window, when she snuck into Killbank, when she stole the statesman's shine and got away with it. Spots of color danced on the edges of her vision as she stared into the dark. The sounds of the vengeants' cries ran together in her ears in a single high-pitched hum. Any moment now—

"I think I hear someone coming!" Mallow hissed.

Aster wet her lips, tightening her grip on the rope with slick hands.

"Remember, if this goes sideways, you and the others get out of here while Zee and I hold off the brag," she murmured to Clementine, her heart racing.

"I'm not leaving you," Clementine insisted.

Before Aster could argue, Zee's voice drifted up from the distance.

"Watch your head, now, there's a low branch here."

And a reedy man's voice Aster didn't recognize: "The dead *take* you, you said they were nearby—"

"Well we can't be right under the raveners' noses, now, can we? Just a little further."

"—Gone and ruined my good shoes. These Luckers of yours better be worth it."

"Get ready," Aster whispered to the others. She recognized Zee's easy stride, even in the dark. The gangly shadow behind him moved far less gracefully, cursing every other step. How heavy would a brag that tall be? Enough to snap the rope? *Dammit, Zee, you should've found a flyweight.*

Too late to do anything about it now. They were only a few feet away. Aster widened her stance. Dug her heels in. Zee slowed his pace. Held his lantern high.

"Perfect night, though, isn't it . . . ?" he said.

That was the signal. Aster and the others pulled with all

their strength. The rope jumped. Tightened around the brag's ankles. He let out a screech as his legs were wrenched out from under him. The girls worked quickly, pulling hand over hand, lifting him higher and higher until even his long arms couldn't reach the ground. He hung upside down like a side of beef.

"*What the ripping hell!*" he shouted. "*Help! Somebody!*"

Aster glanced back at the others to make sure they could hold him without her. Clementine gave her a single nod. Aster unsheathed her knife and walked over to the brag, her movements swift but steady. She crouched back on her haunches, held the blade to the brag's heart.

"You're gonna want to quiet down," she said evenly.

The brag stopped his cries for help. The whites of his eyes shone. "Who the rip are you?" he demanded. His gaze flickered towards Zee, who stood back with his arms crossed. "Are you with her?"

"Don't look at him. Look at me," Aster ordered.

The brag said nothing, but recognition flickered across his face as his gaze fell on her favor.

"By the dead, you're one of them girls who . . ."

"That's right," Aster went on, unable to help half a grin. "And if we dusted Baxter McClennon, we certainly won't hesitate to dust you. So you just sit tight while my partner here cleans out your pockets, and this will go easy for you."

She nodded at Zee, who went to work. Some of the brag's belongings had fallen to the ground, but his coin purse was still buckled to his waist. Zee also helped himself to the brag's pocket watch and revolver. The brag, as instructed, kept his eyes on Aster. They brimmed with hate.

"You'll pay for this," he promised. "McClennon'll make sure of it."

"What did I tell you?" Aster snarled.

He quieted, a scowl bristling beneath his moustache. Unlike the statesman, Aster had never seen this brag before. But she'd seen a hundred like him. He would be a small-time landmaster with a single mine to his name and a dozen or so dustblood families working it. Not theomite, or he'd have a ring like Baxter's, but gold maybe, or silver. Some kind of money that grew from the ground. He was the type of brag who could afford to visit the welcome houses as often as he wanted, but he'd have to claw for attention from the more powerful men there. Then he'd take out his anger on the women, leaving them broken by morning.

It'd probably pleased this man, thinking he'd found a way to cheat the system for a night. Rich folks were always the most miserly. Zee had chosen well.

"All right, we're done here," Zee said, tucking the last of the haul into a sack.

"Good," Aster said, still holding the brag's stare.

"Done here, too," Clementine echoed. She and the others emerged, having tied off the end of the rope to a tree trunk. It would give eventually, or the brag would work his way free, but not until they were long gone.

Aster was filled with a heady rush of triumph. She sheathed her knife and stood.

"If you call for help, I guarantee the vengeants will come running before any of the townsfolk do," Zee said, slinging the sack over his shoulder. "Best just sit tight until morning. You'll be fine."

The brag turned his baleful stare towards Zee. "McClennon'll see to you, too!" he promised. "*All* of you. Ripping degenerates. Sprung from cutthroats and thieves. The blood always tells. *The blood always tells—*"

Aster kicked him swiftly across the jaw, her heart pounding against her chest. He let out a loose moan but said no more. If he'd kept talking, she might've done worse. She let out a sharp exhale, looked up at the others. Zee, carefully neutral. Tansy, wincing instinctively. But Mallow, Clementine, and Violet—nodding. Aster smiled.

"Glory to the Reckoning," she said, tipping her hat at the brag, and she and the others disappeared into the wailing dark.

CHAPTER ELEVEN

The days wore on, each one blending into the next like fine desert sand. Condors climbed through blank blue skies and gathered in trees stripped bare by the wind. Lizards skittered through the grass and sunned themselves on sheets of rock. And every morning, the sun rose bloody over the mountains and Aster woke a little stronger. She'd worked past the soreness that came with riding and hiking for hours without end, and she'd worked past some of the fear, too, that came with life on the run. Life in the welcome house had been just as dangerous and unpredictable, in its way. A brag could turn violent at a moment's notice. A ravener might decide to toy with you just because he was bored. Zee seemed surprised at how quickly they were adapting to living rough, but Aster wasn't surprised a bit. They were all of them used to worse.

The exception, of course, as always, was Violet. Her withdrawal clearly was making her miserable, even if she'd never admit it, though she never missed an opportunity to complain about anything and everything else. Aster still rode with Clementine most days, but sometimes she found herself craving Violet's company, prickly as it was. With everyone else, even Clem—*especially*

Clem—Aster felt the need to be the strong one. But Violet had no patience for pretense, and she saw right through it anyway. Aster could let her hurts out in the open air to breathe.

One afternoon, the two of them were practicing their marksmanship together. Zee had suggested the group stop early for the day once they'd reached Annagold's Falls. The landmark put them about halfway through the Scab and a quarter of the way to Northrock. Two weeks of travel so far with perhaps one week to go—once they were free of the Scab, Zee said, they'd be able to ride the rails the rest of the way to Northrock.

Until then, these falls would be the last source of fresh water for miles. Clementine, Zee, Tansy, and Mallow were all busy bathing in the massive lake, their whoops and laughter carrying across the sparkling water. Violet and Aster had decided to use the spare time to set up a makeshift shooting range on the shore opposite the campsite, both of them armed with revolvers they'd stolen from brags along the way. They'd robbed three more brags since Drywell, and they'd since learned that drawing a six-shooter was the surest way to get a man to cooperate. Aster didn't want to waste this rare opportunity to practice her marksmanship—the roar of the waterfall would more than cover the sound of their gunshots.

Which was a blessing, because Aster couldn't seem to hit this target to save her life.

"How is it I'm better at this than you?" Violet asked—not that she was much good, either. Her shots went wide of the stack of rocks they were both aiming for.

"I'm just letting you win like I did with Clem when we were little. She used to be a sore loser. *You* still are."

"Bullshit. I might believe you're not really trying, but it sure as the dead isn't on account of me."

A crack of gunfire, and an instant later, the stack of rocks was blown away. Violet let slip a smug grin, lowering her weapon. The petals of her favor twitched in the wind.

"Be a dear and go set them back up for me?"

Aster muttered some choice words but stalked off to do as she was told. In truth, Violet was right—Aster *was* holding back, and it wasn't because she gave a rip about letting Violet win. It was because she hated the sudden shock of a loud gunshot, hated the way a revolver jumped in her hand like a living thing that might bite her. It only took a few minutes before she'd be sick with unease, cold sweat crawling down her neck and making a slippery mess of her hands. Her vision would blur in and out of focus, and her mind would go sideways, like a wheel jumped out of its rut. She couldn't trust herself to shoot straight when she got like that. She could barely trust herself to breathe.

No matter how many times she held a gun, she still preferred the knife, steady in her hand.

Aster piled up the rocks, sighed, and returned to Violet's side. Violet tilted her head at her curiously, her smug grin fading.

"What?" Aster asked, wary.

"Are you gun-shy? Is that the problem?"

Aster scowled. "I'm not any kind of shy, Violet."

"No, I just mean . . . it's a phrase folks use, to describe anyone who's particularly jumpy. Because they have good reason to be, because they've seen too many ugly things in their time. It doesn't have to be about guns at all—although it can be, apparently, I guess."

154

"What the hell are you talking about?"

"Listen, I'm just saying, I get the same way sometimes. Gunfire doesn't upset me much, but I can't stand the smell of cigar smoke, because it reminds me of the brags. I can't stand it when Zee touches me, even if it's just to help me down from my horse."

Aster's heart began to race, as if it were a wild animal trapped in her chest. She pretended to busy herself with reloading her revolver. Violet had gotten more open lately, the fog of Sweet Thistle that'd always shrouded her beginning to clear as she weaned herself off the drug. Aster knew the clarity was a good thing—but she didn't always like that it made it easier for Violet to see the rest of them, too.

"The raveners always had guns on them," Violet went on. "Maybe you can't help but think of them when you see one. Or did something happen with a brag once? He threatened you or something?"

No, he had loaded his gun with a single bullet, put the barrel in her mouth, spun the chamber and fired. A twisted game some brags apparently liked to play. Aster hadn't dared fight back. Not a night went by that she didn't feel powerless, but this . . . she could still remember the taste of metal on her tongue, the click of the wheel as it went around and around. Her whole body recoiling from the threat of death, her mind flashing back through her short and brutal life. Harsh words, rough hands, anger and fear and anger and shame and anger—

"By the *Veil*," Aster swore at last, giving up any pretense of reloading her weapon. She holstered it heatedly. "Look, I'm just better with the knife, all right? Can we leave it at that?"

"*Fine*, fine. Hey, let's head back to camp anyway. I'm getting peckish."

Aster swallowed, relieved, though she tried not to show it. "It'll be biscuits and beans again tonight. You're not too good for that anymore?"

"Of course I am, but it can't be helped."

They walked in silence for a time, boots squelching in the mud as they traced the shoreline. The air off the lake had a clean, earthy smell to it, and the cool dampness it left on the back of Aster's neck was a small mercy. She stared at her reflection in the water's glassy surface. It might have been a stranger's. Her hair, which she'd once carefully styled every week, was now brushed back into a fraying low bun and stuffed under a bandit hat. The softness of her face had sloughed away, leaving sharp cheekbones and a hard chin. But her eyes—her eyes were as dark and desperate as always. Old woman's eyes. *Seen too many ugly things in their time.*

"How do you hide it so well?" Aster asked Violet softly.

"What do you mean?" She sounded tired, her shadow dragging behind her.

"You said there're little things that upset you now, but you must hide it well, because I've never noticed. Even back at Green Creek, you never seemed bothered by any of it. I know the Sweet Thistle must've helped you, but . . ." Aster cut a glance at her. "There were times when you even seemed to *enjoy* yourself."

Violet shrugged a little. "Maybe I did. What of it? You think I'd have been better off angry at the whole world and everyone in it? How's that worked out for you?"

156

Aster's face heated, her temper rising—but, of course, that was Violet's point.

"It scares me," Aster admitted then. "My anger, I mean. I'm scared it's already burned up everything good inside me. I'm scared it'll burn anyone who gets too close. And I'm scared . . ." Well, what the hell? She'd already said this much. "I'm scared it's all that'll be left of me when I'm gone."

"Like the vengeants?"

Aster nodded. Hallowers disagreed on whether a vengeant was something your soul turned into upon death, or if it was just something your soul shed and left behind on its way through the Veil. It was the former fate that frightened Aster the most—to be lost in her anger for time untold, with no memory of who she'd been or what'd been done to her. Vengeants were not conscious spirits that only lashed out at those who'd hurt them. They were mindless rage. They hurt everyone.

"Well, at least you let yourself feel your anger," Violet said. "I can't seem to feel anything anymore." She kicked at a rock on the ground, no longer looking at Aster. "It was easier at the welcome house. Being head girl, there was always something to keep me busy. I was *good* at my job. I'm not good at . . . *this*." She gestured to the whole valley. "I'm not used to having all this time to think. All this . . . emptiness and quiet. I'm useless out here." She faced Aster again. "I hate it."

"You miss Green Creek?"

"Sometimes a little." She nodded to herself. "Sometimes a lot."

A sickening feeling curdled in Aster's stomach. She tried to remind herself that the welcome house was the only home

157

Violet had ever known, and Mother Fleur her only family. Perhaps it had taken her more courage to leave than Aster was giving her credit for.

"Why'd you come with us, Violet?" Aster asked, and it occurred to her then, for the first time, that *Violet* was Violet's only name—she had no true name that had been given to her in a life before the welcome house, no secret self she could retreat to at the end of the night. "Honest, now: What are you doing out here?"

But by then they had reached the other side of the lake and were nearing the camp. Violet straightened her shoulders and slipped on her mask of cool detachment.

"I already told you. I'm looking for Lady Ghost."

As suspected, it was biscuits and beans for supper. But tonight there was an added treat: fresh-caught trout from the lake. Zee skinned the fish and crouched down to cook it over the campfire. Clementine stood behind him, kneading his shoulders, her piano-quick fingers playing over him with a natural ease. It was the kind of "hospitality" skill they'd all had to learn in the year leading up to their Lucky Nights. Aster bristled but said nothing.

"Where are Tansy and Mallow?" Violet asked. She sat primly on a saddle blanket, combing out her wet hair. She'd dismissed Aster entirely. "I didn't see them when I was washing up just now. Did they drown, or what?"

Zee scanned the lake. There was no sign of them. "They're probably just drying off and getting dressed."

"Certainly taking their sweet time."

"Can you blame them?" Clementine asked. "This has been

158

our first chance to clean up proper since Green Creek. I was starting to feel filthy."

Zee snorted. "Please! You all were *maybe* a little grubby. At the *most*. It takes longer than two weeks for honest filth to settle in."

"Unbelievable. Do you even bother washing when you're not surrounded by a bunch of pretty girls?" Clementine asked.

"Sometimes not even then. Depends on what we're getting up to."

Aster shot him a lethal look. Her marksmanship was about to improve damn quick. Clementine must have suddenly remembered Aster was there, because she snatched her hands back from giving Zee a neck rub and took a seat.

"It's almost dark," Aster said stiffly, turning the conversation back towards Tansy and Mallow. "I don't like the idea of those two wandering around by themselves."

"Well, they know not to stray too far," Clementine said, though Aster heard a note of worry in voice, too. Just yesterday they'd come across a pack of coyotes picking through the remains of an elaborate camp, flies swarming a half-eaten body—some fairblood adventurer with romantic visions of conquering the Scab who'd gotten more than he bargained for.

"You want me to go look for them?" Zee asked.

But then, before Aster could respond, Tansy and Mallow stumbled into the camp from behind the brush. Their faces were flushed, their hands tangled together. They quickly dropped them as they stepped into the firelight.

"Kind of you to join us," Violet said

"You all weren't waiting on us, were you?" Tansy asked, her cheeks growing pinker.

Clementine's eyes lit up with impish glee. "Violet here was worried sick."

"Shit, we should have said something," Mallow muttered. "We just . . . got distracted and lost track of time."

"I bet you did," Clem said.

Something in Aster thawed. She'd seen the way Tansy and Mallow looked at each other back at Green Creek. Secret touches, wordless conversations. In the welcome house, they'd had to bury what was between them. Out here, it'd been allowed to grow.

Aster smiled faintly. "It's fine. Go on and sit down, your supper's getting cold."

They all settled in to enjoy their meal, watching the last of the day's sunlight pour over the red-rock cliffs. Zee told them the story of Annagold, the young woman the falls were named for. It was said she'd fallen in love with a dustblood stableboy, and when her father had caught them together and sold him to the mines, she'd thrown herself over the edge of the falls in grief. You could still see her remnant on clear evenings, a face in the mist rising up from the water.

Soon that started everyone on their favorite ghost stories. Violet told them about the remnant that haunted Mother Fleur's suite, the bitter old woman who had been the housemistress before her. Tansy told them about the vengeants' victims she'd helped her mother care for—some who'd only needed stitches, others who'd lost limbs, all of whom were considered lucky to have survived at all. And Aster and Clementine told them about their grandmother, who had haunted their house for two weeks after she passed. It should have eased their grief to have

160

her remnant near, but instead it had only made it plain just how much they had lost, and in the end they were relieved when she found her peace and moved on.

The tales grew taller and taller until they finally came tumbling down. By the time they were done, the moon hung high above them and the dead were howling at the stars. Everyone retreated to their corners to sleep, Mallow and Tansy linking pinkies as they walked together.

Clementine watched them with a look that was half happiness, half longing. Aster studied her sister carefully. Clementine clearly wanted what they had—and she wanted it with Zee.

She wrapped her hair for the night and crawled into her bedroll next to Aster.

"You know, this isn't so bad, Dawn," she said. Aster stilled at the sound of her true name. "Maybe we don't even need to find Lady Ghost. Maybe we just find some quiet little valley and live off the land."

Well, that was wishful thinking, though Aster couldn't blame her for it. But the minute they stopped running, the raveners would catch them.

"We'll never be safe so long as we're branded. We have to get rid of these favors," Aster murmured, knowing this might also be wishful thinking. Sometimes, she still couldn't fight off the fear that the promise of it was too good to be true. Still, even in moments of doubt, she'd stopped questioning their journey. Out here, they were finally living on their own terms. Doing what they wanted, going where they pleased. That was something, no matter what was waiting at the end.

Clementine touched the side of her cheek. "Zee thinks they're pretty. I was telling him how much I hate that I can't cover mine up, but he said I shouldn't be ashamed of it."

"Easy for him to say. He doesn't have to live with one," Aster said pointedly.

"That's not how he meant it! He just meant—he just wanted to make sure I knew he doesn't think less of me—of any of us—the way most people do."

"And do you care much, what Zee thinks?"

Clementine hesitated. "So long as we're stuck traveling together, we might as well be on good terms, don't you think?"

"I think we still don't know him well, and that ought to make us cautious."

"Maybe *you* don't know him that well yet, but I've had plenty of time to talk to Zee now that you and Violet are in cahoots," Clementine said.

"We're not in *cahoots*, Clem. We're just—we're helping each other. But you're clearly looking for something more than that with Zee."

"And what's so wrong with that?" Clementine turned so she was facing Aster. "I can tell you're happy for Tanz and Mal. Why can't you be happy for me?"

"Because unlike Zee, I've known Tanz and Mal for years, and I care about them, and I trust them."

"You don't trust *anyone*. You don't even trust me to be able to think for myself. You want me to be just like you, so fearful of the world I don't live in it at all."

The words hit Aster like a slap in the face. She swallowed around something sharp in her throat.

"That's not true," she said in a low voice.

Clementine looked as if she wanted to take her words back, but she steeled herself and continued. "It is so. I've been dying to talk to you about Zee, but I didn't because I knew this was how you'd react. This is how you react to everything."

"I just don't want you to get hurt."

"Everybody gets hurt. And I've *been* hurt."

Not yet, you haven't. Not like I have.

Aster took a shuddering breath. "Well, it's my job to try and keep you from getting hurt again. I didn't have anyone to look out for me. And I wish every day that I had. That's why I work so hard to look after *you*. I love you too much to leave you alone." But Aster thought about what she'd confessed to Violet earlier, her fear that her anger would burn anyone who tried to get too close. What if her anger at Zee was driving her own sister away?

"Even so . . ." Aster continued, "I'm sorry if I ever made it feel like you can't talk to me. That's never what I wanted. You ought to be able to talk to me about anything."

"It's okay. I know," Clementine said quietly. She picked at the grass rather than meet Aster's eyes.

"I promise I don't mean to be so hard-headed. Sometimes it feels like I can't help it. But I'll try, hear?"

Clementine sighed. "It must be exhausting, only being able to see the worst in everything like that."

"It is." Aster's voice cracked, and she covered it with a cough. Clementine reached across the space between them. Aster took her hand. It wasn't right, that Clementine should have to comfort her. It was supposed to be the other way around.

But Aster needed this. Violet might have been the only one who understood what she'd been through, but Clementine was the only one who cared.

"Well, you don't have do it alone anymore," Clem said. "You have *me* to look out for you now. And Mallow and Tansy and maybe even Violet. And Zee. He's good people, Dawn." Clem squeezed her hand. "I promise. Have faith."

Aster nodded. She took her hand back to wipe her eyes before the tears could fall.

"You're just saying that because you think he's fine," Aster said, laughing softly.

Clementine grinned. "He *is* fine. Don't you agree?"

"He's all right, I guess."

"He's two parts puppy dog, one part wolf."

"He's a skinny old stray we can't get rid of."

Clementine seemed to hum with happiness. Aster let out a long breath that left her feeling cleaner and lighter.

"Come here," she said. Clementine scooted closer and Aster wrapped her arms around her. They lay there in silence, listening to the lullaby of the bullfrogs in the lake. A few moments later, they were asleep.

Aster woke to the sudden roughness of a hand shaking her shoulder. She bolted upright as if she'd been stabbed with a cattle prod, her hands pushing off the attacker. It took her a moment in the darkness to realize it was just Zee. She could feel no relief at the sight of him—only anger, and a loose, lingering fear.

"You keep your damn hands off me," she snarled. "What the hell do you want?"

It was only then that she noticed Zee's eyes were wide with a terror she'd never seen in them.

"Aster, we have to go, *now*. There's a ravener hunting party less than a mile away."

He turned to alert the others before she could ask any questions.

"Come on, Clem, we have to run." Aster started tying up her bedroll, moving automatically. It felt like she was wading through a nightmare. The vengeants' keening rang in her ears.

"What hour is it? What's going on?" Clementine asked through a haze of sleep.

"Raveners in the valley."

Clem snapped awake. She leapt to her feet and helped Aster pack their things.

"I was keeping watch from the top of the hill when I saw them," Zee explained as he tacked up his horse. "We can lose them, but we have to hurry."

"How the hell did they find us in the first place?" Violet demanded. "Isn't it your *job* to—"

"I don't know! Maybe the firepit was too shallow. Maybe we didn't double back far enough yesterday. All it takes is one mistake."

"Let's just be grateful you saw them in time," Aster interrupted as she saddled up. They couldn't afford for Zee to lose his bearings, not now. This panic was unlike him, and she didn't want it spread to the others.

And then, Aster heard it—the thunder of hooves and then the unearthly shriek of the raveners' steeds.

"*Hurry*," Zee begged. There was no time to try to hide the

evidence of their campsite, no time to plan a strategic retreat. They simply had to run.

The second everyone mounted the horses, they galloped away, guided by the yolk of the moon. Zee traced the lake's shoreline. Mud kicked up beneath the horses' hooves, and the air was thick with mist. Aster wiped it away from her eyes, straining to see into the dark. They were approaching the cliffs.

"There's a bridge at the top!" Zee said over the roar of the falls. "If we can cross it and cut it behind us, they won't be able to follow over the gorge. But we have to be quick."

Aster swore under her breath. There were too many ways for this plan to go wrong. If the bridge was out—if the raveners caught them before they reached it—if they fell down the cliffside trying to race to the top—

They started single file up the steep, narrow path cut into the side of the ridge. Sheer rock face rising up on one side, a long drop on the other. Soon they had to slow down or risk slipping over the edge. Aster spared a glance over her shoulder, anxiety burning a hole through her stomach as their pace slackened. She could just make out the shapes of four raveners on horseback, circling the campsite. And though they were too far away for her to feel their influence, a rash of chills ran down her arms.

If we'd waited even a minute longer . . .

Aster's scalp prickled as she remembered the last time she'd been at a ravener's mercy. Blood turning to ice in her veins. Bones humming with agony—

No. Focus.

Aster faced forward again. She concentrated on the sound of hoofbeats clattering over shale. Trained her gaze squarely on Violet's back ahead of her. Zee led them around a sharp hairpin turn, the first of several zigzagging up the cliffside. They were almost as high as the tree line now. The air grew cooler and thinner with every step, and the wind tugged at Aster's limbs. They rounded the next turn, slowing to a near crawl.

"Can't we go any faster?" Mallow begged.

"Not unless you want to take a tumble," Zee said sharply. "But the raveners will have to slow down, too. We'll make it, I promise."

The sudden shriek of hellhorses pierced the night air.

The raveners had started up the cliffside.

"I HAVE EYES ON THEM!" a gravelly voice shouted. "THEY'RE HEADING TO THE TOP OF THE FALLS."

"*Zee*," Aster urged.

"Just follow me!"

They rounded another turn. Hooves pounded with the sound of rolling thunder below.

Aster glanced over the edge, her head spinning at the dizzying drop.

The raveners were gaining.

"By the Veil, they're too fast for us," Clementine cursed.

That was because hellhorses were half again as big as any natural horse, twisted by raveners' magic to be able to keep up the tireless pursuit of their quarry. They were as vicious as their owners.

And they weren't slowing down at all.

The beasts let out another earsplitting shriek, piercing enough to cut through the vengeants' keening. Aster struggled to keep control of her own horse as it faltered at the sound. By

167

the time they rounded the final turn, the raveners were only a few hundred yards behind.

"All right, pick it up, we're almost there!" Zee shouted. He broke out into a gallop as they reached the top of the cliffs, a high, cold wind whistling over the flat expanse of dust and drygrass. The ground sloped down towards a crack in the earth forged by the river that fed the falls. Aster's stomach flipped as her own horse ran with reckless speed towards the gorge.

"Do you see the bridge?" Clementine asked her, the wind tearing her words away.

Aster opened her mouth to respond when a gunshot rang out, shattering the night.

She whipped her head around. The raveners had reached the top of the cliffs, too, rising up out of the dark. They were still too far back for their shots to hit, but they wouldn't be for long.

The dead protect us, Aster prayed desperately, whipping back around. The bridge finally came into view, suspended over the air by two lengths of rope. Would it even hold them?

No time to worry about that now.

Zee slowed down once again as he began to cross, the wooden planks echoing hollowly beneath his horse's hooves. Mallow and Tansy followed him, then Violet, then Aster and Clementine. It swayed and groaned sickeningly under their weight. Aster made the mistake of looking over the edge. The bridge was only about fifty feet across, but it was at least three times as far down to the river shimmering below.

"Shit, shit, shit, shit," Violet was chanting to herself.

"Don't look down," Aster warned. She could sense her horse growing more and more skittish the further out they went, and she murmured soothing words to it, hoping it didn't sense the fear in her own voice.

They were a little over halfway across when its back hoof punched through a plank of wood.

Aster grabbed for its mane as the horse's rear dropped lower. Vertigo rushed through her head, terror through her belly. Clementine let out a screech and gripped Aster around the middle so tightly that it hurt.

"*Clem!*" Zee shouted.

Her jaw set, Aster leaned forward to help right the horse's balance. It scrambled and regained its footing, caught up to the others.

"What happened?" Tansy asked in a high voice.

"We'll be fine, *go*," Aster panted. The raveners would reach the bridge any second now.

More gunshots rang out from behind. Aster urged her horse forward as fast as possible over the rest of the bridge. Reached solid ground once again.

"Aster—" Zee began.

"I know." Aster jumped down from the saddle, grabbed her knife, and began sawing away at the rope. Her limbs still trembled from their near fall. Sweat poured down her neck.

"STOP RIGHT THERE," one of the raveners roared.

Aster looked up. The raveners were only a few lengths away from the bridge now.

The blade cut through the first rope. Aster began on the second.

"Zee, get them out of here," she ordered.

169

"We're not going anywhere," Clementine insisted.

The crack of a gunshot echoed, sudden pain searing Aster's cheek. She let out a cry. Almost dropped the knife. "*Zee*—"

Then the second rope snapped, and the bridge dropped away. The raveners skidded to a stop at the edge of the other side of the gorge, guns raised. Aster stood, breathing hard, cupping the bleeding side of her head. She was afraid to move. Zee wheeled around and pulled up next to her, drawing his gun. Mallow and Violet did the same.

For a moment, the two groups stood in tense silence across from each other. Then one of the raveners raised a lantern—which meant, Aster realized, that he wasn't a ravener at all. Raveners could see perfectly in the dark. The man stared at them from across the gap, well built, with paper-white skin, a long, straight nose, and a thick red moustache.

Something about him . . . He looked familiar.

Aster tasted bile. "Help me up," she murmured to Clementine.

Slowly, without turning her back to the man and the raveners, Aster climbed into the saddle behind her sister. Her head swam with pain. Her stomach heaved.

The man smiled thinly and gestured to the raveners behind him, who lowered their weapons.

"Don't worry, Luckers. This isn't where you die," he called across the gap, his words echoing down the gorge. "We still have much to discuss, you and I. My family needs answers. The *people* need answers. We'll meet again, I guarantee it. And when it's your time, you'll know."

The truth hit Aster like another bullet.

McClennon.

That's Jerrod McClennon.

That statesman said he was after us and here he is.

"G-go," Aster stammered to Clementine. She threw a panicked look at the others. "Go."

They turned and rode until the thunder of the falls fell away behind them.

"Are you *sure* that was Jerrod McClennon?" Zee asked the next morning. They had ridden through the night to be sure they lost their pursuers, and now, at last, they had stopped and dismounted under the trees to catch their breath.

Aster tried not to wince as Tansy cleaned her torn cheek with alcohol and stitched it up. The tug of the thread sent spikes of pain through Aster's face.

"It was him," she said through gritted teeth. The memory of Baxter's lifeless face was so clear and sharp in her mind that it had been impossible to miss the family resemblance. Not to mention—"He said his family wanted answers. He must be a McClennon. And Jerrod is the one that man said followed us out of Green Creek."

Mallow rubbed her eyes with the heels of her hands. "Which one is he again? The bastard who owns all the mining camps or the bastard running for governor?"

"The one running for governor. Baxter's uncle."

"Ripping hell."

"If he wanted to kill us, he would have," Violet said grimly. She was clenching her hands into fists and releasing them, over and over, sweating as she did when she was craving Sweet Thistle. "They're going to take us alive."

171

"They're not going to take us anywhere," Aster growled.

"We'll wish we were dead."

"That's *enough*."

They all sat in silence for a moment. Aster looked at Clementine, who was curled up with her knees to her chest. Her stubborn smile had fallen. She had been close to silent for hours.

"Clem," Aster said more softly, "this isn't your fault."

"How isn't it?"

"It's *my* fault," Zee said, shaking his head. "I never should have let them get that close."

"Listen, this is McClennon's fault, and no one else's," Aster sighed. Yesterday had been such a beautiful day in a beautiful place, and they'd *all* let their guard down. Swimming in a clear lake, stealing kisses in the forest, swapping stories by the fire . . . like the paradise beyond the Veil, the paradise they deserved.

And then McClennon and his raveners had tried to drag them back to hell.

He'd better hope, for his sake, we don't cross paths again, Aster thought.

Next time, he would be the one getting stitched up. She would see to it.

CHAPTER TWELVE

Three days later, they struck the town of Scarcliff.

By now, they had their robbery routine near perfected. Five guns in any man's face was usually more than enough to make him compliant, and the brag they'd jumped last night had surrendered the moment he saw they had him surrounded. Still, as they sat around their camp the next morning and counted the shine they'd stolen from him, Aster couldn't help but feel a worm of frustration working through her.

She could already see it wasn't going to be nearly enough.

"You said he was a bank manager?" Aster asked Zee. It was a scorcher of a day, and her shirt clung suffocatingly to her sweat-soaked skin. The shade of the mountain pines offered precious little relief.

Zee nodded. "Told me he just started up at the Scarcliff branch a couple weeks ago," he said. "I talked to every man in the reception room. He ought to have been the richest one there."

Before this last robbery, they only had about 750 eagles to show for all their efforts—they were over halfway through the Scab but nowhere near their goal. At this rate, they were never going to make it to five thousand eagles by the time they got to Northrock.

And so as they'd approached Scarcliff, Aster had told Zee to find the wealthiest man in the welcome house, rather than simply going with the first one he could convince. It had been a risk, Aster knew, asking him to spend so much time in the welcome house and let himself be seen by everyone there. But their situation was growing desperate. She couldn't close her eyes without seeing McClennon's thin-lipped smile.

And as long as they had these favors, there would be no escaping him.

". . . Thirty-two eagles, total," Mallow announced, looking up from the pile of coins with disgust.

Aster cursed, scratching at her cheek where Tansy had stitched up the bullet wound. Where were all the brags who boasted about carrying hundreds of eagles at a time? Had that all been empty bluster?

"All right, but what about his watch? We can sell it," Clementine suggested hopefully.

"It's a piece of shit," Violet said, throwing the pocket watch into the pile. "Fake gold. Cheaply made. I don't know why he was so attached to it."

Besides his coin purse, the only other valuable they had found on the brag was his watch. He had begged them not to steal it, claiming it was a family heirloom. He'd pleaded for the watch more desperately than he had his own life.

Aster had taken it anyway, just on principle.

"Look, obviously it's not going to be enough to keep robbing brags, even if they're bank managers," Mallow said impatiently, sweeping the coins back into the purse. "Next time we ought to just rob the whole ripping bank."

Tansy huffed a laugh.

"Speak sense, for the sake of the dead," Violet scoffed.

"No, wait, maybe she's onto something," Clementine said, her eyes lighting up. "Think, we could get the rest of the shine we need and then some."

"Banks are guarded by lawmen, and the shine's locked up in a safe," Zee said carefully.

But Aster's mind was spinning with the possibilities. If they could get past the lawmen somehow, if they could break open the safe . . . they'd never have to rob another brag again. They could make straight for Lady Ghost in half the time it'd take them otherwise.

And a hell of a lot of landmasters would lose their shine.

That would certainly wipe the smile off that bastard McClennon's face.

"We should at least talk about this," Aster said. "We're running out of time, and we're running out of options. Did you get a good look at the bank in Scarcliff, Zee?"

"Slow down, hear? I don't think this is a good idea. I think—"

Maybe it was the heat beating down on Aster's neck, maybe it was the sickening pain lacing through her cheek, or maybe it was the frustration curdling to a trapped-animal fear in her gut, but she had no patience for Zee telling her what to do. *His* life didn't depend on finding this shine.

"I didn't ask you what you thought, Zee. I asked you about the bank in Scarcliff," Aster snapped.

A flush of red bloomed beneath the brown of his cheeks.

Violet snorted, but Clem shot Aster a dirty look.

"Go on, what were you going to say?" Clem asked him.

"I just think we need to be more cautious now than ever," Zee mumbled. "Yes, I got a good look at the bank in Scarcliff, but trying to rob it . . . there's too much you can't control, too much that can go wrong."

"Well, unless you have a better way for us to come up with over four thousand eagles in the next week, we don't have a choice," Aster argued.

"I bet the bank won't be guarded as heavily at night," Tansy said, perhaps trying to broker a peace. "Breaking in after dark has to be less of a risk than trying to hold it up during the day, right?"

"Yeah, but the shine will still be locked up in a safe," Zee replied. "And we don't have the tools to break into it or take it with us. This is a dead end, Aster."

"It doesn't have to be," Aster persisted. "Look, it's true that if we take this risk, we might get caught. But if we don't do *something*, we'll *definitely* get caught. We need that shine to help us disappear."

Zee set his jaw. "It's too dangerous."

A plume of anger rose in Aster's throat. She climbed to her feet. "I need a word with you," she said through her teeth.

"Leave him alone, Aster," Clementine said sharply. "He doesn't have to be a part of this if he doesn't want to."

"*Now*."

Zee and Clementine shared a look, a wordless conversation passing between them. Aster's anger flared even hotter. But then Zee stood up and let her lead him out of the campsite.

Little brown crickets jumped out of their way as they stepped through the underbrush. A slender black grass snake slithered out of their path.

Once they were out of earshot of the others, Aster stopped and faced Zee, crossing her arms.

"I know you mean well, Zee," she began, straining to keep her voice even, "but when you challenge me, you only make things worse. I don't have time to convince you to help us. You just need to do it."

He sighed and took his hat off, wiped his forehead with his sleeve. His skin was glazed with sweat. "I know, and I'm sorry. But I can't let you get us into something we can't get out of."

"There is no *us*, Zee," Aster snarled, stepping forward. "*You* don't have a bounty on your head. *You* don't have a favor on your neck. *You* can walk away from this. *We* can't. This is just a job for you. But for us, this is life and death. So you don't get a say, hear?"

"You talk like I have nothing to lose," Zee said with exasperation. His energy had seemed bottomless from the day they'd met him, but now, finally, he was beginning to show signs of exhaustion. "I have people to look out for, too, you know. How am I supposed to ever find my sisters if I get caught robbing a bank? How am I supposed to provide for them if I'm a wanted man? You say this is just a job for me, that I can walk away, but it's not, and I can't. This job is the best chance I have at saving my family."

Aster faltered, watching as Zee began to pace back and forth.

"If that's how you really feel, then why have you been helping us rob the brags?" she asked defensively.

"Well I wasn't exactly happy about it, was I? But it felt like the right thing to do in the end. Robbing a bank, though . . . it's one step too far. You have no idea how hard I've worked to avoid a criminal life. My father, he sacrificed *everything* to finally get our family out of our dustblood debt. I can't afford to get us back into it."

"That only happens if we get caught, Zee. But we won't. Because we can't."

He stopped pacing. Looked at her levelly. Aster sighed, relenting.

"We're going back to Scarcliff to rob that bank," she said. "But if the whole thing makes you that uncomfortable, you don't have to come with us. You can wait out here, have the horses ready so we can make a quick getaway. You shouldn't go back into town anyway. People might remember you from last night."

Zee hesitated. "Do you really believe that, or are you just being nice to me because Clementine told you to be?"

Aster's temper flickered at the mention of her sister. "I really believe it. But while we're on the subject, I'll let you know I don't appreciate you using Clem to team up against me."

"I'm not *using* her, I'd never—" Sudden understanding dawned on Zee's face. It shifted to sympathy. "Is that why you're so upset, Aster? You're . . . afraid of me still? Afraid for your sister? Because I promise you I'd never hurt Clementine. You're the only one who could understand how much I care for her."

Aster tightened her jaw. *Don't you dare compare us. You've known Clem for two weeks. I've loved her since the day she was born.*

But no. That wasn't the point she needed to make. Aster swallowed the last of her anger.

"I just want the best for Clem, same as you want the best for your sisters," she said softly. "Listen, Zee . . . I know you're risking everything to help us, and I'm sorry if it ever seems like I don't appreciate that. I do, more than I know how to say. We never could have made it this far without you. But I need you to trust me on this one, all right?"

Zee was silent for a moment. He slid his hat back on his head.

"Wait outside with the horses," he said, a hint of his smile returning. "I reckon I can manage that."

Aster's shoulders dropped with relief. "Thanks, Zee. Truly. Let's get back to others and start planning how we're going to do this—"

Mallow crashed through the underbrush, her face cracked in a grin.

"Sorry to interrupt, but you two have to come see this," she said excitedly. "We figured out why that brag was clinging to his pocket watch so tight—there's a slip of paper inside it with a string of numbers on it."

Aster furrowed her brow in confusion. "So . . . ?"

"*So* why do you suppose a brand-new bank manager would need to remember a bunch of numbers? And why do you suppose he'd be so afraid of someone else finding them?"

Aster and Zee exchanged glances. He seemed to realize it just as she did, his smile widening.

"That's right," Mal answered. "We reckon it's the code to the safe."

* * *

They spent the rest of the day preparing, setting out for Scarcliff a little after midnight. Now they stood at the foot of the town's deadwall, a current of nervous excitement running between them. Rather than take their chances at the checkpoint, they were going to climb over the wall. From the far side of its scarred stone, the sounds of nightlife rose up like bubbles in a champagne glass. On the near side, vengeants cried out for blood, held back only by the glittering theomite dust in the mortar. Zee crouched over his iron grappling hook, double-checking the knot in the rope he'd tied to its end. Mallow restlessly flipped the chamber of her six-shooter open and closed, open and closed. Violet leaned back against the wall, staring up at the stars. She'd just had her dose of Sweet Thistle for the night, and she was the calmest of them all.

"There, I think that ought to do it," Zee muttered. He stood up and gave the grappling hook a few experimental swings.

"Watch it! You'll take someone's eye out," Tansy hissed.

"Sorry."

Zee gave himself some more room, swung the grappling hook around until it gathered enough speed, then released it. It caught on the top of the wall with the sound of a pickaxe hitting rock. He gave the rope a couple tugs.

"All right, who wants to go first?" he asked, raising a brow. The wall was about fifteen feet high.

"Violet—you go," Aster ordered.

"Why me?"

"Because I *said* so. And don't forget to roll when you land."

In truth, it was because Violet could stand to have her favor

180

covered the longest, thanks to the Sweet Thistle. Every second counted here.

Violet cursed and wrapped her face with a dustkerchief, scrambling up the wall gracelessly. She swung her legs up and over the top and jumped down on the other side, landing with a dull *thump*. Tansy and Mallow went next, then Clementine. Finally, it was Aster's turn.

"You'll be here with the horses?" she asked Zee, handing him the theomite ring.

He gave her a single nod. "I'll be here."

Aster grabbed the rope. It was rough beneath her hands, the stone gritty beneath her boots. Her stomach flipped at the sensation of being parallel to the ground. She couldn't help but hesitate for an instant before she jumped down to the other side of the wall. It was a shorter drop than the one from the welcome house window to the haycart, but it would also be a harder landing. She reeled up the rope and threw the grappling hook down first so they'd be able to use it again to escape. Then she sucked in a breath and pushed off the ledge.

Ripping HELL, she thought as she landed. She'd ducked and rolled when she hit the ground, but it still rattled every bone in her body.

"Are you okay?" Tansy asked.

"I'm fine." Aster stood and shook off her dizziness. There were no buildings this close to the wall, and their group was well hidden in the darkness for now, but they had only twenty minutes, at most, to get this done before their favors burned through their fabric and gave them away.

"Remember, once we get into town, just act natural," Aster

reminded everyone. "If you try too hard to be inconspicuous you'll only end up drawing more attention to yourself."

"No one's going to look twice at us," Violet countered, waving her hand. "They'll assume any strangers wandering around Scarcliff were already cleared at the checkpoint."

"Let's hope," Tansy muttered.

They set off to find the bank.

"Where did Zee say it was again?" Clementine asked in a whisper. They ran, low and fast, through the outskirts of Scarcliff. The blacksmith, the carriage repair shop, the holy house and its graveyard—all the buildings shuttered for the night.

"On the north side of Main Street, next to the lawmaster's office," Aster answered. The proximity had to be intentional. The law would be able to respond to a break-in within moments.

Even so, her mood began to lift with the beginnings of the rush she felt every time they went after a brag. Her ears alive to every subtle sound in the dark, her skin itching with anticipation, her heart beating like a battle drum in her chest. In these moments, she couldn't see in her mind's eye the faces of the ones who had hurt her, couldn't feel anything but an intense focus on the job. It was the starkest opposite of the deathlike detachment that had overcome her when she'd been trapped in the welcome house.

Let them come, she thought.

She was ready.

Finally they reached the tightly packed cluster of Main Street, where they slowed to a brisk walk. Two rows of shops faced inward on a dirt road crowded with well-dressed men filtering in and out of the saloons, gambling houses, and welcome house.

Aster lowered the brim of her hat and started down the road.

Mallow scratched at her favor beneath the dustkerchief. "Which side is north?" she asked urgently, cutting her eyes back and forth.

"On our right," Aster murmured. Her breath caught as she spotted the Arkettan flag hanging outside the office. "There."

They pushed their way past the people on the street, Aster's stomach churning every time a man's body brushed up against hers. The urge to bolt coursed through her. She forced herself to ignore it. *Focus.*

Her favor began to prickle beneath her dustkerchief.

They passed the lawmaster's office. Aster led them by without slowing, facing forward even as she cut a glance at the building from the corner of her eye. A single lawman was on duty out front, swatting away the moths that had swarmed to his lantern. There would be other lawmen inside, though, babysitting whatever drunks or petty thieves had been locked up for the night, and still more on patrol. Towns in the Scab were always heavily guarded—they had to be, folks figured, in a place where the children of the world's worst criminals lived.

Well, they're right to be worried tonight.

Aster didn't slow as they passed the bank, either—they had another stop to make first. But she scouted it out, too. The bank was an unassuming building with a simple stone placard out front:

RED ROCK BANK
~SCARCLIFF BRANCH~

A large window looked in on a waiting area, and beyond that, the teller's cage. Aster could just make out the dark shape of the safe in the corner. Since they couldn't get past the cage, the plan was to break in through the back of the bank. The commotion would almost certainly bring the law running.

Which was why, first, they were going to find some brags to take hostage: they needed the leverage.

Two doors down they came to a saloon. Aster stopped and nodded imperceptibly at the others. They walked in through the double doors.

The inside of the saloon was stifling, cherry-wood floors scuffed from the soles of a hundred shoes and half-lit gasoliers hanging from a tin tile ceiling. The smell of alcohol and smoke and sweat hit Aster like a wall as soon as she walked in. The men's voices around them were magnified tenfold. Talking, laughing, joking, cursing. Hands slamming down on tables. Glasses clinking together. She had not been in a room like this, utterly surrounded, since Green Creek. She stopped short in the doorway, panic rising up in her belly, filling her lungs until her chest threatened to burst. Her vision doubled until the whole room turned into a soft blur of yellow lamplight and brown shadows. Her thoughts ran together like ink in the rain.

"Aster." The voice sounded like it was coming from a thousand miles away. She didn't even recognize it. "*Aster.*"

Her vision refocused. It was Violet, standing in front of her, slapping her cheek gently.

"Snap the hell out of it, Lucker," Violet hissed.

The harsh words cut through Aster's haze. Aster curled her lip. "I'm *fine*," she snarled back, shoving Violet's hands away.

She clung to the brief flash of anger, though, and one look into Violet's eyes told her that Violet had known exactly what she was doing in provoking her: bringing Aster back to life. Aster swallowed. "You see any brags in here, or what?" she asked, her voice quavering.

Violet jerked her head. "There's a table of men over there who look like the type," she said, letting her hair down and unbuttoning the top of her shirt. "I'll flirt with them a bit, find out if they're brags, and lure them out to you if they are. You all go out back and wait for me."

Aster nodded gratefully and led the others through the maze of tables towards the back door. Violet was the only one of them who could pull this off—not just because she could play the part most convincingly, but also because she was the only fairblood among them. The brags were much more likely to believe whatever lies she told them.

And to think we almost didn't bring her with us out of Green Creek, Aster thought. The pins and needles of her favor had escalated to steady burn, and soon it would begin to glow with dull red heat.

They filed out the back door, boots *clomping* on the wood of the back porch. There was only one other person out there, a man leaning against the wall and sucking on a cigar. He took a long drag and blew out a ribbon of smoke. He paid them no mind—yet.

Aster took a steadying breath of cool air.

"All right, everyone, weapons ready," she murmured. Mallow, Tansy, and Clementine drew their revolvers. Mallow was the only one of them who'd learned how to shoot growing up, but the others had been practicing the past few weeks whenever they could.

Aster drew her knife. Damned if she was going to freeze up again tonight.

Two minutes later, the back door squeaked and swung open. Violet walked out, followed by the three young men, smartly dressed in checkered waistcoats over shirts with silver sleeve garters. Derby hats cocked back, watch chains glinting at their hips. The tallest had a baby face and an entitled smirk on his lips. Aster knew their type, had seen them all too often. Her anger grew hotter.

Focus, she repeated to herself.

"I *told* my friends there'd be some decent men in this town," Violet was saying to them, her voice pitched high. "I can't wait for you to meet them . . ."

Click-click-click.

Mallow, Tansy, and Clementine put the guns to the brags' heads and released the safeties. The men staggered backwards and let out low curses.

"What the *hell*—"

"Is this a damned joke—"

"Shut up," Aster ordered. "All of you."

The man who had been smoking dropped his cigar and opened his mouth to cry for help.

"Not so fast," Violet said calmly, drawing her own revolver on him. "You breathe a word of this to anyone, and—"

He snapped his mouth shut and darted back into the saloon before she could finish the threat.

If they weren't in a hurry before, they certainly were now.

With Aster and Violet standing guard, Clementine, Mallow, and Tansy bound the brags' hands behind their backs, then jabbed them in their spines with the muzzles of the guns. Aster led them away from the saloon, walking as fast as she could without breaking into a run.

"You're a ripping dustblood," one of the brags observed as they passed through a pool of light, revealing his own shadow. His voice dripped with venom. "My father's a lawyer. When he hears of this—"

Aster whipped around and slammed his jaw with a backfist. For a terrifying, thrilling moment, she saw herself following it with a plunge of her blade.

"Not another word out of you. *Any* of you," she ordered. "Or the dead help me, I will geld you with this dirty knife."

They all shut up then, walking in silence. Aster's head swam with a rush of power. She saw flashes of doubt in the others' eyes as they exchanged glances. They wouldn't be able to pull the trigger if the time came. She knew that with sudden certainty.

But Aster was becoming more sure of herself by the second. Let *these* men feel what it was to be utterly helpless. Let *them* cringe with shame and beg for mercy. If it came down to her friends' lives or the brags', Aster wouldn't hesitate for a heartbeat.

They reached the bank's back door. By now Aster's favor felt like it was burning a hole in her skin.

"Do it," Aster said to Violet.

Violet walked up to the door, aimed her gun at the lock, and shot it. The noise was tremendous, but the door didn't open when she shoved it with her shoulder.

"*Damn it,*" she swore.

Shouts rose up from Main Street. Violet shot the lock again and again, until her gun was empty.

"Watch out," Aster growled. She kicked the door square, and at last it flew open. She wet her lips as she waved everyone through the doorway. The pain from her favor was beginning to make her lightheaded.

"You're dead as dogshit," Mallow's brag said gleefully. "The law'll catch you for sure now."

"The hell did she tell you about being quiet?" Mallow snapped, pistol whipping him upside the head. But Aster could hear the fear in her voice. Her always-steady hands trembled.

The inside of the bank was dark and stuffy with the smell of dust. They'd entered on the inside of the teller's cage, behind the grate that looked out onto the waiting room. A neat row of desks with cash registers lined the half wall. Aster turned to her left and spotted the safe. It was taller than she was and three times as wide.

Aster ran over to it and knelt to open the lock. She could hear several lawmen outside the front of the bank now, working to break the door open.

34, 8, 27, 46, 52.

The wheel clicked as she spun it. She must have been spinning too quickly, though, because the safe didn't open.

She repeated the sequence, her movements measured.

"We're running out of time," Clementine said urgently. "We have to get out of here before they come around back and surround us."

"It's fine," Aster said shortly.

"She's right, though. Let's just abandon these three fools and run," Mallow agreed.

"Let me *concentrate*," Aster ordered.

34, 8, 27, 46, 52.

34, 8, 27, 46, 52.

The safe wasn't opening.

The lawmen broke through the front.

"Hands up!" one of them roared.

"We have hostages!" Aster shouted right back. "You all just stay back!"

34, 8, 27, 46, 52.

Nothing.

Judging from the sound of it, there were lawmen crowding around the back door now, too, awaiting orders. Violet met Aster's eyes and gave her head a short shake. Aster's throat grew tight.

"Why the *rip* isn't this working?" Aster asked herself, kicking at the metal safe. It wasn't *fair*. It'd never been *fair*. This was her shine. They *owed* her. *Everyone* in these twice-damned mountains owed her.

But what if this isn't actually the code to the safe at all? What if this string of numbers is for something else entirely? They'd so desperately wanted this to be the code, so desperately *needed* it to be that . . . Aster's head pounded; her favor burned.

"Hold up a second, that 7, look at it," Tansy said then, quietly, peering over Aster's shoulder. "I think it's really a 1?"

Aster's mind stilled. She studied the numbers more closely. *Ripping hell.*

She tried the safe one more time: *34, 8, 21, 46, 52.*

It clicked open.

Aster's knees went weak with relief. She hurriedly untied the sack at her waist and began loading gold and silver ingots into its mouth.

"Orders!" one of the lawmen shouted. There were now at least half a dozen lawmen on the other side of the teller's cage, guns raised, and another three standing guard at the back door.

"Hold!" the lawmaster answered. He was in the front. His next words were addressed to Aster. "Bank robbery's a capital offense!" he called out. "But you let these three boys go and we'll work something out."

"Aster, if they get a clear shot, they're going to kill us," Violet murmured.

"Don't worry, they won't—"

Before she could finish, a surge of pain from her favor caused Aster to double over, coins spilling from her hands. She'd pass out soon if she kept it covered. Tightening her grip on the sack, she turned away from the safe. Pain was written on the others' faces as they struggled to stay upright, their skin glowing through the fabric of their dustkerchiefs . . .

"By the Veil, they're Luckers—" Clementine's brag yelled.

Aster whirled around and punched him, but it was too late. Their cover was blown.

"It's the Green Creek girls!" one of the lawmen confirmed.

"Do *not* let them escape! Is that understood? We need them alive!"

Aster swore and ripped her dustkerchief away. The relief from the worst of it was instant, though the pain and glow would take a while to fade completely.

"We don't want to hurt these gentlemen!" Aster called to the lawmaster. "Just let us pass, and we'll let them go."

"You know we can't do that," the lawmaster said.

"Then these men's deaths will be on your hands."

"Well, we've reached an impasse, you and I," the lawmaster replied coolly. "But don't worry—I've sent for our welcome house's raveners. They'll sort you out."

Aster's blood froze as cold as her favor was hot. Lawmen were one thing. But if raveners got involved, it was over. They would break the girls' minds, drag them away.

She glanced back at Tansy, Mallow, Violet . . . and Clementine. Words weren't necessary. With one shared look, they all knew what to do.

Bam! Mallow fired a shot above the heads of the three lawmen in the back doorway. The men ducked for cover. *Bam!* Another warning shot and the air swirled with gun smoke and panic.

"Out of our way!" Aster yelled at the lawmen.

One by one the girls took off through the doorway, abandoning the hostages, Aster sprinting out last with the sack of shine held tight in her fist. Boots slapped the ground, dust kicking up around them. Mallow fired off two more warning shots behind her.

The lawmen had given chase, and now began firing back.

A bullet whizzed by Aster's leg. Another hit the ground between her feet. The law was trying to incapacitate them, not kill them. Their only advantage was that the orders were to take them alive.

"Mallow—take—them—out—" Aster panted between breaths.

"You mean . . . ?"

"No—just—stop them!"

Mallow grimaced, but she skidded to a stop, turned, and fired off her last three shots while the rest of the girls kept running. Aster glanced over her shoulder. Two of the lawmen went down, clutching their legs. But the third shot had gone wide, and the last lawman was still on them.

"Shit," Mallow murmured, catching up to the rest of them. She sounded sick.

"Give her your gun, Tansy," Aster ordered. They were cutting through the outskirts of town now.

"Aster, I don't think—" Tansy began.

"*Just do it.* Unless you want to shoot him yourself."

"Give it here," Mallow said quietly. She took Tansy's gun, turned, and brought down the last lawman. But Aster could hear the clamor of hooves not far behind—the lawmaster and the other officers had mounted up to pursue them.

And the raveners would be along for the ride.

Almost to the deadwall now. Weaving through the graveyard. Every breath Aster took was like swallowing fire. Her muscles were turning to jelly, and the sack of shine kept banging into her leg. She was certain she could feel her brain bouncing in her skull. The pain of her favor had weakened her, had weakened all of them. They couldn't keep this up. If they didn't make it back to their own horses, they'd be caught.

"I see them! They're at the edge of the boneyard!" one of the lawmen shouted.

There was the grappling hook. Zee would be waiting for them on the other side.

Thank the dead.

Aster hurried, swinging and releasing the grappling hook. It glanced off the wall and clattered to the ground.

"Aster—"

She swallowed, tried again. This time it stuck.

"All right, everyone up," Aster said. Tansy went first—it was only then that Aster saw her cheeks were wet with tears. Violet went next, cursing as she did so. Then Clementine, begging Aster to be careful. Then Mallow, leaving Aster alone.

Aster slung the bag of shine over her back. *You're going to have to leave it,* a small voice said. *No way you're getting over the wall with that thing, not before they catch you.*

Shots rang out. The mounted lawmen had almost reached her.

But damned if she was going to let this all be for nothing.

Aster clenched the neck of the sack between her teeth. Climbed up the wall. Reached the top. Threw the grappling hook down so the lawmen couldn't follow her. Then she dropped the sack and fell after it, landing in a heap. The others helped her up, their expressions shattered by fresh panic.

"What?" Aster asked, holding back her bile. "What's wrong now?"

No one answered. They didn't have to. She could see for herself.

Zee and the horses were nowhere in sight.

CHAPTER THIRTEEN

"Where the hell is he?" Aster demanded, running to the edge of the woods. The moon was high in the sky by now, painting the trees with silver light. They couldn't wait around for Zee here; the Scarcliff raveners would be on them any minute.

"I don't know," Clementine said, her voice raw and broken. "He wouldn't have abandoned us unless it was an emergency. You know he wouldn't."

Aster exchanged glances with Violet. What if he *had* abandoned them? What if he had finally decided they were too much trouble for their worth, and left them here to die?

Or what if Clementine's right, and he's in some kind of trouble?

On the other side of the wall, the roar of horse hooves grew louder. The lawmen had arrived.

"We'll go back to camp, see if he's there," Aster decided.

"But we already packed it up—" Tansy began.

"Well, where else would you have us go?" Aster asked roughly. "Those lawmen are at the wall, and their ravener friends will have no trouble getting over it. We *can't* stay here. That old campsite is one other spot Zee would know where to meet us. We'll see if he's there and then figure out what to do."

"All right, but Aster, we don't have the theomite ring," Violet said.

Shit.

The realization knocked the last of the fight out of Aster. She became suddenly, singularly aware of the rising and falling cries of the vengeants just beyond the tree line. You got used to the sound of them, growing up in the Scab. You learned to ignore them like you learned to ignore the rush of your own blood in your ears. But pretending the vengeants didn't exist didn't make them go away.

If Aster led everyone into that forest unprotected, they'd be torn apart.

"To hell with it," Mallow swore then, plunging into the trees before Aster could stop her. "I'd rather let the dead have me than those bastards back there. Camp's only half a mile away, we can make it."

"Wait!" Tansy cried, running after her.

Clementine looked at Aster in shock. "Aster, I—I have to go with them," she stammered. "They won't be able to see the vengeants coming. And Zee—"

Aster nodded. She motioned for Violet to follow them. "Come on!"

Violet hesitated, as if weighing another option. Clearly, though, there wasn't one.

They dove into the black teeth of the forest.

It was much harder running through woodland than it had been running through Scarcliff. The rocky, uneven ground threatened to throw them off balance with every step, and the thorny branches of the low-lying scrub bush clawed at their

195

arms and legs. The moonlight was only just bright enough to see by. Aster tried her best to keep up with the others, though her hard landing had shaken her. They were still close enough to the deadwall that they hadn't been swarmed by vengeants yet, but any moment now—

And then, there they were. Their attention surrounded Aster, cold and craving. It crawled over her skin like a voltric current. The temperature dropped.

Tansy shrieked from somewhere up ahead.

"Sophia!" Mallow shouted—Tansy's true name. Clementine put on a burst of speed and disappeared into the darkness.

"Ripping hell, Aster, you just couldn't have let us run a normal heist—" Violet said through her teeth.

"Shut up!"

Aster and Violet caught up to the others: Tansy was curled up on the ground in a ball, her hands wrapped protectively around her head. Mallow crouched at her side, begging her to get up. Clementine looked around them with the wild eyes of a rabbit in a trap.

"Is she hurt?" Aster asked.

"No, she's just—she just panicked," Mallow said. "I've never seen her like this." Mallow had never sounded as young as she did then. An unnatural wind had started up around them, tugging at the hems of their clothes.

"You have to get her to calm down!" Clementine said shrilly. "They're attracted to fear, they're coming!"

"How many are there?" Aster demanded.

"I count seven right now. They're circling like vultures. There'll be more on the way. They— *Violet, duck!*"

Violet screamed and dropped to the ground. An instant later invisible claws raked the trunk of the tree she'd been standing under. The wood cracked and splintered with an explosion of sound. The vengeant shrieked like a motherless child, then took off with heavy wingbeats that buffeted the air.

"*Have mercy, have mercy, have mercy,*" Violet prayed. Aster ran over to her, grabbed her, and lugged her to her feet.

"Come on, we have to keep going! It's our only chance!"

"We'll never make it," Violet said dully.

The air around them grew colder still. Aster's sweat froze along the small of her back. Tansy, screaming. Mallow, pleading. Violet, losing faith. Aster, losing her mind. Clementine staggered back as she watched the vengeants circle faster and faster, churning up a storm that stripped the needles from the trees. They were so loud now, so close, that Aster could barely hear herself think.

Violet's right, Aster realized then. She let out a weak trickle of laughter.

We're not going to make it.

Mallow grabbed Tansy's hand and helped her climb, shaking, to her feet. The girls circled up, back to back. Aster drew her knife for the last time, though it would do nothing to save her.

And then Clementine suddenly broke away, dodging the grasp of the vengeants' claws.

"Clem, what are you doing? *Clem!*" Aster shouted.

"Grayleaf! It grows at the base of pine trees."

Aster struggled to understand. She was uncoupling from reality. It seemed to take all her effort just to make her mouth work.

". . . Grayleaf?" she repeated.

"She's right, we can burn it, keep the vengeants back," Mallow

197

said. She looked at Tansy and seemed to make a decision, steeling herself before running after Clementine. "We're going to make these bastards sorry they ever came for us."

Finally Aster realized what they meant. It lit up a flicker of hope.

"I'll help them," Violet said. "You stay with Tansy and get the fire started."

Aster nodded and turned to face Tansy.

"I'm sorry, Aster," Tansy whimpered. She dropped down and started searching for kindling. "I'm so sorry. I've seen what vengeants do to people and I just—I just froze."

Aster dug in her coat pocket for a book of matches. "It's all right, Tansy," she said softly. "I froze back at the saloon. I almost froze again just now. It's happened to all of us."

Tansy piled together the kindling she'd found. Aster struck a match with shaking hands. She ran through her memories of Zee's advice about building a fire. Which wood would burn bright, which would burn hot, which would burn the longest or produce the most smoke—none of that mattered now. All that mattered was burning enough grayleaf to drive the vengeants back.

"The raveners, they knew this was what I was most afraid of," Tansy went on. "They'd make me see—"

"Don't worry about them. Don't worry about anything. Just think of a song, Tansy, hear? I promise we'll get you out of this."

Clementine ran up and threw the first fistful of grayleaf into the fire. The smell of the smoke sweetened immediately.

"There's more where that came from," she said, dashing back into the dark.

Violet was next. Then Mallow. Aster was tending the fire in a crouch, making sure it burned as long as possible. The vengeants seemed to be retreating. Their hellish screams echoed with frustration.

By the Veil, we might actually survive this after all—

"*Watch out!*" Clementine cried.

A flash of movement in the moonlight. A hiss of leaves in a wake of wind. Mallow let out a scream harrowing enough to match the vengeants'. Aster's skin crawled. Never, even in all her years at the welcome house, had she heard such a desperate sound. She leapt to her feet.

"MAL!" Tansy cried.

She and Aster ran towards where Mallow's scream had come from. A vengeant had grabbed her by the shoulders with its invisible talons and was dragging her up into the air like an eagle with its prey. Tansy held Mallow's ankles desperately. Mallow thrashed against the vengeant's cruel grip. Screamed again. Bite marks appeared across her midsection as a second vengeant attacked. The blood glittered black in the firelight.

"Help!" Mallow begged. "Please!"

Tansy was shoved away with an impatient swipe and went flying half a dozen feet back. The vengeant pulled Mallow higher and higher.

Aster sprinted after them, ignoring her own pain. For a brief instant, the vengeant passed through a shaft of moonlight and Aster saw it in all its terrible beauty: the grinning, antlered skull, the wings made of smoke, the too-long fingers that ended with too-long claws. Mallow's face was a mask of terror.

A gunshot shattered the night. Aster stumbled in her shock and fell to the ground, hard. Picked herself up. But it was too late. Mallow was nowhere in sight.

A second gunshot, then a third.

What the hell is going on?

Clementine, Tansy, and Violet caught up to her. Why had they left the safety of the fire? Now they were all going to die.

"Dawn—" Clementine's voice, as dull and distant as if Aster were underwater. Clementine shook her shoulder. "Dawn, come back, we have the ring—"

A fourth gunshot. Zee appeared an instant later, muscling his way through the group. Shotgun cradled against his shoulder, eyes cold with focus. He lowered the weapon and helped Aster to her feet.

"Do we have everyone?" he asked.

"No, Mallow is still out there," Clementine said. Tansy was shaking, her face wet with tears.

Zee turned to Aster. "Which way did they take her?"

Aster's lips quivered. She couldn't seem to make them move.

"*Aster.*" Zee's voice was gentle but firm. He looked her in the eyes. "Which way?"

She pointed. Zee ran off without hesitation, raising the shotgun once again. He disappeared into the darkness.

Aster blinked, slowly coming back to focus. She was overwhelmed with the sudden urge to cry. She swallowed it painfully.

"What happened?" she asked the rest of them.

Violet looked as frightened as Aster had ever seen her. "The smoke from our fire," she said. "Zee tracked us down. We have the ring now, we're safe."

"Kind of him to finally join us," Aster snarled. But she knew her anger was just a balm for her fear.

Two more gunshots rang out.

"Mallow—?" Tansy asked.

Aster shook her head, feeling sick. "I don't know."

"Zee will get her back," Clementine murmured. "He has to."

"Where the hell has he been?"

"He didn't have time to explain himself," Violet answered. "But he told us to mount up. We can't stay here. The raveners will have seen the smoke, too."

Aster's breathing slowed. "All right, then, we better go. Can everyone make it?"

Violet and Clementine were unhurt, although Tansy was limping from being thrown back by the vengeant. She leaned on Clementine for help. Aster had busted her knee open and skinned her palms, too. She ignored the dull throbbing of her injuries and forced herself to stay in the present. They returned to the fire, where the horses were waiting.

After what seemed like an eternity, but was probably only a few moments, Zee joined them, carrying Mallow across his shoulders. Tansy ran to meet them with staggering steps.

"Is she alive?" Tansy choked through her tears.

"For now," Zee said grimly. He set her down. His face was drawn. "But she's losing a lot of blood, Tansy."

The group worked together to ease Mallow into the saddle, the wails of the dead rising and falling in the distance.

"There was a patrol working around the outer perimeter of the deadwall," Zee explained. "I had to make a run for it so they wouldn't catch me."

He leaned back against the wall of the shallow cave where

they'd retreated, his face drawn with remorse. Aster, Clementine, and Violet sat in a circle around him while Tansy began to dress Mallow's wounds by the light of a lantern. She had asked the others to give her space to work, but they couldn't help but look over worriedly as Zee told his story. Mallow still hadn't woken up.

"Did the patrol see you?" Clementine asked, chewing her lip.

Zee nodded. "It's hard to escape attention when you're trying to herd four scared horses into the woods. Luckily the two lawmen didn't follow me far—they weren't equipped to deal with vengeants—but they kept me on the run long enough that I missed you all." He swallowed, leaning forward to clasp Clementine's hand. "I'm so sorry, Clem. I'm so sorry I wasn't there—"

"I'm just glad you're all right," she said, putting her hand over his. Clementine looked upset by the story, but Aster was relieved that was all there was to it. "We thought you'd been hurt." *Or that you'd abandoned us.*

"It could've turned out a lot worse, that's for certain," Zee admitted. "We're going to have to be more careful from now on." He sat back and pulled his knees up, wincing. "In fact, it'd be dangerous to stay here much longer. The raveners will be able to track us here from the fire."

Aster tensed, defensive. "We didn't know what else to do. The grayleaf was all we had."

"No, no, you all did right," Zee reassured her. "I couldn't have done better myself. We just have to keep going, is all." He looked over to Tansy. "Mallow—can she travel?"

Tansy looked up at them, her eyes red and swollen. Mallow lay unmoving beside her. There was a sickly green sallowness beneath her brown skin, and her chest rose and fell with painful slowness. Every inch of her body was covered with scrapes and bruises from being dragged through the forest and dropped from the air. Deeper cuts from the vengeant's claws had carved wickedly into the muscles of her shoulders. They'd been sewn together with thick black stitches and wrapped with clean white cloth.

But worst of all was the crushing bite to her side. Tansy had removed her shirt and wrapped her up as best she could, but already the bandages were soaked through with blood. Aster's stomach twisted with sympathetic agony. Her wounds seemed small compared to Mallow's.

"I—I don't know," Tansy stammered. "It was dangerous bringing her even this far. I was able to clean and bandage her shoulders, but this wound on her side—" Tansy's voice broke. "We only have basic supplies out here. She needs a hospital."

"Hey, easy," Clementine said, crawling over to Tansy to soothe her.

"This is all my fault. I lost my courage when we were trying to get away."

No, Aster thought. *It's all my fault for getting us into this mess in the first place.*

I was too reckless. I almost got everyone killed. Violet. My sister. And Mallow . . . I did this to her . . .

"The vengeants would've caught up to us anyway." Clementine shot Aster a meaningful look. "Right?"

"Absolutely," Aster said, forcing the damning thoughts away. "It's not your fault that Mal got hurt—if anything, it's to your credit that she might still make it."

"*Might?*"

"No—that's not what I meant—"

"Oh no, I can't lose her," Tansy went on, now clutching Mallow's hand. She shook her head. "I can't do this without her. Mal's been there for me from the beginning. My first night at the welcome house I couldn't stop crying, and she stayed with me until I fell asleep."

"I remember that," Violet murmured. For once, she kept any critical thoughts to herself.

"So I have to stay with her now until she wakes up," Tansy said. Her voice steadied. "I can't expect you all to stay, too. Not if the raveners are coming. But at least if they catch us, we'll be together."

"Tansy, no. We're not leaving anyone behind," Aster said firmly. She turned to Zee. "How long until the raveners get here?"

He let out a long breath. "They have no trouble moving in the dark, and we didn't take time to cover our tracks. I'd give us half an hour, at best."

Tansy began mixing together ingredients in her mortar. "Then I'll hurry."

"What are you making?" Zee asked.

"A stimulant. The sooner she wakes up, the sooner we can assess her injuries. It might not work, but . . . I have to try."

Tansy poured the mixture into a tin mug and stirred it with water from her canteen. Then she held it carefully to Mallow's lips and coaxed her to drink. She coughed but didn't wake.

"Give it a minute," Clementine said into the strained silence.

Tansy shook her head, looking sick now herself. "You all are going to have to leave us."

And then Mallow cracked her eyes open and spoke, her voice brittle but her words clear.

"Next time you want to get me out of my clothes, Tanz, don't feel like you have to wait for me to be dragged halfway to hell first."

"Mal?" Tansy looked at her in shock. Then a fragile smile broke out over Tansy's face. "Mal!" She leaned down to pepper Mallow's forehead with kisses. Clementine and Aster met each other's eyes, relief passing between them. Zee flashed a tired smile of his own, and Violet visibly relaxed.

"Easy, I'm still pretty delicate," Mallow said, laughing. But then it turned into a ragged cough that left her lips flecked with blood.

"Careful! Here, have some water. How do you feel?" Tansy asked. She smoothed the bangs away from Mallow's forehead and gently poured water into her mouth from a canteen.

"Feel like . . . I just got run over by a ripping train . . ." she said. She tried to prop herself up on her elbows and winced from the effort. Clementine helped her. "*Dammit*. Something's . . . broken."

"Your ribs. You're lucky you didn't puncture a lung. I'm still not convinced you didn't. You're not in any kind of shape to ride," Tansy said.

"As long as she's safe to be moved, I can strap her legs to the saddle to help keep her upright. But someone will have to help her," Zee said. He was already on his feet.

"Let me ride with her," Aster said to Tansy. Guilt still nibbled away at her heart. "You've done enough already, Tansy, and you need to rest. I'll make sure she stays awake."

Tansy nodded gratefully, though her eyes never left Mallow's face. She wet a rag and pressed it to Mal's forehead. Wiped away the sweat.

"Where . . . are we . . . going?" Mallow asked.

Aster felt a swell of admiration. She recognized the exhaustion on Mallow's face, and she recognized, too, her determination to bury it. Both of them clung to their toughness, and for Mallow that had always seemed to mean literal, physical strength. When she'd woken up with nightmares back at the welcome house, she'd done pullups on the rafter beam until tiredness took her once more. When she'd been too overwhelmed with anger to laugh it away, she'd shadowboxed until sweat dripped down face. Her vulnerability now clearly frightened her, even if she wouldn't let it show.

But Tansy was right. *She needs a hospital.*

"I know some people who might be able to help," Zee said. "It'll take us out of our way, and they're not . . . *proper* doctors, I'll warn you, but I'd trust them with my life. And they won't turn us in."

"How do you know?" Aster asked.

"Because the law is after them, too." Zee ran outside to get to work.

Violet curled her lip. "He's taking us to a bunch of *criminals*?"

But it was the best thing Zee could've said to convince Aster. She offered Violet a shrug. "Don't worry, Violet. You'll fit right in."

The stars wheeled above them as they rode away from Scarcliff and made their way down into the pocket of darkness that was the valley below. Aster rode with Mallow, holding her carefully around the waist. They had to take it slow, but at least they were on the move. Mallow started to nod off every few moments, and Aster jostled her awake every time. Tansy had said it might be dangerous for her to fall asleep in her condition.

"Aster, for the love of the dead, stop poking at me like a damn frog," Mallow swore thickly.

"Sorry. Doctor's orders."

"Doctor's too clever for her own good."

Aster smiled faintly. "You ever catch frogs as a kid, then?" Anything to keep her talking.

"Bugs, sure; lizards, hell yeah. But frogs—never. My dad's side of the family, they're descendants of the Nine. It's one of our nation's beliefs that frogs are good luck because they're a sign of rain in the desert."

The Nine: that was how folks referred to the confederation of nine nations that had lived on this land before the Empire seized it and renamed it Arketta. Those who had resisted had been imprisoned and sent to the Scab to work—the first dustbloods. Even after the Empire's fall, they hadn't been released from their debts.

"My brother, he'd even croak like a frog sometimes when we were little," Mal went on. "As if he could trick the sky into thinking it was time for a storm." She laughed a little at some memory.

Like most Good Luck Girls, Mallow had never talked much about her family. But still, Aster was surprised she'd never known Mallow had a brother. Her heart ached to think how much she must miss him.

"A brother," she echoed. "Older, or younger?"

"Twin."

By the Veil.

"We used to joke that our souls got switched at birth—I should've been the boy and he should've been the girl. He was always so damn tenderhearted. He told me once he wanted to be a songbird when he grew up because their only job was the make the world more beautiful. The other kids would try to give him hell and I always had to give it right back." She let out a wet cough. "His name was Koda. He's dead by now, probably. The mines aren't kind to boys like him."

The words hit Aster like a punch to the gut.

"Mallow—I'm so sorry. I didn't know."

She shrugged. "We've all lost folks." But Aster could hear that she was trying to hide her pain once again. A hole that deep was best avoided.

"I tell myself, though, that if Koda was *really* gone, I would've felt something when he passed, you know?" Mallow went on. "Just like he might feel that I'm hurting right now. Might wonder what the hell trouble I've gotten myself into this time."

Her words began to slur and her head lolled. Aster nudged her gently.

"I suspect he'd be proud of you," Aster said.

"Yeah, I like to think so." Mallow sighed. "You're lucky you have Clem in all this."

Aster thought about what her sister had told her by the lake. About how they had to look out for each other now. "You're our family, too, Mal."

Mallow didn't respond, and for a moment Aster worried

she'd nodded off once again. But then she spoke, sounding more conscious than ever. "Kaya," she said. "Just so you know—Kaya. That's my name."

Aster smiled a little to herself. "Dawn," she replied.

The woods had begun to thin out, and Zee sent word back that they were almost there.

Thank the dead, Aster thought. It was nearing the small hours of the morning. Mallow wasn't the only one who needed rest. A moment later Aster spotted the unmistakable outline of a sizeable town ahead—but no lights, strangely. No sounds of life, either.

"Ghost town," Mallow said, answering Aster's silent question.

"What good's a ghost town to us?" Aster asked impatiently. Some towns died as soon as the mines that supported them were used up, leaving nothing but abandoned buildings and the lost remnants still living in them. Certainly there'd be no open doctor's office out here.

"Maybe Zee's people are squatting here?" Mallow suggested.

Well, if they were, they'd be fools. Ghost towns had unhealthy reputations. Folks disappeared, went mad, died mysteriously and became ghosts themselves.

"I don't like it," Aster mumbled back.

They rode into the town proper, passing its collapsed deadwall, their hoofbeats echoing down the empty brick streets. Snarls of drygrass grew through the crumbling mortar. A flagpole line clinked softly in the wind. A dozen dust storms had left a layer of grit thick as snow on every surface, and every building they passed had broken windows, or a collapsing roof, or a door knocked in like a punched-out tooth.

No one spoke, as if they were all afraid to break the silence. They left the fairblood part of town behind and came into the outlying mining camp, where the dustbloods had lived in shacks practically stacked on top of one another. Something like ground-fog curdled around them.

Remnants. Aster could just see their blurred human outlines from the corner of her eye. An old woman sweeping her porch. A child running after a ball, over and over. Aster's skin prickled. A lot of folks had died unfulfilled here. Just as many had probably died angry.

Which meant there might be vengeants, too.

As if they needed another round with those.

Enough, she thought. She spurred the horse ahead and pulled up next to Zee. He'd stopped to look at something carved into the side of a tree: a symbol of some kind, what looked like a scorpion.

He smiled but didn't say anything.

"Zee," Aster snapped, "what the hell are we doing here?"

"And is it much farther?" Tansy jumped in. "Mal really needs to rest."

"Well, we better be riding at least a little bit farther, because if you think I'm spending the night *here*, I've got news for you," Violet said.

"Not here," Zee said, turning his smile towards them. Then he pointed up ahead, down a crooked dirt path, to the pitch-black mouth of an abandoned mine.

"There."

CHAPTER FOURTEEN

"Have you lost your damn mind?" Violet hissed at Zee.

"What? Didn't you spend your first night on the run in an old mine?"

"*Barely*. We didn't go any deeper than the entrance," Aster said. The only thing worse than spending the night in the ghost town would be spending it underground.

"Just trust me," Zee said. He led his horse down the path towards the mine, leaving them little choice but to follow him.

"I'm going to kill him," Aster muttered to Mallow.

"Hey, I'll hold him, you hit," she offered, sounding weary.

Zee paused at the mouth of the mine. There was that symbol again, carved into the timber. He climbed down from his saddle.

"All right, friends, on foot from here," he said. "Leave the horses. Our hosts will send someone up for them." He lit a lantern and held it up. The rest of them hurried to dismount, Tansy and Clementine propping Mallow up as best they could.

Zee started down the tunnel, the steep descent making his gait awkward and uneven. Rocks as big as a bear's skull were strewn across the ground. A makeshift pathway of planks laid end-to-end cut through the debris, but years of neglect had left the wood warped and rotting. Somewhere up ahead Aster heard the trickle of water and the shifting of falling soil. The sounds made her scalp crawl. The air down here was cold and close, like the soft, damp breath of an undead thing.

"How are you feeling?" Tansy whispered to Mallow.

Mallow wet her lips. "About ready to collapse."

"Well, fair warning, this shaft runs about half a mile—" Zee began.

"Half a what now?"

"*Dammit*, Zee."

"Ripping hell."

"*Jackass.*"

He elected not to finish his thought. The girls stopped talking, too, each seeming to retreat into her own place of silent concentration. Aster focused on her breathing, keeping it slow and steady, wrinkling her nose at the smell of the grave. She was all too aware of the crushing weight of earth above them. By now the entrance to the mine was just a pinprick of moonlight growing fainter with every step. Her only consolation was that there didn't seem to be any dead down here—unheard of, for a mine this old.

At last they reached the end of the shaft, the ground leveling out into what seemed to be a central chamber that split off into multiple tunnels. Zee held his lantern high—

"TURN AROUND, STRANGERS," a man's voice boomed out from the dark. A constellation of headlamps hovered in the darkness ahead, but Aster couldn't make out the faces below them. "YOU'RE STANDING ON SIX KEGS OF BLASTING POWDER. ONE MORE STEP AND WE'LL

BLOW YOU ALL TO HELL."

Aster looked down at her feet in alarm. Sure enough, the ground beneath them was freshly turned, as if something had been buried there. A detonation cord sprouted up from the soil and spiraled away into the dark. She started to take a step back instinctively, then stopped herself, panic fluttering in her belly. She glared daggers at Zee.

What the hell have you gotten us into?

Zee raised his hands in a gesture of surrender. "Easy," he said, his voice clear and calm. "Name's Ezekiel Greene—Zee. I'm a friend of Sam Daniels. I was helping this group escape to Northrock when we got ambushed by some vengeants. One of us is hurt bad, needs urgent medical attention."

"WHAT'S THE WATCHWORD?"

Zee frowned. "Since when do you all have a watchword?"

"SINCE EVERY BASTARD AND HIS DOG STARTED COMING AFTER US LOOKING FOR A BOUNTY. YOU HAVE FIVE SECONDS TO CLEAR OUT—"

"Hold on now!" Zee cried. "Is this or isn't this a base camp of the Scorpions? And are you or aren't you a refuge for folks on the run from the Reckoning? I know your code. I was there the day Sam swore to uphold it. You'll not find anyone more deserving of your hospitality than these women here."

The Scorpions? Aster had never heard the name, had never heard of *anyone* standing up against the landmasters' law and living to tell that tale. Who were these people? Where had they been the day she and Clem had been stolen away? She shifted her weight, straining to see these strangers' faces.

A brief silence. Then: "I'M SORRY, BUT WE SIMPLY CAN'T

ACCEPT ANYONE WHO ISN'T BROUGHT TO US BY OUR OWN PEOPLE."

"You turn us away, you're leaving an innocent to die."

"INNOCENTS DIE EVERY DAY."

"Not today, they don't!" Aster shouted. Mallow was losing consciousness, sagging against Clementine, and her stitches had just broken. She was losing blood again, fast. "Stop hiding in the dark! Show your face! Come look my friend in the eye when you turn her away."

More silence. One of the headlamps started forward and the others followed. Footsteps echoed with military precision. Aster swallowed, glancing at Clementine, who looked right back at her with eyes widened by fear. Zee's mouth was a line.

The strangers stepped into the circle of the lantern light.

Half a dozen rough-cut young men, all of them Aster's age or a little older. Like the girls at the welcome house, they were dustbloods whose families had been brought to Arketta from all over the world, though they all shared a certain weariness that ran deeper than their worn-out clothes. They wielded pickaxes and pistols, shotguns and knives. The boys in the back had greased their faces, the better to blend into the dark, but the leader's face was bare—half russet-brown skin, half leathered red scarring from a burn.

In his hands was a long-barreled rifle.

"Don't want to have to use this," the leader warned.

Then suddenly one of his partners elbowed him in the side.

"It's the Good Luck Girls from the posters, Cutter," he whispered. "Them that killed McClennon. See their favors?"

Recognition flickered across Cutter's face. Aster stiffened, ready for trouble. A long, tense moment passed. But then Cutter smiled slowly and lowered his weapon, gesturing for the others to do the same.

"Ladies—gentleman—my deepest apologies," he said, dipping his chin in a bow. "On behalf of the Scorpions, welcome to Camp Red Claw. We're honored to have you."

Running the length of the main tunnel was a minecart that'd been modified to carry passengers. It couldn't fit them all at once, so Tansy and Mallow were taken first, to be swiftly escorted to the medical ward. Then Cutter returned for the rest of the group. He took hold of the lever that powered the cart, pumping it up and down, up and down, slowly rowing them along the rails. The rush of air slipped up Aster's sleeves as they gathered speed. Her stomach lifted with every bump and dip. And as much trouble as it had been to get here, she couldn't help but admit how much of a relief it was to let someone else take responsibility for their wellbeing for a night.

"My apologies again for the misunderstanding," Cutter yelled over the *click-clack* of the wheels. Shaggy black hair fell to his shoulders, and now that he'd let his guard down, his brown eyes shone as if he were always on the edge of good-natured laughter. "We never use that mineshaft ourselves anymore, so whenever we hear someone coming down it, we know it's a trespasser of some kind. Used to be just curious folk, the kind who go poking around old ghost towns instead of steering clear like their mothers told them to. But lately we've had raveners, too, and up north they've had spies trying to pass themselves off as hotfoots. Just two weeks ago Camp Blueback was attacked from the inside."

"Hotfoots?" Violet asked. She seemed more than a little uneasy with the night's turn of events.

Cutter tilted his head. It wasn't the kind of question any dustblood would have to ask. But Violet wasn't a dustblood.

"Yeah, you know, runaways. Folks trying to escape the Reckoning and live in hiding. They stick together in camps like this one, hidden all over the Scab. They don't always *stay* hidden, of course—just last month a camp west of Briarford got busted up and every single soul in there was killed. But it's the best we can do until . . ." Cutter's eyes flashed.

"Until what?" Violet demanded.

Zee and Cutter exchanged a look. Zee nodded. "You can trust them."

"Until we finish connecting the mines underground so we can take people out of Arketta and into Ferron, where dustblood debts don't exist," Cutter finished. "No way in hell to get across the border, heavily as it's guarded, so we're going under it."

Aster stared, checking to make sure Cutter wasn't joking. The stories she had heard growing up, about how you could cross the length of the Scab through its mines if you knew the way . . .

Maybe not quite stories after all.

Like Lady Ghost? she wondered.

But no, that was different. There was nothing about building these underground camps that required unnatural power. Undoing a curse like a favor, though . . .

No. That was different.

"So the hotfoots are the people on the run, and the Scorpions are the people who shelter them?" Violet asked, shaking her head. "And your goal is to one day help smuggle them out of the country altogether so they never have to answer to the law?"

Cutter either didn't hear the disapproval in her voice or didn't care. "Damn right!" he said, his grin sharp as a knife. "Which means we're wanted by the law, too, of course. That's why we call ourselves Scorpions—we have to live underground, only come out at night. But we're still plenty dangerous to anyone fool enough to cross us."

The minecart slowed as they neared the end of the tunnel, which shone up ahead with warm yellow light. Cutter eased them to a stop and vaulted out over the side, then offered his hand to help Aster and the others climb out. Aster's stomach turned at his touch, even though she knew he meant well.

"I sent someone ahead to let Captain Daniels know the situation is under control," Cutter went on. "He'll want to talk to you first thing tomorrow morning, but for now, let's just get you all to your beds. I know you've had a long night."

Thank the dead. They were all exhausted. Aster wanted nothing more than put this endless night behind her.

But then they stepped out of the tunnel, and she was shocked back into wakefulness.

Aster had expected the camp to be little more than a collection of bunks stuffed in an old abandoned supplies room or two. From what she knew of mines, they were miserably close and cramped. Their journey so far had only confirmed that.

Now, though, they'd entered an underground city.

A yawning cavern stretched out ahead of them, maybe a thousand feet across and a hundred feet high. Though the roof bristled with stalactites, some big enough to spear a hellhorse, the ground had been scraped and smoothed into an even surface. Ramshackle wooden shanties clustered around the perimeter, while a larger building towered in the center: the meeting hall, Cutter explained, where everyone took their meals and assignments. He also pointed out the stables, where their horses were being taken, and the medical ward, where Mallow was being seen to, and the underground lake, where everyone drew their water. Mining lamps were strung across buildings and between them, chasing away the shadows. And standing in the town square, sculpted by an expert hand: a red-clawed scorpion made of theomite-streaked stone.

That's how they keep the vengeants away.

Like the crude iron guardians people propped outside their houses, but far more beautiful and powerful.

"By the *Veil*, you could all be rich as kings if you took that to market!" Clementine murmured, eyes widening at the sight.

"Ah, but we'd be dead kings, because it's the only thing keeping us safe from the spirits down here," Cutter said with a chuckle as he led them through the narrow walkways. "Most of us used to be miners, so we know how to find traces of theomite, even in mines that have been abandoned. There's never enough, though."

"Are all the Scorpion camps this big?" Aster asked.

He shook his head. "This is actually one of the biggest ones— four dozen souls here. We're lucky we found this cave system so close to the abandoned tunnels. Most of the other camps are much smaller, can only support one or two families at a time."

Cutter stopped in front of a house with a hole in its roof, fiddled with the doorknob, and led them inside. It was sparsely furnished: six stacked bunks and a table with a lamp. Their saddlebags and supplies had already been sent ahead for them.

"The family that was staying here just got moved along to Camp White Eye last week. I'm sorry about the roof. Been meaning to get it fixed."

After two weeks of sleeping rough, these accommodations felt almost luxurious.

"It's perfect," Aster said, her exhaustion returning.

"Thanks, brother," Zee agreed.

Cutter grinned. "If you need anything else, I'm right next door." He pointed to a house with a flag hanging from the front—a black circle with nine spokes against blue fabric, the banner of the Nine. That flag alone would've been enough to get him executed aboveground.

Things really were different down here.

"I'll see you tomorrow," Cutter said, and he left them.

Aster exhaled, and Clementine wrapped her in a hug, her sister's relief seemingly too deep for words. Clem pulled away after a heartbeat. "Do you think they'll be able to help Mallow?" she asked.

"I trust them to do better for her than anyone else could," Aster answered carefully. She shared her sister's anxiety, but she didn't want to show it.

"Mal is tough. She'll get through this," Zee promised, taking off his hat for the night. "And they've seen worse here, believe me."

Aster crossed her arms. "Right, go on and say it, then. Get it off your chest."

"What?" he asked innocently.

"That you were right to bring us here. I obviously had my doubts."

"*I* still do," Violet chimed in. She had already climbed up to

219

one of the top bunks and was sitting in the corner, balled up with her knees to her chest. Her shadow hovered protectively over her shoulder. "We've had no choice but to break the law. These people . . . they've made a life of it."

"'These people' just welcomed you into your home," Aster reminded her.

"They almost blew us to bits."

"Well, who hasn't wanted us dead, by this point? I thought they showed admirable restraint."

Violet *hmph*ed and lay down with her back to them. Aster and Zee smirked at each other.

"Anyway, I mean it. Thank you, Zee," Aster said. "You've saved our lives. Again."

The rest of them picked out bunks and settled down for the night. It had been so long since Aster had slept in a bed that the softness of it shocked her, even if the mattress was lumpy and prickly with hay. Compared to the woods, the quietness here was profound. No crickets or bullfrogs, no wind in the trees. The vengeants' cries had been reduced to a distant murmur. The darkness, too, was completely devoid of stars, and looking up through the hole in the roof was like looking upon the Veil.

Maybe this is what it feels like—to be dead and buried, she thought.

The idea should have filled Aster with dread, but instead she just felt a sudden and overwhelming peace: she was beyond the reach of the living. They couldn't hurt her here. She fell into her deepest sleep in years.

CHAPTER FIFTEEN

Morning came too quickly. There was no sunrise to wake them, but the sound of a breakfast bell rang out through camp and startled Aster out of her sleep. She bolted upright, squinting in the lamplight. Mallow and Tansy's beds were still empty—they must have spent the night in the medical ward. Aster's stomach clutched with panic.

Zee was already up and jumping into his boots. "Cutter stopped by, said Sam was waiting for us in the meeting hall, along with Tansy and Mallow. Don't want to keep them waiting."

Oh, thank the dead: Mal had made it. Her death would have been on Aster's head; Aster felt this with sickening certainty now. The others looked to her to lead, and she had put their lives in danger by forcing the bank robbery. Even if that hadn't been the reason Zee had been discovered, the ugly truth still remained: she'd let herself get reckless. She'd lost sight of what mattered most.

Keeping her sister and the others safe.

She swallowed. "Right, then, we'd better hurry."

The camp was much more lively now than it'd been when they'd first arrived in the small hours of the morning. Most of the hotfoots appeared to be young men like Cutter, but there were a couple of families milling around, too, children chasing each other through the narrow walkways or tugging at their mothers' hands. An old man sat on a little stool in front of his house, stitching up a hole in his hat. Three young girls played skip with a rotting old rope. Aster was reminded of the rundown mining camp where she'd grown up, but there was something subtly different about this place, as if a cloud had blown clear of the sun. Everyone stood straighter, laughed louder, met one another's eyes as they passed.

They're not afraid, Aster thought at first, but then she realized that wasn't quite right. They still had plenty to be afraid of, as Cutter had made clear enough last night. But they weren't *ashamed*. There was no one here to look down on them, no one they had to prove themselves to. Aster was suddenly sure this was how dustbloods would have looked before they'd had their shadows stripped away—before they'd been known as dustbloods at all.

Zee fiddled with his cuffs as they neared the meeting hall, rolling them up and back down again.

"What's wrong?" Clem asked.

"Just nervous, is all. I haven't seen Sam in ages. What if we hardly know each other anymore?"

"How'd you and Sam meet?" Aster asked.

"I first crossed paths with him five years ago around Black Valley. He was on his way back to one of the camps after a hunting trip, but he'd slipped while scaling a rock wall and broken his leg. I still have no idea how he survived such a long fall—and maybe he wouldn't have if we hadn't come along to

222

help him, who knows. But he's had quite the reputation ever since—too stubborn to die."

Aster didn't give a rip how Sam had survived his fall. She was more concerned with the timeline of the story.

Five years ago?

Zee had said he'd only been a rangeman for two. He'd said he'd started the work when his parents had died so he could support his sisters.

"What were you doing out in Black Valley?" Aster asked. She tried to keep her voice casual, despite the stirring in her gut.

He would have only been twelve or thirteen at the time. Had he been alone? Had his father been with him? What business did a gambleman have in the middle of the woods with his son?

But before he could answer, Sam Daniels himself broke through the meeting hall doors.

Aster knew it was him right away, even though they hadn't yet been introduced. He walked with the confident step of one who wore authority comfortably. He was tall, dark-skinned, and unlike the other Scorpions, he wore fine clothes: a black waistcoat over a black shirt with a black gambleman's hat on his head—the only burst of color was his red necktie. He had a nose that looked as if it had been broken more than once and a smile that was equally crooked. A gold-plated handgun hung at his hip. He couldn't have been older than nineteen or twenty, but he had the eyes of someone three times his age.

Then he smiled at the sight of Zee, and became a boy again.

"Ripping hell, am I happy to see your ugly mug," Sam said. Zee grinned back, and they pulled each other into a hug and clapped each other's backs.

223

"It's been too long, brother," Zee replied.

"You must tell me everything," Sam agreed. "But first, we eat. Come with me." He turned and waved for them to follow.

The inside of the meeting hall was filled with long tables and young men hunched over plates of biscuits and beans. For a moment, Aster was gripped by the same heart-stopping panic that had seized her at the saloon in Scarcliff. Dry mouth and wet palms, a light head and a heavy stomach. She was outnumbered here, surrounded, exposed. But here, unlike in Scarcliff, she was able to reassure herself: These men were not brags or raveners or lawmen. They were allies. They had taken her in.

Aster collected herself as they made their way towards a serving table set up at the end of the room. Behind it stood a stocky, tight-jawed boy who looked like he might have been Sam's brother. Sam's hair was short, but this boy was bald as a doorknob, lamplight glinting off his smooth brown scalp. He was the first Scorpion Aster had seen who looked genuinely unhappy—angry, even. *What's his problem?* she wondered. He scowled at the short line of people who waited for him to heap the food onto their plates.

And at the end of the line—

"Mal!" Clementine shrieked. She ran forward to embrace Mallow, who smiled tiredly and wrapped her arms around her. Mallow's movements were stiff and pained, but otherwise she seemed to be doing far better. Tansy, too. Her eyes never left Mallow, as if to keep her from disappearing, and every few moments she broke into an unaccountable grin.

"Thank you for this," Aster said to Sam, her chest loosening.

Sam shrugged. "The work is its own reward," he said. "I've

reserved a table for us, here. You and your friends help yourself to a plate and join me when you're ready."

Aster, Violet, and Zee joined the others in the line. Hunger clawed at Aster's belly. She held her tin plate out to the unsmiling boy, who slopped a spoonful of beans onto it without a word. But his eyes lit up when he saw Zee.

"Good to see you again, Greene," he said, his voice surprisingly soft. "We all figured you were dead."

"Yeah, well, can't get rid of me that easily," Zee said, a hint of red in his cheeks. Aster supposed he wasn't used to this much attention.

"What business brings you here?"

"Just helping these folks get to Northrock," Zee answered, gesturing at the others. "Ladies, this is Sam's brother, Elijah."

"Eli," the boy corrected. His face had set once again, but his voice was still gentle. "You all can call me Eli."

The group took their seats with Sam, who was busy writing something in a journal. He closed it and spread his arms in welcome. He was missing the last two fingers on his left hand.

"Aren't you fixing a plate?" Zee asked.

"I don't believe in breakfast. A cold cup of water does me fine. Keeps my mind clear."

"I forgot how fussy an eater you were."

Sam let out a shocked laugh. "Insulting me under my own roof? You forget I know plenty of damning stories about you, too, Greene."

Although Sam was clearly ribbing him, a flash of genuine fear crossed Zee's face. Clementine raised an eyebrow, grinning. "What *kind* of stories?"

But Sam had already waved this off. He had an underlying restlessness to him, like a lizard skittering across hot sand. "So, brother, has the hunter truly become the prey? Tell me how you came to work for Arketta's most wanted criminals in half a century."

Zee, the hunter? Aster frowned.

Of what?

Zee didn't answer, instead launching into the story of how he'd met them. Aster stayed quiet, letting the others do most of the talking. She struggled to contain the panic that had begun to eat away at her insides like a swarm of locusts. She felt surrounded, outnumbered. Zee may have felt safe around all these young men, but that didn't mean she did. Violet, too, remained completely silent, picking at her food. Her sullenness from last night had only deepened.

"Well, I'm glad you found time to visit us," Sam said when they finally finished. "I only wish it were under better circumstances."

"Ah, you know I would've stopped to say hello anyway," Zee replied, seemingly more at ease now.

Aster opened her mouth to speak. She was hoping Sam would tell them his own story now. But then he stood, taking up his journal.

"There's been a collapse in one of the southern tunnels that needs clearing out, so I'm afraid I have to leave you now. But I insist we celebrate tonight with a feast. I'll have my brother break out the good liquor. Until then, rest up, wash up—treat this place as your home."

He left them.

Clementine nudged Zee as soon as Sam was out of sight. "I don't see what you were so nervous about. They clearly love you here."

"Yeah, you never told us you had *friends*. I honestly thought we were your first," Mallow snorted. But then she broke into a cough, and Tansy was quick to grab her hand.

"Easy, Mal. You need to get back to bed."

"Only if you're coming with me."

Violet rolled her eyes. "Don't get excited. They're stacked bunks. But I'm going to head back to the house now, too, if you two want to follow me."

Aster wasn't surprised Violet wanted to hole up until supper, but in the end, everybody decided to go back except for Aster herself. She didn't blame them—the dead only knew when they'd have a chance to rest like this again—but she also wasn't quite ready to join them. Violet's words by the waterfall echoed in her head. *I'm not used to having all this time to think.*

You had to keep running, that was the trick. If you stopped, your troubles would catch you.

Maybe she could take this time to count up their shine—she was itching to know how big the take from the bank had been. But some part of her didn't want to risk the Scorpions finding out they had their shine on them. Sam *seemed* honest enough, but still, she didn't know these people. Not really, not yet.

I'll find someone around here who'll tell me more about this place, Aster decided instead.

And if they could tell her more about Zee, too, so much the better.

As the rest of her group trickled out of the meeting hall,

Aster's gaze wandered over to Sam's brother, Eli, who was busy clearing off the serving table now that breakfast was over. A grubby rag was slung over his thick shoulder, and he scrubbed at the scarred wood every time he found a spill. He hadn't seemed like much of a talker when they were introduced, but who else would know more about the Scorpions than the captain's brother?

Aster started towards him.

"Need some help?" she asked, clearing her throat awkwardly.

He looked up at her. Narrowed his black eyes. "No."

"Sam says you're preparing a feast for tonight, so I find that hard to believe."

"Believe whatever the hell you want." He piled the platters on a pushcart and wheeled it to the kitchen door. His words struck Aster. Her hurt soon turned to anger. She had just been beginning to believe this place really was a refuge, and here this asshole was treating her like the mud on his boots.

Aster jumped in his path. Crossed her arms. "You have a problem with me?"

"No—I—" He seemed genuinely surprised.

"I didn't come all this way just to be judged by the likes of you."

He held his hands up for peace. The lines on his palms ran deep. "I'm not judging anybody. I'm sorry if I—I'm not like my brother—I'm not good at conversation. That's why he greets the newcomers and I just make the food."

Aster softened, stepping out of his way. She followed him into the kitchen. He didn't protest.

"Well, I'm not good at conversation, either," she muttered,

warmth flushing her face. "I was just . . . kind of curious, I guess. I always heard about hotfoot hideouts growing up, but I never thought I'd actually see one. But if you don't feel like talking . . ."

"When did I say that? Listen, if you really want to hang around, I'm not going to stop you," Eli said. "You want to wash the dishes? Because I sure as hell don't. Here."

He tossed her his cleaning rag and pointed to a washtub. Aster half regretted her own stubbornness, but she supposed as much as the Scorpions were doing for them, she could manage to wash a few dishes.

For a few minutes they worked together in silence, her washing and him drying, but it was an easy silence, and the task was soothing. Eli didn't look at her. He didn't touch her. He didn't seem to expect anything of her. It was an unspeakable relief.

"How long have you and Sam lived here?" Aster asked eventually. She was used to making idle conversation with men, but Eli acted nothing like the brags at the welcome house. They loved to hear themselves talk. Eli would clearly have to be drawn out.

Eli's scowl deepened. "Lived in Red Claw about a year," he said, "but we've been with the Scorpions much longer. They took us in when we were just a couple of hotfoot kids. Sam fell in love with the lot of them, decided to join up. Didn't take him long to work his way up the chain to captain."

"And who's above him?"

"It's not like that. The Scorpions don't have a single leader. Every camp has its own captain, its own rules, its own way of doing things. We work together as best we can."

"Sounds . . . messy."

"It is," he said shortly.

Aster was undeterred. "So, if Sam's the captain of this camp, that makes you second-in-command, right?"

"Cutter's second-in-command. I just work here."

They'd finished with the dishes, and now Eli jerked his head for Aster to follow him into the pantry. The room was lined with shelves of food, from dry goods and salted meat to bags of beans and barrels of wine.

"It's like living in a giant root cellar down here," Eli explained. "Cool and humid all the time. Keeps everything fresh. I figure we make chili pepper stew tonight. That'll mean chopping a lot of vegetables."

"Fine by me."

In truth, Aster's mouth was already watering at the thought. They hadn't eaten a proper meal since leaving the welcome house. Eli handed her a netted cap to hold back her hair. Aster fit it over her head as best she could, feeling like a fool. Eli smiled faintly.

"Ought to just shave it all off like I do."

"We can't all go around looking like a billiard ball."

He handed her a sack and they began to gather vegetables: peppers, onions, tomatoes, garlic, and sweet red potatoes.

"Where'd you get all this food? Do you grow it?" Aster asked, wrinkling her nose at the sharp scent of the onions.

He shook his head. "We have to make regular supply runs aboveground from friendly vendors, and we trade with the other camps, too. It's impossible to grow much of anything besides mushrooms and mold in these caverns."

230

"You like it, living like that? Living . . . down here?"

Eli was quiet for so long Aster assumed he hadn't heard her. He slung a heavy bag of beans over his shoulder with deceptive ease. "You feel like you have to say yes to a question like that," he answered finally. "There are folks dying to get taken in by the Scorpions. But I wasn't made to live underground. None of us were. I miss the sun. I miss weather. Wind and rain. The smell of trees. Everything."

"You get to feeling like you're already dead and buried," Aster said, thinking of the uncanny feeling that had overwhelmed her last night.

Eli looked at her squarely for the first time. "Exactly. I hate that they've chased us down here. That this is the best any of us are supposed to hope for."

Like Green Creek, Aster thought suddenly. Women were supposed to be grateful if they got taken away to live in a welcome house. Men were supposed to be grateful if they escaped to a hole in the ground.

"Will you try to escape to Ferron when the time comes?" Aster asked. "When the tunnels are done, I mean?"

Eli shook his head. "Don't think so. My brother says we owe it to our own to stay and fight the landmasters. We're blessed that we can. Not everyone's able to." Eli sighed. "And I know he's right. It's only that sometimes I wish we didn't have to fight at all. Feels like I've been fighting since the day I was born. I'd rather've grown up slow, like kids are supposed to do."

It was as if he'd pulled the thought out of Aster's own head, one she hadn't even realized she'd been thinking. But if she acknowledged the weight of what she'd lost, it would crush her.

"You wish you could start your whole life over," Aster said, almost to herself.

Eli nodded. "With a whole new body that they never broke down and a mind that hadn't made any bad memories yet. Yeah . . ." He laughed softly. "I think about that a lot."

Unsettled, Aster followed Eli back into the kitchen. They began chopping up the onions and soaking the beans. For a moment Aster felt as if she were a daybreak girl again, washing and peeling until her skin was raw. But of course, there were no raveners here to force her to work faster and fill her with dread. And she would actually get to enjoy the food she made.

"What about you? What's your plan?" Eli asked eventually.

Aster hesitated. "Trying to find Lady Ghost," she replied, starting in on the peppers. "She's this woman who can get rid of favors." It sounded absurd when she said the words out loud, and she found herself getting defensive before Eli could laugh at her. "One of the girls with us, Violet . . . she has an in with her."

Eli raised an eyebrow. "That so?"

Well, it was a stretch of the truth, certainly. But not an outright lie, Aster hoped. "You know anything about Lady Ghost?" she asked.

Eli shook his head. "Nothing more than the basic story. Growing up I'd come across women who'd aged out of their welcome house and tried to remove their favors—burning them off, most times, or cutting them out—but none of them had any luck. Left their faces scarred and their favors more painful than ever. Not to say the same'll happen to you," he added quickly, cutting his eyes over to Aster. "I'm sure Lady Ghost knows what she's doing."

"Right," Aster mumbled, though now she wished she hadn't asked. Wished she hadn't pinned so much hope on a woman they knew so little about. A woman who might not even exist.

Eli was adding spices to the beans now. "Anyway, Zee's good people for helping you all get to Northrock," he said, seeming to try and lighten the mood.

"Right . . . and do you know Zee well?" Aster asked, hoping she sounded casual. Might not do for Eli to know how curious she was about Zee's past . . . or that she was certain Zee himself was lying about it.

Eli shook his head. "Not like my brother does. I tend to keep to myself."

Damn it.

"I have nothing but respect for him, though," Eli went on. "Him taking you to Lady Ghost reminds me a little of what we hope to do for folks one day, helping hotfoots cross the border."

With that, an idea cut through Aster's brief disappointment.

"Eli . . . what if we worked together?" Aster asked slowly.

"What do you mean?"

"The Scorpions are fighting to help dustbloods, right? That includes most Good Luck Girls. You ought to help them, too. And *we* could help *you*. The landmasters visit the welcome houses and we know them better than they know themselves. We know their comings and goings, we know their plans. Imagine—"

But Eli was shaking his head.

"What?" Aster demanded.

"Nothing, sorry, it's just—well, you and your friends are special, seeing as you got rid of McClennon's boy and you've been giving the law hell. You're legends around here. But you'd have a hard time getting some of the guys to work together with any other Good Luck Girls."

Aster bristled. "What's that supposed to mean?"

He must've seen the look on her face, because he backtracked. "Forget I said anything."

"Whatever I'm thinking is worse than the truth."

Eli said nothing, brow knitted as he chopped the garlic.

A warning crept up the nape of Aster's neck, raising her hackles. "Eli . . . am I safe here?" she asked carefully. "My friends, my sister . . . are we safe?"

It seemed to take Eli a moment to understand her meaning, but as soon as he did, he rushed to reassure her. "Of course," he said. He set his knife down and faced her. "*Always*, Aster. My brother, he'd never allow anyone to hurt you. Neither would I, for that matter. That's not how this place works. You're safe here. Always."

She let out a breath that was half relief, half exasperation. "Then what the hell are you talking about? Why shouldn't the Scorpions help girls like us?"

Eli sighed, picking up the knife again. "There's just this . . . resentment some men carry, when it comes to the Good Luck Girls. One of my bunkmates, for example, Ian—when he heard you all were here it got him to talking about the girls he'd grown up with who ended up in the welcome house. And his words about them were . . . less than kind."

". . . Well? What'd he say?"

"I'd rather not repeat it."

"Eli, I've heard things that would make even your hair

234

curl. Don't treat me like some child. Tell me what your friend said."

Eli looked down at his big bear-paw hands. The knuckles were scarred white. At last he spoke. "He's not my friend," he said, his mouth a line. "And what he said was, 'We were breaking our backs down in the mines, but at least that was honorable work. Good Luck Girls sell their souls, lying with the landmaster so they can live in his mansion and drink his wine. They're two-faced traitors who deserve what they get.'"

Aster clenched her jaw. She drew in a measured breath through her teeth.

"And what did you say?"

Eli shrugged. "I told him if he was going to act like an ass, he could spend the night in the stables. For all I know he's still there."

Aster exhaled.

"How many are there who think like him?" she asked in a low voice.

"Not all of us," he said quickly. "Not even most of us. But . . . enough. That's what I hate most about the Reckoning, I think. The way it makes desperate folks turn on each other. You're right—we need to be helping each other. It's the only way."

Well, too bad, because I don't feel like helping these fools anymore.

"The thing is," Eli continued, "it's not just men like Ian who are the problem. There are . . . practical reasons we haven't been able to help the Good Luck Girls, too." He hesitated. "It's hard enough helping miners run away from the tenant camps, but to help girls escape welcome houses . . . those places are

235

locked down like military forts. It's near impossible to get in, let alone out."

"Right, I know."

They were silent for a long moment, peeling potatoes, listening to the water bubbling in the pot. That was how Aster felt—boiling with anger. Her favor burned. How dare any of them think of her as a traitor? She'd never wanted any of this. They had no idea what they were talking about. *They* were the traitors for abandoning the people who needed their help the most. For giving up without ever even trying.

"You're right to be angry," Eli said at last. He had moved onto dicing the tomatoes.

Aster looked at him sidelong. "I didn't realize I needed your permission."

"It's not like that. I just—I admire you for it. It's like I said. Everyone's telling us to be grateful. It's hard to let yourself be angry anyway, you know?"

Aster swept her potato peels into a compost bin, wondering if she should answer truthfully. But as honest as he'd been with her, she supposed she could return the favor.

"It scares me, though, Eli . . . how angry I am, all the time," Aster admitted. "Just two days ago we robbed this bank in Scarcliff. And I got so . . . so consumed by my anger—at the brags who were cursing us, and at the landmasters whose shine we were stealing, and at the lawmen who were trying to capture us—that I wasn't thinking straight. I was so desperate to hurt *them* that I didn't care if *I* got hurt, too, see? And my recklessness almost got my friend killed. That's how we ended up here." She shook her head, her stomach turning. "I don't think they blame me, but I blame myself. Sometimes I think I'd be better off if I didn't care about anything." She was thinking of Violet now—Violet and her cold detachment. "Maybe I'd be happier, at least."

Eli sucked his teeth. "I don't know. You can't help but care about some stuff, and pretending you don't never solves the problem," he said thoughtfully. "But anger . . . anger gets things done. Sometimes, at least. You just have to make sure *you're* using *it*, and never the other way around. That's when you get reckless, that's when you end up hurting yourself and the people you care about. But the anger alone doesn't make someone a bad person, I don't think. It just makes them human." Then he looked at Aster with glint of mischief in his eye. "So . . . you robbed a bank? You're going to have to tell me more about that."

That managed to bring a smile out of her. Aster relaxed, just a bit.

"Let me start at the beginning."

Evening fell upon the camp, and Aster rang the bell to let everyone know that supper was ready. In the end they'd prepared three vats of chili pepper stew, along with cornbread and cold root brew. People trickled into the meeting hall in twos and threes—the Scorpions, the hotfoots, and finally, Aster's own group. They all looked much more well rested, even Mallow.

Aster ran over to meet them.

"Aster! Were you really working on supper all day? How are you not ready to drop?" Tansy asked, her eyes brightening at the spread of food on the serving table.

Aster glanced back at Eli, who had already taken up his post behind the serving table like a pianist about to play his favorite tune. She smiled. "I had help."

In the morning the mood in the meeting hall had been subdued, everyone still dragging themselves out of sleep or focused on the day ahead, but now chatter and laughter echoed throughout the room. At one table someone picked out a haunting melody on their guitar, while at another a group sang a drinking song:

"*A drink to get rich, a drink to get wed, a drink for the living, and two for the dead!*"

Sam Daniels arrived after most had taken their seats, greeting everyone he passed by name. He joined Aster and the others at their table, along with Cutter and several of the younger Scorpions. Once everyone had been served, Eli slid in at their table, too. After spending all day in the kitchen, Aster had thought she'd all but lost her appetite for the meal in front of her. But with the first taste, her hunger returned. The rich red stew and fresh cornbread made her stomach cramp with raw want.

After they finished eating, a boy named Lewis broke out a deck of cards. He had smooth, golden skin and long, black hair gathered in a tail. He began dealing the cards, the corner of his mouth tilted up in a smile.

"Come on, Lewis, we can't play cards, there are ladies present," Cutter said.

"Sounds like someone's just afraid of losing to a girl," Clementine taunted.

Cutter crossed his arms. "Sam. Tell him I'm right."

Sam was already organizing his hand. "Loser does the dishes tonight."

"What's the game?" Tansy asked excitedly. They'd all seen the men at the welcome house play cards in the gambleman's room, but none of them had ever been allowed to play, of course.

Lewis began explaining the rules. Aster was too tired to follow him—her long day was finally catching up to her—but she agreed to stay up a little longer and look over Clementine's shoulder.

"I don't get it," Zee complained once Lewis had finished with the rules. "You need to start over and explain it to me like I'm five."

"Wait, wasn't your dad a great gambleman? How are you so bad at this?" Clem teased him.

Zee opened and closed his mouth, seemingly too caught off guard to form a response. Sam raised his eyebrow at Zee, but said nothing.

"He—I never—" Zee stumbled.

"You'll catch on, *Ezekiel*," Mallow said impatiently. "I just want to know what we're betting with. Because we're not risking any of our shine, that's for damn sure."

"No, of course not," Lewis said. "Let's say we bet with . . . secrets. The winner of each round gets to ask one of the rest of us a question."

Aster and Violet exchanged glances. Aster didn't like the sound of that. She could imagine what kind of questions a bunch of young men might have for some Good Luck Girls.

But she didn't protest and, as the game progressed, was relieved to find that *these* young men mostly seemed curious about their journey. Apparently they'd already heard about it from travelers and read about it in the papers, though the story had clearly warped with each telling.

"So how'd you rob the stagecoach?" one of the boys asked Violet.

"Well, it was just a private coach, strictly speaking . . ."

"Did you really hang a brag for crossing you?" another asked Mallow.

"Well, from his *feet*, but, yeah."

"Is it true that they call you The Knife?" a third boy asked Aster.

She allowed herself a faint grin. "If they do, that's news to me."

She supposed she should have had a little more faith in Eli's taste in friends.

The boys were good-natured enough about answering the girls' questions, too, about the Scorpions' life underground and the dangers they faced here. Aster had already learned most of what they had to say from Eli, but it was interesting to hear others talk about it. Not everyone shared his longing for a life aboveground. They'd found happiness here.

Eventually, though, as the night wore on and they grew more comfortable with one another, the questions turned to the welcome house.

"All right, this question is for . . . Tansy. You've been quiet. How'd you end up at Green Creek?" one boy asked finally.

Sam and Aster both shot him a warning look, but then Tansy spoke up.

"No, it's okay. It's a question I've asked myself," she said quietly. "We didn't have much of a choice, though. My mother passed suddenly, and we needed the money."

Mallow nodded, her hand folded over Tansy's. "My folks just told me it was my responsibility to do my part. There was no question of me saying no when the scouts came to our door. We felt lucky I'd been chosen."

Aster and Clementine met each other's eyes. Aster knew neither of them had told their story to the others yet. They hardly spoke about it themselves—Aster felt differently than Clementine about the family they'd left behind, and neither seemed to want to open old wounds by trying to convince the other to see things her own way.

"Our family honestly believed we'd be better off," Clementine said carefully. "The welcome house scouts . . . they're good salesmen. They promised that we'd never go hungry, that we'd always have the best medical care in the country. And they promised Aster and I wouldn't be separated. It seemed too good to be true."

"Because it was," Aster muttered. Clementine missed their family desperately, Aster knew. She blamed the landmasters for her suffering.

Aster, though, blamed their family. They should have known better. They should have loved them too much to sell them off. She would never have sold her own daughters to a welcome house, no matter how desperate things became. Aster would rather have gone hungry at home than live the life they'd abandoned her to.

You are too hard on them, Clem always argued. *It's not their fault there were no good options.*

No good options—like Eli had said. Maybe her parents had been facing hardships she hadn't been aware of. Maybe the

241

welcome house really had felt like the lesser of two evils. The thought had always weighed on Aster uncomfortably.

But it's still an evil. They ought to at least have recognized that.

They played another round, and this time Eli won. He looked at Aster, and he seemed to see the question tugging at her heart.

"Do you ever think about trying to find your family now that you're out?" he asked in his soft voice.

On this, at least, Aster and Clementine agreed.

"What good would it do? We're wanted by the whole country. We'd only get them killed," Aster said. However she felt about them, she didn't want that.

"Maybe after we get our favors removed and lay low for a long while, then we could try to find them, but for now . . ." Clementine just shook her head.

Lewis crossed his arms. "And what about you, princess?" he asked.

Violet looked up from her cards in surprise. "Who, me?"

"Who else? The landmasters work damn hard to make sure it's only dustbloods who get swept up in the welcome house system. So how'd you end up there?"

"Ignore this fool, Violet, it's not even his turn," Sam said, waving him off. Aster thanked him silently. She suspected Violet was just as uneasy talking about her past as Aster herself was. But to her surprise, Violet spoke up, a hint of her old defiance creeping into her tone.

"You think I haven't suffered?" she asked Lewis, sharp as a whip.

"I never said that," Lewis said evenly.

"Neither of my parents were dustbloods. You're right about that much. Sometimes a fairblood family has a run of bad luck and has to sell their daughter away. That's how my mother ended up in the welcome house."

"Wait, your mother was a Good Luck Girl, too?" Cutter asked. "But don't the doctors—"

"Something went wrong when they operated on her," Violet said before he could finish.

"Or maybe they just weren't willing to cut a fairblood girl," Lewis pointed out.

Violet curled her lip, and it looked like she was ready to argue the point, but then she faltered. "I've . . . I've wondered that myself. If it was an accident. If *I* was an accident. Maybe they thought they were doing her a kindness. I doubt she'd agree they did, though."

"So . . . your father was a brag, then?" Sam asked, putting the pieces together.

Violet nodded. "A steel magnate, Tom Wells. When he found out he'd gotten my mother pregnant, he promised to buy her out of the welcome house—and not just keep her, like other brags do, but actually marry her. Take her to live with him in his gilded mansion on the highest hill in Northrock. It's the kind of thing Good Luck Girls dream about. It seemed too good to be true." She looked at Aster and echoed her words. "Because it was."

Aster furrowed her brow. She had known Violet's father was a brag, but she hadn't known the details.

"My mother waited six years for him," Violet went on. "Six years—she was in love with that man. But he never came back to the welcome house, and when she realized that he never

243

would, she killed herself. Left me nothing to remember her by but the bedtime story she used to tell me and her suicide note." Violet shrugged then, and took a drink of root brew. But Aster saw her jaw clench as she swallowed.

"I can see how crushing that would have been for her," Cutter said quietly. "Thinking she'd get out and have a real life, freedom—"

"Freedom?" Aster said, turning to Cutter. "She'd still have been marked by a favor. Would have been a man's property for the rest of her life. Issued some fancy identification she'd have to show to any lawman who saw her out on the street. Don't ever think that any Good Luck Girl finds *freedom* in Arketta."

Cutter looked down at his hands.

Aster turned back to Violet, who shifted uncomfortably.

"And your father never came back for you, either?" Lewis asked into the silence. "You've still never met him?"

"Not yet." A strange darkness flickered over Violet's face. A strangeness that Aster had never seen before. "But one day."

Sam's expression softened. "I'm sorry for your loss," he said.

There were murmurs of sympathy all around. They had all lost something. That was why they were here.

So much suffering in the Scab, Aster thought, taking a sip of the root brew and savoring its sweetness.

It was time they left these mountains behind for good.

CHAPTER SIXTEEN

They left Camp Red Claw early the next day.

As much as she wanted to put the Scab behind her, Aster was reluctant to go aboveground again. Traveling in the mines could be treacherous, yes, but traveling in the woods was even worse. Still, they had no choice—the Scorpions hadn't yet finished their tunneling through the Scab, and couldn't have taken them much further north.

"It's not so different, your work and the Scorpions'," Clementine said to Zee as they made their way up a new mineshaft, leading their horses by the bridles. The mouth of the mine was still just a distant spark of daylight, and Eli escorted them, his face hidden beneath a soft-brimmed hat.

"What do you mean?" Zee asked.

"Well, you both help people cross the Scab," Clementine explained. "The only difference is, the Scorpions' people are on the run from the law."

Aster's and Eli's eyes met. Perhaps he, too, was remembering their conversation.

"That's actually why we work together, you know," Eli said quietly. "Rangemen and Scorpions. Most rangemen are dustbloods, so they try to help when they can. But Zee's one of the best I've met."

"Not *the* best?" Zee said, indignant.

Eli smiled. "Your cardplaying skills leave a little to be desired."

Zee and Eli were leading the group, while Clem, Tansy, and Mallow followed and Aster and Violet brought up the rear. Everyone else seemed as well rested as they'd ever been—even Mallow wasn't limping too much—but Violet's eyes were hollow, her face drawn. It was as if all of the truth telling last night had drained her.

"You doing all right?" Aster murmured.

Violet didn't look at her. "I'll do better as soon as we're out of this ripping mine. Crawling around in the mud isn't exactly my idea of a good time."

Well, it was better than being torn apart by vengeants. She could at least show a little gratitude for the hospitality they'd been shown, Aster thought irritably. But, at the same time, she knew Violet well enough by now to understand that her bitterness was usually something she hid behind.

"Your mother . . ." Aster began. "What was she like?"

"Pretty clear, isn't it?" Violet snapped. "A fool for loving a brag, and even worse for leaving her daughter with nothing but a cursed favor on her skin."

Despite the harsh words, Aster could hear the love in her voice.

"The story she told you . . . the note she left—" Aster gently prodded.

"I don't want to talk about it," Violet cut her off.

Aster didn't push further. It wasn't as if she wanted to

246

talk about it, either. But after spending the day with Eli, she supposed she could see why it might have been a good idea. Talking . . . it helped.

The slope steepened, and conversation tapered off as everyone leaned into the incline. Though the air was cool, sweat had already broken out along the groove between Aster's shoulder blades. No doubt once they got outside in the heat, her whole body would be covered.

Back to reality, she thought grimly.

At last they reached the mouth of the mine. This mineshaft had let them out in the woods, on the opposite side of the hill from where they'd entered. Eli went first, checking for raveners before waving the others through. The horses whickered excitedly as they stepped out of the darkness.

"All right, this is as far as I go," Eli said once they were all out.

"I can't thank you all enough," Zee told him. "You'll let your brother know how grateful I am for his help, won't you?"

"We ought to be the grateful ones. You brought a lot of joy with you, let us keep a piece of it."

Zee smiled and touched the brim of his hat. Then he mounted his horse. Mallow and Tansy did the same. Violet squinted in the sunlight, her shadow stretched out behind her like a battle flag. Then, taking a drink from her canteen to steel herself for the day ahead, she too climbed into the saddle.

Aster and Clementine were last. Aster lingered, wanting to thank Eli as well, but, as always, the words didn't come easily. He seemed in no hurry to return to the camp, raking his hat off his head and closing his eyes as he let the sun paint his face. For the first time since Aster had met him, he seemed to be at peace.

"Eli," she said finally, not wanting to break the moment. He opened his eyes, and she cleared her throat. "You thank your brother for me, too, hear? It's not often we meet honest men like you two. We'll miss your company."

"And we yours. Wander well, Aster."

He dipped his chin in a bow, and Aster climbed up into the saddle behind Clementine, her gaze cast forward as they rode into the thicket of the woods.

Aster stacked the silver coins by tens as she counted them, her lips moving silently. *Ninety-one, ninety-two, ninety-three, ninety-four . . .*

Clementine was counting, too, double-checking her math. It was late afternoon, and they had come to rest beneath the low-spread branches of an old tree. Aster had been both dreading this moment and impatient for it—the moment when they would find out if they'd stolen enough shine for Lady Ghost.

"We shouldn't have spent so much buying fresh supplies from the Scorpions," Tansy said, watching anxiously.

"We needed that stuff. And Sam gave us a good deal," Zee argued.

"Shut up and let me concentrate," Aster muttered. They were almost done, and she had no patience to start over.

One hundred eleven, one hundred twelve, one hundred thirteen . . .

Aster placed the last coin on the last column.

5,114 eagles.

"Five thousand one hundred and fourteen?" Clem asked tentatively.

A relieved smile broke over Aster's face as she nodded, confirming the number.

It was official—assuming that Violet's information was correct, they had enough shine to have their favors removed.

"So we don't have to rob anyone else?" Violet asked. She seemed detached despite the good news, turning over a fossil of a seashell in her hand.

"Not as long as we're careful with our shine," Aster replied, sweeping the coins back into their purse.

"We still *could* rob another brag, though . . . just, you know, for the hell of it," Mallow suggested, grinning.

"Mal, no. You almost died last time," Tansy said.

"Almost. I'm still here, aren't I?"

Aster shook her head. "The bank was a mistake. I shouldn't have forced it. No more big risks like that."

"A mistake? How? It got us the rest of our shine," Mallow argued.

"It also almost got us caught," Violet said dryly.

Aster couldn't even argue with Violet this time. She drew the coin purse closed and looked up at the others, letting the glow of her excitement warm her and fuel her courage.

"Listen, I've been thinking . . . I've been meaning to . . . I owe you all an apology," she finally managed. *There. It's out.* "I got reckless back in Scarcliff, and you all paid the price."

Tansy furrowed her brow. "You think we blame *you*? You're the one who got us out of there."

"Yeah, the rest of us were ready to give up, but you stayed strong," Mallow agreed.

"Well, there's a difference between strength and stubbornness," Aster said.

"Aster—" Clementine shook her head. "I'd be dead if it weren't for you. We'd all be dead, a dozen times over."

Aster glanced at her sister.

"We've all made mistakes out here," Clem went on. "But we also know we all want what's best for each other. That's what matters. It's not like back at the welcome house, when Mother Fleur was always trying to set girls against each other. There's trust here."

"Yeah, and *you* can trust *us* enough not to let you make too big a fool of yourself," Mallow said. "So try not to worry too much."

Even Violet was nodding now, and the glow in Aster's chest grew just a bit brighter.

"Thanks for that," she mumbled self-consciously.

Night fell. Though Aster already missed the relative safety of the Scorpions' camp, there was something comforting about the familiarity of their routine. Biscuits sopped with bacon grease. Blankets rough but warm. The dead howled but kept their distance. The stars glittered like tears.

The next day they set out for Clearwater, the last decent-sized town in the Scab. It had been three weeks since they'd fled Green Creek. Three weeks of racing through the Scab, which they'd never once left in their entire lives, and now they were almost through it. Beyond it stretched the green valley of northern Arketta, and already the woods were changing as their group neared the edge of the mountains, leafy oaks and ash trees taking over from the bitter-bark pines, dry red dirt slowly turning to rich brown soil.

Clearwater was also the last town until Northrock that would have a welcome house—outside of the Scab there were very few dustbloods, and very few Good Luck Girls as a result.

This would be Zee's last chance to find his sisters.

"Are you sure you want to risk me going into Clearwater?" Zee asked as they rode towards town. They were about a mile out, and the sun was just beginning to descend in the sky. "We already have your shine, and we're almost out of the Scab. I can come back this way myself, after taking you to Lady Ghost."

"You're going now," Aster said. After their close call in Scarcliff, it was tempting to make a straight line for Northrock. But she was all too aware of what Zee had sacrificed in helping them—if there was even a chance that they could help him find his family, Aster was going to take it.

Zee was clearly relieved, though he didn't say so. "All right," he agreed. "You all just wait for me here, then, and keep an eye out. If there's trouble, go on without me. I'll catch up."

Zee spurred his horse forward while the others dismounted and took cover in a stretch of low bushes. The Bone Road was just visible through the trees, winding down towards Clearwater.

Violet tied up her horse. "I hope he finds his sisters, but I don't reckon he will," she said to no one in particular.

None of her usual biting commentary this time, just a simple statement of fact.

"Where do you think they are, if not at a welcome house?" Clementine asked, worry plain on her face.

"Who knows?" Mal muttered. "Dustblood girls go missing in the Scab all the time. The law never wastes much time looking for them."

"But it's probably a good thing if they're not at the welcome house, right?" Tansy said to Clementine. "That means chances are they're being taken care of by decent folk somewhere . . . hallowers, maybe, or the Scorpions . . ."

"Or they're already dead," Violet said shortly.

"By the Veil, Violet, can't you go *ten minutes* without ruining someone's day—" Mallow began.

"*Quiet!*" Aster whispered suddenly. She'd seen movement out of the corner of her eye. A ravener was coming up the Bone Road on a hellhorse. The girls all ducked behind the bushes, hands falling to their weapons.

"Oh, the dead protect us," Tansy said under her breath.

A wagon trailed behind him, iron bars forming a cage over the wooden base. Only one prisoner sat inside—a girl no older than ten.

A welcome house recruit.

Aster heard Violet swear as she locked eyes with Clementine.

"Even with all five of us, we won't be enough for him," Tansy muttered. Raveners didn't feel pain or fear, which made them far more dangerous in a fight than a normal man. That was why Aster had always run from them instead.

"So we're just supposed to sit here and let him take her away?" Mallow asked. "No, I say we ambush him. One clear headshot, and he's done."

"You won't get a clear shot," Violet said darkly. "And not much else will stop him."

They looked to Aster, who swallowed. It was one thing to take a relatively small risk for Zee and his sisters—Aster felt like she owed them—but to run a much bigger risk to save a stranger?

And there were other factors to consider, too. Where were they supposed to take the girl afterwards? How would Zee find them? What would they do when the law came running? They certainly couldn't afford another run-in with them.

We'll take the girl with us until we figure something out.

Zee said he'd catch up to us if there was trouble.

And the law won't be able to follow us into the woods, not once the vengeants are out.

But the ravener . . .

He swayed on the back of his hellhorse, the snout of a rifle poking over his shoulder. Aster could already feel his mental influence pressing against her mind. He was radiating despair to keep the girl subdued.

Aster's gut churned with anger, hot and acidic. If they did nothing, then within the next day this girl would be maimed by a doctor, scarred with a favor, and tortured until she lost all will to fight back—to say nothing of the work she'd be forced to do in the months and years ahead.

"So, Aster? What do we do?" Clementine asked.

Aster set her jaw. "We're going to do whatever it takes to save her," she said. Her heart hammered in her chest, not with anger, but with the sudden certainty that what they were about to do was exactly right. "Hurry—we can't let them get into town."

Quickly, the girls wrapped dustkerchiefs around their faces and loaded their revolvers. As they did, Aster explained her plan in a whispered rush:

"Mallow, you use the sling-stones to stop the hellhorse, then Violet and I will run up behind him and free the girl. Once she's safe, Clem and Tansy can open fire and we'll all make our escape into the woods."

The others stared at her, eyes steely. They were doing this.

"I'm still hurting, so I can't make any promises about my aim," Mal warned as she searched the saddlebags for the sling-stones. The weapon consisted of three cords of braided rawhide with spiked weights on the ends. When thrown, it would tangle itself around an animal's legs. Zee had used it to hunt small game when a gunshot would have given them away.

Whether or not the weapon would be enough to take down a full-grown hellhorse, Aster had no idea.

The ravener was only a few lengths away now.

"Back up," Mallow whispered. She began swinging the sling-stones in a circle over her head. They whirled through the air with a low *whup-whup-whup*. She'd only have one shot.

The ravener passed in front of them. Rust-red eyes, sandy stubble painting his jaw. No mercy in that face.

Then, his body tensed. He *turned*—

Mallow released the sling-stones. They flew through the air, low and fast. Wrapped around the hellhorse's front legs and bit in deep.

Yes!

The beast reared, letting out an unearthly screech. It landed awkwardly but didn't lose its footing. Still, it was stopped for now, thrashing in an attempt to free itself. There was no time to lose. Aster ran out onto the road with Violet following on horseback. They made their way to the wagon. The girl appeared despondent and slow to react, the ravener's hooks still deep in her mind.

Don't worry, little one, Aster thought, bile rising in her throat from her indignation.

I'm going to save you like I couldn't save Clementine.

I'm going to save you like I couldn't save myself.

The ravener climbed down from his saddle. Soothed his horse, knelt to inspect and untangle its forelegs. He didn't look up as Aster took out her pistol. A trickle of sweat ran down Aster's temple, and she willed herself not to freeze, aiming the gun at the cage's padlock. "It's okay," she whispered to the girl, who stared without speaking. Aster glanced one last time at the ravener. He moved slowly, seemingly unconcerned. Something about his unhurried movements raised Aster's hackles.

"Do it," Violet murmured from her saddle.

Aster trained her eyes on the padlock again. She pulled the trigger.

The air exploded. Aster jolted back as metal flew and smoke filled the air. Coughing, Aster pulled open the cage door and scrambled onto the wagon.

"Who—who are you?" the girl asked, her words half slurred. Her eyes showed shock, but she hadn't so much as screamed when the gun went off right beside her.

"My name's Dawn," Aster said quickly, not sure why she gave the girl her true name. "We're getting you out of here."

She took the girl by the hand and hurried them both down onto the road. The ravener was now standing, facing Aster at last.

"You've injured my horse," he said calmly, wiping blood away on his pants. "I will kill you for that."

He hit her with a spear of pain through her chest as though her heart were being crushed in a giant's fist. Aster screamed as she fell to the ground, curling in on herself. Her gun clattered out of her hand. Fear roared through her head.

"*Take her! Get her out of here!*" Aster shouted to Violet as she struggled to climb back to her feet. But Violet collapsed, too, falling from her saddle like a sack of grain.

The first gunshots rang out from the others as the ravener started towards the girl, who stood frozen to the spot, watching him with blank terror. Bullets found his ribs, his thigh. He didn't flinch, just slowly pulled his own rifle off his back. Aster fought against the sickening dread that washed over her as she crawled towards the girl.

"No!" Clementine cried then.

She ran out from the cover of the woods, a flash of movement in the corner of Aster's vision.

No, Clem, Aster thought desperately. *Take the others and run.*

Clementine raised her gun. The ravener snarled and shoved her back with the butt of his rifle. Blood poured from Clementine's nose. Aster leapt up with a fury she'd never felt before, his hold on her slipping away. An animal snarl escaped her lips. She grabbed her knife from its sheath and lunged—

He spun with frightening speed and slammed the heel of his hand into her chest before the blade could find its mark. Aster's legs flew out from under her. The air left her lungs. The ravener seized her mind once again, this time with a crushing hopelessness that made her throat swell with tears.

They were all going to die here. Aster knew that then.

She had tried as hard as she possibly could have, and they were going to die anyway.

Through the blur of her tears, Aster saw Mallow and Tansy run out of the woods, guns raised, firing at the ravener's head. The pistols clicked emptily as the bullets ran out before they hit their mark.

In the distance, shouting.

The law was coming.

"Let's see your face, dustblood." The ravener crouched down over Aster, pulled her dustkerchief away. His cold, slick fingers brushed her cheek. Aster's stomach heaved.

The ravener's eyes sparked with recognition.

Aster moved before she could think. He was hesitating, wondering what to do with her, but she had no such uncertainty. She had known the second she saw this ravener that she would kill him if she got the chance. Had known, since her first night at the welcome house, when the raveners had tortured her into submission, that they would never show mercy and would never deserve the same.

"*Glory to the Reckoning,*" Aster whispered to him, making the words a curse, and she swung the knife. This time it landed, burying itself in his throat. He seized, his orange eyes lighting up with panic and his hands flying to the wound. Aster shoved him off of her and retched into the dust. He gasped for air, his breath wet, a ghastly rattle growing quieter and quieter. Until finally, there was no more breath at all.

"Aster!" Clementine rushed over to her. She was clutching her nose, blood pouring out from between her fingers.

Damn him, Aster thought.

He had touched Clementine, hurt her. Aster wanted to kill him twice.

"Are you okay?" Clem asked. She reached out and grabbed Aster's hand, pulling her to her feet.

"I'm fine." Aster coughed. "Where's the girl?"

Clementine pointed. Violet was already helping the girl up into the saddle.

Thank the dead, Aster thought.

As if in response, they started up their howls.

"All right, then, let's get going before the law gets here," Aster said. Together, they returned to the woods and mounted up, leaving the ravener behind in a spreading pool of his own cursed blood.

CHAPTER SEVENTEEN

It took over an hour for Zee to join them at their emergency meeting point, a narrow crevasse in the cliffs. When he rode up to the shelter, it was at a speed Aster had never seen from him before. He brought his horse around to an abrupt stop and slid down from the saddle. The barrel of his vengeant shotgun was still smoking.

"Were you followed?" Aster asked calmly. She was not here, in this moment and in this place, not really. She was floating somewhere outside herself, just a few inches to the left, as she had been since she watched the life leave the ravener's eyes.

Zee shook his head. "Only by the dead." His breath came out short and hard. He limped into the shelter—three long furrows from a vengeant's claws had ripped into the meat of his thigh, and his denims were soaked with blood.

Violet grimaced. "Ripping *hell*. Join the others."

The others were gathered farther back, being patched up by Tansy in turn. Clementine's nose was still bleeding. Mallow had opened her stitches again. And the girl—the girl was in shock. Her skin was rough with sunburn and insect bites and scratches.

Zee stopped short at the sight of her.

"Who the hell . . . ?"

"You told us to come here if we got into trouble—well, she's the trouble," Aster said. "We'll explain more later. Go get yourself cleaned up."

Violet gave Aster an odd look.

"You're awfully relaxed. If I didn't know better, I'd say you slipped yourself some Sweet Thistle," Violet said in a low voice.

The words seemed to come from far away. Aster turned to face her. "Good thing you know better, then," she said coolly.

She tried to walk past her, but Violet grabbed her by the arm. Aster shook her grip off.

"Don't touch me."

"Are we going to talk about what happened tonight?" Violet persisted.

"What's there to talk about?"

"You *killed* a man."

Aster's stomach rolled.

"I did what I had to do," she muttered. "And that 'man' sold his soul a long time ago to become a ravener. I just killed an empty husk."

"Well, even so. It's a hell of a thing. And you're acting like it's nothing."

Aster wheeled around on her. "*You're* going to preach to me about being too callous? Really, Violet? Where was this sympathy when you were ratting girls out to Mother Fleur? Why'd you wait until now to grow a ripping conscience?"

Aster felt as if she wasn't in control of her own body anymore, words pouring out before she could even think them. A shaky feeling settled over her, as if her joints were coming loose, and chills raked up her arms.

By the dead, maybe I really am losing it.

Violet's mouth was a hard line.

"I wasn't blaming you, Aster. I was just . . . making sure you were okay," Violet said stiffly.

She stalked off before Aster could reply, leaned against a tree and took out her Sweet Thistle.

Forget her, Aster thought mulishly, though she still felt sick. There were more important matters at hand.

Aster walked over to where the others sat huddled together. Tansy worked on Zee's leg. Mallow was rewrapping her own wounds. And the little girl clung to Clementine's side, dried tearstains streaking her cheeks. Clem washed her face with a damp cloth. They had managed to coax the girl's name out of her earlier—Adeline—but not much else.

"Are you hungry, darling?" Clementine asked her.

Adeline said something unintelligible.

"Sorry?" Clementine said.

"A little," she said more clearly.

Aster sat next to her and wordlessly handed her a dry biscuit. Adeline nibbled at it with a sound like a mouse chewing at the floorboards.

"Where are you from, Adeline?" Aster asked softly.

She swallowed. "Yellowwood . . . but the man with the pretty eyes was taking me to live somewhere else. Somewhere my father said I wouldn't be hungry anymore."

"A welcome house?" Aster asked.

Adeline nodded.

261

"Well, we're from a welcome house, too," Aster said, gesturing to the other girls. "And the truth is, it's not as nice a place to live as that man probably told you and your father." She paused, looking at Clementine, wondering how to explain it to the girl. She'd never been good with words, and she didn't feel up to the task of comforting anyone right then.

"The hunger's in your soul, not your belly," Clementine said, seeming to understand Aster's silent plea. "And that's much worse."

The girl turned her button-black eyes to Clem. She had no reason to trust them, Aster realized. Bad enough she'd been taken from her home—now she'd been kidnapped by strangers. But something about the softness of Clementine's voice seemed to soothe Adeline. She began to cry again, quiet, leaking tears—they seemed more from her being overwhelmed than anything.

"I want to go back home," she said.

"If you go back to your father, he'll get in trouble," Clementine said carefully. Deals with the welcome houses couldn't be undone. In theory, a family could buy their daughter back—that was one of the ways fairbloods justified the whole practice—but the price was more than any dustblood saw in a lifetime. "And then the law will take you to the welcome house anyway. Do you have any other family, though? Someone who could maybe hide you?"

The girl seemed to think about it. "My auntie," she said finally. "She lives in Two Pines."

Aster looked to Zee to see if he recognized the name. He nodded.

"It's a little town about half a day's ride from here. Your auntie works on the tenant farm there, Adeline?"

Adeline nodded.

"Well, should we try to take her there?" Clementine asked Aster in a hushed tone. "We can't bring her with us to Northrock. It's too dangerous."

"It'll be dangerous getting her to Two Pines, though, too," Aster murmured back. "It takes us out of our way, and we'll risk exposing ourselves. And what if her aunt wants to send her back to the welcome house?"

"Then we'll tell her. We'll tell her why she *can't*," Clem said.

Aster hesitated. But she hadn't saved this girl just to get her into more trouble by bringing her to Northrock.

"All right, then, Adeline, we'll take you to your aunt first thing tomorrow," Aster said. "You just get some rest for now, hear? It's been a long day. Don't worry. We'll take care of you."

Aster left her in Clementine's care, letting out a long breath. She spread her bedroll and climbed into it. That shaky feeling still hadn't left her. She looked over to where Violet sat at the entrance to the crevasse, her face turned to the wind to cool her skin from the fevered sweat of her withdrawal. Violet, the only one who had seen Aster's deathly calm and recognized it for what it was—mortal exhaustion. The same kind that would fall over Aster after a particularly bad night at the welcome house. Violet had probably felt it herself a hundred, hundred times.

I wasn't blaming you, Aster. I was just . . . making sure you were okay.

I'm not, Aster thought then.

I'm not okay.

It was a simple thought, but there was something huge and terrifying in it. She couldn't afford to think that way. She had to be strong. Weakness was not an option, had never been an option. Clementine was counting on her. Mallow and Tansy. And now this girl—

But the thought repeated itself, louder. It had escaped. She couldn't put it back.

I'm not okay.

The words carried her on a dark current into an uneasy sleep.

The next morning they woke early and rode for Two Pines, weaving their way north through the increasingly dense forest. The green of the trees deepened, and the soil darkened, softening beneath their step. They were very near the edge of the Scab now. There were fewer lawmen in Arketta proper, but also fewer dustbloods. Even with their favors covered, they would draw unwanted attention.

Aster tried not to worry about that yet. It was enough to worry about getting Adeline home safely. Now the young girl was riding with Tansy, whom she'd taken a liking to, while Mallow rode with Zee.

"You excited to see your auntie, Adeline? What's her name?" Tansy asked.

"Ruth," Adeline said. The night's sleep seemed to have done her good, and she looked around the forest with clear delight, pointing out every bird and beetle. Aster supposed, like most folks, she had never ventured outside her hometown—until now. "I've never met my auntie," Adeline went on, confirming Aster's suspicions, "or at least, not since I was a baby. But my ma talked about her all the time. Said they were like peas in a pod growing up. She passed last year—my ma. Vengeant got her."

"I'm sorry to hear that," Tansy said. "I lost my mother, too."

Aster and Clementine rode behind them in an easy silence. Aster was feeling a little more clearheaded now that it was daylight, having shaken off whatever malaise had gripped her last night. It was probably just leftover effects from the ravener attack, she decided. She was glad she'd dusted the bastard.

"It's strange to think we're about to leave the Scab," Clementine said, pulling a waxy, star-shaped leaf from one of the trees as they passed. She pressed it to her nose and inhaled. Neither of them had ever seen this much green before. "Did you ever think we'd get this far?"

"Just been taking it day by day," Aster confessed. At the beginning of all this, the idea of finding Lady Ghost had seemed about as likely as running away to the moon. But now . . .

"You think we'll ever go back home?" Clem asked. "I don't. But it's so hard to imagine never returning."

"You don't want to find Ma and Pa?" Aster asked carefully.

Clementine was quiet for a moment. "I think they'd want us to be happy," she said finally. "I think they'd want us *alive*. Even if that meant we'd never see them again. I mean, that's why they sent us to Green Creek in the first place."

But Aster heard the longing in her voice. There was no way to know if their parents still lived in the same camp, if their parents were even alive themselves anymore. Aster had mourned their loss the day they'd abandoned her. But Clementine, as always, still held out hope for the best. Maybe she imagined their whole family living happily together again one day.

Aster knew better.

It was about midday by the time they reached Two Pines. After a long discussion, Violet and Aster decided to go on alone to meet Adeline's aunt—there was no reason to risk everyone's safety, and a big group would only draw attention. Zee and the others would wait for them in the forest at an arranged meeting point while Aster and Violet rode into the tenant farm.

"Let me do the talking," Violet muttered as they went down the road. "No one's going to believe you're an honest rangeman—or an honest anything, for that matter."

Aster bristled. "If anything, *I'm* going to have to be the one who vouches for *you*. This woman's going to see your shadow and slam the door in your face. And who could blame her?"

Violet let out a little *huff*. Their plan was to convince Adeline's aunt that they were rangemen who had found the girl abandoned. Mallow had shown them how to wrap their chests flat, a habit she herself had taken up ever since leaving Green Creek, so that they might more easily pass as men. And Zee had given them his rangeman's badge, which could be shown to authorities to prove they weren't vagrants. As long as they got out before their favors burned through their dustkerchiefs, their cover would remain intact.

Even so, Aster's throat tightened with mounting apprehension. She hoped Adeline's aunt would be too excited to see her niece to question the people who'd brought her.

Aster followed the signposts down a side road that led to Mr. Cottenham's farm, where Adeline said her aunt worked tending fields of tobacco. The farm was about a mile and a half east of Two Pines proper, where the fairbloods lived. The shanties that lined the sea of tobacco leaves reminded Aster exactly of the house she had grown up in—cheaply and impatiently built, the wood weathered and cracking, the roof beginning to hunch in on itself, as if in apology. There was no deadwall to protect these homes from the vengeants, only crude iron wardants and bunches of dried grayleaf hung from the windows. Several families sat outside on benches, eating their midday meal and drinking dipperfuls of cool water from the well.

Aster and Violet dismounted from their horse before helping Adeline down.

"Afternoon, gentlemen. Don't often get strangers around here," said an older man who looked at them suspiciously from underneath his sunhat. He was working a wad of chaw around in his mouth. His eyes flicked down to Violet's shadow, but he made no comment.

"We're looking for a woman named Ruth," Violet said briskly, slipping into her most authoritative tone and flashing the rangeman's badge. "This girl here is her family." She gestured to Adeline.

The man's expression softened at the sight of the young girl. "Ruth Sheppard?"

Adeline nodded, and the man smiled. "I'll take you to her."

He led them through the camp. The workers wore their exhaustion like heavy coats, and two raveners walked up and down the rows of tobacco, making sure no one fell behind or tried to start any trouble.

Ripping hell, Aster thought when she saw them.

That was the last thing they needed.

The man brought them to a house with a tidy little flower garden outside and an iron wardant twisted into the shape of two girls skipping together. Adeline looked at it curiously, mimicking the pose.

"Keep still now, Addy," Aster murmured. She wet her lips as the old man knocked on the door.

"Ruth's usually home right about now, but she might have gone next door," he said. "She and Ms. Crane have been known to play cards during their midday meal with some of the other ladies. Can't tell Mr. Cottenham, of course. He wouldn't like it to know any of us were gambling with his money, let alone a bunch of women . . ."

But then the door opened. A woman with gray-streaked hair and weathered brown skin stood in front of them, thin as a rake, with the same dark eyes as Adeline.

"Walter? Who are these two?"

"I was hoping you would know. They say this girl is family of yours."

"Auntie Ruth?" Adeline asked, stepping forward tentatively.

The woman's hand went to her throat. Her eyes widened with shock. "*Adeline?*"

Walter smiled. "I'll leave you all to it, then. You know where to find me if you need anything."

Ruth ushered them into her house and closed the door. Aster was struck by an almost physical longing as she looked around—replace Ruth's spun-wool blankets with her own mother's, and they might have been in Aster's childhood home.

Ruth wrapped Adeline in a fierce hug, kissing the crown of her head. Tears streamed down both their cheeks.

"I never thought I would see you again," she said, releasing Adeline so she could get a better look at her. Aster's body flooded with relief. Ruth wanted the girl. That much was clear. "I don't understand how this is possible—I got a letter from my brother-in-law saying he was planning to sell Addy away to a welcome house. I did everything I could to convince him not to, offered to take Addy in myself, even, but he said he needed the shine, and that was that."

Ruth smoothed the girl's hair with her fingers. Adeline's face was split with a grin. Never once, despite their efforts to cheer her up over the past two days, had Aster seen Addy smile before this. It made Aster's heart swell with a joy that she herself hadn't felt since . . .

Well, since she had been Addy's age.

"She looks so much like my sister when she was little," Ruth went on, standing back up with difficulty. "That's us out front, you know—the two wardants playing skip. Did you know her, or . . . ?" A cloud passed over her sunny excitement. "How *did* you come by Adeline, anyway?"

"We're rangemen," Violet said smoothly. "We work together. We came across Adeline on our way north for a job. Seemed she'd been abandoned by the ravener who was supposed to take her to the welcome house."

"But why?"

Violet shrugged. "Who can guess at the reasons a soulless man does anything? Maybe a more lucrative job opportunity came up. Regardless, it wouldn't have felt right to leave Adeline alone out there."

"Yes, of course," Ruth said absently. But the cloud was

darkening. "So you—you stole her from the welcome house system, then? She's here unlawfully?"

Aster hesitated, her own smile faltering. "Would you rather us take her back?"

"No, of course not. My sister would want me to look after her girl, I'm sure of it. But . . ." She hesitated, then lowered her voice. "Someone will come for her, won't they? The welcome house, or the law? Both? And if you all found me this easily, then it's only a matter of time before they do as well."

Adeline had begun looking around her new home, opening the drawers and cabinets, seemingly unaware that she was still in danger.

"Do you all have anywhere else you can go?" Violet asked, sharing an uneasy look with Aster.

Aster wasn't sure what she'd been expecting when they attacked the ravener, guns blazing. She'd been certain it was the right thing to do, but had no plan for what would come next. And then, after, she'd hoped Adeline's aunt would know what to do. But everything the woman had just said was true. What if Aster and Violet were just handing her a death sentence?

And Addy . . .

Aster stared at the woman, mouth dry. "You need to leave. Go somewhere else."

Ruth blinked. "I . . . I suppose I could try to get us far enough away to start over in another town," she began. "We could change our names maybe, our look . . . but I don't have the shine for something like that. No shine at all really." She looked around the little house. Aster realized almost nothing in it was even Ruth's to sell—like the house itself, all the furniture, dishes, and clothes would have been loaned to her by the landmaster, Mr. Cottenham, and the total cost added to her family's debt.

"I can promise to love her like my own daughter, but I cannot promise to keep her safe," Ruth went on. "Maybe . . . maybe it would be better for her to go to the welcome house. At least they'll be able to take care of her—"

A stab of fear in Aster's gut. A memory rose up in her mind from where she'd buried it, clawing its way back to the surface like a monster that refused to die. The moment her parents had told her they were selling her and Clementine off to the welcome house, the betrayal that had broken her so completely she had never been able to put herself back together.

You'll be better off there, Dawn. Her mother's voice, deceptively soothing and sweet. *I promise they'll take care of you.*

"Wait," Aster interrupted then, so quickly she forgot to mask her voice. She covered it with a cough. "Let my partner and me talk it over."

Aster nodded at Violet to join her outside, trying to hide how shaken she was. She closed the door behind them. Violet put her hands on her hips, squinting in the sunlight.

"What's there to talk about?" she asked. "We can't do anything more for these people."

"We can. We have to." Aster went over to their black mare and reached into the saddlebag. She pulled out the coin purse, heavy with all the shine they'd collected since Green Creek.

Violet's eyes widened. "No . . ."

"Violet, we don't have a choice. They'll come here, they'll come and kill the aunt, you know they will. And then they'll

271

take Adeline back to the welcome house. They need to go somewhere else, and not a damn hole in the ground waiting to get killed. They need to be able to start a new life far enough away that the raveners will give up looking for them. And for that they need shine, lots of it. Or it'll all have been for nothing. "

"If you don't—if we don't keep that shine for ourselves, then your whole ripping *journey* will have been for nothing," Violet hissed. "Lady Ghost—"

"We can't leave them to die!" Aster kept her voice low, but her anger bled through. "And we can't let what happened to us happen to that girl."

Violet sighed and laced her hands over her head.

"It's not that I don't care. I do. I promise you I'm not the black-hearted bitch you seem to think I am." Aster flinched. Violet clearly hadn't forgotten Aster's harsh words last night. "It's just that sometimes you have to be practical. You have to make hard decisions. And if you don't get your favor removed, you'll die, too, Aster. You all will."

Aster dropped her shoulders. Looked through the window. Ruth had sat Adeline down at the kitchen table and was pouring her some tea, so calm in the face of this sudden upheaval to her world.

They have a chance at the life that was stolen from me and Clementine.

"We'll give them my share at least," Aster offered.

"Don't be a fool. That's not even enough to make a difference. Unless you want to give them Clem's share, too?"

Aster said nothing, but the corners of her mouth tightened.

"That's what I thought."

The breeze blew between them, carrying the sweet scent

of the tobacco plants with it. The farmworkers who'd been eating their midday meal were packing up their things now, getting ready to head back to the fields. Aster's favor burned more intensely beneath the fabric of her dustkerchief. They didn't have much longer.

"Look, it comes down to this," Aster said finally. "*We* can figure something out, we always do. But this is it for them. This is their only chance."

Violet rubbed her eyes with the heels of her hands.

"Damn you, Aster," she muttered.

"The others will understand. If they were here they would make the same choice. " She knew in her heart it was true.

"Of course they would. They're soft like you. And they'll do whatever you tell them, because you're their leader. That's why you have to be practical, like I said. If you'd ever been head girl, you'd know that."

"Don't give me that old song and dance. You were just looking out for yourself back at Green Creek. You've said as much."

"I had to. No one else would." But then Violet seemed to come to some decision, and her expression settled into something that was almost boredom. "Anyway, you do what you want. Give her the shine, if that'll make you feel better. I just want to get out of here."

Aster swallowed and nodded. Relief coursed through her. Still, her mind whirled with doubt as they rapped on the door and waited for Ruth to answer. As blunt as Violet had been, she still had spared Aster the obvious, unspoken truth: there was no way they would make back this much shine in the little time they had left.

But just as true was the fact that, as honorable as their reasons had been, it was their fault Adeline was on the run from the law in the first place.

They'd gotten her into this mess, and they would get her out.

Ruth cracked the door open, looking at Aster and Violet expectantly.

"Thanks for your patience, Ms. Sheppard," Aster said. "We've been talking, and we have a bit of spare shine we'd like to give you. Help you start your new life somewhere else, as far away as you can go." Aster held up the coin purse. "A little over five thousand eagles in here, ought to be enough."

Ruth's eyes widened. "I cannot possibly accept this."

"Please," Violet insisted, and Aster was surprised to hear the genuine goodwill in her voice. "For Adeline."

"I only wish someone could have done the same for my sister," Aster added.

Ruth took the heavy coin purse. Her eyes shimmered with fresh tears, which she wiped away quickly. "I don't know how to thank you—by the Veil—"

Aster held her hands up. "We're honored we could help."

Ruth thanked them again, pulling them both into a hug. A flood of homesickness washed over Aster, followed by a surge of pride and contentedness such as she had never felt. Stealing from the brags had brought a rush of satisfaction every time, true, but this—this was like a solid meal that stuck to your ribs and would leave you full for days. For just a moment, all her pain and shame fell away.

This, Aster thought, letting out a shuddering breath.

This is why I'm here.

That was when she heard the sound of voices from behind them. Aster turned, her stomach dropping. Walter was at the front of a group of half a dozen farmworkers, all armed with sickles and other tools, marching towards the house with purpose.

"I *knew* there was something wrong with you two," he shouted, his voice harsh and accusing. "They're not who they say they are, Ruth! They're the Green Creek girls. That there's one of the stolen horses." He held up a wanted poster as proof. "Grab them, boys!" he ordered, the group within mere yards of the house now. "And remember, McClennon wants them alive!"

Aster didn't have time to process the turn of events, didn't even have time to mount her horse before Walter swung his sickle. Instead, she grabbed Violet by the hand and took off on foot.

"Come on!" she shouted.

They broke out into a sprint across the hardpacked earth, side by side, until they disappeared into the cool green shade of the tobacco fields. Aster's heart kicked in her chest in time with her footsteps, the impact of each one rattling through her bones.

"They won't hurt Ruth and Adeline, will they?" Violet asked, already short of breath.

"They have no reason to," Aster panted back, though she was reassuring herself as much as anything. The posse was hot on their heels, their footsteps pounding into the fields after them.

No chance they'd be able to outrun them for long.

Aster tore off her dustkerchief. Their cover was blown anyway, and the pain only slowed her down. They had to make it back to the forest, back to the meeting point where Zee and the others were waiting for them.

And here we are leading a ripping mob right to them—

"This way," she hissed to Violet, forcing the thought down. She ducked sideways, running across the rows of plants now instead of down them. Their only hope was to lose the men in the maze of green.

Branches whipped against their faces. The scent of the tobacco left Aster's head swimming. A distant shot rang out. One of the men must have had a gun.

And then there were the raveners . . .

"I—see—the end!" Violet said between breaths.

An instant later they broke free of the field. Aster crossed the short strip of open grass that bordered the woods and dove into the trees. The meeting point was still about a quarter mile away.

Aster and Violet covered the distance in a little over a minute.

"Aster? We heard gunshots—" Zee started when they burst through the trees.

"No time to explain. They're on our tail. We have to get out of here," she said. Violet took a grateful gulp of air as they came to a stop. Aster began untying the horses. "We had to leave our horse back there," she went on. "Clem, you ride with Zee; Violet, with me."

The sounds of pursuit rolled towards them like a tidal wave. More shots rang out, along with shouted curses. They couldn't be more than a hundred feet behind them.

"By the *Veil*," Mallow swore as the men poured through the trees.

"There are raveners, too, and the law won't be far behind them," Aster said grimly.

They spurred their horses into a gallop and bolted deeper into the woods. The men in the posse wouldn't be able to keep up with them, but the law would be on horseback, too. The law would have no trouble. And they were probably already on high alert, given the stir Aster had caused in Clearwater.

She glanced over at Zee, whose face was drawn beneath the brim of his hat. He seemed to be thinking the same thing.

"How do we lose them this time?" Aster asked, the wind nearly tearing her words away.

He shook his head, eyes trained on the rushing ground ahead. "It's going to be tough, Aster. There are always extra lawmen at the borders of the Scab."

Clementine's arms were wrapped tight around his middle. "So what are we supposed to do?"

"I have an idea. It's dangerous, though." He finally spared a glance at Aster. "It's near nightfall—the vengeants will be out soon. If I lead them onto the lawmen, the rest of you can escape with the theomite ring—"

"Zee, *no*," Clementine interrupted.

Aster gripped her horse's mane as it stumbled while weaving around a tree.

"—Keep going until you reach the next town, Stonegate," he went on, inexorably. "There's a train station there. It's the first stop on a line that runs all the way up to Northrock—"

"Zee, you're coming with us," Mallow called out, from a bit behind them.

"No," Aster said then, respect settling in her chest. "*I'm* going with *Zee*."

"No!" Clementine cried. "Not both of you."

Zee gave Aster a brief nod. He brought his horse to a stop. Aster and Mallow did the same.

"She's right, Clem," he said softly. "No horse can carry three full-grown riders. Someone has to stay with me."

"Let it be me, then. I'm the one they really want—"

"*No.*" Aster cut her off, already dismounting. "I came all this way to save you, Grace, hear? I'm not giving up on you now."

"Aster . . . are you sure?" Tansy asked. "Maybe we can . . ."

"My decision is final." She had to end this argument now. Their head start over the lawmen wouldn't last long. Clementine climbed down from her saddle, tears streaming down her face.

"Promise me you'll catch up to us," she whispered, wrapping Aster in a hug.

Aster's heart beat hard and fast in her chest. "I don't want you to wait for us. It's too dangerous—"

"*Promise me.*"

Aster had never lied to her sister. She didn't intend to start now. But then she looked up and saw Violet giving her the barest shake of her head.

Sometimes you have to be practical.

"I promise," Aster whispered back, telling Clementine what she needed to hear. Clem exhaled, thanking her, and saddled up behind Violet. "Wander well, friends."

Clementine hesitated, words seemingly caught in her throat, but then Violet spurred their horse forward.

278

The sky had begun to deepen to crimson as the sun sank in the sky. The shadows around them had lengthened and turned black. And, to the south, soft but growing stronger, the sound of a hundred horse hooves in pursuit.

"Good luck," Clementine shouted over her shoulder.

They all took off. Aster and Zee watched them go until they disappeared into the thicket of the forest. Once they were gone, he pulled the shotgun from his back and handed it to Aster.

"Hope you've been practicing as much as you say," he said without a trace of his usual humor. "You're going to need this."

CHAPTER EIGHTEEN

Aster looked at the gun as if it were a live snake in her hands.

"Shouldn't *you* take this?" she asked. Shooting at the padlock had been bad enough, and that was just shooting a small pistol at a damn object.

Zee shook his head as he hurried to find his knife. "Last time I tried to ride and shoot, this happened," he said, patting his injured thigh. "I'd let you take the reins, but Nugget knows me best. You can do it, Aster."

Then he sliced open the palm of his hand.

"*Zee*—what the hell—"

"We have to draw the vengeants to us."

"They're not living things. They can't even smell blood." He'd lost his mind.

"No, but they're attracted to pain and fear, and it won't take much to whet their appetite. We're already plenty afraid." He winced, handed her the knife. "You do the same."

"Zee . . . I don't know about this . . ."

As she spoke, the sun dipped below the horizon, and the forest was plunged into darkness. The vengeants began to wail, low at first, then louder and louder. Aster's pulse roared between her ears.

She cut her palm.

Aster saw the blood before she felt the pain—and what an awful lot of blood it was. Soon her whole hand was painted red, rivulets running down her wrist and up to her elbow. The wound beat in time with her heart. Her palm burned as if it were on fire. Zee gave her a bandage to wrap herself with, but already she was beginning to feel lightheaded.

"Stay sharp," he said. "Once the vengeants are almost on top of us, we'll lead them onto the law. We'll get out of this, I promise."

She wondered if he was lying, too.

The lawmen were getting closer, making no effort to mask their approach. Every few seconds, they repeated the same shouted warning:

"ATTENTION. YOU ARE UNDER ARREST. DROP YOUR WEAPONS. COME FORWARD WITH YOUR HANDS UP."

What if the law reached them before the vengeants did? What if there weren't enough vengeants to stop them? What if—

Zee climbed into the saddle and helped Aster up so they would be ready to run once the lawmen were close enough. She almost dropped the shotgun as she took her seat behind him. It was harder to hold it with her injured hand.

"How many rounds are in this thing?" she asked shakily. The vengeants were coming for them, too, she could sense it, their wings buffeting the air and churning it into short, choppy gusts.

"Six rounds," Zee answered, stroking Nugget's neck to soothe her. "It takes a long time to reload—too long. So don't shoot unless you have to."

Their breath fogged in front of them. The temperature was dropping, fast. Even so, a bead of sweat trickled down Aster's hairline. She wiped it away with the back of her wrist. Stared into the dark, flinching at every movement. She did not feel any safer with this gun in her hands. She might as well try to shoot down a thunderstorm.

Then she saw it—an oncoming flash of silver cutting through the moonlight, covering the distance fast as a coyote. She raised the gun—

"*Wait*," Zee said. He wheeled the horse around, and the vengeant just missed them, claws whispering past Aster's face. "We don't want to scare them off yet. We need more to come."

How many?

Because the forest seemed to be boiling with vengeants now, branches snapping as they rushed forward. Their high, gibbering screams rolled over Aster like a wave. Her scalp tightened. Her heart punched through her chest. She felt, more than she saw, another vengeant diving for them from above—

"NOW!" Zee ordered.

She swung the shotgun upwards and fired blindly into the dark. The shot ripped through the night with a roar of noise and a flash of fire, and the kick of the gun practically knocked Aster off the saddle. The vengeant let out a wounded shriek and fell back, but another was right on its heels. Zee finally dug his spurs in and the horse bolted, leading the vengeants after them.

The wind tore at Aster's face as they galloped towards the lawmen. She held back the rush of panic that always seemed to come when she fired a gun. Held back the vomit heaving up her throat. She couldn't afford to lose herself. Not now, not here.

"Hang on!" Zee said, and he pushed them even faster, into a gallop. Branches scratched at their arms and legs. Aster's bones rattled from the pounding of the horse hooves. She sensed at least two vengeants keeping pace with them, one on either side. Aster hesitated, not sure where to aim. Then the one on the right lunged, sank its fangs into her calf, and *pulled*—

Aster screamed. Fired the shotgun twice at her attacker, and then a third time, to drive off the other vengeant on the left.

That's over half the shells gone already.

"Are you okay?" Zee shouted.

"I'll be fine," Aster barked back. But her leg throbbed, and her vision swam.

Human shouts rang out from up ahead. They'd heard the gunshots.

"All right, we're almost there," Zee said. And sure enough, Aster could just make out the dark shapes of mounted lawmen riding towards them from about a hundred feet away. Two dozen men, at least, a few of them carrying grayleaf torches— enough to ward off a vengeant or two each, but certainly not enough to drive back the horde Zee and Aster were bringing down on them.

"STAND DOWN!" the lawmaster in front shouted.

Zee kept riding.

The first scattered gunshots rang out.

"I thought they weren't allowed to kill us," Zee snarled, ducking his head.

"I guess they'd rather bring in our bodies than let us escape again," Aster said grimly. Her leg was soaked with blood now from the vengeant's bite, and another vengeant was catching up to them, its wingbeats heavy and powerful.

Fifty feet away from the lawmen now.

"*Damn it,*" Zee cursed, reeling backwards into Aster. He clutched his shoulder. He'd been shot. The horse staggered without his guidance. Their speed flagged.

Shit—

Aster whirled around and shot the moonlit vengeant above them just as it dove for the kill, claws outstretched and jaws yawning. It squealed, and its form flickered as it turned and fled.

Twenty-five feet. Zee had taken up the reins again, breathing raggedly as he did so. They gathered speed. Hurtled towards the posse of lawmen.

"STOP RIGHT THERE—"

Zee let out a wild, desperate yell. Aster aimed her gun over his shoulder and fired her last shot, forcing the lawmaster to duck out of their way. And then they barreled through the patrol, a horde of vengeants at their heels.

Madness.

A volley of shots rang out around them. Aster and Zee both ducked, covering their heads. Men shouted as they were attacked by vengeants, dragged down from their horses or carried up into the trees. The screams of the living and the dead rose in a chorus that curdled Aster's blood.

It didn't take long for the lawmen to turn and run—not after Aster and Zee, but away from the teeming horde. People scattered in all directions. The smell of blood and gunpowder thickened in the air. Zee took advantage of the confusion, leaving the vengeants and their new prey behind. Aster felt a flutter of hope as they turned north. Towards Stonegate. Towards their friends.

We did it.

Aster reeled with a rush of elation that swept away her fear. For a time, both of them were silent, listening to the rhythm of the hoofbeats and the fading sounds of the chaos they'd created. Then Aster's weariness hit her like a hammer, and it was all she could do to stay upright. Zee fumbled for his canteen with his good hand and took a drink.

"You know what Clem's gonna say when she sees us, don't you?" Zee said finally, wiping his mouth and passing the canteen back to Aster. She heard the smile in his voice.

Aster smiled back, despite everything. "*I told you so.*"

Once they were clear of danger, Aster and Zee stopped to clean and dress their wounds as best they could. Zee ripped off a piece of his shirt to make a sling for his arm, while Aster did the same to bandage her calf. Then they reloaded the shotgun, saddled up, and continued riding for the rest of the night, following the others' trail. The sooner they caught up, the sooner they all could leave the Scab behind.

Aster rode in a half-sleeping haze, her head lolling with the horse's every step. She was beginning to feel like she had on the night after she killed the ravener. Disconnected, unreal. *Not okay.* The vengeant attack, the lawmen's gunfire, the roar of the shotgun in her hands—it was all getting to be too much.

But to Aster's surprise, Zee's presence was helping her stay grounded in the moment. She still wasn't entirely comfortable being near him, and she suspected she never truly would be. And there was still something about his past that she knew he wasn't telling them, something he was ashamed of, or afraid of, or both. But she had her own fair share of secrets, and she knew what it was to be silenced by her own fear and shame. Aster trusted Zee, she realized, more than she had ever expected to when she'd first met him.

She had not believed it was possible to have that with a boy—an honest friendship.

"Zee," Aster said tiredly, talking to keep herself awake. "With everything that happened, I never got a chance to tell you . . . but I'm sorry you never found your sisters."

Zee didn't answer, and Aster wondered if he'd heard her, wondered if she'd even spoken or if she'd just dreamed the words. But then he replied, his voice soft as the early morning light pouring into the forest.

"Me, too."

"What will you do now? After you're done with us?"

"I haven't given up on them," he sighed. "And I never will. But the trail's gone cold. I checked every welcome house in the Scab, and there was no sign of them. It's like they just . . . vanished."

A chill crept down Aster's spine. Not knowing what happened to your family—that was almost worse than losing them outright. You couldn't grieve, couldn't move on.

Clementine would probably say, *You'll figure something out, I know it*, or *I'm sure they're together, wherever they are*. And she might even actually believe it. But Aster couldn't summon the words. False hope was too cruel a gift to give a friend.

"Well, if there's ever anything we can do to help, you tell me, hear?" she said instead. Zee's sisters deserved freedom just as much as she and Clem did, or Mallow and Tansy, or Violet, or Adeline, or any of the other hundreds of Good Luck Girls in the Scab.

"Thanks, Aster," Zee said, sounding surprised. "I'll make sure I do."

They reached Stonegate just as the sun had risen properly over the valley, and they stopped at the top of a ridge, looking down at the town below. It was by far the biggest they'd seen yet, and rather than a deadwall, it had a giant stone arch in the middle of town. Zee explained that the arch represented the gateway into and out of the Scab, even though, in actuality, folks arrived at and departed from the train station on the east side of town. The tracks wound north, glinting in the light like a ribbon of steel. The train waited in the station.

But where were Clementine and the others?

Zee dismounted and knelt to check the trail he'd been following. Now that it was daylight, Aster could see just how exhausted he looked, his face drawn and his movements slow and pained. She knew she looked as bad or worse.

"Their trail stops here. They didn't go into town," he said uncertainly.

"So they're waiting for us, like they said. But where?"

"They must be nearby."

Aster dismounted and joined him in looking around, worry cutting through her foggy-headedness. What if someone else had found their trail? Had they been captured? Or maybe some accident had befallen them—

Then Clementine's voice cut through the silence.

"They're here! They made it! I told you all they would."

Aster whirled around. Clementine had emerged from the trees on foot, running towards them. Mallow, Tansy, and Violet were right behind her. Aster barely had time to exhale with relief before her sister wrapped her in a crushing hug.

"Good to see you, too," Aster said with a tired laugh, and it was only then that she realized just how close she had come to never seeing Clementine again. Her throat tightened, and she swallowed back a teary feeling.

Clementine released her and turned to hug Zee next, then stopped short when she saw his arm in a sling.

"The hell happened to you?" Mallow asked, eyes widening.

"We'll tell you all about it," Zee said. "But first, we have to catch that train."

He pointed to the freighter in the station.

Violet scowled. "Does it have to be *that* train? We've had a hell of a long night, Zee. We only got here about an hour before you."

"Afraid so," Zee said. "That'll be the last freighter running until tonight. During the day they run passenger trains—no chance of us stowing away on one of those."

"And no chance of us hanging around here until nightfall undiscovered," Tansy concluded.

"Exactly. But once we're on the train, we can rest up all the way to Northrock. It's a full day's ride. Where are the horses?"

Tansy and Mallow hurried back into the woods and led the horses out. Aster and Clementine traded places once again, so Aster was riding with Violet and Clementine was riding with Zee. Then they made their way down the ridge until they were on the edge of town and rode parallel to the tracks, sticking to the woodland for cover. They weren't going to get on the train at the station, Zee explained—too many eyes. Instead, they would jump on as it rounded the first bend. The train would have to slow down there to make the turn.

Still . . . it would be moving. Aster didn't care for that. This was a rushed plan, like the bank robbery. Something was bound to go wrong.

The train let out its first whistle. It was leaving the station.

"Come on, we can't let it get ahead of us," Zee urged. But their horses were tired, and they couldn't be coaxed to go any faster. It wasn't long before the train began to overtake them, its engine bulling ahead on the tracks twenty feet to their left. Some of the cars were wooden, their paint fading into the grain. Others were open at the top, carrying mountains of coal. Black smoke belched from the chimney. The wheels gathered speed with a sound like rolling thunder. Aster felt as if they were chasing down a demon from hell.

The bend in the tracks was just ahead.

"All right, get ready to dismount!" Zee called back. He angled closer to the tracks, until they were riding right alongside the train. The cars roared past them, the wind tearing at their hair and clothes.

It's going too fast. We'll never be able to catch it, Aster thought desperately. Unwanted images flashed in her mind: Tansy dragged under the train's wheels, Mallow dashed against its sides. She gritted her teeth and shook her head.

Zee brought his horse to a stop as they reached the bend. Climbed down from the saddle.

"Take only what you can carry on your back," he shouted over the noise. "Where's the shine?"

Aster and Violet exchanged glances. The shine was with Adeline and her aunt.

"We've got it," Violet said to the others, reading Aster's face.

They had all dismounted now and were filling their knapsacks as quickly as they could. The end of the train was in sight.

"There, 24-67," Zee yelled, wetting his lips. He pointed out the next upcoming boxcar, blood-red paint peeling from its wood. Someone would have to climb the ladder on the side, he explained hurriedly, in both shouted words and gestures, unlatch the door, then slide it open for the rest of them.

And obviously, with his arm, Zee wasn't going to be the one to do it.

Aster glanced at Mal, but Mal was still injured, too. And so was Aster herself, with her leg—

"I'll do it," Clementine said in a voice barely audible over the roar.

"Clem, no," Aster began, her heart kicking.

But her sister was already stepping forward, climbing through the knee-high grass and onto the spit of gravel that lined the tracks. The rocks crunched beneath her boots. She closed her eyes, mouthing a prayer. The boxcar was three lengths away, coming around the corner at about the speed of a cantering horse.

Or a person running near as fast as they could.

"Everybody get ready to run!" Mal cried.

The boxcar rattled past them. Clem ran with it, leapt up, and grabbed the ladder, flakes of rust falling from beneath her fingers. She climbed quickly up to the top. The others kept pace with the car, Aster hobbling as fast as she could with her injured leg. As soon as the train was around the bend, it would speed back up.

Aster would never catch it then.

Now on the roof of the car, Clem lowered herself onto her belly, unclasped the latches at the top of the door. Tried to lug it open.

"It—it's stuck," she yelled, stammering.

"Unstick it then!" Violet barked.

The train was beginning to accelerate.

Clem finally forced the door free. It slid open with a crash. She climbed down from the roof and swung inside, landing in the hay that lined the floor.

"Tansy, come on! I've got you," she shouted, holding out her hand.

Tansy was leading the group. She pumped her knees faster, grabbed Clementine's hand, and jumped. Clementine pulled her into the car safely.

Violet was next.

"*Shit, shit, shit,*" she yelled with every step, pushing herself into a sprint. She held out her hand and Clem and Tansy pulled her into the car, too. Mallow took her turn, then Zee. He let out a loud yelp as they grabbed him by his injured arm.

Now it was just Aster.

The train had rounded the bend. It was picking up speed. Aster forced herself to keep up, even as her leg stabbed with pain.

"Come on, Aster, you're almost there!" Clementine cried, though Aster saw the fear in her eyes.

Aster cursed herself, cursed the burning in her lungs and throat, cursed the throbbing pain in her leg. She reached out for Clementine's hand. Grabbed it.

She stumbled.

Her legs gave way.

She screamed.

Clem held on tight as Aster tried to scramble to her feet. Her legs burned, dragged behind her, gravel tearing at her clothes and skin.

The wheels were terrifyingly close, sparks flying by her face. The roar of them drowned out all thought other than pure, wordless fear. Aster tried again to regain her footing, but the train was moving too fast. She was going to be dragged to death, or cut in half on the tracks.

And if she didn't let go, she would bring Clementine with her.

I'm sorry, Grace, Aster thought, loosening her grip. I'm so sorry.

Then, suddenly, she felt a strong hand clamp down around her wrist. Zee's. And then Violet's hand over Zee's. Mallow's and Tansy's.

"*PULL!*" Clementine shouted.

Aster felt herself lifted up. They drew her up into the car.

Aster let out a sob as she landed flat on her stomach, the wood scraping against her skin. She crawled forward, and Clementine closed the door behind them, sealing them in the dark. A rush of relief coursed through her, a heady euphoria that, for an instant, overwhelmed all her pain.

How many times, how many ways, had the Scab tried to beat her over the years? To beat all of them?

Now, at last, they were leaving it behind for good.

"That was dangerous," Aster coughed once she'd recovered enough to sit up. Her head still swam with giddy disbelief, but she tried to regain her composure. "You should have left me behind."

Violet rolled her eyes—Aster couldn't see it, but she sensed it. "You're welcome," Violet snorted, as if in confirmation.

Aster smiled. *Thank you*, she thought. *All of you*.

CHAPTER NINETEEN

It wasn't exactly comfortable riding in the boxcar. The air was dark and dusty, the cargo rattled in its crates, and the floor shook with every bump on the tracks. There was a remnant in there, too, the foglike figure of a rail worker who sat in the corner, having a smoke and casting a vague but overwhelming sense of longing. But Aster was too tired to care, and she fell asleep within minutes.

When she woke, Aster didn't know how many hours later, Clementine was the only other one up. Keeping watch. She sat with her arms wrapped around her knees, staring at the remnant—not with fear, but curiosity. Aster sat up straighter against the crate she'd been leaning against, wincing at the stiffness in her leg.

"Talking to ghosts again, Clem?" Aster asked softly.

Clementine offered a faint smile that was just visible in the light streaming through the slats in the wood.

"Listening, more like," she said. "This one's name is Calvin. He's been here a long time."

"Well, if you all hadn't saved me, I might've ended up a ghost on this train, too," Aster said. "Thanks again for . . . you know . . ."

"Oh, please. As if I would ever leave you behind. Can you believe we've almost made it?"

"Well don't go and jinx us, we're not there yet," Aster said. There was still the small matter of all the shine they had to make up, not that Aster was ready to talk about that yet. She wasn't even ready to *think* about it. "You really believe we're going to find Lady Ghost at the other end of this train ride?"

"I know we will."

"What are you going to do once you get your favor removed?"

Clementine's fingers went to the side of her neck. "I think the first thing I'm going to do is go into a cake shop. Get one with buttercream frosting."

Aster snorted. "What, to celebrate?"

But Clem wasn't laughing. "No, just—just to do something normal. Something other girls get to do. Go shopping in the city, order something from a bakery, walk around freely. And all of it without everyone staring at you and—and hating you."

There will still be plenty of hate left to go around for a couple of dustblood girls, Aster thought, but she kept it to herself. Because Clementine was right.

Whatever else happened, at least they'd be free.

"What about you?" Clementine asked. "What are you doing once your favor's gone?"

Aster thought back to her conversation with Eli. *Sometimes you wish you could start your whole life over.*

"It's hard to even imagine," Aster said, her voice barely carrying above the rattle of the wheels below. The air was thick with the scent of sawdust, starting a tickle in her throat. "I know we can't have children, but maybe . . . I don't

295

know . . . I like the idea of giving a girl the kind of life we didn't get to have."

"Well, it's not as if it's too late for you to have that life," Clementine said, looking at her oddly. "We're still young."

But it did feel too late, Aster realized, and the thought filled her with an unbearable sadness. She shoved it away forcefully. There wasn't time for that.

"Aster—Dawn—" Clementine began, but then the train went over a big bump, shaking everyone else awake.

Thank the dead, Aster thought, relieved she'd been freed from the heavy turn the conversation had taken. Tansy and Mallow, who had been curled up against each other, both sat upright with a jolt. Violet cursed as she was sent rolling across the floor. Zee snorted like a startled bull.

"Did we jump the ripping tracks?" Violet asked.

"No, but we're really flying," Zee admitted, rubbing his eye with the heel of his hand. "We must be crossing through the Goldsea now."

The Goldsea was a flat stretch of prairie near Arketta's northern border, where forests dominated once more.

It meant they were almost there.

"Did we miss anything interesting while we were out?" Tansy asked.

"Not really," Clementine answered. "Aster and I were just talking about Lady Ghost, and what we're gonna do once these favors are gone."

"Did Aster mention anything *else* about Lady Ghost?" Violet asked.

Aster glared at her. Clementine wrinkled her nose. "Like what?"

"Like how you're supposed to pay her now that all the shine is gone."

The words hung in the air, the truth of it suddenly heavy in Aster's chest.

"But I thought you said you two—isn't it in the—?" Tansy stammered, before Aster had managed to speak.

"What the hell are you talking about, Violet?" Mallow asked more impatiently.

Aster sighed. "I've been meaning to tell you all . . ."

And then she told them everything—about how Ruth's joy at seeing Adeline had turned to fear once she understood what would happen to them if they couldn't escape. About how, without the shine, Adeline would have been even worse off for them having saved her.

"I never would've made such a big decision without you all, but it was life or death for them," Aster finished.

But it'll be life and death for us too if we can't make up for it, she thought. When she made the decision she was certain the others would have done the same, or at least she told herself that. But now, trying her best in the almost dark to gauge her friends' reactions, fresh doubt seized her. Tansy looked stunned. Mallow was scowling. Clementine stared at her hands.

"You were there, Violet," Aster said desperately. "Tell them how it was."

"Oh, it was the right thing to do, I don't doubt that," Violet replied. "Even if it wasn't the *smart* thing. But now we have to figure out what to do next."

They were all quiet for a moment. Aster's heart hung at the top of her throat.

Then Mallow nodded, slowly but surely. "I'm glad you all did it," she said. "I would've done the same. But without that shine . . ."

"Without the shine, we came all this way for nothing," Tansy said, her voice thick.

Clementine shook her head. "No, we'll make those eagles back. We'll find a way. We always do. Rob another bank—"

"What, in *Northrock*?" Mal asked. "This isn't the Scab anymore. All the banks up here will have top-of-the-line security—"

"Well, what else are we supposed to do?"

"—and look at us now. I've been tossed around like a rag doll, Aster got her leg chewed half off, Zee's been shot to hell—"

Zee spoke up for the first time then, as if his name had shaken him out of his stupor.

"Use the ring," he said.

They all stared. When no one spoke, Zee repeated himself.

"Use the theomite ring to pay Lady Ghost," he said more firmly. "It's worth at least five thousand eagles. She'll take it."

"Zee—no," Clementine said immediately. "We're supposed to use the ring to pay *you*."

"You've already sacrificed too much," Tansy agreed. "You used up all your father's shine on us, you got yourself in trouble with the law, you left your horse behind . . ."

"We owe you," Mal finished.

"If I was only in this for the pay, I would've given up a long time ago," Zee replied, leaning his head back against the wall. "You all are family to me now . . . maybe the only family I have left. So until I find my sisters . . ." He looked

298

back at Clementine, twining their fingers together. "Let me get you to Lady Ghost, Clem." Then his gaze swept around the circle. "All of you."

Aster felt her old protectiveness rise up again—not of Clementine, this time, but of Zee. "We're not letting you walk away empty-handed," Aster insisted, surprising herself. "There has to be another way."

"There isn't," Zee said, equally insistent. He held out the ring. "Please, Aster, just let me help you all. Let me finish this. Believe me, it's the least I can do after . . ." He stopped himself. ". . . It's the least I can do."

Aster took the ring uncertainly, trying to see past the shadows to read Zee's expression. What had he been about to say?

Something about whatever it is he's been hiding from us.

Something so ugly he was willing to give up the theomite ring to atone for it.

Aster shifted, sitting up straighter.

"Zee," she said, slowly and carefully, as if treading on broken glass. "Look, we all have secrets here, and you're entitled to one or two of your own. I . . . I've made my peace with that. But if you've been trying to make up for something by helping us . . . if that's the real reason you won't take the ring . . . I think we have a right to know. Because I think of you as family now, too, and I need to know that it's real."

She swallowed, her face suddenly warm. She hadn't been expecting to speak so honestly. Zee opened his mouth to answer, but Clementine beat him to it.

"For the love of the dead, Aster," she demanded. "What more does Zee have to do to prove to you he's a good man—"

Zee pulled his hand away from hers. "No—Clem—she's right," he said, speaking as if each word cut him. "I—I haven't been completely honest with you all."

Aster's lips parted as she let out a sharp, pained breath. The others grew still, the air in the boxcar suddenly heavier than it had been before.

"What do you mean, you haven't been honest with us?" Clementine asked into the stunned silence. Aster couldn't read her sister's face in the dark, but she could hear the tremble of hurt in her voice. "Zee—"

"You *are* family to me," Zee said, taking his hat off and turning to her. "Every word of that was true, Clem. It's my first family I haven't been entirely honest about. My parents. My father." He looked around at all of them, the whites of his eyes shining. "He wasn't a gambleman. He was a ravener."

For an endless instant, no one spoke.

"Your father . . . what . . . ?" Aster murmured.

"He hunted down welcome house runaways. And he used to take me with him. That's how I learned how to track. That's where we got all our shine," Zee finished.

"And that's why you're so keen to help a bunch of welcome house runaways now," Violet said through her teeth. "To clear your conscience."

"That's not the only reason—" Zee said desperately.

But Aster no longer heard his words, a hum rising in her skull. It was as if the Veil had dropped from in front of her eyes, and Aster saw Zee clearly for the first time.

The cloud of guilt that clung to him, no matter how selfless he acted.

The discomfort that seized him whenever someone asked him about his life before becoming a rangeman, the inconsistencies in his answers.

The panic that overwhelmed him whenever raveners were near—the only time he ever showed raw fear.

Aster's stomach turned, and it wasn't just the sway of the boxcar nauseating her.

Zee's tone turned pleading. "I wanted to tell you all a thousand times. But I didn't want you to think—I was just a boy, he made me go. But I never wanted to help him. I hated every minute of it—"

"Did you kill anyone?" Mallow asked tensely.

"No! Of course not."

"But your father did. Your father killed girls like us," Clementine persisted.

Zee faltered, then nodded. "Girls like you, and girls like my sisters," he said helplessly, his voice growing thick. "I only wanted to do right by them. The shine was supposed to get us out of debt—"

"That's enough," Aster said before he could go any further. She did not have the energy to soothe Zee's guilt. Nor did she want to. She felt no relief at having been proven right about him, only an overwhelming exhaustion that settled over her like a sickness.

"I am sorry," he said finally. His hat was still in his lap, and he put it back on as if to help hide his face. "I'm sorry for what I did, and I'm sorry for lying about it for so long."

Well, he's sorry. I guess that counts for something, Aster thought, bitter.

"You said your father died—how?" Tansy asked, her voice barely above a whisper.

Zee let out a loose breath. "He killed himself," he said. "Being a ravener, it takes a . . . a toll. Mortals aren't built to endure the power that comes from beyond the Veil. It eats away at your soul. You can't understand unless you've seen it happen to someone you love. My father went into the business so he could get us out of debt once and for all, but he started losing his memories, his emotions, his desires . . . everything that made him *him*. He used to build model boats and take them down to the creek for us to race. He would sing my sisters to sleep. All of that went away. It was like he was turning to stone. My mother passed one winter and he didn't so much as shed a tear. He shot himself later that year—not out of grief, I think, but emptiness. He might as well have already been dead."

No one spoke. They had all had their share of tragedy, and they had all experienced a ravener's cold indifference. But the idea of watching a loved one slowly lose themselves to the curse . . . it was a horror Aster had never considered.

You're not the one who grew up being tortured by them, last I checked, she'd once told him.

But maybe he *had*.

"I'm sorry, Zee," Aster said finally, some of her anger easing. "You should have told us. But I'm sorry all the same."

"I see why you didn't want to talk about it, though. It's a hell of a thing," Mallow muttered.

But Zee's attention had turned back to Clementine. "Clementine? You're so quiet," he said, swallowing. "What are you thinking?"

"I think . . . I think maybe you were as much your father's prisoner as anyone else," Clementine managed, not looking up at him. "But I wish you hadn't kept it a secret from me. I would've understood. I *do* understand. You have to trust me."

"She's right, Zee," Aster said with a sigh. "You think we don't know how it feels to want to leave your whole past behind?" The others murmured in agreement.

"Honestly, I thought you would hate me," Zee admitted.

"I hated that I could tell you were *lying* to us," Aster said. All the worst men were liars. They would tell you that up was down and punish you for arguing otherwise. The welcome house had been a lie, too. The whole damned Scab had been based on a lie—the lie that said dustbloods deserved whatever bad things happened to them.

Aster didn't think she could stomach even one more lie.

"Well, you have my word—nothing but the truth from here on out," Zee said. "So believe me when I tell you this: I'm going to get you all to Lady Ghost, not because I want your shine, and not because I want your forgiveness. I just want to see you win."

Once the train slowed down in the outskirts of Northrock, they jumped out. It wouldn't do to be caught stowing away. But that meant they'd have to cover the last couple of miles into town on foot, through pastureland. Aster's injuries had stiffened from sitting for so long, and every step now sent a pulsing ache through her body. The ground was uneven and pitted with puddles. The grass stood as high as their waists in places. It was slow, treacherous going, and so different from

303

the mountains they'd left behind that Aster felt like she'd stepped out in another world entirely.

"Water all over the damn place. Even the air feels wet," Mallow muttered.

"Even so, I'm not going to be able to wash the smell of cattle patties off my boots for *weeks*," Tansy replied, disgusted.

"Just be happy it's cows out here instead of vengeants," Aster said.

It was long after dark by now, but they hadn't heard a single vengeant yet. Aster had always known that, outside the Scab, vengeants were rare as a two-headed snake. But it was still uncanny, after hearing their chorus every night, to be met with silence now. Did fairbloods truly live like this, fearlessly, free to wander out after dark without so much as a second thought for the dead?

In Northrock, it wouldn't even be dark—not truly. It was a proper city, a modern city, the only one in Arketta that used voltricity to power itself. Even here, still a mile out, they could see its halo of blue-white light, blotting out the stars. The skyline stood out starkly, like the teeth of a key.

Another world.

At least in the Scab, Aster had known what to expect. What dangers were waiting for them here?

Aster turned to Violet, who was walking a little apart from the rest of them. At the beginning of all this, Aster would have expected as much. But now, it struck her as unusual. Here was a perfect opportunity for Violet to complain about their surroundings or remind them that her father was some bigwig in the city, and she was letting the moment pass without so much as a single comment. Violet hadn't been this reserved since their

304

night with the Scorpions, which had been understandable—they had been strangers, and Violet had stuck out as the only fairblood among them.

But she's used to us, so what is it this time?

Maybe she was just itching for some Sweet Thistle—this would be her first night going without it after weeks of tapering off.

Or maybe she was nervous about meeting Lady Ghost. If there was something they should all be worried about, Aster needed to know.

She picked her way across the grass until they were walking side by side.

"You ready for tomorrow?" Aster asked.

Violet looked up at her suspiciously. "What do you mean?"

"Nothing, only—"

"I know where we're going."

"I never said you didn't." But Aster didn't give up. "Is it something about Lady Ghost that's bothering you? Are you worried she won't be there?"

Violet flashed her a slanted grin. Their boots whispered through a shallow cattle wade. "A little late to be asking that, don't you think?"

"You know how much I hate it when someone answers a question with another question."

"All right, then—no, I'm not worried about Lady Ghost."

"Well, you're worried about something. I see it in those beady little eyes."

"Since when do you care?"

Aster dropped the humor, laid a hand on Violet's arm. "Hey. I'm just making sure you're okay," she said.

But Violet just snorted. "A little late to be asking that, too."

What's that supposed to mean?

"Violet—"

"Aster!" Zee called from up ahead. "There's an abandoned barn here. We can hole up there for the rest of the night."

"Let's do that," Aster called back. They had spent too much of the night traveling to try to find Lady Ghost before sunrise. She gave Violet a final look before running to join the others.

Inside the dilapidated old barn, they climbed up to the hayloft to avoid the rats that had taken up residence below. They'd had to leave most of their supplies behind when they got on the train, so they were back to sleeping under thin blankets and eating dried food. The smell of damp and rot hung heavy in the air, and Aster felt as if she were breathing into a dirty rag.

But this was it—the last night on the road.

By this time tomorrow, they'd be with Lady Ghost.

By this time tomorrow, if all went well, if the promises were real, their favors would be gone.

"I'll take the first watch," Violet volunteered as everyone staked out their sleeping areas.

Aster furrowed her brow. "All right, if you're sure. But wake me if you need anything."

"Unless you have a luxury hotel room to offer me, I don't think that'll be necessary," Violet replied dryly.

Well, if Violet was back to being an asshole, that had to be a good sign, Aster figured. Aster drew the blanket up over her shoulders and settled in for what she was sure would be a restless night of sleep. She was nervous about tomorrow, of course, but beneath that, there was something else, fragile as a soap bubble—excitement.

It's not too late for you to have the life you wanted, Clementine had said.

Maybe she was right. Maybe it wasn't. Once their favors were gone . . .

Aster drifted off, allowing herself to dream of the possibilities for the first time. But just as she slipped into the deepest reaches of sleep, someone was shaking her back awake.

Clementine. She crouched over Aster, her eyes were wide with panic.

"Aster, get up!" she whispered urgently. "It's Violet. She's gone."

CHAPTER TWENTY

Aster threw her blanket off and leapt to her feet. Violet was supposed to be on watch. Why the hell wasn't she here?

"Violet?" she called out into the darkness, to no response.

She reached for her knife at her hip, fear already mounting in her gut. But the knife was missing, too. She scanned the wooden plank floor for it, knowing she wouldn't find it.

"What's going on?" Tansy mumbled as Clementine jostled her awake.

"Violet's gone," Clem said.

"Gone?" Tansy said, sitting up. "She probably just went to relieve herself."

"Not with my knife, she didn't," Aster replied. "Violet?" she called out again, futilely.

Now Mallow and Zee were sitting up, too. "Maybe she took the knife because she was scared of the dark. You know how she is," Mal said.

But then Aster noticed something tied to the empty knife sheath—a neatly folded envelope sealed with wax.

What the rip is this? Whoever had written this letter, it hadn't been Violet. They had no envelopes or sealing wax out here.

And this wax was cold and hard as a button—it had been dry for a long time.

Aster pulled the envelope free and sliced through the wax with her thumbnail, possibilities racing through her head: Someone had kidnapped Violet. This was the ransom note. The paper was so soft with age it scarcely crinkled as she unfolded it. It was too dark to make out the words.

"Somebody light a match," Aster said, dread creeping up her throat.

After what felt like endless seconds, Zee found and struck a match. It lit with a quiet *hiss*. Aster leaned into the light. The ink had faded, but Aster could just make out the words written in a spidery script.

"*My Dearest Violet,*" Aster began, her voice subdued, "*I'm not sure when you'll read these words, but whenever you do, know that I love you more than anything and can't bear to be away from you. But I have a chance to escape and find us a better life, and I have to take it. If the worst happens and I don't make it back to you (for only the worst could keep me from coming back!), keep telling yourself our bedtime story. Tell yourself every night. Because the seraphant is waiting, and the words will guide you to her. I love you always. Ma.*"

"Wait a minute . . ." Clementine murmured as Aster finished. "Violet told us that her mother left her a letter before she died. Before she . . . killed herself. Maybe this is it."

Tansy shook her head slowly. "I don't know. These don't sound like the words of a woman who's about to take her own life at all."

"All right, but why did Violet leave us this letter in the first place? And where is she *now*?" Mallow asked.

"Could she have left us to find Lady Ghost on her own?" Tansy murmured.

Aster's stomach dropped at the thought. She reached for the theomite ring around her neck, exhaling when she felt it was still there.

"No, she couldn't have, or she'd have taken the ring as payment," Aster said. "She must have gone somewhere else."

Mal huffed. "Well, how the hell are we supposed to find Lady Ghost without her?"

The match went out. Zee lit another. Aster looked over the letter again, her skin prickling with growing frustration.

Our bedtime story . . . the words will guide you to the seraphant . . .

"Does anyone remember Violet saying anything about a bedtime story?" Aster asked. She was beginning to think "the seraphant" might be code for Lady Ghost, and that this letter was meant to lead them to her.

But that still didn't explain why Violet had left them, or where she was now.

"I'm pretty sure Violet mentioned the bedtime story the same night she told us about the letter," Clementine said. "We were with the Scorpions, all of us talking about how we ended up at Green Creek."

"Violet didn't *tell* us the story, though, so what good is this letter to us?" Mallow demanded.

"Think back, what did she tell us that night?" Tansy asked.

They all fell silent for a moment, remembering. The second match went out, its smoke coiling in the dark.

Violet's mother was born to a poor fairblood family and sent away to Green Creek, Aster thought.

And because she'd been a fairblood, the doctor hadn't cut her.

Eventually she'd gotten pregnant with Violet and fallen in love with the father, a wealthy brag.

He'd promised to take her away from the welcome house so they could live together as a family.

But instead, he'd abandoned them, and Violet's mother had killed herself out of grief.

"Violet's father was a steel magnate, right?" Zee asked, seeming to run through the same facts in his head. "What did she say his name was?"

"Tom Wells," Tansy answered.

"And she said he lived in Northrock, remember? In a gilded mansion on the highest hill," Clementine added.

"Well, we're right outside of Northrock now. Maybe she . . ." Aster stopped, remembering Violet at Camp Red Claw when they were exchanging stories with the Scorpions.

And your father never came back for you, either? You've still never met him?

Not yet. But one day.

There had been something strange in Violet's eyes when she'd said it. A darkness. A secret. And, maybe, an intention.

"Maybe she never meant to go with us to Lady Ghost at all," Aster said slowly. "Maybe she went into Northrock to find her father."

"Is Lady Ghost even *in* Northrock, then?" Mallow demanded. "Or did Violet just make the whole thing up to get us to take her to the city?"

Aster shook her head, swallowing around a hot coal in her throat. After everything they'd been through together, everything they'd shared with one another—what if Violet had been using them the whole time?

Either way, this letter was useless without her.

Aster closed her eyes against angry tears. Violet had betrayed girls before. She'd built a reputation for it. But, even for her, this was beyond belief.

Something wasn't right.

"You all stay put," Aster said evenly, pocketing the letter. "I'm going to find her."

Aster donned her coat and bandit hat and stole away into the night. She only had a few hours until sunrise, and she'd have to go back into hiding come daylight.

Which meant she had to hurry.

Aster hopped the low fence that surrounded the cattle pasture and ran down the gentle slope towards the river bordering Northrock. The Mercy. It looked to be at least half a mile wide, its current smooth and sinuous. Aster skidded to a stop as she came to the riverbank, her boots squelching in the mud. The stench of the water made her stomach churn. She would be swept away if she tried to swim across, Aster was certain of that. And any bridge might well have a checkpoint with the law, just like the deadwalls in the Scab. How the hell would Violet have made it to the other side?

Aster ground her teeth. She could see the highest hill in Northrock from here, could see the silhouettes of the manor homes that looked down over the city from their perches.

But they couldn't have felt further away.

She would take her chances at a bridge.

Aster ran along the bank until she came to a stone one that crossed the Mercy at a spot where it narrowed. She ducked behind the bushes, her mind racing. She'd have to wait for a delivery cart to pass and jump in the back. She prayed it wouldn't take too long for one to come. Zee had said most deliveries to the city were made overnight, but they'd been talking about freight trains. She had no idea if the same was true for deliveries on the road.

I don't have time for this, she thought, impatience clawing at her insides. The longer she waited here, the more likely Clementine and the others would be discovered, or Violet would move on from wherever she had run to, or the sun would rise and—

Someone was coming up the road. Aster tensed, readying herself. But it was a private coach, like the ones they had robbed. No way she would be able to climb on the back without being noticed. She let out a frustrated breath and ducked back down, waiting for the carriage to pass.

The minutes ticked away slowly. The road remained empty. The black water below rushed by with an endless roar. Aster's muscles were beginning to ache from crouching for so long, and the vengeant bite in her calf throbbed sickeningly in time with her pulse. Fatigue dragged at the edges of her mind, making her eyes droop and her thoughts scatter.

Then, just as Aster was about to give up and make a rush across the bridge on foot, checkpoints be damned, she heard another carriage coming down the road.

And this one was a delivery cart.

A milk wagon, Aster saw a moment later, packed with big metal drums of milk and cream. The top was open.

Aster tied her dustkerchief around her face. Braced herself on the balls of her feet. As soon as the wagon bumped up onto the cobblestone bridge, she made her move, dashing out and climbing onto the back. Once she was sure the rattle of the wheels had been enough to muffle her impact, she freed one of the rough blankets wedged beneath the milk cans and used it to cover herself.

The time it took to cross the bridge felt endless. Sweat poured down Aster's neck despite the chill in the air. She froze when the wagon stopped. She could hear the lawmen's voices asking the driver for his name and permit. Lantern light swept over the back of the wagon, seeping in through the fibers of the blanket that covered Aster. Once, twice. After an interminable silence, the lawmen waved them through.

Aster exhaled. She counted to a thousand, wanting to make sure they were well clear of the lawmen, then jumped out of the cart.

"*Hey!*" someone shouted. But Aster pushed her way past the people on the street and ducked into the first alley she came across, running as fast as she could go. The damp and dark reminded her of walking down the mineshaft, but instead of rocks and rotten wood, here there were trash cans and broken bottles to dodge. Aster glanced behind her, making sure she wasn't being followed, then slowed to a walk, smoothed her shirt, and returned to the main streets.

So this is Northrock, she thought, taking a moment to scout

out her surroundings. The buildings here were as tall as the trees in the Scab and left the brick streets below cloaked in shadows. Even now, long after sundown, the streets were clogged with people—double-decker horse-drawn buses, vendors hawking their wares, lawmen on foot and mounted, men in bespoke suits stumbling out of a gambling hall, men in rags begging by the doors. The blue-purple glow of the voltric streetlamps bathed the whole city in otherworldly light. They hummed just at the edge of her hearing.

Aster struggled not to let herself become overwhelmed—by the light, by the noise, by the heavy smells both sweet and foul. As hard as she tried to blend into the crowd, she could tell she stood out in her muddy rangeman's outfit. She lowered the brim of her hat, letting herself be carried by the tide of people. She had no idea how to get where she was going, but if she didn't hurry, her favor would give her away to all these people.

Panic began to press in on Aster from all sides. There were too many bodies brushing up against hers, too many eyes raking over her face. Her head swam. Sweat coated her palms. She pushed against the people crowding her. Struggled to stay focused. She didn't have time to lose herself, not tonight. She had to find the gilded mansion on the highest hill—

Somebody grabbed her by the wrist. Aster bit back a scream.

"The law's on to you. Follow me," the stranger whispered in her ear, then they released her wrist and pushed past her. The voice belonged to someone wearing a patched black coat worn gray at the elbows, collar turned up against the night air. Aster only had enough time to see there was no shadow at the stranger's feet before they disappeared into the crowd.

Aster's heart had leapt into her throat. She swallowed it back. She had no reason to trust this person, but it only took one glance behind her to see that two lawmen *were* watching her, and one of them had already dropped his hand to the nightstick at his belt. She cursed and ran to catch up with the stranger.

"Who the hell are you?" Aster growled. She could see now that her companion was a young dustblood woman about her age, with eyes black as the night and a short, sharp nose.

"Points for effort. You were at least *trying* to be discreet. But you'll find sneaking around the city's a hell of a lot different than sneaking around the Scab."

"How'd you know—"

"That dustkerchief is the first giveaway. There's no dust up here. Plus you're dressed like you stepped off the cover of a penny novel about the mountains. But most damning is that wide-eyed wonder you're looking around with. Everyone gets it their first time in the city," the girl listed off, continuing to lead them expertly through the crowd. "I've been tailing you since you jumped out of the delivery cart. There's a few of us that sleep rough in the old mill down the street, and the law will look for any reason to arrest us and send us to the Scab. So I can't have you starting trouble around here."

Aster bristled. "I'm not here to start trouble. I'm looking for someone, and I don't have time—"

"Do you even know where you're going?"

Aster hesitated.

"Let me help you. One dustblood to another."

"I don't have anything to pay you with."

"Sure you do." The girl held up Aster's pocket watch—the one that had been in her back pocket only moments before. Aster swore and reached for it, but the girl snatched it away and offered her free hand instead. "My name's Cora."

Aster supposed she couldn't complain too much when she herself had stolen the watch from a brag. But still . . .

". . . Pleasure," she muttered, shaking Cora's hand, though she wasn't about to reveal her name back. "I need to get to Tom Wells's manor. Tonight. He's a steel magnate. Do you know him?"

Cora raised her eyebrow. "Sure, he lives uptown with all those other wellborn bastards. He has men guarding the place day and night. I can get you close, but then you're on your own."

Aster nodded, trying to ignore the fear gnawing at her gut and the pain eating away at her favor. She followed Cora down an alley like the one she had come through earlier. She kept her fist curled at her side, wary. For all she knew, this girl was leading her into some kind of trap. But Aster was desperate. She had no choice.

"What do you want with Wells, anyway?" Cora asked as they moved through the bowels of Northrock.

"Don't worry about it."

"No need to be touchy."

But Aster wasn't in the mood for conversation. She rubbed at the side of her neck with her shoulder, trying to ignore her favor. "We need to hurry."

Cora nodded and picked up the pace. The further uptown they went, the cleaner and quieter the streets became. There were no rats in these alleys, no drunks passed out on the curbs.

They were definitely heading in the right direction. Aster felt a brief rush of relief, grateful her trust had been rewarded.

"Anyway, if you're planning on staying in Northrock, you're going to need to learn how things work at some point," Cora said eventually. "It's dangerous for a dustblood up here."

It can't be worse than the Scab, Aster thought.

"I'm not. Staying in Northrock, that is," she muttered. But then she relented, grateful she'd found someone in this strange place willing to help her. "But . . . thanks. I appreciate the concern."

Cora shrugged. "You've clearly got some skill if you managed to escape the Scab and make it all the way here. My friends and I could use someone like you, if you ever change your mind."

Cora came to a stop then. They'd reached the end of an alley that opened on to an empty courtyard. Mansions stood on every side, large stone buildings aglow with yellow light from gated windows. At least half a dozen guards patrolled the area.

"Tom Wells lives in that one," Cora said, pointing to the mansion directly ahead. "This is where I leave you. Good luck."

Aster swallowed. "Right. Thanks." She turned to say goodbye, but Cora had already disappeared into the darkness.

Aster was on her own. And if Violet wasn't here . . .

No, there wasn't time to think like that.

Aster darted out of the alley before she could second-guess herself again, sticking to the shadows for cover. These guards were mortal men, not raveners, but it would still be tough to avoid them.

Sneaking around the city's different than sneaking around the Scab.

318

Aster picked up a broken brick underfoot and hurled it as far as she could to the opposite side of the courtyard. It landed with a *crack*. The nearest guard ran to investigate. Aster hurried along the perimeter until she'd reached the other side, then squeezed between the bars of the iron gate in front of Tom Wells's house. A short path led up to the front door, splitting around a small decorative fountain. Aster crept forward, focusing on the trickle of the water rather than the hammering of her own heart.

Almost there.

Movement up ahead. Aster froze. Reached for her knife instinctively and cursed when she remembered it wasn't there. Someone was sitting on the porch, mostly obscured by a large bush.

Aster hesitated. It wasn't a lawman or a guard, she could tell that much. But whoever it was would probably shout for help as soon as they saw her.

Or they might know something about Violet. Aster had come this far. She wasn't leaving without answers.

It was only once she got closer that she realized the person on the porch was Violet herself, hunched over, crying softly. Holding Aster's knife to her own throat. Violet had removed her dustkerchief, and the blade pressed against her favor.

"Violet?" Aster whispered, shocked. She pulled down her own dustkcherchief so Violet would recognize her, but she didn't move any closer. She was afraid of scaring Violet into hurting herself.

What in the name of the dead is going on here?

"I . . . I couldn't do it," Violet stammered. "If I were still on the Sweet Thistle, I could've done it, I think. But I feel too damn much now. I couldn't make myself."

"Violet, I have no idea— What are you talking about?" Aster asked, edging closer. Violet had lowered the knife, but her knuckles were still white from gripping it.

"I saw my father, Aster. With his real daughters. There were two of them, about half my age. They looked just like me—just like *him*—the same hair, the same eyes. He hugged them and kissed them and swept them up into his carriage. They're living the life *I* was supposed to have. I watched it all from right here." She used her knife to point at the low-lying shrubs that framed the house like frosting on a cake, the blade trembling in her hand.

It was as if Violet were speaking another language. Aster struggled to piece the words together to make sense of what she saw before her: Violet, with a knife pointed at herself. All the anger that had driven Aster to come here, all her sickening fear of betrayal—it drained away slowly, to be replaced by a feeling of unreality. She didn't know what she'd expected to find, but it certainly hadn't been this.

"I don't understand," Aster said finally.

Violet looked up at her. Her eyes were rimmed red, the blue of them bright with tears.

"I came here to kill him, Aster," she said, each word hard and clear as a diamond. "I came to Northrock to kill Tom Wells for what he did to my mother, and then to kill myself to end all the suffering he's caused me. But I couldn't do it. I wasn't strong enough. Even after everything we've survived since Green Creek, I wasn't strong enough."

Her voice cracked, and a fresh sob racked her body. She buried her face in her hands. Aster finally closed the distance between them, sitting next to her on the porch, as hidden behind the bush as she could manage. After a brief moment of uncertainty, she placed her hand around Violet's shoulder and let Violet lean into her.

"Violet, you're about the strongest person I know," Aster said—and she meant it. Violet had been many things, but she had never been weak. She had never let anyone see her fear back at the welcome house, and even since leaving, she had never let it stop her. "The fact that you didn't go through with this only proves it."

Violet shook her head. "I failed. I've wanted this for years, Aster. My whole life. Most nights it was the only thing that kept me going. I knew I had to live long enough to watch that man die. I never hated any brag as much as I hated him. And when I saw you and Clementine were getting ready to run away, I realized it might be my only chance to get to Northrock and make him pay." She let the knife drop from her hand in frustration. "And I failed. So what's the damn point? Tell me. Why am I even still drawing breath?"

"Because you *deserve* to be here," Aster said urgently. "Violet, hear me now: you don't need a *thing* from Tom Wells. Not his mansion, not his carriage, and *certainly* not his acceptance. And you don't need his remorse, either, hear? You can walk away without it and you'll still be whole."

"That's easy for you to say," Violet muttered.

"No, actually, it isn't." Aster set her mouth. "You know me, Violet. When have I ever turned my back on a fight? I came all this way just now to fight *you*." Violet raised her eyebrow and coughed out a laugh. "I thought you'd left us for dead back there."

"No, I'd never! I—I left the letter. My mother's letter," Violet said quickly. "I wasn't lying about Lady Ghost. She's real. My mother always said so. Didn't it explain everything?"

Aster furrowed her brow. "Not exactly." She pulled the letter out. "This *is* the letter you're talking about, right? Your mother's last words before she took her own life? I have to admit, it doesn't read like that kind of note at all. Maybe you left us the wrong one?"

"No, there was only the one . . ." Violet said, staring at the brittle paper as if it might bite her. "What . . . what did it say?"

Aster hesitated. "What do you *think* it says?"

"When . . . when my mother gave it to me, she said it would tell me how to find Lady Ghost when I was older, if we couldn't go together, like we planned." Violet paused. "See, she'd always told me that when we went to live with my father, he'd pay for us to get our favors removed, because he was rich. But she said the letter was just in case, and not to worry." She wiped at her eyes with the back of her hand before continuing. "But the day after she gave it to me . . . that's when she died. When she left me. Alone. And . . . and I . . . I don't know. It was another year before I even learned how to read, and by then I was too afraid to read it, to see what else my mother said. Knowing why she . . . killed herself."

Violet hesitated. "Can you read the letter out loud, Aster? I'm still . . . I can't."

There was an almost childlike fear in her voice that Aster had

322

never heard from her before. But there hadn't been anything in this letter for Violet to be afraid of, had there? Aster held it to the moonlight and began to read the words uncertainly, watching Violet from the corner of her eye.

Violet let out a wracked sob before Aster could even finish. "She was trying to *save* me?" she choked out. She snatched the letter from Aster, looked over it herself. "I've always thought she abandoned me, but here she says she wanted—she would never—"

At the sound of the pain in her voice, the last of the anger Aster had felt towards Violet melted away.

"Violet," she began, working through her own confusion, "are you *sure* your mother killed herself? If this letter is the only proof you have . . . it's just, it's clear she had other plans."

Violet took in a wet breath. "Mother Fleur was the one who told me how my mother died. I never had any reason to doubt her . . ." But doubt had crept into her words now. "Mother Fleur lies. I know that. I'd even help her tell her lies sometimes. But she never lied to *me*, Aster. She was different with me. She said she loved me the way my mother never did. She said my mother regretted I had ever been born, and that was part of why she killed herself—because my mother could never have him, and because she could never love me, not when I'd only remind her of the man who broke her heart. It's my fault she killed herself."

Ripping hell. Aster felt sick.

"Violet, listen," Aster said. "Whatever your mother did or didn't do, it was never your fault. *Never.* You have to know that."

Violet blinked at Aster and just shook her head.

"Mother Fleur must have just been saying those things to control you," Aster went on. "To keep you loyal."

"Then it worked," Violet said hollowly. "I didn't want to believe her at first. Of course I didn't. But then she told me—I remember her words exactly—she said, *If it ever seemed like your mother loved you, it was only because she was very good at faking things she didn't feel. As all Good Luck Girls must be.* As I have been, ever since."

Sudden understanding hit Aster like a gut punch. "So . . . all this time, you thought that the letter . . ."

"I don't know, Aster!" Violet said, sounding frustrated now. "I tried *not* to think about it at all. But, yes, deep down, I thought the letter would be some sort of confession of not loving me, of regretting that I was ever born. That she'd wanted to get it off her chest before crossing the Veil." She folded the letter carefully and tucked it away. "You have to understand, I never would have left this with you if I didn't honestly believe what my mother first told me, too: that it shows the way to find Lady Ghost. I wanted that much—*needed* that much—to be true. I just didn't realize her directions would be hidden in our bedtime story."

Violet picked the knife back up and handed it to Aster, whose mind spun.

Had Violet really been so certain that the letter would lead them to Lady Ghost, given the lies she'd believed about her mother? Aster studied her face. Violet looked utterly exhausted, unable even to find relief in this moment from all the pain that had come before it. And seeing her bloodshot eyes and tear-streaked cheeks, Aster couldn't bring herself to question

Violet any further—maybe she had truly believed in Lady Ghost deep down, or maybe she'd just convinced herself to believe, because it was the only way she could make it through her grief. Aster would never know for sure, and in that moment she realized it didn't even matter. Not anymore.

"Anyway," Violet said, heaving a sigh, "if you want to forget the whole thing and leave me here for the law, I won't blame you. I'm as bad as Mother Fleur, lying to you all. And it's not as if I have anything left to live for, anyway. My real mother's still dead, after all."

"Violet, no. You're coming with us. Mother Fleur is . . . she's wicked, for what she did to you. And the brags are wicked too, for all the pain they caused. But I'm damned if I'll accept that wickedness is what it takes to survive this life. We've only made it this far because we trusted each other and looked out for each other. So that's what we're going to keep doing, hear?" Aster swallowed, realizing the words were as much for herself as they were for Violet. "As much as they've taken from us, they still haven't taken that. We still have our humanity. And that's more than they can say."

Violet was quiet for a long time. "I don't know. You were right, you know, back in Clearwater. I was cruel to you and the other girls. I was willing to do whatever it took to make things better for me. Because I just—I always resented that this life had happened to *me*, right? This wasn't supposed to happen to *me*. The fairblood girl with the rich father." She shook her head, curling her lip in disgust. "But this life shouldn't have happened to *any* of us. And I made it even harder for you all. I would've been just as bad as Mother Fleur one day. I would've been worse." She looked at Aster squarely. "I know it's not enough, and I know it's too late, but I'm sorry, Aster. For all of it."

Aster's throat tightened with tears. She swallowed them back, surprised at the sudden rush of emotion. She hadn't realized how much she had needed this from Violet, how long she had been waiting for it—an honest apology, a promise to be better.

"Well, if you want to make it up to us, I can't think of any better way than getting us to Lady Ghost like you promised," Aster said with a forced chuckle. She looked up at Violet with a faint smile. "So are you coming back to camp with me, or do I have to drag you there?"

Violet laughed gratefully and Aster helped her up from the porch. They crept back towards the gate.

And then its doors flew open, and a tide of lawmen with rifles poured through.

CHAPTER TWENTY-ONE

Aster sat in the back of the lawmen's wagon, her hands cuffed but her head held high. Violet sat across from her, her face pale as ash in the gloom. They each had a lawman at their side with a rifle ready in his hands. Aster's heart thrashed against its cage, but her mind remained clear. Now that the worst had happened, she felt strangely calm. At least Clementine and the others were safe.

You'll get out of this. You'll see them again, Aster told herself.

The alternative was too terrible to think about. She had to shut it out, think only of how they would escape. She tried to communicate this to Violet through her eyes alone, but Violet was still too wretched to respond, her gaze glassy and unfocused and her hair hanging in her face. Her apathy frightened Aster more than anything else. It was as if she had already given up.

The wagon bumped over something on the road. Aster shifted her legs to steady herself and was immediately jabbed in the side by the lawman to her left. She clenched her jaw. There were no windows in the wagon, but Aster could tell they had been traveling a long time—longer than they ought to be to make it to the local jail, even in a city as big as Northrock.

So where the hell were they going?

Aster swallowed back the fear rising in her throat. At last they came to a stop. One of the lawmen got up and shoved the back doors of the wagon open, hopping to the ground. The others led Aster and Violet out.

Northrock was still visible in the distance, a warm glow against the dark, but they had traveled to the outskirts of town and now seemed to be on a lush estate. The grass was thick, the air sweet with the smell of a garden. Aster shivered as the wind slipped up her sleeves.

"This way," a lawman said, spinning her around roughly. Now Aster faced the manor itself, built of unyielding white stone that towered three stories high. Aster looked at Violet once again, to see if she had any idea where they might be, but Violet's eyes were still downcast. She seemed to be murmuring something to herself. A prayer?

The lawmen marched them forward.

Aster's boots crunched along the gravel walkway. She couldn't fight with her hands bound. If she ran she would surely be shot. But she grew more and more certain, with every step she took, that if she walked into that building she would never come out again.

At last they reached the front doors. A man stood waiting for them outside. He wore a perfectly tailored pinstriped vest, but his crisp white sleeves were rolled up to the elbows, as if he'd been working with his hands. Sky blue eyes peered out from beneath the brim of his bowler hat.

Aster barely held in a surge of bile. The last time she'd met those eyes, they'd been staring at her across a gorge.

"Mr. McClennon," the lawman behind Aster greeted him. "We have the girls. Where would you like them?"

Jerrod McClennon.

Aster's resolve cracked. There could be no good reason for his requesting them to come to his private estate instead of taking them to jail. And it was surely against the law, but who was going to stop him? She watched helplessly as shine exchanged hands between McClennon and the lawman. Violet finally locked eyes with Aster, as if she, too, was beginning to realize how desperate the situation had become.

McClennon led the group along a stone path around the massive house, to a cellar entrance guarded by two raveners emanating dread. The raveners leaned down and opened up the doors to reveal a yawning passage of stairs.

We'll meet again, I guarantee it.

And when it's your time, you'll know.

Aster knew.

She began to struggle in earnest, trying to pull her arms out of the lawman's grip, her heart rabbiting in her chest. It didn't matter if it was futile. She would rather die here, fighting, than trapped down in that cellar.

"None of that now," McClennon chided, and immediately one of the raveners turned his gaze to her and plunged a dagger of fear into her chest. It spread like frost, leaving her numb and shaking. "You'll conduct yourselves like ladies during your stay here."

Aster gritted her teeth against the pain beating in her skull and the rush of panic in her blood. She hardly even felt it when the lawman removed her handcuffs. He shoved her forward, and one of the raveners grabbed her by the shoulder, leading her down the stone stairs after McClennon. The other ravener followed with Violet, who stumbled in the dark. The raveners could see perfectly, of course, but McClennon used a lantern. Aster could just make out the rooms ahead by its light.

Prison cells.

McClennon set the lantern down on a table and fetched a ring of keys from a hook on the wall. Aster wet her lips, searching desperately for any escape. She began to struggle again in the ravener's grasp, but he kicked her swiftly in the back of the leg, buckling her knee.

"You'll be wondering why I've had you brought here, no doubt," McClennon said conversationally as he searched for the right key. The raveners mounted their pressure against her mind. "It's because you girls are special—not the first ones to escape a welcome house, of course, but certainly the first ones to kill family of mine in the process. So it seemed only fitting that I handle your case personally. Mr. Mason down at the lawmaster's office was happy to oblige."

"What is this place?" Violet asked, her voice flat. It was the first time she'd spoken since they'd been captured.

McClennon found the key he was looking for and took his time opening the padlock to the nearest cell. "I have several raveners in my employ guarding the estate. I allow them to practice their craft down here on volunteers. It's fascinating work they do."

Aster's stomach churned. "Volunteers?"

"Dustbloods will do just about anything if you offer to pay

off their debts. Everyone has a price—but you know that, of course." He nodded his head towards the cell. "In you go now. We've got a long day ahead of us tomorrow."

Aster and Violet filed in, too weakened to resist, and McClennon turned the lock with a click. He left without so much as a second glance, taking the lantern with him—but the raveners stayed, and Aster could sense them watching her still. The cellar doors slammed shut.

Aster and Violet found each other in the dark and slid down to sit on the hard-packed dirt. At first neither of them dared speak, not with the raveners listening, but it was a comfort just to hear Violet's steady breathing.

"How are you feeling?" Aster finally whispered.

Violet let out a long sigh. "It's been a hell of a night, that's for damn sure." Aster sensed Violet turning to face her. "Thank you, though, for . . . earlier . . ." Whether she was being vague for the raveners' sake, or for her own, Aster wasn't sure.

"Of course," Aster said. She reached for her hand and gave it a squeeze. It was a promise: *We'll get out of this.*

Violet squeezed her hand back as if to say, *That's a sack of bullshit, but thank you for it anyway.*

They fell silent again.

Thank the dead Clementine and the rest of them aren't here, Aster thought again. It was her only consolation, and she clung to it. Zee had promised to stick with them. Even if they couldn't find Lady Ghost, maybe he'd take them back to the Scorpions.

Even now, after everything, it wasn't yet too late for them.

Aster tried to stay awake, but her exhaustion was catching up with her. It would be nearly morning by now. She bit her thumb, hoping the pain would be enough to keep her conscious. The dread was deepening in her belly, and it wasn't just from the raveners—it was from the idea of being left alone, in the dark, at the mercy of others. Falling asleep would only leave her even more vulnerable.

But it wasn't long before the cold seeped into her skin, and the dark ate away at her mind, and she gave into the weariness that had settled over her.

When Aster woke, she had no idea how much time had passed. But McClennon was back, his lantern light shining in their faces.

And he wasn't alone.

"Thought you all could use some company," he said, and he swung his lantern light to reveal who was behind him.

Tansy, Mallow . . . and Clem.

The last of Aster's courage left her then. She might have endured anything as long as she'd known Clementine had escaped. But now—

McClennon opened the cell and forced the others in with Aster and Violet. Then he relocked it.

"I told you girls we'd meet again. Now I've got the whole bouquet, don't I?" he said, chuckling to himself. "You know the best thing about Arketta? A person gets just as much or as little as they deserve in this country. The days of the Empire and its tyrant kings are no more. Instead the working man rules himself, and if he pays his dues, he can live like a king himself. Glory to the Reckoning, indeed." McClennon paced back and forth as he spoke, gesticulating as if addressing a formal audience. "You all are young, you take that kind of opportunity for granted. You resented the welcome house when others might have died to take your place. You wanted freedom without putting in the work for it first. And worst of all, you disrespected the very laws that keep our society whole. You *killed* an honest man. I understand it's in your blood to behave criminally—the science says you can't help yourselves—but still . . ."

None of them moved or spoke as McClennon trailed off. The two raveners stood on either side of him, running a low current of fear through Aster's blood. It was nothing to the anger rising inside her. She curled her lip, riling at McClennon's words. His lies. He was taking his time getting to the point, and she dreaded to think what punishment he'd see fit to dole out at the end of this little speech.

He crossed his meaty arms. "Fortunately for you girls, I'm a merciful man. I believe in second chances, in redemption. Our country was founded on those ideals, and it's those ideals I will hold up as your governor. I understand that the one who murdered my nephew is the only real criminal here. The rest of you are just followers, weak-minded and spineless, as your people tend to be."

He paced again. Once. Twice. Then continued, "Clearly, the circumstances point to Clementine, the girl lucky enough to have been selected by Baxter. But I would hate to exact punishment without knowing beyond a doubt. What kind of governor would be so disrespectful of our citizens' rights? So, as soon as you tell me which one of you killed Baxter—Clementine or not—I promise that the rest of you will be safely returned to Green Creek to continue your work."

"You should let all of us go," Aster said, before anyone else could speak, before Clementine could out herself. She didn't believe for a moment that McClennon's promise was genuine, but if there was any chance they could all get out of this alive, she had to take it.

But McClennon just speared her with a distasteful look. "It was murder, as determined by the law, and that law is clear on how murderers must be dealt with. I expect the execution will be a rather big show. The public will demand as much. But there's no reason for the rest of you to sacrifice yourselves for her. So, who was it?" He looked at each of them in turn. They all froze, exchanging glances. Aster saw fear in each of their eyes, but determination, too. None of them was going tell.

Then Clementine shifted slightly. Aster grabbed her hand.

"Fine," McClennon said finally. "I'll ask again tomorrow." Aster let out a tense breath as he began to walk away, but then he stopped and turned around.

"Oh, and like I told you—a person gets just as much or as little as they deserve here. So if you want to eat, you'll have to work for it. I'm sure these two will be happy to help you with that." He nodded at the raveners, his smile twitching upwards once again, and left up the stairs.

As soon as the cellar door closed behind McClennon, Aster drew Clementine into a hug.

"How the hell did they find you all?" Aster asked, shaking with equal parts anger and fear. The raveners were still with them, eyeing them silently. McClennon had left the lantern this time—not as a kindness, certainly, but so the girls could see well enough to go about their "work." Aster shrank from the slow crawl of their gaze.

"We got worried about you," Mallow answered. She clutched at her side, wincing. "We went into the city to try to find you. But it was swarming with lawmen."

"And Zee?" Violet asked, anticipating Aster's next question.

Clementine cut a glance at the raveners. "He . . . went off on his own. We asked him to. There were places he could look that we couldn't, him being a man."

"I'm sure McClennon would have brought Zee here if he had him," Tansy murmured. "So I think there's every reason to believe he hasn't been caught."

"And every reason to believe he has no idea where we are," Mallow added darkly.

Aster's heart sank even further. There could be no counting on him to help them out of this, then. Not that she suspected he could have, anyway. McClennon had said he had several raveners guarding the property, probably not even including the two he'd stationed down here with them.

"I've been thinking, and I . . . I want to volunteer to take the blame for this," Clementine said carefully. She couldn't openly admit anything with the raveners listening to their words and reading their emotions, but, if the welcome house had taught them anything, it was how to talk around a ravener.

"No," Aster said.

"None of us can take all the blame," Tansy agreed.

"I can," Violet mumbled, but Aster cut her off with a look.

"*No*," she said again. "You're with us now, Violet. All the way." She swept her gaze around to the others. "None of us

335

are taking the blame. We'll figure something else out."

But Aster's words rang hollow in her own ears, and probably to the others, as well. If it came down to it, she would take the blame herself. She had known that since the moment she saw Baxter's body on Clementine's bed.

It won't come to that, she told herself. They'd always found a way. The slag-glass lamp. The Sweet Thistle. The bank. The train.

But they were out of options now.

"Maybe Zee *will* find us," Clementine said softly.

Aster and Violet locked eyes. They couldn't speak freely, but they didn't need to in order to communicate their understanding of the bleak truth.

They were on their own.

CHAPTER TWENTY-TWO

Morning arrived, though they couldn't tell it from their underground cell. Their only sign that the sun had risen was the arrival of a houseboy carrying a pot of hot cereal. He kept his dark eyes on the floor.

"You'll remember what Mr. McClennon told you," one of the raveners said to them. He was the younger of the two. "This isn't a free ride here. If you want this food, you'll have to provide payment."

"Go dust yourself," Mallow said. Aster grinned faintly.

His eyes flashed with malevolence. "Have it your way," he shot back, and a wave of misery washed over them. Aster's chest tightened. Her throat grew thick with tears. "We'll be back come nightfall," he said. "Hopefully you'll have seen reason by then."

He passed a pitcher of water to them through the bars, but he left the food just out of reach, the smell of it making Aster's stomach cramp. The raveners and the houseboy left without another word. Aster dug the heel of her good hand into her eyes, wiping away the tears. She could barely even feel any relief that they'd been left alone.

"Looks like we'll only be guarded overnight," Tansy said quietly. "Maybe the raveners have more important work to do."

"Thank the dead," Mallow muttered. Her face was pale.

Aster didn't mention the thought that occurred to her: that McClennon had probably sent his raveners after Zee, and that he would not have left them alone down here if he weren't certain they couldn't escape.

But at least they could talk freely now.

"Everyone doing all right?" Aster asked.

They all murmured assent, though they looked about as lively as the bag of kittens Clementine had once saved from drowning back at home, before the welcome house.

"So," Clem said, looking between Aster and Violet. "We never heard the whole story. Where did you disappear to last night, Violet?"

Aster shifted on the hard floor, quiet. This wasn't her story to tell. After a moment, Violet swallowed and told it herself, her voice growing stronger as she spoke. She left nothing out—not her plan to kill her father and then herself, not the lies she'd believed about her mother, not the regret she felt for the way her own resentment had made her treat the other girls. Clementine, Tansy, and Mallow listened without speaking, their faces shifting from shock to sympathy to uncertainty. Maybe they weren't ready to accept Violet's apology for the way she'd treated them in the past—but maybe, given the circumstances, they felt like they had to.

Then, finally, Tansy broke the silence.

"Thanks for telling us, Violet," she said. "I . . . I'm sorry for everything that happened to you and your mother. What Mother Fleur did to you—"

"She hurt all of us," Violet said flatly. "I'm the only one who helped her."

"You're not that person anymore, though," Clementine countered.

"Yeah, Violet, we never could have made it this far without you," Mallow said. "I'm glad you're here. I mean, not here, in this cell, but, you know . . ."

Aster and the others nodded in agreement.

"And another thing, Violet," Aster said. "Maybe now you can tell us your mother's bedtime story. The one that's supposed to tell us how to find Lady Ghost."

"What for?" Violet asked, her voice hollow.

"So we can figure out where she is," Aster said, stating the obvious.

Aster had no idea how they would ever get the chance to look for Lady Ghost again, but that was beside the point. They needed to keep believing they could.

Violet gave her an almost imperceptible nod, as if she understood what Aster wanted from her. "Well, the story always began the same way," she said. "*Once there was a seraphant who lived in a castle made of theomite, set amongst ten claws.* After that it changed every time. A different orphan girl would be in trouble—she'd have fallen down a well, or gotten lost in the woods, or been kidnapped by a bandit, or something. She'd call out the seraphant's name, and the seraphant would appear, save her, and offer her the chance to come live in the castle with her. *And there they were safe as the stars in the sky,* that's what my mother always told me."

"The seraphant must be Lady Ghost," Aster began, voicing the thought she'd had when she first read the letter in the barn. "Desperate girls seek her out to save them."

"That makes sense," Clementine agreed, fiddling with her bracelet. "But there're no castles made of theomite in Arketta, of course, so what could that mean?"

"And the ten claws," Mallow added. "What're those supposed to represent?"

Violet shrugged. "My mother never explained any of those things, and I was too little to question them. I just loved the idea of living in a glittering castle with a bunch of other lost girls and a kindly ghost. I didn't know it was *Lady* Ghost."

Aster stood up and began to walk around the small cell. Lady Ghost lived somewhere where there was a lot of theomite. That much was clear.

"A mine, maybe?" Mallow said. "Do you think she lives in a mine, like the Scorpions?"

"You could be right!" Clementine said.

"That's what I'm thinking," Aster agreed. "But if it *is* right, how will we know where to find it?" *As if we'll ever have the chance.* Aster tried to ignore the nagging voice in her ears.

"That must be where the ten claws come in," Tansy said. "You don't know any other details, Violet?"

Violet shook her head. "Of course, I was young. Maybe I just don't remember."

"Well, we'll figure it out," Clementine said confidently. No one replied, as if they all wanted to let themselves enjoy the fantasy a little longer.

"Where are you all going to go once you get your favor removed?" Tansy asked.

"I'm building a nice cabin in these north Arkettan woods somewhere," Mallow said immediately. "The Scab can go straight to hell for all I care. You're staying with me, right, Tanz? We can have a nice quiet life."

"So long as I can take up medicine in some way," Tansy said. "I never realized how much I still have to learn until we left the welcome house."

"It's the city for me," Clementine said. "A place like Northrock, with that many people . . . I could just . . . disappear." She shifted uncomfortably. "And I'd bring Zee with me, of course."

Aster said nothing. The idea of Clementine wanting to bind her life to Zee's would have upset her beyond words once, but now she saw him as her own brother. She would want him to be there for Clementine.

"What about you, Aster?" Tansy asked.

"I'd go with Clem," Aster said quietly. A dull sense of loneliness had crept into her chest. Mallow had Tansy, and Clementine had Zee . . . back at Annagold's Falls, she had told Violet that she couldn't imagine herself getting that close to anyone, and that was still true. But she hoped it would not be true forever, if they got out of here. The welcome house had already taken so much from her.

But she would always have family in Clem, at least. And, perhaps . . .

"I might—I might try to join up with the Scorpions," Aster said, thinking about what her sister had said—that it wasn't too late for her to live her own life. "They could do a lot of good for welcome house recruits, and rip them if they think we're not worth the help. I'll teach those fools otherwise. Someone needs to look out for girls like us."

"Like the seraphant in the story?" Violet asked, raising an eyebrow.

Aster laughed self-consciously. "Maybe. I mean, we did help Adeline. Maybe she'll have a better shot at a happy life now. I certainly hope so, at least." Aster's neck burned, and she glanced back at Violet, eager to get the attention off herself. "What about you, Violet? Your favor's gone—what's the first thing you're doing?"

Violet looked at Aster levelly. And to her surprise, Violet smiled.

"As long as you all will have me, I'll be happy just to stick with you."

The raveners returned that night. Aster's stomach growled at the scent of the food the houseboy had brought this time— baked sweet potatoes swimming in butter.

"Well, ladies, what'll it be?" the younger ravener taunted. "Have you come to your senses?" The older of the two raveners never said so much as a word, but somehow he frightened Aster even more. His were the eyes of the dead.

"We're not hungry," Aster said flatly.

"Are you ready to confess to your crimes?" the older one asked, his voice as soft as shifting sand.

"That'll have to be a no as well."

"I'm sorry to hear that," the young ravener said, sucking his teeth. He snapped his fingers at the houseboy, who jumped skittishly. "Go on and let Mr. McClennon know there'll no confession tonight." He turned back to the girls. "We'll be here all night if you change your mind. You can end this whenever you want."

Aster and the others settled onto the cold, hard floor to try to sleep, but every time Aster found herself nodding off, the raveners would give her a prod in the mind, a quick stab of panic. She jolted awake every time, shaking and nauseated. She refused to give them the satisfaction of seeing her upset, but it grew harder and harder to keep her composure as the night wore on. She held back curses and wordless screams, fought the urge to make a rush for the bars of the cage, determined to remain brave for the others.

Worst of all, without sleep, there was no relief from the hunger that clawed at her belly.

By the time morning came and the houseboy returned, Aster had hardly slept—and neither, from the looks of it, had anyone else.

The houseboy kept his eyes lowered, as always, as the raveners asked the girls if they were ready to give up and trade their services for food. There were no sharp replies this time, only hollow, hateful silence.

"Have it your way," the young ravener said, shrugging. With that, the girls were left alone, like the previous morning. The minute the cellar door shut, the air loosened.

"By the Veil. I feel sick," Clementine murmured.

"We should try to sleep while they're gone," Tansy said. Her hair had fallen out of her braid, and her eyes were bloodshot.

Aster said nothing. She had been hungry like this before. They all had, probably, except for Violet. She knew from experience she could go another day without food if she had to. But with the raveners denying them sleep, too . . .

"Anyone who wants to eat should eat," she said finally. "We're giving McClennon what he wants if any of us die."

"We're also giving him what he wants if we offer ourselves up to those dead-eyed bastards," Mallow said. "I didn't come all this way give in now."

Aster and Violet exchanged glances. The others had never been with a brag before. Their resistance was understandable. But Aster . . . she'd already crossed that line to survive, and if there was a chance she could save them now, she knew she'd do it again. Still, the thought made her ill in a way none of the raveners' magic had managed to. Mallow was right. They had not come all this way for that.

"Anyway, Tansy's right," Aster said. "We ought to sleep now. The dead know we won't get any tonight."

But even without the raveners tormenting her, Aster struggled. Memories from the welcome house rose to the surface of her mind, buried horrors that the raveners had churned up—and with those memories came all the sorrow and shame Aster kept hidden in the deepest reaches of her heart. It swelled in her chest, threatening to suffocate her, doubling the fear the raveners had already forced on her.

She drifted in and out of consciousness, her dreams as frightening as reality.

It seemed an eternity before the raveners returned with supper. By then Aster had no appetite, even as the smell of food made her stomach wrench. There was a wild animal inside her gut, slowly devouring her.

"Confess," the younger ravener ordered, all humor gone now. Perhaps McClennon had put pressure on him to get results.

But the girls remained silent.

They refused the food as well, and the houseboy left it on the ground just outside their reach. The food from the day before had begun to turn, and flies swarmed to it, their whining driving Aster mad. The pitcher of water had been refilled, but quenching their thirst only made Aster's hunger that much sharper.

That night the raveners toyed with them once again—but this time, they gave them visions. This was the older ravener's specialty, apparently, a rare gift. He sent brown-black roaches long as a finger crawling up Aster's legs, gave her festering wounds gleaming with maggots, sliced along the veins in her arms and made her watch the blood run free.

Aster screamed. All of them screamed. She knew none of it was real, but she felt the skittering of the roaches' legs, smelled the rot of her own flesh, swam with dizziness as if her lifeblood were truly draining free. The young ravener grinned to see they'd finally broken through her guard, but the older ravener never said a word, never moved, sat still as stone as he tortured them.

Morning came.

"Confess," the younger ravener ordered.

Aster shook her head. She barely had the strength to move at all. Last night's ravening had been even worse than the torture that she, like all girls, had been subjected to in order to break her spirit when she first arrived at the welcome house.

He jerked his chin towards the houseboy, eyes to the ground

as he held a steaming platter of eggs and biscuits. "Eat," he ordered again.

Aster looked to the others. Tansy sobbed quietly. Mallow had the stunned look of a rabbit in the shadow of a hawk. Clementine's eyes were closed as she hugged her knees to her chest. Violet's expression was one of grim concentration. But they all shook their heads as Aster met their eyes.

He curled his lip. He racked them all with sorrow as his parting word, then turned to leave with the others.

"What did he make you see?" Aster asked.

"Snakes," Clementine said immediately. When she opened her eyes, they glistened with tears. "Rattletails. I could feel the poison in my veins. How did he know? Can he . . . can they read our minds?"

"No, they just have a good instinct for what frightens us," Violet murmured.

"My brother was dead," Mallow said. Her voice was listless. "He looked like he'd been beaten to death. His face—" She turned to Violet. "It wasn't real, was it? Do they know something I don't? About Koda—"

"No, none of it's real," Aster said quickly. "Like Violet said, they just know how to mess with us."

"Hell if I'm going to be able to sleep after that," Mallow said.

But they tried. When evening fell and the raveners returned, Aster reminded the others that they would need their strength for the night ahead, nearly begging them to let her at least offer herself up in return for a meal. But they were resolute.

"I promise we'll make it out of this," Aster said to them as the houseboy left. "I promise. Stay strong."

"You don't even believe your own words," he sneered.

She glared at him, steeling herself.

But in her heart, she knew he was right.

Three more nights and days passed without food or proper sleep. The ravenings grew more gruesome every night. Aster was treated to visions of Clementine rotting away, to the deepest loneliness and the keenest fear, to the sensations of drowning and of burning alive and of being crushed to death. By their sixth day in McClennon's custody, she was barely conscious. Her hunger had grown so fierce she'd retched. Her tongue felt thick and heavy in her throat. Exhaustion made specters dance in the corners of her vision. She couldn't tell where the raveners' work ended and her own suffering began.

They were all in bad shape, but Clementine seemed to be the worst. Aster hated McClennon for doing this to her, and she hated even more that she was so completely helpless. She wiped the vomit away from Clementine's chin with her own shirt sleeve, wishing there were anything more she could do.

"Aster," Clem said as the houseboy left with their breakfast, her voice thin with exhaustion, "Aster, it's no good. I have to tell them."

"*No*," Aster said, though, in truth, she'd been considering turning herself in, too. They couldn't last much longer. "McClennon won't let us die. He can't. Then he never gets the satisfaction of having broken us. And he never gets his answer. He'll have to stop this eventually."

"Or he'll think of something worse," Violet murmured.

Aster couldn't even bring herself to be angry. She knew Violet was right. But she could hardly say so.

"We'll get out of this—" she began.

"I swear to the dead, Aster, if you say that one more time," Mallow growled, cutting her off. Her lips were cracked, her eyes bloodshot.

But Aster refused to give in. "We *will*. Clementine, look at me," she said, because her sister had begun to cry. "Remember what I told you on your Lucky Night? Before all of this? I gave you that rattletail bracelet and told you that you could survive anything. You'll survive this, too, Clem, I promise. I'll get you out of here."

Clementine looked at the bracelet, running her finger along the intricate diamondback pattern. She still seemed to be holding back tears, but then, suddenly, something in her expression flickered. She slowly unhooked the hairpin that held the bracelet together.

A smile spread across her face like wings spreading to take flight.

"All right," she said, struggling to keep her voice steady. "Which one of you Luckers knows how to pick a lock?"

Aster carefully tore the hairpin free from the bracelet. It was made of flexible metal, and with a bit of effort, she was able to break it in two—one piece to provide leverage like the turning of a key, and the other to coax the tumblers into place. A brag had once told her how he'd picked the lock to his former lover's house. Aster remembered details.

But she'd never done it before herself.

"Can you even see what you're doing?" Clementine asked.

"Well enough," Aster muttered. She knelt next to the heavy padlock and stuck the makeshift lockpicks in. It was awkward positioning, her head craned so she could see the keyhole. Everyone grew suddenly silent as she worked, listening to the scratch of metal on metal.

Nothing.

Aster took a steadying breath. "Let me try again," she said, keeping her voice light. "We don't know which way the key turns. It might need to go the other way."

She started over, the picks slipping in her sweaty fingers.

"How long until the raveners come back?" Violet asked tensely.

It was impossible to tell what time it was. They might walk in any minute. And even if they didn't, Aster still had no idea how they would escape the estate without being caught.

One thing at a time.

"I think it's starting to give," Aster said suddenly, excitement rushing through her blood.

The lock clicked, fell free.

"*Hell* yes. *Hell* yes," Mallow said.

Aster turned and grinned at the others. "By the Veil, we did it—"

The cellar doors swung open, letting in a cascade of fading sunlight.

Heart in her throat, Aster hurried to put the lock back, her hands shaking. She finished. Looked up.

And realized it was too late.

The houseboy.

He held a pitcher of water and was staring at her with his wide brown eyes. Aster tensed, meeting his stare. If he turned to run back to McClennon and rat on them, there was no way they'd be able to pick the lock again in time to stop him.

She wet her lips, holding her hands up.

"You have to hurry," the boy said. His voice was clear and firm. "McClennon's men just left the property. They think they found the rangeman south of here. They don't know when they'll be back."

Clementine made a desperate sound. Aster struggled to understand.

"You're saying the raveners are gone?" she asked, still tense.

"I'll leave the cellar doors unlocked," he answered. He slid the pitcher of water through the bars and left before they had time to question him further. The doors slammed shut.

Aster looked at the others and saw her own shock written across their faces.

"Do you think he's right?" Tansy asked. "There're no raveners on guard right now?"

"He also said Zee is somewhere nearby," Clementine said. "We have to find him before the raveners do."

"No, we have to get as far away from this place as possible," Violet said gently. "Zee can take care of himself. You know he can."

"We don't even know this houseboy is telling the truth," Aster pointed out.

"He saw us messing with the lock," Tansy countered. "And rather than threatening to punish us, he told us to make a run for it now because this might be our only chance."

"Yeah, but *he could have been lying*," Aster repeated. "This

350

could all be a trap." She'd been suspecting McClennon might try something else soon—maybe this was it. Let them think they'd found their freedom, then find them all guilty of the crime of attempted escape. Aster knew enough to question such a sudden turn of good fortune.

Clementine was already trying to pick the lock open again. Mallow glanced at Aster.

"Do you really think we can't trust him?" she asked.

Aster hesitated. The houseboy hadn't been like the raveners. She thought about how he hadn't laughed at their suffering or tried to convince them to confess. How he'd always averted his eyes when the raveners pressured them into giving up their bodies. How he had likely suffered at McClennon's hands, too, how he was perhaps a prisoner in his own right.

But, more than that, Aster found herself thinking of Violet, of Zee, of Sam and Eli. People Aster had trusted despite her fears, people who had rewarded that trust. There were times when refusing to give folks a chance could be more dangerous than putting your faith in them. Times when you couldn't do it alone. Times when you needed help.

And Aster sensed, even if it frightened her, that this was one of those times.

"No," Aster said finally, "I think we can trust him." She leveled her eyes at Clementine. "And I think he's right. We have to hurry."

Just as the houseboy had promised, he'd left the cellar doors unlocked. Aster winced at the groan they let out when she pushed them open, but then the fresh air hit her, cool and clear as a creek on a summer day. By now it was dark outside, cold stars scattered across the sky. Aster shivered as wind blew down the stairwell, turning to look back at the others crowded on the steps behind her.

"On the count of three," she whispered, hoping they didn't hear the fear in her voice. "One—two—"

They ran.

Aster allowed herself a brief moment of relief as they stole away into the shadows, running alongside the house. There were no raveners in sight. Still, they had to assume one or two had been left to guard the property, and they could be anywhere.

"Which way, Aster?" Tansy whispered. They crouched low as they ran over the thick carpet of grass underfoot, going wide around the pools of light spilling out of the manor house's windows. The smell of earth was heavy in Aster's nose.

"We have to find Zee," Clementine answered for her.

"And we will, but first we have to get well clear of this place," Aster said. "The boy said the raveners were after Zee right now—how are we supposed to fight them all?"

"We can't just leave him!"

"*Quiet*," Aster pleaded. "We'll find somewhere to lie low and figure out what's going on. We can get help and come back for him. Or maybe he's staying one step ahead of them, and we can find some way to catch up with him."

"But—"

"We can't run *towards* the raveners, Clem," Mallow interrupted. "Not without our weapons or our horses or— Listen, if anyone can outfox those bastards, it's Zee. Have a little faith in him."

Clementine let it go, though Aster could tell she was still

worried. Aster was worried too—not just for Zee, but for themselves. They were in no shape to run for long. Adrenaline was keeping her going for now, but already her head was spinning and her limbs shaking from nearly a week of food and sleep deprivation.

Thump. Aster turned at the soft noise. Violet lay on the ground.

"*Violet!*" Aster cried in harsh whisper. They ran back to her. She was crumpled on the grass, her face death-pale and her eyes half-lidded and unseeing. Aster slapped her cheek gently. Violet moaned but didn't come around. "Violet! Help her," Aster said desperately, wheeling around to Tansy.

"I—I don't know—if I can," she stammered. "Stopping the Sweet Thistle, then going so long without food—I think it was too much for her body to handle."

"Come on, then," Aster said, "grab her legs."

Aster's heart pounded painfully, and even with each of them on one of Violet's limbs, they barely had the strength to lift her. She felt dangerously close to fainting herself. Blackness ate at the corners of her vision as she struggled to hang on to Violet's arm. And as soon as they managed to make it a few steps, Violet began retching.

"Quick, set her down, get her on her side!" Tansy ordered. "She'll choke."

Gunshots in the distance.

The raveners were coming.

Oh, by the dead—

"Aster." Violet coughed weakly. She'd woken up. "Leave me here."

353

"Hell no—"

"I can't keep up. I—" She shuddered and retched again, dry heaves. "I don't want you to die. Just go—"

"Shut up, Violet, we're not going anywhere without you," Mallow said angrily. She tried to pick Violet up again, but her arms trembled violently.

"I see their trail!" a man's voice cried.

Aster looked at Clementine, panic coursing through her veins. Her sister would die if they didn't leave right now.

They all would.

"For once . . . in your damn life . . . just do as—as you're told," Violet begged.

Aster met her eyes, shaking her head.

No. They'll kill her. No—

Violet's eyelids fluttered again. Her stare was unfocused.

"Aster—" Tansy whispered.

"We're leaving." Aster's voice sounded faraway in her own ears. She squeezed Violet's hand and stood back up before she could change her mind. "Follow me."

No one spoke as they ran away. And though her throat tightened with tears that refused to spill, Aster did not look back.

CHAPTER TWENTY-THREE

There was no way they'd be able to outrun their pursuers long in the shape they were in. Aster couldn't even feel relief when they crossed over from the terrifying openness of the grass to the relative shelter of the woods. She had no idea where they were going, only that they had to get away from McClennon.

They all slowed to a walk as they made their way through the snarl of underbrush, climbing over roots and ducking under branches. They had no lantern to light their way, and the light of the stars was only just bright enough to see by. None of them spoke, the silence heavy as a tombstone.

You're with us now, Violet. All the way. Aster's own words echoed in her ears.

McClennon had made a liar of her.

A sudden rustle came from up ahead. Aster froze, signaling for the others to do the same. A silhouette of a man appeared between the trees, holding a rifle.

He lowered it slowly. His grin flashed in the dark. "And here I was thinking I'd have to break into the house."

"Zee," Clementine exhaled, her voice shaking. She ran forward and he swept her in a hug—and then, clearly to her surprise, he drew her into a kiss, too. He laughed self-consciously as she pulled away.

"I—I thought I lost you," he said. "What's wrong?"

"Violet," Clementine said miserably. "She—"

"She stayed behind," Aster cut her off. They didn't have time to celebrate finding Zee, and they didn't have time to despair over leaving Violet behind. If they didn't escape now, her sacrifice would have been for nothing. "We have to keep going."

Someone had to make the hard decisions.

"Shit," Zee murmured. But he didn't hesitate, motioning for them to follow him deeper into the woods.

"We heard the raveners were after you," Tansy said. She sounded short of breath. They all did. Then again, it was near a miracle that they were standing at all.

"They were—they are," Zee replied. "After I realized you all had been taken by McClennon, I tracked you to the estate. I kept trying to find a way past the raveners guarding the property, but they were too vigilant, and I always had to retreat before I had a chance to sneak through. One of them finally spotted me tonight, and a minute later they were all after me. I've managed to stay ahead of them, but I had no idea where to go—until I heard you all stumbling through the woods just now."

"Do you have food?" Mallow asked.

"Food?"

"McClennon starved us," Clementine explained.

"Ripping bastard," Zee said blackly. "There's an old abandoned holy house where I've been sheltering. Got a bit of food left over. I'll take us there now."

They told him the story of their captivity as they hiked

356

through the forest as fast as they could. Aster felt like a sleepwalker moving through a nightmare. She was terrified that the raveners would catch up to them, especially since they were on horseback while she and the others were on foot. But Zee remained focused, guiding them through the dark and hiding their trail as they went.

"Here we are," Zee said finally, pointing out the holy house. It was where the help who worked the McClennon estate had once worshipped, Aster suspected. There were some rundown houses as well. She wondered where the servants lived now. Something about the empty buildings boded ill.

But anything was better than McClennon's basement.

"We can only stop for a moment," Zee warned as Tansy collapsed onto one of the benches. "The raveners will find us if we stay the night here." He ducked behind the pulpit and retrieved a knapsack and a canteen. Passed them around. Inside the knapsack were salt pork and dried bread. Aster had never been so happy to see the tasteless food in her life.

"We should go to straight to Lady Ghost from here," Clementine said around a mouthful. "Violet told us how to find her."

"Really?" Zee asked.

"Well, sort of," Aster said, forcing away the hurt in her heart. "She gave us a clue. What do you know about a place called the Ten Claws? We think Lady Ghost might be hiding out in an abandoned theomite mine there."

It suddenly seemed foolish to hope there was anything to this—that the Ten Claws existed, that Lady Ghost lived there, that Violet's mother had known these things and that they had interpreted her story correctly. It suddenly seemed like these were the foolish hopes of people who desperately needed something to cling to. And maybe they had been all along.

But then, to Aster's surprise, Zee nodded slowly.

"The Ten Claws?" he echoed. "I don't know that name. But there *are* two hills north of here that the locals say look like a pair of cat's paws, and a mine in the valley between them. I'd say it's worth a look, at least."

"Is it close?" Aster asked. She held her breath. They might have another month-long journey ahead of them, for all she knew. One they'd be hard-pressed to survive.

But then Zee's grin flickered back to life. "We can be there by the day after tomorrow."

Aster knew they'd reached the right place the moment she saw the two hills in the distance. They weren't the dusky red rock hills of the Scab, but the deep green of the forests of northern Arketta, the gray rock spiking up into ten jagged peaks. They stood stark against the blue sky.

Aster's hope soared as high as the hills themselves, a sudden lightness in her chest that felt like falling up. She tried to quell it. The past two days had been endless, creeping through the woods, eating whatever food they could find, and sleeping rough without the comfort of their blankets or bedrolls. Aster still hadn't recovered fully from her captivity—or from the shock of losing Violet. None of them had, it seemed. She felt brittle, unsure of herself, her mind like a broken mirror that had not quite been pieced back together fully, her body like a scarecrow rattling in the wind. They had come so far, endured so much, that she was not sure how she would find the strength to keep going if it turned out Lady Ghost was not here. The whole story might be just that—a story. Or worse, a trap, created to lure gullible fools to the hands of the law.

Aster's fear was a familiar old friend at this point. It only wanted the best for her. But she'd learned, since leaving Green Creek, that it wasn't always right. It had taken courage to run away from the welcome house, and it would take courage now to finish the job.

"Are we sure it's the right place?" Clementine asked. Her fingers had traveled to her favor, tracing the ink there. Like Aster, she seemed afraid to hope too much.

But Aster nodded. "Looks like a pair of cat's paws to me. As much as any hills could, at least. Have you ever been here, Zee?"

"No, but I've met other rangemen who have," Zee said. "They say it's hell in winter in the valley. The town here dried up a long time ago."

There was no reason not to keep going, but they all stood silently at the edge of the trees, hesitating, gripped by the same fear.

Then Aster took a step forward.

The air was cool and crisp up here, not as bitter as the cold that descended on the Scab after sundown, but chilly enough that Aster's skin prickled beneath her shirtsleeves as they left the shelter of the trees and made their way to the abandoned town below. Since it was still daytime, there wasn't any sign of the remnants that had no doubt claimed the town for themselves. Aster didn't care to imagine the place at night. She still couldn't help but feel like she was being watched as she walked silently through the maze of empty buildings.

Finally Zee led them to the mouth of the mineshaft. There were no symbols here carved into the timber to mark it as any place special. He paused at the entrance, seeming uncertain, but perhaps not wanting to say anything. Aster pushed past him gently.

"Come on," she said, her voice steady. It had been just over a month since they'd lit out from Green Creek, over a year since Aster's Lucky Night, a full decade since her parents had sold her away. She nodded to herself. "We've waited long enough."

Zee lit a lantern and they descended the mineshaft. It was even more rundown than the shaft at Red Claw—there was no plank path to guide them through the rubble, and at one point they even had to climb over a cave-in. No one spoke, but the silence between them was as charged as the air during a thunderstorm. Aster could sense their mounting excitement and worry with every echoing step.

When they reached the bottom of the mineshaft, two young women were waiting for them—each armed with voltric rifles.

The woman on the left had shaved her blond-white hair in a close military crop, while the woman on the right had wrapped her thick black hair in a dustkerchief. Both had favors —birds of some kind. Aster's stomach dropped, disappointment crushing her heart in its fist. If they had favors . . . if Lady Ghost couldn't actually remove the curse . . .

Was Lady Ghost even here?

Someone clearly was. Behind the two women was a tunnel sparkling with warm yellow lantern light.

Neither smiled, neither spoke, waiting for them to declare themselves.

Aster swallowed. "We're here for Lady Ghost," she said without much hope. She turned to show them her own favor. "We . . . we've come a long way."

Finally the woman on the left smiled slightly. They both lowered their weapons. The woman on the right waved them forward.

"Follow me," she said.

The two women led them down the tunnel to an open space about the size of Green Creek's reception room, with mining lamps strung from the ceilings and spilling light into every corner. The room reminded Aster a little of the meeting hall at Red Claw—filled with rows of long tables with a shorter table at the head where the leaders would sit. Several smaller tunnels branched off from this central chamber, perhaps leading to sleeping and storage spaces. About twenty women sat at the longer tables, chattering over their supper, but the head table was empty save for a single older woman who stood and started towards Aster and the others. She wore a black dress with a gray sash. Her skin was withered and white, her hair thin and ashen, wisping around her hollowed-out face. A hush fell over the crowd as she neared Aster.

Aster felt an absurd urge to curtsy or to bow or to thank her or apologize. Her throat swelled with tears. It was real, then, the story was real, Lady Ghost was *real*—

"Welcome," the woman said, smiling gently. "I'm Lady Ghost."

Aster reached out to shake her hand, but then the blond woman beside her spoke up.

"And I'm Lady Ghost," she said.

361

"And I'm Lady Ghost." The dark-skinned woman wearing the dustkerchief.

The women sitting at the tables spoke in a chorus. "I'm Lady Ghost."

Aster looked around in confusion. She turned to Clementine.

"I-I don't understand," Aster stammered. "Is this some sort of joke? A test—?"

"It's the truth," the older woman said. "There has never been just one woman named Lady Ghost. It's all of us, working together. The stories you've heard—we've all helped to tell them." She nodded her head towards the front of the room. "Come sit with me, and I'll explain."

The two women who had escorted them returned to guard the mineshaft as Lady Ghost—what was her real name, Aster wondered—walked back to her table, slowly, as if it pained her. Aster and the others exchanged glances. They seemed just as confused as she felt, but that excited energy was still there, humming stronger than ever.

Finally, they were about to get some answers.

The other Lady Ghosts resumed eating and talking amongst themselves. Aster couldn't help but notice, though, as she passed them, that they all had favors—some more faded than others, but still . . . maybe it took a long time to remove them? Years, even? Aster scratched at her neck self-consciously.

"Here," Lady Ghost said, gesturing for them to sit. They all slid onto the bench opposite her. Mallow, Tansy, and Clem were practically buzzing with anticipation, but Aster remained reserved—she couldn't stop thinking of Violet, whose faith had led them here. Yes, she had led them to Northrock for her own purposes, but she had always believed she'd be leaving them with the directions for how to come here. Zee was fidgeting with his sleeves, looking as uncomfortable as Aster had ever seen him. Maybe he felt as out of place here as Violet had among the Scorpions.

Aster sat directly across from Lady Ghost. And she, too, had a favor, Aster saw: a trail of faded gemstones dotted her cheek and neck. Doubt crept into Aster's heart once again.

Lady Ghost followed her gaze. "There's no getting rid of them," she said, answering the unspoken question. "That's just another part of the myth, I'm afraid. But for most of the girls we help, their favors haven't kept them from finding other work in Ferron."

"Wait . . . Ferron?" Clementine's voice was high, breathless.

"That's what we do here—we help girls borderjump to Ferron and start new lives. There are still plenty of wrong-minded folks there—it's not perfect, I won't lie to you—but there are no dustblood debts there, no welcome houses, no tenant mines, no raveners, no vengeants, no landmasters. You'll finally be free."

The five stared in disbelief. For a moment they were all silent. The Scorpions were years away from finding safe passage to Ferron, and no one else had even come close.

"You're serious?" Clem whispered.

"I didn't think it was possible," Mallow said, shaking her head.

Lady Ghost smiled. "A lot more is possible in this world than you might think."

"Except getting rid of our favors," Aster said. The words popped out before she could stop them.

She couldn't help but feel a certain amount of defeat—they

had come all this way to get their favors removed, and now she knew they never would. The prospect of escaping to Ferron couldn't stop the question brewing in her gut: How could she ever truly leave the welcome house behind when it was written on her very skin?

You were never going to leave it behind, no matter how far you ran, a small voice whispered back. The thought filled her with grief, which she expected, and relief, which she didn't. At least, at last, she could stop running.

Green Creek would always be a part of her whether she wore its favor or not. She couldn't change the past.

But neither did she have to let it decide her future.

"Yes," Lady Ghost said quietly. "Except for that."

"Borderjumping," Clementine said, sounding uncertain, "does it cost a lot? Because—"

Lady Ghost shook her head. "There's no set fee. When this all started, it cost us about a thousand eagles a head to borderjump and make the arrangements in Ferron. But we never expected the women we helped to reimburse us for all of that, and now we're better organized, so really . . ." She held her palms up. "Whatever you can spare is appreciated. But all you really need to give us is your answer to the question: Would you like us to help you find a new life across the border?"

"Well, hell," Mallow said. "I'll take it." Tansy laughed. The two turned towards each other for an excited kiss, then pulled apart, breaking into wide grins. Then they turned towards the others.

"Ferron! We're going to Ferron!"

Aster warmed at their excitement. While this wasn't the dream they had all held on to during endless days on horseback and in McClennon's cellar, maybe that was just because it wasn't the dream that had been offered. Looking at Tansy and Mallow, Aster could see this was even *beyond* what the two had dreamed about.

"Can Zee come?" Clementine asked Lady Ghost. "We never would have made it here without him, and he's in just as much danger with the law as we are now for helping us."

"We'll figure something out, then," Lady Ghost said, smiling at Zee, whose expression relaxed with gratitude. He and Clementine embraced each other, eyes closed. Zee stroked the back of Clem's head. She buried her face in the crook of his neck. And for a moment Aster's chest swelled with emotion at the sight of them, all of them, happy and heading towards freedom.

This was what they'd risked everything for, and this was worth every bit of hardship it'd taken to get here.

Clem reached out for Aster's hand, and Aster let her take it as the four started peppering Lady Ghost with questions.

"What's life like in Ferron?"

"Is it true they have voltric trains that run underground?"

"Will we be able to see a moving picture show?"

Aster was full of questions too, but of a different kind. Why wasn't she as excited as the rest of them? Why couldn't she share this moment? She was still thinking of Violet, but of course so were the others, and that was only part of it anyway. There was more to it. Violet wouldn't be the only girl they were leaving behind. There were others. Girls whose faces she had never seen, whose names she would never know. Aster thought of Adeline, locked up in a prison cart. They had managed to save her, but there were so many more like her, on their way to the welcome houses or imprisoned within them.

And Lady Ghost will keep fighting for them. They're not your responsibility. Clementine is. You got her out of that place. You deserve to be free.

Everyone deserved to be free, though. Everyone deserved to feel this.

Aster looked around at her friends, all of them too excited to notice that she'd grown quiet, isolated by her indecision. Her stomach knotted painfully.

If Clementine's your responsibility, it means you can't leave her. She still needs you.

Did she, though? She had Mallow and Tansy. She had Zee. She had herself. Clem had grown up over the past month, as hard as it was for Aster to accept that. She would understand.

I'm tired, Aster thought. It was her final argument, and it nearly convinced her. All she had wanted, all her life, was to escape the Scab. She could spend the rest of her life in Ferron with the people she loved. It was as sweet as any dream she'd drawn up for herself as a little girl—sweeter, because this was real.

But then she remembered her conversation with Eli, the truth he'd spoken, his voice soft but sure. He'd said he felt like he owed it to others, no matter how unfair it was that any of them should have to fight at all.

Aster had wanted to help dustblood women the same way he and his brother helped dustblood men. The Scorpions and

Lady Ghost had already done immeasurable good alone. But if someone could bring them together . . .

"I—I want to stay," Aster said finally, looking first at Clementine, then at Lady Ghost. She swallowed around the stone in her throat. Steadied her voice. "I want to stay in Arketta and fight with you all."

"Aster, *no*. It's too dangerous," Clementine exclaimed before Lady Ghost could reply. "We finally made it here, we can't go back now—"

"I'm sure, Clem," Aster said softly. "I'm going back for Violet—I'm going back for all of them."

For a moment Lady Ghost's expression was serious, but soon her smile returned. "Well, if that's truly your wish, we'd be blessed to have you. But you don't have to decide right now. I expect you'll want to sleep on it."

Aster nodded, though she felt surer with every passing moment.

"You must all be very tired," Lady Ghost said. "Why don't you let me take you to where you'll be staying tonight?"

She stood and motioned for them to follow her.

They spent a week under the Lady Ghosts' care, resting and healing and preparing for their new journey. A wagon would take Clementine, Tansy, Mallow, and Zee to the border-crossing point the following morning. They'd all begged to know the details of how it would work, how it was possible to cross the border that seemingly no other dustbloods could ever cross—but Lady Ghost simply said that, for now, it was better for few to know the details, even amongst people they trusted.

Just in case something went wrong. "But let's just say that it takes a lot of work and bravery, and important connections on *both* sides of the border."

Aster had never known she could feel so happy and so sad all at once.

Clementine crawled into her cot, and Aster wrapped her arms around her, pressing a kiss to the crown of her head.

"Are you *sure* you don't want to come with us, Aster?" Clementine asked. "*Really* sure?"

Aster was quiet for a long time. Then, "I just keep thinking of how many girls like us there are out there. Girls who aren't lucky enough to have anyone looking out for them. It's such a miracle we made it here, Clem. A chance in a thousand. It's long past time someone evened the odds."

"I know," Clementine sighed. "I'm just not ready for us to go our separate ways. I've never not had you."

Aster felt a hitch in her breath. A sudden shot of doubt spiked through her. Maybe Clementine didn't need her anymore, but what if she still needed Clementine? Because Aster knew without question that she never would have survived this journey without her sister's light to clear up her own darkness. She never would have survived the welcome house if she'd had to face its horrors alone.

But Aster would have the other Lady Ghosts . . . and she would have Clementine, too. Time and distance meant nothing beyond the Veil. In some way, on some plane, they would always be together.

Tears wet Aster's cheeks. When was the last time she'd cried? She could not even remember. "When the time is right, I'll come back for you," Aster promised, her voice barely a whisper. "We *will* be together again, hear?"

Clementine nodded, and Aster could tell she was crying, too. Aster held her even closer and kissed her again, and a few moments later they fell asleep.

CHAPTER TWENTY-FOUR

Three weeks later

"You're sure about this?" the blond woman asked—Robin, her name was Robin, Aster had learned.

Aster had learned a lot in the last three weeks—she'd learned how the Lady Ghosts were able to sneak girls across the border, and about the fairblood working in a government office who was part of the plan. She'd learned that her bunkmate reminded her of Clementine, and that this was sometimes comforting and sometimes unbearable. And she'd learned just how many risks the Lady Ghosts were taking each and every day they did their work.

But there were some things she didn't know for sure and would just have to take on faith because she felt them in her heart: that the others had settled in Ferron, that they were starting their new lives there. And that this, what Aster was doing, was exactly what she needed to do.

Aster nodded, trying not to look at the needle in Robin's hand, or the ink at her side—Veil ink, the kind used to create tattoos that couldn't be hidden, that burned bright when you tried. Her first favor had been nothing short of a violation.

They had held her down, they had hurt her, they had left their mark on her forever. But as much as they had taken from her, they would not take her future. This favor would be different. This fight was one she'd chosen. No more running, no more hiding . . . and no more shame.

"I think you must be the first one to do something like this," Robin muttered as she gently cleaned Aster's neck and face with a cloth. "It'll certainly set the other girls talking."

"The other girls are always talking," Aster said with a half smile. By now she'd had a chance to meet them all, and soon she would be one of them, doing the work that needed to be done. "Let's give them something worth talking *about*."

"All right, then, relax," Robin said, matching her smile. Then she pressed the needle to Aster's skin. Aster stayed still. It burned, but no more than her favor did when covered. But this—this she would be proud to show. It would represent everything she'd overcome. Her time as a daybreak girl, when she'd dreaded the coming of the light every morning, and her time as a sundown girl, when she'd dreaded its fading. Her whole life as a dustblood, standing in the sunlight without a shadow at her feet.

No longer would she stay in darkness to hide who she was.

When Robin was finished, she smiled at Aster. "You okay?" Aster nodded. Robin led her over to the mirror and Aster stared back at her own face. Her skin was a richer brown from their weeks on the road. The scar on her cheek was ragged as the Scab itself. Her eyes were older, but they shone bright with new possibility. She saw not Aster staring back at her, but Dawn, the girl she'd once been, and the woman she hoped to be.

And there on the side of her face, stretching down into her neck, tracing rays of light around the petals on the edges of her cheek: her favor transformed into a spreading sun.

Acknowledgments

The acknowledgments for a debut novel could easily be as long as the novel itself. I have so many people to thank for bringing me to this point in my writing life, and I am incredibly grateful for every single one of them.

First of all, I want to thank the Dovetail editorial team, Lynn Weingarten and Marianna Baer. You two are mission control—*The Good Luck Girls* never would have gotten off the ground or survived the turbulence without your constant guidance. I can't thank you enough for the brainstorm sessions, the pep talks, and the thorough and thoughtful feedback. This is a story about, among other things, the power that comes from understanding your own anger and fear and turning it into something good—thank you for helping me translate mine into these pages.

I also have to thank my amazing editor Melissa Frain, whose support has been unwavering from the beginning. Just as big a thanks to the rest of the Tor Team—Melanie Sanders, my eagle-eyed copyeditor; Saraciea Fennell, my publicist; and Elizabeth Vaziri, editorial assistant—from one assistant to another, I know nothing could get done without all your hard work.

To my other mentors in YA publishing, a huge thank you for bringing me into this world and helping me navigate it. Cheryl Klein—I never would have made it out of our corner of the Midwest if you hadn't given me the opportunity to work with you and encouraged me to continue pursuing my writing. Jill Santopolo—your guidance has given me so much more confidence in my work, and I never would have had the opportunity to write *The Good Luck Girls* if you hadn't pointed me in the right direction. All the thanks to you both.

I'm equally grateful for my wonderful New School MFA family, who gave me the community every writer needs to stay sane. A special thank you goes out to Darcy Rothbard, critique partner, for reading my worst first drafts, for talking through plot holes with me over drinks, and for answering my frantic texts at 3 A.M. I never could have gotten through this without all of your guys' help.

I've also had some of the best writing teachers in the world over the years. Every writer says that, but that doesn't make it any less true! To Mary Klayder especially, I can't thank you enough for all the love and support you showed your students. You gave me so much courage to speak my truth. And to Mrs. McCormick—the first teacher I had who looked like me and the first one who told me I had something special to offer the world through my writing—thank you for giving this Black girl the hope to dream.

I buried myself in research for this story, and there were a handful of books that were particularly helpful:

The Half Has Never Been Told: Slavery and the Making of American Capitalism by Edward E. Baptist

Slavery by Another Name: The Re-Enslavement of Black Americans from the Civil War to World War II by Douglas A. Blackmon

Bury My Heart at Wounded Knee: An Indian History of the American West by Dee Brown

Wicked Women: Notorious, Mischievous, and Wayward Ladies from the Old West by Chris Enss

Gateway to Freedom: The Hidden History of the Underground Railroad by Eric Foner

Sex Trafficking: Inside the Business of Modern Slavery by Siddharth Kara

Girls Like Us: Fighting for a World Where Girls Are Not for Sale, an Activist Finds Her Calling and Heals Herself by Rachel Lloyd

These resources were invaluable to me, and this story is infinitely better for them. Thank you so much to these writers. Thank you, too, to my patient sensitivity readers, who helped me to tell the emotional truth. Any mistakes in the text are my own.

And, finally, I'd like to thank my family, for all their endless love and support. You've been reading my stories since I was writing them in crayon and binding them with staples. This one belongs to all of us.

Charlotte Nicole Davis

Charlotte Nicole Davis is a recent graduate of The New School's Writing for Children MFA program and is currently working as an editorial assistant at Bloomsbury USA Children's Books. She grew up in Kansas City, which was once the Wild West but today is mostly just fro-yo shops. She now lives in a little apartment in Brooklyn.

Charlotte says: 'I didn't want to tell a story about racism, necessarily—there's plenty of that on the news—but a story about a black girl and her sister finding freedom? Young women of all types getting into good trouble? Underdogs coming together to stand up against the rich and powerful? That sounded like exactly what the doctor ordered.'

HOT
KEY
BOOKS

Thank you for choosing a Hot Key book.

If you want to know more about our authors
and what we publish, you can find us online.

You can start at our website

www.hotkeybooks.com

And you can also find us on:

We hope to see you soon!